A DETECTIVE INSPECTOR

MURDER BY MISTLETOE

NEW YORK TIMES #1 BESTSELLER **TONY LEE** WRITING AS

JACK GATLAND

Published by Hooded Man Media.
Cover photo by Paul Thomas Gooney

First Edition: December 2022

PRAISE FOR JACK GATLAND

'This is one of those books that will keep you up past your bedtime, as each chapter lures you into reading just one more.'

'This book was excellent! A great plot which kept you guessing until the end.'

'Couldn't put it down, fast paced with twists and turns.'

'The story was captivating, good plot, twists you never saw and really likeable characters. Can't wait for the next one!'

'I got sucked into this book from the very first page, thoroughly enjoyed it, can't wait for the next one.'

'Totally addictive. Thoroughly recommend.'

'Moves at a fast pace and carries you along with it.'

'Just couldn't put this book down, from the first page to the last one it kept you wondering what would happen next.'

Before LETTER FROM THE DEAD...
There was

Learn the story of what *really* happened to DI Declan Walsh, while at Mile End!

An EXCLUSIVE PREQUEL, completely free to anyone who joins the Declan Walsh Reader's Club!

Join at www.subscribepage.com/jackgatland

Also by Jack Gatland

DI DECLAN WALSH BOOKS

LETTER FROM THE DEAD

MURDER OF ANGELS

HUNTER HUNTED

WHISPER FOR THE REAPER

TO HUNT A MAGPIE

A RITUAL FOR THE DYING

KILLING THE MUSIC

A DINNER TO DIE FOR

BEHIND THE WIRE

HEAVY IS THE CROWN

STALKING THE RIPPER

A QUIVER OF SORROWS

MURDER BY MISTLETOE

BENEATH THE BODIES

KILL YOUR DARLINGS

KISSING A KILLER

PRETEND TO BE DEAD

ELLIE RECKLESS BOOKS

PAINT THE DEAD

STEAL THE GOLD

HUNT THE PREY

FIND THE LADY

TOM MARLOWE BOOKS

SLEEPING SOLDIERS

TARGET LOCKED

COVERT ACTION

COUNTER ATTACK

DAMIAN LUCAS BOOKS

THE LIONHEART CURSE

STANDALONE BOOKS

THE BOARDROOM

AS TONY LEE

DODGE & TWIST

For Mum, who inspired me to write.

For Tracy, who inspires me to write.

CONTENTS

PROLOGUE

Everyone knew Santa Mick.

It wasn't that he was famous; it was more a case of him just being around all the time, especially at the Berwick Street soup kitchen on a Tuesday night. Always in line, rain or shine, always smiling, and always with that bloody silly red hat on his head.

Most of the rough sleepers who knew him didn't know why Santa Mick started wearing the hat, assuming it was probably found one night before Christmas a few years back, likely when an office worker dropped it while staggering out of a Christmas party, or maybe tossed it away. After all, "Father Christmas" hats were ten-a-penny these days, with every shop and market stall in London selling red fabric cones of cheap felt, with white felt around the bottom and the barest attempt at a fluffy white ball at the tip. The first one people saw him wearing had been that little bit too large for Santa Mick, but he'd worn it anyway, even going so far as to sing carols while he was sitting outside St Pancras Station asking for money.

Lewis Hoyle assumed it was *then* that Santa Mick realised the hat was his lucky charm, because people gave more money to the smiling, singing man in the Father Christmas hat than they had the previous days. And, weirdly, it made Santa Mick a lot happier, and actually nicer to be around, than the previous, bloody miserable Just-Mick.

Lewis had known Santa Mick for about five years now, since before the hat, even. Back then he'd been *Mickey Fish,* a name given to him because of his habit of hanging around Billingsgate Fish Market, to the east of London and near Canary Wharf, hoping for gifts of discarded boxes of fish from the sellers, which he'd then carry into London and sell to the cheaper and less-fussy restaurants in the area. Of course, as grand as the plan was, this rarely ever happened, but he gained the occasional crabstick on his adventures, and more importantly, a horrid fishy smell that followed him around for years.

Hence *Mickey Fish.* You always knew when he was coming, because the smell arrived ten seconds before he did, and the others in the queue for food at the soup kitchen would hum the "Jaws" theme when he approached.

In fairness, Mick took this all in good humour, even joking and humming along with them.

Lewis had been working on the streets for years now. Pretty much since the St Benedict Soup Kitchen had started. The charity was named after *Saint Benedict Joseph Labre,* the patron saint of the homeless, who travelled Europe in the Eighteenth Century, even living on the streets for thirteen years before dying on them, collapsing on the steps of the Santa Maria de Monti Church in Rome. The kitchen was Lewis's home, and the streets were a place he felt comfortable to walk through, speaking to the men and women forgotten by London, offering them support, advice, and the word of God when needed, just like St Benedict had done almost two hundred and fifty years earlier. Winter was the worst time, as many of the homeless on the streets wouldn't go to shelters, preferring to risk hypothermia on the ground rather than the possibility of a stabbing or mugging, losing their closely held items, in something that was little more than a dorm room.

Lewis understood this, too.

And with Shaun, an ex-homeless man who now worked for an outreach group trying to find actual housing for these people, he would spend the days and nights with the homeless, feeding them, laughing with them, even learning about them, and taking them for hot meals sometimes at a North London church he was a parishioner at.

Mick, though, had been *different*.

He was in his mid-to-late fifties, although he looked a good decade older, mainly through spending over ten years on the streets. He was slim, but had the look of a man who was once much larger, and his mid-length hair and beard were almost white now, which gave him even more of a "Santa" like appearance when the hat was on. The hat itself appeared around four years earlier, and hadn't left his head since – although Lewis knew this was a lie, as he'd swapped a new one for Mick every couple of months over the last year or two, and, once the hats were swapped, he burned the old one. They were always the same, though, the simple, cheaply made ones. He'd offered a better-made one to Mick once, a "luxury" hat, but Mick had refused it, saying he wanted to fit into the crowd, to not stand out, and "showing off" in a new hat, to use his own words, *wasn't done*. Even Shaun, who knew Mick from his time on the streets, had said never to change the style of hat; Santa Mick was Santa Mick because of it.

And the hat wasn't just worn at Christmas, oh no. Santa Mick wore it all year round, even on the hot summer days, where the felt hat was obviously too warm for him. But Santa Mick didn't mind, and actually enjoyed the confused looks from people. Santa Mick loved Christmas, and Lewis knew he'd been like this in his previous life.

Santa Mick would arrive at Berwick Street every Sunday night without fail, never complaining about the weather, or the time spent queuing, never bitching about his status in life, just carrying on, surviving the best he could while trying to keep his spirits high, even though his body must have been suffering. Lewis knew he'd get beaten up now and then. Usually drunks who, coming out of a pub in August, would see the "stupid man in the red hat" and target him. Santa Mick never complained, never pressed charges. He said it was karma for his past, accepted that it would occasionally happen, and promised the good times always outweighed the bad. Lewis had known little about Santa Mick's past, but recently Santa Mick had been a little more lucid with other members of the team, in particular the St Benedict's one-time helper Mallory when she visited, and Lewis had learned enough from her comments to have a very good idea of Santa Mick's past.

And now, a couple of weeks before Christmas again, Santa Mick was in his element once more, humming "Carol of the Bells" as he waited in line for his soup.

Lewis smiled; he couldn't help himself. Santa Mick had that effect on everyone, no matter what he may have once been. There wasn't much judgement on the street, after all. There was movement to his side. Mina, no older than sixteen or seventeen, her mousey-blonde hair pulled back into a ponytail had seen Santa Mick, and was now rummaging in the bag at the back of the gazebo, tossing off her marigold rubber gloves before returning to her post. Lewis knew what she'd been doing; Lewis himself had done it for years when he first started, constantly washing his hands in antibacterial gel, "just in case". People soon got over this, and he was sure she would too.

At least the gloves were now gone.

Mina came from a church in Hampstead, run by an old friend of Lewis's, and up to this point she had been ladling soup into bowls, now returning to this as, turning to the back of the gazebo as well, he pulled a fresh Father Christmas hat by the bobbled tip out of a bag he had hanging off the rear table, next to the hand gel.

As Santa Mick walked up to the table, Lewis offered it to him.

'Your hat replacement,' he said with a smile. It had become a ritual now, the replacing of the hat, but this time Santa Mick shook his head, almost scared to remove the current, and surprisingly clean-looking hat on his head.

'No,' he said, shaking his head as he stepped back, as if scared Lewis was going to leap across the table and snatch it from his skull. 'I got new one. Lady gave it to me.'

'What lady?' Lewis almost felt hurt, betrayed even that Santa Mick would take a hat from a stranger over him.

'It was an 'elf lady, spoke to me when she walked to work,' Santa Mick shrugged. 'Dunno the name.'

He slurred as he talked, and Lewis could tell from the breath that Santa Mick was a little worse for wear this evening, especially as he was calling some woman he'd met, who walked to work an "elf", although it sounded like he meant "health", like a nurse or something similar. He was a drinker, most of them were, but usually Santa Mick was one of the better ones, probably because he felt the hat deserved better behaviour.

Lewis actually wondered if something else was doing this, but pushed the thought away.

'Oh well, in that case I'll wear it myself,' he smiled, miming the act of pulling on the hat originally planned for Santa Mick, but as he did so Santa Mick's whole demeanour changed, and he snatched at it, pulling it away from Lewis's head, tossing it to the puddled and soaked London street.

'No wearing the hat!' Santa Mick was almost scared, pleading. 'Only Santa Mick wears the hat!'

Lewis looked at the queue behind Santa Mick and saw the same expression he was sure he wore now on his own face.

Santa Mick had never been like this before.

Someone else had given him a hat. But who?

'Mick, are you okay?' he asked, his voice calm and low. 'This isn't like you.'

Santa Mick's eyes widened as he realised his error, and he nodded at a bowl on the table.

'Just want my soup,' he mumbled, looking away from Lewis. Who, deciding that everyone could have a bad day once in a while, looked towards Mina, already ladling out a measure of soup. But, as she passed him a filled bowl for Santa Mick, Lewis was sure he saw her drop something into it, like a tiny drip of liquid from a phial.

Turning to face away from the group, he looked at her.

'What did you drop into the soup?' he whispered.

'Nothing,' Mina frowned. 'Was I supposed to?'

'Show me your hands.'

Confused, Mina opened them.

There was nothing in them.

Lewis matched Mina's frown as he rubbed at his eyes. He'd been up for almost two days now with the planning for the Church Carol Service later that week, and the hot soups for the homeless they'd be giving away during it, and he wondered if now was a good time to get a good night's sleep.

'Sorry, long day,' he said, turning back to the queue, but Santa Mick, his soup and a roll in hand had now gone.

Sighing, Lewis looked down at the hat, discarded in the puddle, but was surprised to see it too was no longer there, taken away from the kerb. Straightening, he spun around, looking for Santa Mick, wondering if the crazy, drunk old man had taken it anyway ...

But Santa Mick was gone.

SANTA MICK HADN'T UNDERSTOOD WHY HE'D BEEN SO ANGRY AT Lewis; the man had always been a good friend to him, and now he'd never speak to Santa Mick again, most likely.

And he'd never give him a new hat.

Placing the now empty cardboard bowl of soup down beside him as he leant against the wall, Santa Mick took off his new hat, staring at it. The blonde lady was friendly when they spoke, she seemed almost familiar, like a relative or something, and it was nice. *She* was nice. It reminded Mick of his life before, but the years of alcohol and drugs had made that nothing more than a foggy, fuzzy memory.

As he pulled the hat back on, he remembered wearing a tie, and he remembered ... Scrooge? *A Christmas Carol*?

Although maybe he'd remembered that from the homeless services he'd been to. He couldn't remember.

Mallory might. He'd spoken to her about it.

Mallory who?

Santa Mick had a moment of fear when he realised he couldn't put a face to the name. *Who was Mallory? How did he know that name?* He knew he'd seen her loads of times. But what did she look like? His memory was shot, and he started to cry, until another name appeared in his mind.

Jacob Marley.

The name burned through his head like a hot knife slicing through, and he clutched at his hat, holding it to his skull as he waited for the headache to subside. But, with the lessening of the headache, a new pain showed itself; a deep, gripping pain in his stomach.

Slowly rising, Santa Mick clenched his stomach. He could feel his guts burning and churning now, and the last thing he wanted to do was shit himself in the middle of Soho. There was a toilet nearby. He could get to Cambridge Circus and sneak into the *McDonalds* ones, they'd find him and kick him out, as they always did, but not before he ejected whatever the hell this was out of his body.

Now shuffling in an almost stumbling, limping walk down Broadwick Lane, past the record stores, restaurants and studios, Santa Mick realised he wasn't going to make it. *McDonalds* was a good five minutes at this pace, and Santa Mick was lucky if he could hold whatever was trying to escape from his gut for another two.

He had a terrible pain rip through his stomach at this, and he decided if he couldn't stop himself shitting in public, then he'd at least find a more secluded place to do it. Turning right into Duck Lane, a narrow cul-de-sac of buildings and rear doors, he followed the wall, aiming for the end, and the large dumpsters waiting there. He wouldn't be able to climb one, but he could squat to the side, in the shadows and out of the sight of most people, forgotten for the moment – especially with the streetlights forgetting this road even existed.

He made it halfway down the alley before he collapsed to his knees with another wrench of pain. Now crawling on all fours, his guts settling a little as the pain in his stomach took over, a knife stabbing into his appendix repeatedly, forcing a whimper from him every time it did so, he almost didn't hear the woman behind him.

'Are you okay, Mick?' she asked, walking down the alley towards him. Santa Mick turned onto his back, pulling himself to a sitting position against the wall, wiping the tears and sweat from his face as he looked at her. She was young, maybe twenties, maybe thirties, he couldn't tell anymore. She wore a checked skirt under a long, padded and hooded Barbour coat, pushed back and revealing her dark-brown hair and pale-grey glasses.

'Food poisoning,' he gasped, still fighting the urge once more to defecate all over the street. The woman didn't seem to notice this as she leaned closer.

'Santa Mick, do you recognise me?' she asked softly. 'Have you seen me before?'

Santa Mick shook his head, not really looking at the woman. There was a chance he knew her, but at the same time his mind was splotchy, with giant holes in both his short-term and long-term memory.

The woman seemed surprised by this answer, but then shook this off and smiled, reaching into her jacket.

'Well, recognising me or not, we can't have you not enjoying Christmas, can we?' she continued, pulling out a small, green bottle. It was the size of the mini bottles that off licences sold whiskies in, the tourist-friendly ones that were also found in mini-bars, not even a good mouthful's worth.

But this bottle didn't have a label on it; in fact, it didn't have anything on it.

'Here, I use this tincture when I have a gippy tummy,' the woman offered. 'It'll sort out whatever's causing the issue, and stop you needing to *go*, if you know what I mean.'

Santa Mick wasn't going to take it, but a wave of nausea and pain ripped through him, and in desperation he snatched it from the woman, opening the top and pouring the small mouthful's worth into his throat. It tasted odd, like grass, but he swallowed, passing the bottle back. The woman, however, had straightened, looking down at him.

'Oh no,' she said. 'I don't need that now. It's gone. But you need to rest there until you feel the effects, okay? I'll see you around, Michael.'

And with that, without even saying goodbye, the brunette woman in the Barbour coat walked out of Duck Lane and back onto the street, leaving Santa Mick sitting on the floor, leaning against the wall.

It was around this point he realised he'd just *pissed* himself.

Santa Mick started to cry deep, bellowing sobs that came from the depths of his soul. Never had he felt so pathetic, so broken, so useless—

He gasped as he realised he couldn't grab his breath, trying to gulp in air through his mouth, but to no avail. His lungs weren't getting any, his windpipe wasn't working and his heart was now pumping faster as he panicked. Managing the faintest of wheezes, he forced himself to his feet and out of the alley, staggering into the street, clutching at his throat, unable to take a breath as he croaked out for help. But the surrounding people were stepping back, staring at Santa Mick, brandishing the small bottle in his hand like a weapon in horror, and he realised with one more crash of shame and embarrassment that his attempts for privacy had been in vain, and he'd now shit himself, feeling it running down his leg as, tears also running down his cheeks, he cried, unable to sob properly, unable to grab oxygen—

And then Santa Mick, or Mickey Fish, or whatever name he was better known as fell to the street, his eyes open, his tongue blue, and his red-felt Father Christmas hat falling off his head and landing in the puddle Santa Mick had collapsed into, the small bottle of tincture beside it.

The people around him stared in shock at what had just happened.

But it was too late.

Santa Mick was dead.

1

BATHROOM SMELLS

As Christmases went, this one was shaping up to be pretty crappy for Detective Constable Billy Fitzwarren.

That said, the last few had been pretty bad, too. Billy had been effectively blacklisted from family events ever since he'd chosen police over family a few years back, and even the constant help from his Great-Uncle Chivalry Fitzwarren hadn't thawed the ice between them yet. For the last couple of years, Billy had mainly kept himself to himself, working on cases, or, with last year, having Christmas lunch with DS Anjli Kapoor. Although that wasn't happening this year, as she was with DI Declan Walsh now, and they would be all loved up and together.

Billy should have been loved up.

Billy should have been happy. He was still dating Andrade Estrada, the incredibly hot Colombian diplomat – or spy, if you listened to DCI Monroe – that had come to him a few months back with a request to connect professionally, which had rapidly turned into far, far more.

The problem was this was ending in a matter of days.

Andrade had only been on a six-month rotation, and this finished at the end of December. As the new year started, so did Andrade's next assignment, which currently seemed to be the office in Barcelona, Spain. Which was doable for a long-distance relationship, but at the same time was another stopgap before Andrade moved once more, six months later, with locations being suggested that included Ghana, Indonesia and Israel.

All of which would be far more challenging locations for travelling to.

But there was another option. Andrade, several weeks earlier, had suggested Billy *go with him*. Which, to be honest, although romantic and exciting, simply wasn't practical. No matter what happened, Billy couldn't keep changing locations every six months if he wanted to build a career.

He knew if he was reunited with his Fitzwarren clan, he could have managed it, as he could leave the force and move into the family business, of which there were several offices around the world. Maybe even work remotely, and the family assets, removed from his grasp, and including the substantial trust fund he was now frozen out of, would become once more available for him. He could spend a good couple of years slumming around, using his family money to create a good life for the pair of them, as Andrade carried on up the diplomatic ladder.

But that was the issue here. Andrade would continue his dream, working upwards, while Billy would stop his own.

He couldn't be a police officer, even if he took a sabbatical to follow Andrade for six months only. He was about to consider going for his Detective Sergeant exam in the following few months, and if he walked away, he'd be placed way back down the line when he returned. And that was even if Monroe allowed him back. He'd already left once before, almost leading Rufus Harrington's Cyber Security department, before being pulled back in.

No. It simply wasn't workable.

There was no way the relationship could feasibly continue once Andrade left the London Embassy.

Billy had kept quiet about Andrade while in the Temple Inn offices over the last couple of months, as he had a lot to decide, especially about his future. He'd only mentioned to a couple of people about Andrade's offer for Billy to go with him, but at the same time, he'd barely spoken to Andrade either about the offer, preferring to retreat into his work, convinced he'd screw up what they had in the remaining time they had it, anyway. He'd decided not to go with Andrade, as he had a life here, and even if they didn't speak to him half the time, he had family. However, being the coward he was when personal confrontation was involved, Billy had delayed telling Andrade this decision until the last minute, instead putting off the conversation every time they'd found themselves entering it, always finding something else, something nicer to change the subject to, and now there was only a couple of weeks to go before Andrade left forever, and Billy still hadn't discussed their future with him at length.

Not that Billy wanted to hurt Andrade, after all, even the unit had accepted him now, no longer making "spy" jokes – at least in Billy's presence. Anjli and Declan had even managed a second date with them, one that didn't end in a murder being reported and the evening ending quickly, like the first one they'd had. But they'd been given orders that, if the subject of "the future" came up, they were to change the conversation any way they could.

If Andrade wanted to stay in the UK, then Billy would

have done everything within his power to make sure this happened. He had even considered asking Andrade to marry him, simply to give him access to becoming a British Citizen through marriage, but Andrade was a Colombian diplomat who wanted to rise to the level of ambassador eventually, and Billy was just a copper who wanted a quiet life.

Andrade had an apartment in Central London, off Mayfair; it wasn't far from the Colombian Embassy and was an open lease for whomever held the role Andrade was currently in. When Andrade moved on at the start of January, another diplomat would move in, the same way Andrade had moved in when he first arrived.

Billy had been to the apartment exactly one time during their relationship; although Andrade was openly gay, he hadn't wanted to push the official regulations involving relationships of either sex, and so most of the time he'd visited Billy in the house Billy currently rented in Wanstead, in East London, or they'd gone out into Central London for meals, often using Andrade's expense account, even though Billy could perfectly pay his own way. Billy had always felt there was something *wrong* here, that Andrade was hiding something from him, but at the same time he didn't want to consider something like this, as to suspect Andrade of anything was to suspect him of *everything*. And then he'd be just as bad as Monroe, going on about secret handshakes and codes, as if the miserable sodding Scot hadn't remembered Billy was a bloody *Freemason*, and had enough of those, anyway.

However, for most of November, Andrade had become more distant, especially as his time in London lessened to where it could be easily counted in weeks and days, and over the last few days in fact, he hadn't been answering Billy's text messages at all, the phone calls going to voicemail. He'd wondered whether Andrade had learnt through some other source that Billy wasn't coming with him and so had decided to cut all ties, but this was fundamentally silly, as the only people who could have told him anything were in the Unit, and Billy now never talked about personal things there; the offices had been bugged by enemies too many times now for him to feel comfortable doing this, even though he swept them daily.

And so, after a small glass of Dutch courage, Billy had thrown caution to the wind and made his way to the apartment door one evening, and politely and nervously pressed the buzzer.

Nothing.

Billy checked his watch; it was almost nine pm. Unless there was some kind of event on at work, Andrade would have been off the clock.

Perhaps he was out? Maybe he'd found someone else, and just hadn't bothered to tell Billy?

No, Billy shook away the answer. *He would have said goodbye.*

And, after a couple more attempts at buzzing Andrade's door, Billy decided, on the spur of the moment, to try something stupid.

This time, he buzzed another number.

After a moment, there was a click through the intercom.

'Hello?' the voice spoke through it.

Billy pulled out his warrant card, showing it to the camera embedded at the top of the buttons.

'DC Billy Fitzwarren, City Police,' he said. 'I'm trying to get hold of Andrade Estrada, but he's not answering the door and I'm worried he's unresponsive.'

'Is he in trouble?'

'Are you his boss or an immediate relative?'

'No.'

'Then I can't talk about the case,' Billy lied.

After a moment, the door buzzed, and Billy pushed through it, already taking the steps to the second floor, two at a time. He didn't really think that anything had happened to Andrade, but there was now also a fear that whoever let him in was now contacting the police, just in case, and the last thing he wanted was to be caught there with no reason to actually be there – he had to be swift right now.

In and out, before anyone realised.

By the time he reached the door to Andrade's apartment, the man whose voice had let him in stood beside it.

'Look, I'm the superintendent for the building,' he said, his voice shaky and worried. 'If anything's happened, I need to know.'

Billy couldn't really ask him to leave, and so decided to play the gamble and nodded, banging on the door.

'Andrade?' he shouted. 'You in there?'

Just as before, there was nothing. No answer, no noise. Andrade was either out, or being very, very silent.

After a moment, Billy looked back at the superintendent.

'Do you have a key?' he asked.

'Do you have a warrant?' came the expected reply. This was, after all, a place of residence for a foreign diplomat. There was no way to know what secrets could be picked up from a quick scan of any room, and Billy was actually grateful the man still kept to his principles, even if it was causing him issues.

'I only need a warrant if I want entrance to the premises, and that's not the case here,' Billy replied. 'Look, I'm worried,

Andrade is a contact who's stopped responding to messages—'

'He working with the police?'

'What?'

The superintendent waved at Billy.

'For the police to be here, I'm guessing he's working with you on something?'

'I'm sorry, I can't answer that,' Billy replied, and he wasn't lying for a change. He couldn't answer that, as to do so would be to lie, or to confirm that he was in a sexual relationship with the man. And, if that came out, this wouldn't look that innocent. He'd look more like a crazed, spurned lover, banging on their ex's door.

Christ, is that what I'm doing here? Billy thought to himself, while quickly passing the suggestion aside.

'Look, all I'm asking is you open the door, stick your head in quickly and check he's not dead or something,' he eventually replied, now getting nervous. *Maybe something was wrong here? Maybe he was right to get in?*

'Is he likely to be dead?' the superintendent looked horrified, but was already pulling his ring of keys out, hunting for the relevant one. 'No, don't tell me. Ten seconds.'

'Thanks,' Billy relaxed a little as the superintendent opened the door, but then tensed as he saw a spatter of something red on the hallway floor. 'Shit.'

'What?' the superintendent wrinkled his nose. 'God, someone's spilt wine on the carpet.'

'I think I should come in with you,' Billy paused the old man before he could enter. 'I've seen that before. It's not wine, it's ... well, it's the colour of dried blood.'

'Blood?' the superintendent stepped back, the door opening, showing a smudged and wide smear of what looked to be blood in the carpet, heading from the living room towards the bathroom to the left. And, at the same time, there was a strong smell of excrement, like someone had a terrible stomach and hadn't flushed afterwards.

'Yeah, like something's bled a lot in there,' Billy replied. 'It could be an animal though, maybe a rat or—'

'We don't have rats in here,' it was spoken haughtily, the superintendent, furious someone would even consider his apartments to be rodent-infested.

'Well, then it's something worse,' Billy replied, already steeling himself for what he could find in there.

Andrade hadn't replied to his messages for days now.

The blood was more than a small animal would have.

The superintendent shuffled his feet, looking at the floor.

'I'll let you look,' he eventually suggested, obviously reluctant to enter now the chance of seeing something horrible looked more likely. And slowly, with a growing sense of dread, Billy entered the apartment.

The smells of excrement and blood were emanating from the bathroom, the first door on the left, where the smear of blood on the carpet ended, and Billy paused beside the closed door, forcing himself *not* to take a reassuring breath, purely because the act would have filled his lungs with more of the putrid smell. Instead, he held a hand over his mouth, and twisted the doorknob, slowly opening it, looking at the bath, and the body within—

It wasn't Andrade.

That this was the first relieved thought in Billy's head was bad enough.

That he hadn't recoiled to the fact there was a dead, naked man in Andrade's bath was worse.

There was no water around him, and someone had

slashed his throat downwards, rather than across, his tongue pulled out through the gaping wound towards the sternum. The blood had streamed out of this vicious cut, covering his chest and running down to his feet, which had been torn apart, the toenails removed, the blood in the carpet likely from when whoever did this, dragged the poor bastard into the bath to finish him. The victim had also shit himself with fear of death, and as Billy couldn't see any other major wounds on the body, he assumed the throat cut had been the method of death; a manner of execution known as a *Colombian Necktie.*

Stepping back out of the bathroom, trying not to touch anything else, Billy looked back at the superintendent.

'Don't let anyone in here,' he said. '*Anyone.*'

Pulling out his phone, he dialled the first number on his contacts list, staring at the sliver of bathroom he could see through the almost-closed door as he waited for the phone to connect. There was a mirror above the sink, and through it he could just see the hair on the head of the body, he averted his eyes so he—

'Guv, it's Billy,' he said as the call was finally answered, backing away further, as if the body was causing issues with his phone signal. 'I'm at Andrade's apartment and really need some coppers here right now.'

Ignoring the smell now, he took a deep breath, immediately regretting it before continuing.

'I think I've walked into a bit of a diplomatic incident.'

2

CHRISTMAS BELLES

Detective Inspector Declan Walsh stared across the ballroom at current PM Charles Baker and wondered for the fifteenth time that evening *why the hell he was here.*

No, he *knew* why he was here – Baker had asked for him. It was the first of the many Number Ten Christmas Balls the Government held, and Declan had been invited, alongside half a dozen Tory donors, a couple of middle-of-the-road pop stars – although considering most of them hadn't been famous since the nineties, Declan was sure there was another term for them by now – a TV presenter or two, and David Bradbury, currently the Chief Superintendent of City of London's police, Declan's *boss's* boss, also currently looking as equally unimpressed as Declan was to be there.

In fact, it was Bradbury, seeing Declan alone, who made the first move, walking over to him, a glass of orange juice in a champagne glass in his hand. He was taller than Declan by a hair's breadth, his short grey hair whiter at the temples. He wasn't wearing his usual glasses, but was in full uniform, the diamonds on the black epaulettes of his jacket showing his rank.

'DI Walsh,' Bradbury said by introduction. 'Miserable bloody shindig, isn't it?'

Declan fought the urge to reply with his first thought, that his grey, off-the-rack suit was probably worth less than half the female guests clutch bags, as the suits were all bespoke, the hair styled by men who were known as artisans rather than barbers.

In fairness, the costs of many things were worth more than his suit. His phone was worth more than his suit, and it was the basic model.

'Politics, sir,' he smiled humourlessly. 'You ever consider it?'

'Me?' Bradbury almost laughed. 'Walsh, I'm a career copper. If I became an MP, I'd be citizen arresting half of Commons by the end of day one.'

Declan gave a half-shrug at this.

'I can think of worse things,' he replied.

'How's your unit doing?' Bradbury changed the subject as he grabbed a small pastry *something* off a tray as it passed by. 'You've all been quiet of late. That concerns me.'

'No crimes of note lately,' Declan sipped his own glass of orange juice. 'In some respects, that's nice, but in others ...'

'Yes, I get that,' Bradbury nodded. 'Sophie – I mean Detective Superintendent Bullman has been keeping me appraised recently.'

Declan forced a smile off his face, hoping to God his superior hadn't noticed it. The Temple Inn's Detective Superintendent had been coy when talking of her professional relationship with Bradbury, and the consensus was that Bullman and Bradbury were seeing each other secretly. He was a long-time widower, and she – well, to be honest, Declan still didn't know that much about her, even though she'd been his boss, or at least connected to cases he was involved in for over a year now.

She ... she was an enigma. And the less said about it, the better.

'I hear there's been some arguing though,' Bradbury smiled now, and Declan frowned for a moment before realising what he meant.

'Oh, you mean the weddings?' he asked, shaking his head. 'Yeah, you could say that. DCI Monroe and Doctor Marcos haven't set a date yet, and it'll likely be next year, but DCI Farrow from Mile End is kicking off a fuss, saying the Guv is trying to steal his thunder, because he's getting married in a couple of months, and nobody's talking about it.'

'He's marrying your ex-wife, isn't he?'

Declan nodded.

'He is, sir,' he replied. 'And before you ask, I'm fine with it. Henry Farrow is a good man. Worked with him for years before I moved over to Monroe. He'll look after Liz, and Jess too, when she's around. Although knowing my daughter is now Jessica Farrow will be a tough pill to take.'

'He worked with your Alex Monroe too, didn't he?'

'Yes sir, back in the day. He was a DI then, I think.'

'You sure the miserable Scot didn't do this deliberately to piss on his chips?' The language was coarser than Declan had expected, but it made a valid point.

'I hope not, sir,' Declan puffed his cheeks out. 'All I know is they're going to have a hell of a bun fight as they try to outdo one another. And personally? I'm not taking sides. I'm staying the hell away from all of it.'

'No plans to settle down again? Move on like Elizabeth has?'

Declan froze for a moment.

'No, sir,' he replied slowly. 'DS Kapoor and I, we ... we're still finding our feet. It's comfortable right now. I'd be scared to break it.'

'Probably for the best,' Bradbury smiled. 'What would I know, anyway?'

He stopped, however, as a man started walking across the ballroom towards them. Charles Baker, the current Prime Minister of the United Kingdom was an arrogant, vain man, in his mid-to-late fifties, wearing a modern and obviously bespoke navy-blue suit, a blue striped tie slightly clashing against it, his lustrous white hair giving his tanned face an almost ageless appearance. He had a glass of champagne in his hand and a wide smile on his face.

'You made it,' he said, walking over. 'Welcome to my party. First one of the Christmas season, I'd reckon!'

Bradbury raised his glass in a motion that could be taken either as a *thank you*, or as a mocking toast, and although Declan was convinced it was the latter, Charles took it as the former.

'Got to admit, I'm surprised I'm here,' Declan replied. 'Especially considering the last time we spoke.'

Charles forced a smile here, but it looked sickly and incredibly fake. And Declan knew exactly why. A few months earlier, after a rather harrowing serial killer case that almost cost one of his team their career, Declan had confronted Charles Baker in his office, explaining he knew how far Baker had gone to push public support towards one of his crime bills during the case, using the deaths to his advantage, a fact his overeager assistant had thrown

Declan's way by accident. Declan had got his way in the end, but the last words from Charles Baker had been incredibly final.

'Once you leave this room, we're done. I've had my fill of blackmail, even from you. With this last favour, we're through.'

But now, they seemed to be friends again.

'I spoke words harshly and in haste,' Charles explained, waving around. 'You saved many of the people here, it was only fair I give you your time in the spotlight.'

'In other words, you found a more political use for me,' Declan replied curtly, keeping his voice low to make sure nobody saw his anger, but finding it harder to keep Bradbury, standing beside them, from seeing it.

'Is it hard to believe I've changed?' Charles asked, hands out. 'I have, I promise.'

He pointed across the room where, to the side and in the corner, a slim, nervous man stood, awkwardly, sipping at a glass of water. His suit looked borrowed, his brown, fuzzy beard now tidied and his glasses no longer broken, Shaun Donnal looked very different from the man he'd been the last time Declan had seen him, although that had been over a year ago, when he'd been homeless, armed, and on the roof of a stately home.

'See? I even bring old friends to my parties,' Charles grinned. 'I'm working with Shaun on a homeless outreach programme. Can you believe that? Me, working with Labour?'

'If I recall, you used to be Labour too,' Declan replied.

'Yes, but we both went in such disparate directions,' Charles sniffed dismissively. 'But that said, I did forgive him the gun he aimed in my face.'

'A calculated act aimed at distracting your true enemy,

and one that saved your life, if the reports described it correctly,' Bradbury interjected.

Charles scowled a little at this.

'Always a pleasure to see you, Bradbury,' he muttered.

In return, Bradbury raised his glass once more, and Baker decided to ignore him for the moment, fully turning back to Declan.

'Anyway, we were working together, and he was coming tonight, and he asked if you could be here. He wanted to speak to you. Seems you've been avoiding his calls.'

'I've not,' Declan replied, looking from Charles to Bradbury. 'I'm not, I swear. We just have this nightmare receptionist, and she won't put anyone through. I'll speak to him now.'

He hadn't wanted to speak to Shaun, but he'd also noted several of the guests observing Charles Baker spending time with him, and before they snapped off a couple of candid shots on their smartphones and sent them to the press, Declan wanted to be as far away as possible. And so, this said, Declan now made his way through the ballroom, nodding to a couple of middle-aged Conservative MPs who recognised him, even though he had no clue who they were. The chances were he'd saved them at a State Dinner a few months earlier, but he didn't want to stop to ask.

To be brutally honest, the sooner he got out of here, the better.

Shaun Donnal looked up as Declan approached and smiled, holding out his hand.

'Thanks for seeing me,' he said as Declan moved into the corner with him, keeping his voice down low so as not to bring any others into the conversation.

'I hear you've been trying to contact me?' Declan asked, placing his now-empty glass on a tray as it passed, grabbing another orange juice.

At this, Shaun smiled awkwardly.

'Yeah, sorry, I thought that was the best way to get you over,' he said. 'I hadn't tried that hard through, well, *official* routes, because I needed to talk to you about something off the books. But then something else happened, and now I need your help.'

'So, wait, are we talking about something off the books, something you need my help with, or both? Or are they the same thing?' Declan frowned as he looked at the one-time Labour MP.

At this, Shaun shook his head.

'Sorry, yeah, I'm not really helping,' he replied. 'Best I explain. So, since you last saw me, I've spent the last year turning my life around. Found a place to stay, a halfway house, and I've started repairing my relationship with my family.'

Shaun paused, cocking his head to the side as he considered this statement.

'Well, my daughter anyway,' he continued. 'My wife doesn't want anything to do with me. And I get that.'

Declan understood this as well. The breakdown Shaun Donnal had suffered, one that threw him so far off the grid he landed on the streets of London for over a decade, had been because of the belief he'd killed someone twenty years earlier; a belief also shared by Charles Baker, neither man knowing the other blamed themself, while both being lied to by the instigator of the belief, Francine Pearce. However, after Declan had solved the case, and they had cleared Shaun of all wrongdoings, he'd disappeared off the streets. Declan had hoped he'd made a change for the better, and was glad to see he'd been correct.

'Charles actually helped, too,' Shaun continued, bringing

Declan back to the present. 'He found an outreach programme I could get involved with. I've also started training as a counsellor, working with a homeless charity, St Benedict's, and helping the people I used to live with.'

'I'm happy for you,' Declan replied. 'So, what's the problem?'

'Santa Mick,' Shaun explained, and Declan frowned, unsure he'd heard correctly. 'Don't know his name, his full name, we always knew him as Santa Mick, because he always wore a Father Christmas hat on his head, even when it wasn't Christmas. Before that he was Mickey Fish, because he slept near Billingsgate Fish Market and, well, he stunk. The hat was better.'

'Okay, so what happened with Santa Mick?' Declan asked.

'He died,' Shaun looked across the ballroom. 'Found dead two nights ago, on Sunday in Soho. Collapsed in the middle of the street.'

Declan frowned.

'You don't think death by natural causes is the case here?'

'I don't think anybody cares what the case is,' Shaun shook his head. 'I heard rumours people were literally stepping over the body rather than checking on him. But I'd seen him on the streets earlier that day, and he looked healthy as anything. However, a couple of the soup kitchen attendees—'

'Homeless people?'

'You don't find many employed people attending soup kitchens,' Shaun snapped, before calming himself. 'Sorry. Had enough of MPs and their mates looking down on me tonight. Anyway, a couple who were there that evening said he seemed off. He even turned down a new Christmas hat, tossing it to the floor.'

'So, he was off, and then he died,' Declan was nodding slightly as he considered this. 'Still could be any number of reasons why he collapsed, though. But, if we do humour this thought, did he have any enemies?'

Shaun frowned.

'The long-timers look out for each other,' he replied. 'I don't think—'

'The reason we found you last time was because you attacked another "long-timer" with a screwdriver,' Declan raised an eyebrow. 'I don't think it's all puppies and balloons, is it?'

Reluctantly, Shaun nodded.

'Okay, sure,' he said. 'But Santa Mick was different. I never saw anyone speak a bad word against him. I don't know if this is just an overreaction or not, but I was hoping you could look into it?'

Declan sighed.

'Sure,' he said, nodding. 'But I can't guarantee we'll find an answer you like. Give me the details and I'll—'

He stopped as Shaun pulled out a sheet of folded A4 paper, passing it across.

'I wrote everything down,' he explained as Declan took it, opening up the sheet.

'Thanks,' he replied. 'I'll look into this and ...'

His voice trailed off as he continued reading the note.

'What's this?' he asked, looking up at Shaun. '*October 20, 9.45? 100 Wardour Street?*'

Shaun looked away, watching the party for a long moment before replying.

'This was the other reason I wanted to speak to you,' he said. 'The one I knew would have me kicked out of your police station reception the moment I said it.'

He leant in closer.

'I saw her, Declan,' he whispered. 'Francine Pearce.'

Declan took a long breath here, forcing his face to stay emotionless.

'Francine Pearce is dead,' he replied softly. 'She died in Wales, back in June, when the cottage she was hiding in had a gas leak and exploded.'

'That's a lie and you know it,' Shaun hissed, and his face distorted into an expression of cold fury. And Declan knew he was correct. He'd travelled to St Davids, in Wales in early July to investigate the explosion, and all he'd found were the clues he was meant to find, that the police investigating were supposed to find, clues showing Francine Pearce had been eating a fish and chips dinner in her holiday cottage, hiding from the world when it exploded.

It wasn't a gas explosion; Declan knew very well who'd caused it, but he also knew Francine hadn't been there at the time, and that an innocent had died in her place.

He never spoke of this outside the Unit, but he knew without a doubt she was still out there, hiding, planning for the future. Francine Pearce had built her career up through secrets and blackmail, with victims including Shaun, Declan himself and ...

Declan glared across the ballroom now at Charles Baker, nervously watching him while being spoken at by some lobbyists.

This was why Charles Baker had invited Declan. Not as a favour to Shaun, but because he too had a personal reason to make sure Francine Pearce was gone for good.

'It was her, Declan,' Shaun continued. 'I was talking to a *Big Issue* seller, and she got out of a car, a posh one, and looked at me. I froze, but she was looking through me, scanning the road, and she didn't even recognise the man she destroyed. I wasn't worth her concentration.'

'And she went into the building?'

Shaun nodded.

'She'd grown her hair out, the fringe was a parting and she'd lightened it, and she even had these blue-framed glasses on, but even this couldn't hide who she was. She wasn't hiding anymore. And she walked into the building.'

'And what did you do?'

'Ran as fast from there as I could,' Shaun admitted. 'And I sat on this for two months while I worked out what to do.'

Declan looked back at the note. He wanted more than anything to crumple it up, tossing it away before anyone else was hurt, but there was a part of him, a hidden, curious part, which wanted to know more.

'I'll look into it,' he said. 'I'll look into both.'

'There's a number at the bottom,' Shaun pointed at it. 'It's the number of Mallory Reed, she was the one person who possibly knew Mick the best. Lewis Hoyle, he runs the kitchen, he's worth talking to as well.'

Declan nodded, folding the note and looking back up, but Charles Baker diverted his attention, now talking animatedly to both Bradbury and one of his aides, looking over at Declan in what looked to be mild anger. In fact, catching his eye, Charles now walked over to Declan, Bradbury following.

'Your team's started an international incident,' Charles growled.

'How?' Declan was genuinely surprised at the accusation. 'I've only been away from the office for half an hour!'

'We've had a report that DC Fitzwarren has been brought into custody in relation to the murder of a Colombian diplomat,' Bradbury interjected. 'He's your cyber guy, isn't he?'

Declan nodded, already pulling out his phone.

'Dammit, there's no signal here,' he muttered. 'I should check in.'

'Damn right you should,' Charles added. 'Because now I've got the Colombian Embassy claiming diplomatic privilege, and massively pissed off we're even involved in this.'

Declan nodded to Shaun and then to Bradbury, but before he left, he looked at Charles, moving in close.

'I'll look at your problem,' he whispered. 'Both of them. But the next time you try to use me to remove another thorn in your shoe? I'm coming for you.'

'Francine Pearce is a thorn in everyone's shoe,' Charles replied gently.

'Then use your secret Star Chamber thing to get rid of her,' Declan hissed. 'You know, do some sneaky shit. You're good at that, *Prime Minister*.'

And, with Charles Baker worrying about his Premiership, and with Shaun Donnal worrying about a dead man in a Father Christmas hat, Declan left the ballroom, hunting for a signal, and worrying about the state of DC Billy Fitzwarren.

3

DIPLOMATIC ACCESS

IT TOOK ANOTHER FIVE MINUTES FOR DECLAN TO GET A SIGNAL in the maze of office corridors that was Number Ten, and once he had it, he called Anjli.

'What do we have?' he asked by introduction. 'Bradbury just told me Billy's in custody?'

'It's not good, and we're currently having some kind of standoff,' Anjli replied. 'I'll text you the address. It's in Mayfair. Can you get here fast?'

'Already on my way,' Declan replied, disconnecting the call and nodding to a security officer. 'Best place to get out without press, and find a car? I need to get to a crime scene.'

The guard looked Declan up and down.

'DI Walsh?'

'Yes,' Declan frowned. 'Have we met?'

'I was one of the guards told to stop you entering the State Dinner,' the guard was already walking down the corridor in the other direction, waving for Declan to follow. 'Just following orders but it felt wrong. I was glad you got through, saved all those people. Allow me to return the favour.'

Walking down the back corridors, Declan realised he was heading to the exit beside Horse Guards Parade – he'd been here before, when Jennifer Farnham-Ewing had tried her best to return to Charles Baker's side. He hadn't seen her at the party, and it was only now he even thought of her.

'Does Jennifer Farnham-Ewing still work here?' he asked as the guard opened a door, leading Declan outside and waving over to a black Range Rover.

'God no, thank goodness,' the guard smiled. 'Baker finally pulled the trigger on her after the whole Lady Justice thing. I think she works in the Whip's office now.'

'She's still in Parliament?'

The guard shrugged.

'Wherever she is, she *was* in Number Ten,' he replied. 'Believe me, it's a demotion.'

The Range Rover drove up, and the driver looked out.

'What's the deal?' he asked.

The guard turned to Declan.

'You have an address?'

Declan checked his phone to see Anjli had already texted the Mayfair address he needed to get to.

'I need to be here yesterday,' he said, showing the address. 'How fast can you do it?'

'Quicker than your rubbish squad cars,' the driver grinned. 'Get in.'

Declan nodded thanks to the Number Ten guard as he climbed into the car, and before he'd even grabbed his seat belt, the Range Rover was already speeding off, blue lights flashing.

'Don't often get to drive like this,' the driver grinned. 'Hold on, mate.'

Declan did just that, grimacing as they hurtled around a corner on two wheels.

This evening was not going well so far.

THEY ARRIVED AT THE MAYFAIR ADDRESS IN A MATTER OF minutes; the driver ignoring perceived traffic rules and road directions, and screeching to a stop, lights flashing at the edge of a police cordon. Thanking him, Declan clambered out of the car, forcing his rubbery legs to straighten and, seeing Anjli Kapoor across the road, rushed over to her.

PC Esme Cooper, on seeing him, lifted the cordon to let him pass under.

'What's going on?' he asked, looking around at the police, standing outside the building as if waiting to be allowed to enter. 'Why aren't we inside?'

'Because we're not being allowed inside,' Anjli growled, and Declan could see she was only just holding back an explosive rage. 'We've been here fifteen minutes and they've not let a single person in. We're not even allowed to speak to Billy, who their security team has in a room on the ground floor.'

'Do we know what happened?' Declan walked with Anjli towards the main entrance where an equally irritated DCI Alex Monroe stood beside Sergeant Morten De'Geer, his seven-foot Viking frame dwarfing the Colombian Embassy employees who barred the way into the building.

'There was a call from Billy,' Monroe replied. 'He called us rather than 999, which was the first problem. He said he thought he'd caused a diplomatic incident and explained he was needing some friendly coppers on the scene. There was a body in the bathroom, he didn't recognise him, but he was in Andrade's apartment.'

'It wasn't Andrade?'

Monroe shook his head, looking around the scene as he continued.

'No, and by the time we got here, the Colombians had got wind of this and brought their own security in, locking down the whole place. They won't let anyone in, saying it's their issue.'

'It's a murder in London,' Declan hissed. 'How is it—'

'The building's owned by the Colombian Government, boss,' De'Geer interrupted. 'It holds the same rights as their embassies, in which the rooms within are technically not in London, but on Colombian soil.'

'Oh, for Christ's sake,' Declan shook his head in disbelief. 'We're being stopped from entering a potential murder scene because of a territorial pissing contest?'

'It is more than that, Detective Inspector Walsh,' another voice spoke now, a male voice, with the sing-song tone of a man speaking a second language, and Declan looked around to see one of the Colombians now walking towards him. He was in his sixties, his hair a picture of black and silver, his olive skin pocked with scars and small holes, as if he'd really gone mad scratching himself while suffering from chicken pox. He was shorter than Declan was and looked stockier under his suit, but Declan really felt this was all muscle, rather than fat.

This wasn't a sedentary desk worker, no matter what he stated.

'I am Pablo Restrepo,' the man said, offering out a hand. 'I am, what you would call "section head" of the embassy.'

'Head of security,' Declan stated, to a brief smile and nod from Restrepo.

'Spy,' Monroe added icily, and to his credit, Restrepo didn't argue with this.

'Your language is pretty,' he said to Monroe. 'There are better words out there for the term, I'm sure.'

'Oh, I'm sure there are, and I'm also sure you'll be hearing some prettier bloody words from me very soon, if my wee laddie isn't brought out of your building!' Monroe exploded. 'How dare you—'

'Your, what did you say, "wee laddie", Detective Constable William Fitzwarren, was found illegally on Colombian property, in the presence of a dead Colombian,' Restrepo replied calmly, a mellow counterpoint to Monroe. 'We need to confirm he is not a suspect before—'

'*Not a suspect?*' Monroe's Glaswegian accent was gaining strength as he spoke, a sure sign he was about to throw a punch, or worse, any moment now. 'What you need to do, laddie, is allow us into the building to have a look and see what bloody mess you've gotten yourselves into! Where is Andrade, anyway?'

Restrepo looked pained for a moment, and Declan wondered whether this was because of Monroe's attitude, but then he realised it was because the section chief spy was torn – on one side he had rules to follow, and on the other he *really* didn't want to deal with this mess alone.

'Okay,' Anjli, also seeing this, joined in. 'Let's play a game of hypotheticals. Scenarios that aren't real, and see if we can gain something from that.'

'Yes,' Restrepo replied, grabbing onto this idea like a life raft. 'I can do this.'

'Hypothetically, Andrade has been in a relationship with

Billy,' Anjli said, and noted no surprise on Restrepo's face. 'You knew?'

'Let us say the hypothetical we did,' Restrepo replied, shrugging. 'It is not so big a thing for us.'

'And, let's say, hypothetically, Billy loses contact with Andrade for a few days, and comes here to check on him, in the process finding a body. An unknown body.'

Restrepo nodded.

'Hypothetical Andrade has not been seen by hypothetical me for a week now—' he began, but Monroe held up a hand.

'We don't need to tie ourselves in knots here, and I'm sorry for snapping,' he said. 'What can we do to help? We've grown to care for Andrade over the last six months, and we want to make sure he's okay, as well as ensuring the wellbeing of our own man.'

'I cannot let you inspect the scene, until our Ambassador allows us,' Restrepo sighed. 'And he is on a plane returning from Madrid right now.'

'That's okay,' Monroe grinned, looking up at the house as, through the doors, a woman emerged, walking down the steps, pulling off her latex gloves. 'We're really bad at doing the "official" thing, too.'

Restrepo turned to watch the woman as she walked across the road towards them.

Doctor Rosanna Marcos was middle-aged, with olive skin framed by mid-length, untamed, jet-black hair, pulled back with a fluorescent scrunchy, completely failing to match her jeans and comfortable "lighthouse keeper" style jumper. Although the December night was warm, it was still December, but while everyone else wore coats, she seemed fine without one.

'Wait, you know the *Barracuda?*' Restrepo was confused.

'Well, we don't call her that,' Monroe puffed out his cheeks as he replied. 'But Doctor Rosanna Marcos is our divisional surgeon and crime scene examiner.'

Pablo Restrepo looked lost as Doctor Marcos stopped beside him.

'Don't worry, I only deal with you in my off-time,' she said, patting him on the shoulder as she looked back at Monroe. 'I did some freelance work for the Colombians when I was suspended during the Tancredi case, about eighteen months back. They called me the Barracuda. I never had the heart to ask why. But I've helped them out here and there. Always unofficially.'

'Okay, this is something we need to talk about later,' Monroe looked around the group, as if checking he wasn't the only one confused here. 'But did you have time to look at the—'

'I'm going to have to stop you there, Alex,' Doctor Marcos held up a hand. 'I was here in my capacity as freelance crime scene examiner for the embassy, and as such, I'm bound by their rules. If they say you can't be told, then I can't tell you.'

'But you are going to, yes?' Restrepo said with resignation.

'Oh absolutely,' Doctor Marcos smiled. 'Just not with you around. You know, keep the myth going and all that.'

Restrepo held up his hands, swore softly to himself and walked off, speaking softly and quickly in Spanish as he left.

'He says it's best he's not here for this,' Doctor Marcos leant in, speaking softly in that not-speaking-softly way people do when they fake whisper.

'You speak Colombian?' Monroe was genuinely surprised.

'I'd be a pretty rubbish freelance CSI for them if I didn't,' Doctor Marcos looked actually hurt at the implication. 'And it's Spanish, not some mystical dead language of the ancients.

Anyway, with Pablo now gone, I can tell you what I saw. Naked man, mid-twenties, left in the bathtub with a Colombian necktie.'

'Matches what Billy said so far,' Anjli pulled out her notepad and started writing in it as she listened. Doctor Marcos nodded at this.

'Billy's in a reception area, by the way, he's okay but really stressed,' she continued. 'The body was about six hours old, I'd say, but I can't be too sure unless I check with a proper autopsy, and there's no way they're going to let me do that. There's already talk about sticking the body in a box after hosing it down, and sending it home on the first diplomatic plane to Colombia.'

'That doesn't sound sketchy at all,' Declan shook his head. 'I'm guessing they spoke freely because they didn't know you speak the language?'

'Oh, no, they told me everything because I asked,' Doctor Marcos replied. 'I'm a people person. Anyway, the trachea had been sliced down vertically with a sharp blade, and the tongue pulled through the hole before death. The poor bastard was left to bleed out in the bathtub, but the toenails were also gone and there's blood on the carpet, as if they dragged him to the bathroom and any blood on his feet smudged into it. They claimed they didn't know who he is, but they were obviously lying through their teeth, and not wanting to talk about it, so my guess is they knew him well. Anyway, I managed to grab some hair follicles, and I'll be doing my own tests. The one thing they're not saying is they're terrified something bad's happened to Andrade. Nobody knows where he is, and they haven't seen or heard from him since some massive fight in the embassy about six days ago. And no, I don't know what the fight was about. What I can say—'

She stopped as, through the main doors, Billy emerged, alone, shielding his eyes from the lights shining at him.

Seeing the others, he walked over.

'You okay?' Declan asked.

Billy shrugged, silently.

'What are we doing about this?' he asked.

'We are doing nothing,' Monroe replied. 'Bradbury has already laid the law down. We were hanging around until they let you out.'

'They confirmed I hadn't been here earlier, so I couldn't have done it,' Billy said, and the weariness in his voice was clear. 'All I want to do is go home.'

'And you can, after we've finished up something,' Monroe nodded. 'Detective Constable William Fitzwarren, you have thrown us into a bit of a diplomatic incident. And because of that, I've been asked by the powers that be to suspend you, with pay for the time being. Basically, you're off the case, laddie.'

'But Andrade—'

'I get that, but we can't have you using your police time to work on this case,' Monroe said, loud enough for Restrepo, casually standing to the side, having moved closer the moment Billy had arrived, to hear. 'You need to go home and wait for further instructions.'

'But—'

'*We're not working the case, lad!*' Monroe exploded. 'You're a witness in an international murder, and you've thrown us into a ton of shite with your reckless phone call! Go grab your things from the office and go home! *You're suspended!*'

Billy stared open-mouthed at Monroe for a good few

seconds, glancing at the others for support and, not finding any, took a deep breath, turned and walked away from the team, the apartment, and the police cordon.

'Are you happy now?' Monroe snapped at Restrepo who, having the good grace not to pretend he hadn't been listening, now nodded, walking back to his own agents.

'Come on, we're leaving,' Monroe said, walking back to the cordon, where PC Cooper watched Billy hail a cab and leave. 'Before we're blamed for more problems.'

'And where are we going, Guv?' Declan was angry at Monroe for doing what he'd just done; there was no reason for Billy to be treated so harshly. And no matter how hard he tried to hide this, the emotion was there for everyone to see.

'Back to the office to catch Billy before he leaves, you bampot,' Monroe whispered, already typing a message into his phone. 'We need to work out how to solve this case without being *seen* to solve it, and find out what happened to Billy's pretty-boy boyfriend before the Colombians clean house.'

4

MIDNIGHT BRIEFING

'Right then, settle down as we have a lot to go through.'

Monroe had moved everyone into the briefing room the moment they arrived back at Temple Inn, pausing Billy before he could gather his things and leave, aiming him at the glass-walled room, and sitting him in his usual chair.

It was a full house, surprisingly, for the time of evening. Monroe stood at the front of the room, the plasma screen behind him, and with Bullman in her usual place of hovering by the door. Billy was by his laptop, Anjli sat next to Declan, and Sergeant De'Geer, PC Cooper, and Doctor Marcos all sat along the back of the briefing room, waiting for Monroe to start.

'Guv,' Billy replied, half-rising from his seat. 'I'm suspended. I shouldn't—'

'Quit your gabbing, laddie,' Monroe replied, waving him back in his chair. 'I said that to calm the diplomats down.'

'So, I'm not suspended?'

'Oh, aye, you're totally suspended, but we're changing the

rules a little,' Monroe smiled, looking back at the others in the room. 'The Colombians don't want us involved, and are claiming every level of diplomatic immunity they can just to stop us from checking into this. And unfortunately, we cannot, as a City of London Unit, go against these rules.'

He looked at Bullman, who entered the room now.

'Billy, you're suspended with pay until the Colombians decide what they're doing with this case,' she explained. 'Whatever you do on your own dime, in your own time, that's nothing to do with us. I, as Detective Superintendent of the Unit, will keep a link with Pablo Restrepo at all times, pushing for what snippets I can get out of this. If I accidentally pass these to you while you act as a private citizen in this manner, I'll obviously be very apologetic.'

'And how would these snippets be accidentally passed on to DC Fitzwarren?' Monroe asked.

'Oh, did I not mention? PC Cooper will be checking in on Billy now and then, making sure he does nothing silly,' Bullman winked. 'And, of course, as a police officer who's not been suspended, I'm sure she can find ways to assist his mental health.'

Billy looked back at Esme Cooper, who nodded. Declan knew for Bullman to name her so, meant she had to have already spoken to Cooper about this. And it was a dangerous, if good, idea. Billy and Cooper could check out the facts of the case, facts drip-fed to them from Doctor Marcos and Bullman, while privately investigating the disappearance of Andrade Estrada.

'I'd like to take a week's holiday,' Declan put his hand up.

'Yeah, me too,' Anjli did the same.

'I know, we'd all like to help Billy, but we can't,' Monroe shook his head, motioning for them to put their hands down. 'And besides, DI Walsh has found us our next case, it seems.'

'But Billy needs someone with forensics knowledge,' De'Geer looked confused. 'If Doctor Marcos is passing information, then there needs to be—'

'Aye, and there will be,' Monroe nodded at the entrance to the office, through the glass windows. Entering through the double doors, and looking a little nervous as she did so, was DC Joanne Davey, recently of the Last Chance Saloon, and now on indefinite leave.

Declan felt the atmosphere change as she walked into the main office, nodding at Bullman as she made her way to the briefing room door. She'd been with the Last Chance Saloon since the start, and for most of that time had been the right hand of Doctor Marcos, a role De'Geer now served. But it had been her actions in the "Justice" case that had taken her out of the unit, and if it hadn't been for Declan, out of the force altogether.

'Everyone,' she mumbled as she entered the briefing room.

'You okay, Joanne?' De'Geer was the first to ask.

Davey smiled, brushing a strand of red, wavy hair away from her face. She'd cut it short in the months since she'd left, but the fringe was still long.

'I'm doing okay,' she replied calmly. 'Doing therapy three times a week, keeping myself busy. Was looking to get back into the job, thought this might be a good way to get rid of my ring rust.'

She grinned at Billy.

'Or, you know, get fired properly this time.'

'For those in the cheap seats, I'll go over this,' Monroe stepped forward, bringing the attention back onto him now.

'Billy is suspended. For all intents and purposes, we cannot contact him in relation to work, unless it's in connection to something he's already done, prior to the suspension, and something which we need confirmation on. Billy will be on his own cognisance, working in the shadows with DC Davey here, looking into the case we're not allowed to get involved with. PC Cooper will be their liaison to the Unit, and will pass messages from anyone gaining intelligence related to the Colombian investigation. Which, of course, we're not doing. Because we've been told not to. That understandable?'

There was a round of affirmative nods from the officers in the room.

'Okay then,' Monroe looked at Billy. 'You're suspended as of right now. Go to your desk and pick up your personal items, and by that I mean anything you think you'll need over the next few days. Also, take two of the burner phones from my desk, we'll link them together so there's no trail back to us.'

'Sir, sorry, but why do you have burner phones in your desk?' It was Cooper who asked.

'You weren't here when Declan was accused of terrorism,' Bullman replied. 'I only officially came on board after, although I was part of the investigation. We decided, as we have some very heavy hitters out there with a personal issue with the Unit, we should have a way to contact each other if we need to go off the grid.'

She looked at Monroe.

'They've been in his drawer for almost a year, waiting for their chance to shine in the spotlight. Now's a better time than any.'

Billy nodded, rising.

'I'll get my things,' he said, looking at Davey. 'Thanks.'

'Don't thank me yet, I haven't done anything,' Davey shrugged.

'You came when Monroe asked,' Billy walked past her, patting her shoulder as he did so. 'That's a lot.'

'Well, I felt I owed it to you after Walsh saved my career,' Davey nodded at the others in the room. 'So, where do we start?'

As they walked out, Declan chanced a glance at the back of the briefing room. As he expected, De'Geer was watching out of the window, following Davey and Billy as they walked to the monitor station, while Cooper stared ahead, emotionless, doing a rather poor job of hiding any inner thoughts on the matter. It was well known she carried a torch for De'Geer, while he possibly still held one for Davey.

It's going to be an interesting liaison job for her, he thought to himself as he looked back at Monroe, surprised to see the canny old Scott watching him expectantly.

'Sorry, what?' Declan asked.

'I said you'd bring us up to speed on our new case,' Monroe raised an eyebrow, amused. 'Or did you want to share something with the class?'

'I, um, I wondered what we'd be doing for cybercrime help if Billy's not here,' Declan lied, quickly looking for a route out of the hole he'd dug. 'Billy finds out a lot for us, and with him gone for the moment ...'

'We'll survive,' Monroe shrugged. 'Also, we have your daughter joining us for the Christmas holidays, so she can help on that side. She helped Billy restructure the whole thing out there. I'm sure she could start a couple of days earlier. And, if she can't help, we can always call on others. I think Trix Preston is still in our phone book.'

Declan shuddered and then nodded.

'That's fine, I think Jess is a better choice than Trix,' he blurted. 'And I like the idea of her manning the monitors—'

'Because it means she won't be on the streets?' Bullman shook her head. 'Typical dad.'

'I was going to say because she's running double duty right now,' Declan protested. 'What with the wedding.'

'Oh aye, Farrow's wedding,' Monroe smiled darkly. 'I'd almost forgotten that. I mean, he doesn't mention it continually or anything.'

Deciding not to fall into this rabbit hole of a debate, Declan rose.

'I don't have photos yet, so it's probably good Billy's not here to put the photos up,' he said.

'You do know the screen's touch sensitive?' Monroe leant in. 'I only ask Billy to do that, so the wee bairn feels part of the process.'

Declan faltered for a moment, looking at Monroe as the older man backed away, holding his hands up in surrender.

'Your case, your floor,' he said.

Swallowing, Declan straightened, and Monroe moved to where Billy had been sitting, resting against the table Billy usually placed his laptop on.

'I was at a Number Ten party tonight,' Declan started and instantly regretted it.

'Ooh, did you meet the Prime Minister?'

'It must be really cool being so famous.'

'Did you save the country with incredible policing bills?'

'Did you steal an ashtray?'

'Who's the Prime Minister this week?'

Declan waited, sighing audibly, and when the room had tired of ribbing him, he continued.

'While there I saw Shaun Donnal.'

The briefing room was quiet now. Declan looked over at De'Geer and Cooper.

'It was my first case here, and before you were in the Unit,' he said. 'Shaun was a suspect in a murder, a one-time Labour MP who fell off the rails and eventually became homeless, living on the London streets until we proved his innocence in a years' old murder.'

'We know, Guv,' De'Geer nodded.

'We read the Unit reports when we join,' Cooper added. 'All the reports.'

'Oh,' Declan, unaware of this, replied, a little deflated. 'Well then. Good. Anyway, after the case ended, Shaun pulled his life back together. He had reasons to live off the grid, and they'd now gone. As far as I know, and this was from the occasional check-in on him through the police network—'

'He was stalking him,' Anjli said knowingly.

'He saved my life,' Declan argued. 'I felt I owed it to him to keep an eye on him. Anyway, after the Devington case, he got off the streets with help from friends and family. Not his wife, that ended long before, but over the last few months he's been a figurehead in a bipartisan campaign on homelessness, and he's been lobbying Parliament for a couple of charities, while also working in the same soup kitchens that used to look after him.'

'And he was at the party?' Anjli asked.

'Charles brought him in,' Declan shrugged. 'There were a couple of things. I'll come to the second in a minute. The main reason he was there though, is because two nights ago, a homeless man named "Santa Mick" was found dead in Soho.'

'Mick or Nick?' Monroe asked. 'Because the latter is more

relevant to the season. And with the season being such—'

'Mick,' Declan hastily confirmed. 'Apparently this "Mick" was known before as "Mickey Fish" when he camped near Billingsgate, and has been Santa Mick ever since he wore a discarded Father Christmas hat, which, according to Shaun, he wore all year round.'

'How did he die?' De'Geer asked.

'I'm not sure,' Declan admitted. 'I only just found this out as I was called to Mayfair, so I haven't even called the local nick to find out where the body is.'

'Local nick or Mick?' Monroe carried on his terrible joke, but paused at a glare from Doctor Marcos.

'You think you're funny, and I'm glad for you,' she smiled coldly at her fiancé. 'But the rest of us have to suffer in silence.'

Monroe shut his mouth, glowering at the floor as Doctor Marcos looked back at Declan.

'When you do, let me know,' she nodded. 'Me and the Viking will go check it out.'

'All I know is what Shaun told me,' Declan continued, leaning back against the front table, opening up the A4 paper Shaun had given him earlier that evening. 'Santa Mick was well liked, and Shaun hadn't heard of anyone with issues against him, but the man does seem to be an enigma, with no background. One of the soup kitchen people, and by that I mean the homeless lining up for food, said he was actively off that night, almost confrontational, and within an hour after leaving he was seen to collapse in the middle of the street, where he died before help could get to him.'

'Could be natural causes,' Doctor Marcos pursed her lips. 'We need the body to be checked. If it is that, though, we don't have anything.'

'I know,' Declan replied, 'but there's something here, I can't put my finger on it. And it's not just Shaun needing help. He wrote here that a witness saw Santa Mick stagger out of an alley off the street, moments before dying, but that a woman had left only seconds before, at speed, and looking suspicious.'

'How do you "look suspicious", laddie?' Monroe asked.

Declan held up his hands.

'I don't know, but there's a name here, Mallory Reed, who Shaun reckoned might know more about the victim,' Declan tapped on the paper. 'So, I'll be checking in there as well.'

He straightened now.

'It might be nothing, or it might be someone settling scores, knowing nobody will check into it. The fact that Shaun Donnal believed in this so fervently he convinced Charles Baker to bring him to me says there's more going on here. I just don't know what yet.'

'And the other thing?'

Declan paused, trying to work out the best way to explain the second thing.

'He reckons he saw Francine Pearce on a London street in October, almost four months after she died,' he eventually replied. 'Which, I can believe as I know for a fact, as do many of you, that she most likely faked her death.'

'And caused your imprisonment, and almost killed Monroe's nephew, Tom,' Anjli hissed, looking at Monroe as she said this. 'Let me have this one, Guv. I owe that bitch some payback.'

'All we have is a place, a time and a date,' Declan interjected. 'We don't even know if it was her. Shaun spent years on the street. This and the whole Santa Mick thing might be nothing more than trauma taking normal situations and turning them into conspiracies.'

There was a long silence as everyone considered this.

'I know a couple of people in Soho nick, from when I worked there,' Cooper eventually replied. 'They're street-walking coppers, so there's a chance if they were in town two nights back, they were called in on this.'

'Make that call, please,' Declan nodded. 'And, if you can locate it, find out where the body is, so De'Geer and Doctor Marcos can have a look.'

He turned to Anjli.

'Tomorrow, we'll have a look around the area,' he said.

'And check into this location where Francine Pearce was found?' Anjli asked hopefully.

At this thought, Declan shook his head.

'I was hoping the Guv could do that,' he replied, looking at Monroe. 'If I do it, or if the person I live with is doing it, we could lose ground if we do find her. Remember, she's an expert on court cases and how to have them thrown out of court. She could have us down as prejudiced because of what happened.'

'But she also tried to have the Guv killed!' Anjli complained.

'Aye, but that wasn't personal,' Monroe smiled. 'The whole "setting Declan up as an abductor" angle that DS Ross came in to check? That's *totally* personal.'

'Right then,' Declan looked back at Monroe. 'Do you want to finish up?'

'Actually, *I* do,' Bullman stepped more into the briefing room than she usually did. 'I have a bit of a problem, and I need help.'

'Whatever you need, boss,' Declan said as he sat back down.

'We don't have a Christmas party sorted, and it's less than two weeks until the day itself,' Bullman replied. 'Declan's talk of swanky Whitehall parties, and the fact he smells of small-talk and canapes, reminded me. If you know anywhere we can have it, let me know.'

This earth-shaking announcement made, Bullman looked around the room.

'I didn't say it was a big problem,' she said, unimpressed at the lack of interest facing her. 'Go on, piss off home, be back bright and early tomorrow. We need to find a diplomat, stop a killer, find a dead person and solve Santa's murder. You're going to need a lot of sleep if you want to solve the case and stay on his good list.'

5

FREUD POISONING

THE FOLLOWING MORNING, DECLAN ARRIVED TO FIND HIS daughter, Jess, already working at Billy's computer monitor system. Sixteen-years-old and now in her first year of A Levels, Jess wanted more than anything to join the police when she was able and, over the last year had proven to be a pivotal member of the team, far more than the "mascot" some people seemed to think she was. And, having spent days beside Billy, she was probably also the only person in London who knew how to use his sprawling file admin system.

'Morning,' he said as he pulled his overcoat off, hanging it up as he looked around. Apart from Anjli, who'd driven in with him, there wasn't anyone else in the building, it seemed, if you didn't count the desk sergeant in reception.

'Morning Guv,' Jess said, smiling.

Declan winced a little at this; although she was making sure she spoke the correct "police speak" while in the office, he would have liked her to call him *Dad.*

'Where is everyone?'

'DCI Monroe is yet to come in, D Supt Bullman is in her office, and Morten – I mean Sergeant De'Geer – is in Paddington with Doctor Marcos, checking on the body.'

'We found it?' the news surprised Declan, although he wasn't sure why. There probably weren't that many homeless people collapsing dead in London streets right now.

'Yes, but we still don't have a name,' Jess pulled up some details. 'The victim was found on Broadwick Lane in Soho and was taken by the paramedics to St Mary's Hospital. He was declared dead on arrival and placed in the morgue.'

'Doctor Marcos will love that then,' Declan nodded. 'You okay?'

'It's a learning curve,' Jess admitted. 'But it's better than the alternative.'

Declan frowned before realisation hit.

'The wedding?'

'It's stressful for Mum,' Jess turned in the chair to face her father. 'Henry's still convinced Monroe and Doctor Marcos got engaged just to annoy him, and I said this wasn't true as I was there when it happened, but he won't listen.'

'You think he'd listen to me?'

'Sure, Dad,' Jess replied with mock sincerity. 'I'm sure he'll love having his fiancée's ex-husband call him up and give marriage advice.'

'He asked my advice when picking the bloody ring,' Declan muttered, starting up his own computer, but as he did so, he hid a secret smile.

At least she called him Dad this time.

Anjli, having escaped upstairs to make a couple of mugs of coffee, appeared now, passing one over to Declan as she placed her own one on her desk.

'Anything from Billy?' she asked.

Jess shook her head.

'I've not really been told what's going on,' she said, looking back at her dad hopefully. 'Maybe you could tell me what's happening?'

'If Bullman's keeping you out of the loop, then it's for a reason,' Declan replied apologetically, picking up the mug and taking a mouthful of the coffee to draw the moment out. 'I'll ask her when I see her.'

Jess, knowing she wasn't going to get any further, turned back to the computers, already forgetting Anjli and Declan were there.

'You up for a stroll?' Monroe said, walking into the office, his overcoat still done up. Declan, jumping slightly at the voice from behind, tapped his mug.

'Can I finish the coffee first?' he asked.

Monroe paused by the desk, considered this, and smiled.

'Only if you made me one as well,' he said.

Declan went to speak, but it was Anjli who replied, passing her own mug across.

'Here you go, Guv,' she said with a winning smile. 'Just how you like it.'

Monroe took the coffee from her, frowned, and then placed it back on the desk.

'I wouldn't take a lassie's caffeine,' he shook his head. 'Nice try, though. Ten minutes, and then we bounce. Morning, Jess.'

And before Jess could reply, Monroe had already entered his office.

'Anything more from the paramedics?' Declan asked as he sipped his drink. 'In the St Mary's notes?'

Jess pulled up a document, reading it. After a long, drawn-out moment, she looked back at Declan.

'Nope.'

Declan almost laughed at this.

'I appreciate the candour,' he said, finishing his coffee and placing it onto his desk. 'Don't break anything while we're out.'

Back in his office, Monroe was standing beside his desk, and when he saw Declan put his overcoat on, he returned into the main office. By the time he arrived, Anjli had also finished her mug, wiping her mouth with the back of her hand to make sure the froth was gone.

'What's the rush, anyway?' Declan frowned. 'Soho isn't going anywhere.'

'Aye, but the soup kitchen that's giving out hot breakfasts to the homeless right now will be,' Monroe replied. 'And I believe the Lewis chap your friend Shaun mentioned is working the shift, so it's the best time to chat to him.'

'He's not my friend,' Declan grumbled as they walked to the door. 'He's more an acquaintance who held me at gunpoint once.'

'Laddie, that's how all my long-term friends were made,' Monroe laughed. 'Come on, we might even get a bacon roll.'

THE ST BENEDICT'S POP-UP HOMELESS FOOD KITCHEN WAS again at the end of Berwick Street, and where the street food vendors would set up for the lunch trade. In fact, several of the vendors were already setting up, and grumbling loudly about the kitchen still being there, although Declan, as he walked through the market area, listening to the vendors, felt they were complaining more about the clientele of the pop-up kitchen, than of the kitchen itself.

There was still a small queue of people standing waiting, and Declan let them go through before talking. Anjli was originally joining him, but had dropped back a couple of streets ago, deciding to have a quick look at the death site in Broadwick Lane before returning to Declan, and Monroe had gone to check a building on Wardour Street.

Declan could work out easily which of the two servers today was Lewis, primarily as there was only one man serving. He was young, maybe mid-to-late thirties, his hair cut into a short, probably trendy style with product combed in, helping it defy gravity, while shaved at the sides. He was slim, almost painfully so, and wore a blue collarless shirt that seemed a little too big for him. Declan wondered for a moment whether this was rapid weight loss because of illness, but the man seemed healthy in himself, and Declan shrugged the shirt off as possibly a mis-purchase, or even that this was the current style.

Lewis looked up, seeing Declan.

'Coffee or tea?' he asked, and Declan shook his head.

'Oh, no, I'm not here for breakfast,' he said. However, as he spoke this, he saw Lewis's face soften, as he nodded in what seemed to be some kind of misunderstanding.

'I understand,' Lewis said. 'It's always hard for the first time. Pride gets in the way—'

Declan realised with a shudder of horror, that Lewis was under the assumption he was homeless, and quickly pulled out his warrant card, showing it before things got even more awkward.

'DI Walsh,' he said, placing it back away. 'I'm guessing you're Lewis Hoyle? I'm here to talk about Santa Mick.'

At the revelation of the warrant card, Lewis looked horrified, which was to be expected. And, as he whispered to the girl beside him, probably asking her to hold the fort, he pulled off his apron and slipped out of the side of the gazebo.

As he did this, Declan looked down at his crumpled suit and battered overcoat.

Do I really look homeless?

Lewis must have caught the look, as when he walked up to Declan, he smiled weakly.

'I'm really sorry,' he said. 'It's just many of you ... them, many of *them* when they first fall, they try to keep to things they feel comfortable in. You've worked for ten years in a job with a suit and tie, well then you feel more secure when wearing it after you're let go of. So, we get people in suits turning up, without homes, without jobs, but still trying to look as if they do, literally living a lie.'

Declan watched Lewis. He understood the comment, but there was still a small part of him that wanted the man to squirm a little.

'So, Santa Mick,' he said.

Lewis, at this, nodded eagerly, grateful to change the subject.

'Was he murdered?' he asked, not in a mawkish, "need to know" way, but more to complete a silent belief, to know whether or not he was right in his suspicions.

'We don't know yet,' Declan replied quietly. 'We're examining the body now. Once we've done that, we'll know better.'

'But you're still checking into it?'

Declan shrugged.

'An old acquaintance asked me to,' he explained. 'And until we know for sure, I'm willing to look into it.'

'Shaun Donnal,' the name was spoken as a statement rather than as an enquiry. 'I knew him before he cleaned himself up, you know. Used to come to the soup kitchen. So did Minty, the guy he stabbed with a screwdriver.'

'How is ... um, Minty?' Declan asked. After the Devonshire case, he'd lost track of all the little side-cases. Lewis gave a reluctant half-shrug.

'On the streets, same as usual. He now has a story to tell, a small scar to show, and is way more distrusting of strangers,' he said. 'Shaun's been trying to build bridges with him, but it's hard when the guy you're trying to do this with thinks you're going to kill him.'

'And how is Shaun?' Declan asked.

At this, however, Lewis grinned.

'You mean "is Shaun still a hallucinating alcoholic, and is this all one of his fever dreams", don't you?'

Declan gave an awkward half-smile in response.

'The thought was there,' he said. 'I saw him a year ago, just after the case, and he was cleaning himself up, but ...'

'Yeah, I get you,' Lewis nodded. 'He's done good. He's doing the steps, going to meetings, I think whatever secrets he had were no longer important, after you did whatever it was you did. He could start afresh. And we all need that, sometimes.'

'What's your story?' Declan asked. 'Were you ever ...'

'Homeless? God no,' Lewis shook his head. 'I wanted to be a priest, but it didn't work out.'

'How come?'

'Issues with faith,' Lewis replied. 'I believe in God, but there were things I questioned. And you don't really do that. And then a path I thought lost to me reopened up ... anyway, I wanted to help, to serve, and I started helping the charity that does this.'

He waved around the soup kitchen to emphasise the point.

'Over the years I, well, I just stayed,' he smiled, and this time it was a genuine one. 'It was my calling.'

'Well, I'm glad you found it,' Declan pulled out a notebook. 'Can you tell me about Mick?'

'Known him for about five years now, since just before he stopped being Mickey Fish.'

'Billingsgate, right?'

'Yeah, he'd been there a couple of years,' Lewis explained. 'Started turning up in Soho, one of the other kitchens, and became one of those faces you always saw, yeah? And then a year or so after, he gained his first Santa hat. No idea why or how, but it called to him, yeah? Probably helped him when begging or something, and became his lucky charm. But then he carried on wearing it into spring. And then summer. And on and on. I started buying replacements, because the bloody things got filthy, and I'd swap them with him, so he always had an almost-fresh one. I'd buy ten at the end of Christmas, usually at a sale price, ten, twenty quid or so, and update them throughout the year. And, as time went on, the name "Santa Mick" came and stuck.'

'Sounds like you cared for him a lot,' Declan said, looking up from his notes.

'I care for all of them,' Lewis said, looking back at the kitchen and the last people in the queue. 'You can't not, when you see them every day. Even the addicts, who don't know where they are, and try to sell the bread back to you for a hit.'

Declan nodded at this, understanding how someone could do this. When he was a redcap, there were squaddies people classed as lost causes, people he was constantly arresting, but who he would still have gone into battle for.

'He was accepting of his fate,' Lewis added. 'Told me once he didn't mind the abuse, or the beatings he got for wearing the hat all year round, because it was karma for his past.'

'What did he mean?'

'No idea, we never learnt about it,' Lewis shrugged. 'Christ, they didn't even know if Mick was his real name.'

Declan considered this, noting it down.

'Tell me about the last time you saw him,' he continued. 'Three nights ago?'

Lewis nodded.

'It was a normal Sunday night in the kitchen,' he said. 'We were exactly the same as we always were. Mick came up, humming a carol, as he always does, and I had a replacement hat for him, as the last time I'd seen him, it was pretty grimy. But he didn't want it, was saying he'd been given one by a lady who would talk to him when she went to work. A nurse, I think. Or some kind of health professional.'

He blushed.

'I'll admit, I was a little pissed off,' he said. 'I was jealous that someone else had given him the hat. I said I'd wear it myself, but as I did so, he lunged at me, grabbed it, pulling it away and throwing it into a puddle.'

'He was violent?'

'No, but he had been drinking,' Lewis replied. 'And he was scared. After he did this, he was really apologetic, kept saying "no wearing the hat" and "only Santa Mick wears the hat", as if it scared him someone would see me. He was literally pleading, and when I asked if he was okay, he just mumbled he wanted the soup, took it and left.'

Lewis's face darkened.

'I never saw him again.'

Declan closed the notepad, looking around.

'Did he have any enemies?'

'Not that I saw. People liked Santa Mick. He was like a good luck charm.'

Lewis paused, scratching at his chin for a moment.

'There was one thing,' he added. 'The girl working with me. Young girl, friendly, her name was Mina. I was convinced she put a drop of something into his soup, but when I asked her, she said she hadn't, and there was nothing in her hands. I was probably just tired.'

'That's worth looking into,' Declan said. 'Is she here today?'

'No, but the charity will have her details, and she stays in a Rectory in Hampstead,' Lewis replied. 'Wait here, I'll get a card and write a name you should speak to on it.'

As Lewis walked off to do this, Declan spied Anjli walking across the street.

'Anything?' he asked.

'No witnesses in the shops, but there's CCTV cameras at both ends,' Anjli replied. 'Hopefully one of those two have picked something up.'

Lewis walked back, passing Declan a card.

'Call this number, they'll be able to give you details on Mina,' he said.

Nodding thanks, Declan placed it into his pocket.

'One last thing,' he said, looking around. 'Mick said a woman gave him the hat, talking to him when she went to work. That means he had to be somewhere in the mornings, even on weekends. Do you know where he slept?'

Lewis considered this.

'December, he'd be in the shelters,' he said. 'Maybe St Mungo's, possibly Whitechapel, I don't know. I think he spent his mornings in Liverpool Street and worked down Fleet Street? Ended the day with us.'

'Thanks,' Declan shook Lewis's hand, before turning to leave with Anjli. 'We'll let you know if we find anything.'

As they walked away from the kitchen, Lewis already returning and pulling his apron back on, Declan considered what he'd heard. If Santa Mick walked down Fleet Street daily, there was every chance he could have met Declan when he walked out of Temple Inn for a coffee, or a sandwich.

Had they ever met?

Had Declan simply ignored the homeless man?

'I know what you're doing,' Anjli said, glancing at him. 'Stop it. You'll get nowhere, blaming yourself for someone you never even met.'

Declan forced a smile, looking at Anjli.

'Let's go find Monroe,' he said. 'I could do with some good news.'

6

VISITORS BOOKED

MONROE HAD KNOWN FROM THE MOMENT HE ENTERED THE building's reception this was going to be a lost cause situation.

The outside of 100 Wardour Street had matched the surroundings: black wood framing with tinted black windows under a brick four-storey building, with a bar to the right and a gelato shop to the left of it had faced him when he arrived. He had memories of this once being a cigar bar he'd been to, but this looked long gone. And, when he entered through the doors, it was as far from the homely atmosphere of a cigar bar as you could find.

The reception was small, cold, bare, and white. No screens, no paintings or prints, not even a company logo behind the reception desk; it was a company that you came to only if you knew where you were going. And in this case, Monroe was not part of that list.

To the side was a modern-looking, black, backless sofa, almost nothing more than a padded bench, and in front of it was a black, wooden coffee table, unadorned by any of the usual magazines, pamphlets or flyers you'd usually find in a place like this. And, to Monroe's copper mind, this was suspicious. It really was as if the company didn't want anyone to know who they were.

There was a receptionist at the standing-counter reception as he entered, looking him up and down as he walked towards her, as if deciding whether he had the "look" of someone who needed to be here. Deciding he was obviously lost, she faked a weak, obviously insincere smile.

'Can I help you, sir?' she asked with the enthusiasm of someone who really didn't want the answer to be in the affirmative.

Monroe smiled back, a more genuine smile, as he leant on the counter.

'Aye, I'm hoping you can,' he said. 'Who owns this building?'

'Sorry, sir?'

'I mean, which company do you work for?' Monroe looked around. 'I mean, I can't see a single thing that states where I am.'

The receptionist frowned.

'Were you looking for *Bar Casa*?' she asked. 'It's been gone a while now. We suggest the smoking lounges in St. James or Pall Mall.'

'No, that's alright, lassie,' Monroe looked back at her. 'I was asking about the current owners, not the past ones.'

'And you are?'

Monroe smiled, pulling out his warrant card and showing it to her.

'Detective Chief Inspector Alex Monroe,' he said.

Usually, this was the point when the person he was talking to would change their attitude, realising the police were asking questions, but surprisingly, the receptionist almost doubled down on her current dismissive attitude.

'Are we in trouble?' she asked, almost mockingly.

'That depends,' Monroe kept his fixed smile, but the humour behind it had gone. 'On whether you can tell me who owns this place.'

He hadn't seen the receptionist press any buttons, but to the right, an elevator door opened, and a middle-aged, portly man emerged from within. He was in a trendy-looking suit that seemed a little too tight for him, a dress shirt without a tie, and his balding hair was cut short, giving him a surrounding peppered cuff to his bald pate.

'Can I help you?' he asked, walking over to Monroe, stopping at Monroe's side of the reception desk.

'Well, that depends who you are,' Monroe smiled.

'I'm the head of security here.'

'Your name?' Monroe was rapidly tiring of being nice now, pulling out his notebook and pen as he spoke.

'What's the problem here?' the head of security looked at the receptionist.

'The problem here, laddie, is you've avoided telling me your name, while your woman here has avoided telling me the name of your company several times,' Monroe replied now, his tone icy and angering fast. 'Two questions I'd like answered before I continue.'

'My name, DCI Monroe, is Paul Stringer, and I'm the head of security for Robinson Finance,' the head of security, now identified as Paul, replied. 'And as you are a City of London officer, and we're definitely *not* in the City here, I question your jurisdiction in whatever matter you're here on.'

Monroe raised his eyebrows at this. He hadn't said where

he was from, and the receptionist hadn't had time to pass the message.

They knew who he was before he walked in.

'I'm asking questions,' Monroe smiled disarmingly. 'Conversationally.'

'Well, *conversationally*, you can bring us a warrant if you want us to answer anything,' Paul replied.

'Even if I wanted to see a visitor book for, say, October the twentieth at around a quarter to ten?'

Paul didn't answer this, staring coldly at Monroe.

'Aye, didn't think so,' the older detective smiled coldly. 'You see, the problem now, *Paul*, is I was just coming in for a quick social visit, mainly checking out a vague comment a witness to something else made to me. A quick squizz at the visitor book, a smile or two and I'd be gone.'

Monroe moved closer now, face to face with the stockier man.

'But now? Now you've piqued my interest, laddie,' he continued. 'And I'll be back. Tell Francine Pearce the Last Chance Saloon says hi.'

'We have nobody of that name associated with us,' Paul replied, stone-faced.

'Aye, of course you don't,' Monroe nodded slowly. 'Check the visitors' log then. Tell whoever signed in around that time the message, aye?'

'I think you should leave now,' Paul folded his arms as he spoke. 'Before I call the real police.'

Monroe chuckled, holding his hands up and backing off.

'I liked this place a lot more when it was a cigar bar,' he said. 'They were much pickier about who worked here. And it smelled less.'

Walking out onto the street, Monroe straightened his

jacket and took a deep breath. He'd played the calm response in the room, but he was secretly livid and boiling with anger.

They knew who he was. They knew he was coming.

They knew Francine Pearce.

Looking around the street, he glanced back through the tinted windows, seeing Paul Stringer watching him still. And, deciding not to give any clues towards their next steps, he held his hand out, hailing a taxi, before heading back to Temple Inn.

In the reception, Paul watched Monroe leave before pulling out a phone, dialling a number and holding it to his ear.

'It's me,' he said after a moment. 'You were right. They've found her.'

The message given, Paul disconnected, nodded to the receptionist, and then left the floor, returning to the elevator.

There was a lot to do, and little time to do it in.

'You know, I thought you'd have more mahogany,' Davey said, as she looked around Billy's house. 'Maybe some baroque furniture. Definitely a Chesterfield or two.'

'This is one of my great-uncle's houses,' Billy explained as he placed his box of paperwork and peripherals, taken from the office, onto a leather sofa. 'He rents it out usually, it was currently empty, and I needed to get out of my apartment.'

'How come?' Davey looked out of the window at the

Wanstead street outside. 'There's a pub on the corner. We could decamp there.'

'Let's just say they weren't as welcoming to my alternative lifestyle as I'd hoped,' Billy replied. 'And that's word for word, from a letter sent to me.'

'Alternate lifestyle?' Davey frowned. 'You mean being gay?'

Billy shrugged, walking to a door at the end of the living room.

'Want a coffee?' he said.

'I'll have a tea if your butler is around,' Davey grinned. 'Seriously though, isn't this a little far out of the City for you?'

Billy was in the kitchen now, shouting through the door.

'Not really,' he replied. 'Remember, Declan and Anjli commute from bloody Berkshire, and I man the monitor desk mainly, so I don't need to worry about bringing the car in, as I don't need to go out to crime scenes that much. And I can grab the Central Line train into either Holborn or Chancery Lane and walk, or I change at Liverpool Street and catch the Circle Line to Temple.'

'Well, that's just a waste of a chauffeur,' Davey mocked, sitting down on the sofa. 'Can I ask a question?'

'Sure,' Billy walked back into the room with two mugs. He placed one down in front of her. 'If I can ask you one after.'

'You were told Andrade was leaving the embassy at the end of the year, right?' Davey looked around. 'I'm guessing you'd decided not to go with him. That's not the question, just a comment, by the way.'

'Yeah,' Billy nodded. 'It's too much of a nightmare to bounce every six months. And I have my life, my career, everything here.'

'And yet here you are, a couple of weeks before he would

have left, in a house you could leave at any time, having given up your long-term lease,' Davey picked up her mug, blowing on the tea to cool it down. 'Are you sure you don't want to go with him? Because to me, it looks like you're doing everything in your power to clear your desk before you *do* go.'

Billy looked around the room for a long moment.

'I suppose it could look like that,' he admitted. 'It's not supposed to, though. I swear.'

He sipped at his own drink before looking back at Davey.

'Go on then,' she smiled. 'Ask the bloody question.'

'Why didn't you come back?' Billy asked. 'It's been three months since they took you off suspension—'

'You mean since my Detective Inspector blackmailed the sitting Prime Minister to give me my job back?' Davey interrupted.

'Bullman did the same for Monroe.'

'I'm not Monroe.'

'No, you're not,' Billy snapped. 'He made mistakes, and he's trying to make up for them while you hide away and hope they'll swallow you up.'

Davey sighed, leaning back on the sofa so that her head was staring up at the ceiling.

'I thought you'd get it better than the others,' she said. 'You quit as well, remember?'

Billy did. After the whole "Declan is a terrorist" incident, Billy had been forced into a position where he sided against his own friends and had been at the wrong end of a gun barrel one too many times. As such, he'd decided to leave the force and find his own way, something that changed after the *Red Reaper* case.

'I did, but again, I came back,' he said. 'Look, Joanne. We all understand what you did and why you did them.

Christ, Monroe and Declan have both done similar. You could have come back, and you'd have been welcomed. You were used.'

Davey smiled.

'I was never supposed to be there,' she replied. 'They brought me across with Doctor Marcos. I stopped being a DS and became Igor to her Doctor Frankenstein. I've had a lot of time to reflect, and that's not the direction I wanted to go. And I wasn't completely happy there.'

'Are we talking about the job now, or De'Geer?' Billy leant forwards now, cupping his mug of tea. 'Because there was a moment—'

'There's *always* a moment,' Davey snapped. 'That doesn't mean you have to listen to it.'

They sat in silence for a moment.

'We miss you,' Bill eventually said. '*I* miss you.'

Davey gave a faint smile back at this.

'Thanks,' she said. 'It means a lot. And I missed you too, Richie Rich, it's why I offered my services the moment I heard you were offing diplomats. I mean, if anyone in that Unit can help you hide bodies, it's me.'

Billy went to snap back a reply, but realised Davey was finally laughing. Smiling himself, he relaxed.

'How is everyone?' Davey asked. 'Did De'Geer and Cooper get it on in the end?'

'Not yet,' Billy smiled as he shook his head. 'It's like watching baby chicks try to learn to swim. They shared a room on the last big "out of London" case, though.'

'And?'

'Apparently, De'Geer took a shower, and Cooper took a long walk and ended up sleeping in the data hub.'

Davey laughed at this, and her phone beeped.

'It has to be Bullman,' she said, pulling it out. 'I think it's the only number we have in them.'

She read the message.

'Rosanna had a tip from one of the Colombians,' she said. 'They've only just identified the body. The dead guy is called José Almas.'

Billy walked over to a desktop and monitor he had in the corner of his living room, turning it on as he waited for the screen to boot up.

'I've heard that name before,' he said. 'Andrade told me he replaced José in London. So why is an ex-diplomat dead in his apartment?'

'More importantly, how can the section chief claim he didn't know who the body was, when he would have seen him every day?' a new voice spoke, and both Billy and Davey spun to see PC Esme Cooper, her face flushed and angry, standing at the door. 'He would have had a key if he lived there before Andrade, so that explains how he got in. But his face wasn't mutilated, right? Pablo Restrepo would have seen it. And recognised him. Doctor Marcos called it at the crime scene. They lied to us.'

'How long have you been there?' Billy, realising the topic of conversation before the message arrived, asked.

'Long enough to hear how I'm a baby chick,' Cooper replied. 'Not a fan of that, to be honest.'

'Sorry,' Billy said, but before he could continue, his computer burst into life, and he was distracted by the screen.

Davey, however, rose and walked over.

'I asked the question, so don't blame him,' she said, holding out a hand. 'It's good to see you, Esme.'

Cooper shook Davey's hand, but didn't reply, instead looking back at Billy.

'So, what do you have on this Almas guy?'

'Give me a chance!' Billy exclaimed, glaring back at the two women. 'I've only just logged in!'

'The Billy Fitzwarren I knew would have done this *before* he logged in,' Davey mocked.

'Oh, good,' Billy smiled. 'You're bonding with each other over a joint mockery of me.'

Rising from his computer, he walked to the door.

'I'm going to the loo,' he said. 'Esme, there's coffee in the machine and the kettle's boiled.'

This said, he left the room, heading upstairs. He didn't need the toilet, but he needed some time away from people. Since he'd last been here he'd been accused of murdering a diplomat, didn't know where his diplomat boyfriend was, had been held on suspicion, released, suspended, and was now being babysat by colleagues.

He hadn't had a moment alone in over twelve hours.

Walking into his bedroom, he released a sigh, walking to his double bed – no, the double bed he was renting from his uncle – and sat down on the end. He wanted to cry, scream, punch something, all at the same time, even, because he felt completely powerless in the situation. Andrade had been completely off the grid for the last week, and now there was a dead man in his bath.

Had he known about this? Had he been the one that did this?

His train of thought stopped however, as he saw the blood on the corner of the duvet. It was small, a tiny spattering, but it hadn't been there when he left the previous night.

Rising, and slowly scanning the room, Billy saw a similar red smudge, barely noticeable unless you were looking for it, on the door to his built-in wardrobe. Carefully walking to it, he slid it open—

A battered and blood-stained Andrade, crouched against the wall and in black trousers and a white, blood-spattered shirt, stared up at him in fear.

'It's not my blood,' he said, looking at his hands. 'I swear.'

'Is it José Almas's?' Billy said carefully.

At this, Andrade's eyes widened.

'You know?' he whispered. 'I didn't do it, I swear.'

'I believe you,' Billy held out a hand to his boyfriend, and potential murder suspect. 'So how about we get you cleaned up, and you can tell me what really happened?'

7

FIND THE LADY

MONROE WAS BACK AT THE OFFICE WHEN DECLAN AND ANJLI returned from Soho.

'You didn't walk, did you?' he asked, surprised. 'You could have caught a cab with me!'

'That was our plan,' Declan said icily. 'However, we watched you climb into one and leave as we were walking down Wardour Street.'

'Oh, aye, sorry about that,' Monroe looked down at Jess, who he was currently standing beside as she typed on the keyboard. 'I was being watched, and the last thing I wanted was for them to see you with me.'

'A message would have been nice,' Declan said.

At this, Monroe frowned.

'I sent you a message!' he replied indignantly, pulling out his phone. 'I typed it out in the car and everything—'

He stopped as he looked at the screen.

'Let me guess,' Declan sighed as he removed his coat, placing it over the back of his chair. 'You forgot to press *send*.'

Monroe tapped his screen and a little "send message"

noise could be heard faintly . A second later, Declan's phone buzzed. He looked down at it.

I'm being watched. Making own way back. See you at office.

'It doesn't mean the same when you do it after we've arrived,' Anjli said, reading the same message on her own phone.

'It's the thought that counts,' Monroe protested.

Declan walked over to Jess now.

'Did you manage to look into the Mina woman?' he asked.

'Not yet, because you only sent it ten minutes ago,' Jess said, and Declan could tell immediately from her tone she was pissed off. 'I've already had the "oh well Billy would have done that already" speech from the old man of the sea here.'

Declan looked at Monroe, who held his hands up in surrender at this.

'Jess,' Declan said softly. 'Do you need help?'

'No, I'm fine—' Jess stopped, as her brain caught up with her mouth. 'Oh, God. I'm so sorry, Mister Monroe.'

As Monroe made a "it's nothing" motion, Declan crouched beside the chair.

'Billy's been doing this for years,' he said. 'You've helped him here and there. You're allowed to be overwhelmed.'

'It's a little full-on,' Jess admitted. 'Usually I'm doing the scrag work while Billy does all the wizardry.'

'Aye, and because of that, we do throw a lot of the normal stuff onto him,' Monroe admitted. 'Work at your own pace, lassie. Technically, we shouldn't even have you doing this.'

I've got Mina's details,' Anjli said, now on her desk's phone. 'Take that off your list.'

Jess nodded gratefully as Declan looked at Monroe, the pair of them walking away now from his daughter.

'So, is it Pearce?' he asked softly, looking back, making sure Jess didn't overhear.

'I think it might be, aye,' Monroe replied. 'They definitely didn't want me there, and they knew who I was. I've seen a couple of cameras on the street, so the next step is to see if the owners of those have three months' worth of footage we can check.'

His phone buzzed, and looking at the screen, Monroe turned the phone onto speaker.

'You've got me, Declan, and Anjli here,' he said. 'Speak.'

'I'm with Doctor Marcos,' the voice of De'Geer came through the phone's speaker. 'She's had a look at the body.'

'And?'

'She said it's definitely got the signs of poisoning,' De'Geer confirmed. 'She said she'd go into it more when we get back, but it looks like Santa Mick was ingesting things not included in the usual soup kitchen menu.'

'Do we know what, yet?' Declan asked.

'No, but there was one thing that showed,' De'Geer was silent for a moment, and the faint sound of him flipping through his notebook could be heard down the line. 'Viscumin.'

'Never heard of it,' Monroe frowned. 'Should I have?'

'In a way, maybe,' De'Geer was reading as he replied. 'Doctor Marcos said she only knows of it because she was really into *Asterix* books as a kid and wanted to learn everything.'

Monroe frowned, but before he could reply, De'Geer continued.

'Viscumin is the name given to the group of toxic lectins

present in mistletoe,' he said. 'And concentrated, it's enough to kill.'

'Wait,' Declan looked up at this. 'You're telling me someone named "Santa Mick" was killed by a poison made from concentrated mistletoe, the stuff used in Christmas decorations?'

'I'm just saying what I'm being told,' De'Geer sounded reluctant to continue. 'And she said although they found welts and redness on his forehead, that was likely through sweat. However, she also found old bridgework in Santa Mick's mouth, high-end work. She sent the serial number of the implant in to see if she can find – oh, I'm being called away, back later.'

The phone went dead, and Monroe, Declan, and Anjli stared at each other.

'Did he just say high-end dental work?' Anjli said slowly. 'Because this is sounding more and more like Santa Mick wasn't your common homeless person.'

'Mistletoe,' Monroe shook his head. 'I used to kiss girls under it. Never thought it could kill.'

'Well, it could if it fell onto your head,' Jess said. 'And you know, it was, like, still attached to the tree branch.'

Monroe looked back at her, and she beamed back at him.

'I have something, Guv,' she said, as if knowing this would belay any complaints about her terrible joke.

'Come on then, bedazzle us,' Monroe grumbled.

In response, Jess brought up a screen showing Broadwick Street on a CCTV camera.

'The pub Anjli spoke to sent us details on how to access their cloud server,' she explained. 'They keep seven days' worth of footage on it, and it's aimed down the street.'

'Which means we should see Santa Mick's last moments,' Monroe nodded. 'Go on, girl.'

'Ah, well, that's a problem,' Jess admitted. 'I don't know how to scroll forward or backwards. I've texted Billy for advice.'

'It's this button,' Declan said, leaning over and tapping a button on the keyboard, and immediately the screen moved forward at speed. 'I've seen him do it so many times. And that one there is backwards.'

Jess smiled gratefully at her father as she scrolled through the images. It was lunchtime, and daylight, but within a matter of a minute or two, the image on the monitor had darkened into night.

'The soup kitchen would turn up between seven and nine on a Sunday night,' Anjli said, walking over to watch the screen with the others. 'So, we should start to see something soon—'

'There,' Declan pointed. 'Stop the footage.'

Jess did so, and on the screen, a crowd had gathered around the dead body of Santa Mick.

'Okay, now go back,' Declan said, and on the screen the images reversed, people running backwards as, at five times speed, the dead body of Santa Mick lurched to life, disappearing off into an alley.

'Keep going,' Declan insisted before Jess could pause again. 'I want to see him enter the alley – there.'

Stopping the video, Jess hit play, and the team watched as, on the monitor, Santa Mick lurched onto the screen. In the bottom corner now, he leant against a wall, pulling off his hat and staring at it for a moment, before pulling it back on and staggering down the middle of the street.

'He looks worse for wear,' Declan muttered. 'Lewis said he was slurring, so he could be drunk.'

'He's more than that,' Anjli tapped the screen. 'He's clutching his gut. That's stomach pain.'

On the video, Santa Mick paused, staring down the street, and then, as if deciding to take a different path, he turned right, heading down the side road.

'That's Duck Lane,' Anjli said. 'I looked down there. It's a cul-de-sac.'

'Probably looking for somewhere private to, well, you know,' Monroe said. 'Should we forward it until—'

He stopped, as, on the screen, a second person walked down the alley, after Santa Mick. She was young, brunette and wearing glasses, a checked skirt and a hooded jacket, the hood down for the moment.

'She deliberately followed him,' Jess said, reversing the footage again. Now, watching once more and focusing on the woman, they saw her walking towards Santa Mick from the opposite end of the street, and then veering into the lane after him as he lurched away for some privacy.

'Is there a camera down there?' Monroe hissed.

'Unfortunately, no,' Jess shook her head. 'Sorry.'

'It's not your fault, lassie,' Monroe said as, on the screen, the woman hurried out once more, continuing her journey.

'She wasn't there longer than thirty seconds,' Declan checked his watch. 'A minute, tops.'

'Enough time to poison someone,' Anjli mused. 'Although he looked in a pretty bad state before this.'

As she spoke, on the screen, Santa Mick stumbled back onto the street, clutching at his throat. The people passing by stepped back as Santa Mick fell to his knees, silently screaming before falling—

Declan paused the image.

'We've seen enough,' he said, closing the screen. 'Jess doesn't need to see the rest.'

Monroe nodded.

'We need to find that woman,' he replied. 'Even if she didn't do anything, she could help us with what they said down that alley.'

There was a beep as a message appeared on Jess's screen.

'Doctor Marcos just emailed,' Jess read the message. 'They've been able to check in to that dental work, and they got a name. Michael Siddell.'

'Santa Mick is a Michael,' Monroe nodded. 'Do we have anything on him?'

Jess was already checking.

'There was a missing person's report for a Michael Siddell back in 2008,' she said, reading the screen. 'Sixteenth of September.'

Monroe frowned.

'Why do I know that date?' he asked. 'What else is there on this?'

'It says he was forty-eight, married, no kids, worked in the city as an investment broker for ...'

She stopped, looking back.

'*Lehman Brothers.*'

At this, Declan understood.

'That's the reason the date's familiar,' he said, looking at Monroe. 'That's the week the city crashed. *Northern Rock, Lehman Brothers, Merrill Lynch,* the banks fell like dominos. People lost their life savings, and companies laid off hundreds, thousands of workers, even.'

'The bank he's working for collapses, and the next day he disappears,' Monroe nodded. 'Poor bugger probably had his own breakdown. And then for fourteen years he lives on the streets.'

'This means we might have other motives though,' Anjli said, leaning against her desk as she spoke, phone in her hand. 'This might not be someone with an axe to grind against Mickey Fish or Santa Mick, this could be someone hunting Michael Siddell, one-time investment broker.'

'A lot of people were destroyed by the crash,' Declan mused. 'We should look into that. See if his wife—'

'Widow,' Jess was reading the screen still. 'She declared him legally dead in 2015, seven years to the day after he disappeared.'

'Understandable,' Declan replied. 'We should still consider speaking to her, though. See if you can find out anything on his life before his disappearance, and find a photo, send it to De'Geer. See if it matches the body we have on ice.'

He looked back to Anjli, still on the phone.

'Who are you calling?' he asked.

'I've had a message from the front desk to call Waterloo,' she said. 'Apparently they have someone dead there they think's connected.'

'Connected?' Monroe looked at Declan. 'Bloody marvellous. Thanks once more for taking this on, laddie. It's the case that gives on giving.'

Anjli was scribbling details on a notepad as she listened. Then, thanking whoever was on the other end of the line, she disconnected the call, reading the notes.

'Arthur Drayson,' she said, looking up. 'Father Christmas near the South Bank market. Keeled over and collapsed while talking to a kid on his lap, 999 called, but they found him dead on their arrival.'

'Any sign of a blonde woman?' Declan asked. 'Or a sixteen-year-old named Mina?'

'Unsure,' Anjli shook her head. 'It happened on Sunday, though, around six-thirty in the evening. Southwark police are sending us the details, as although the higher ups said nothing was worth checking, their SOCO is convinced there was something dodgy going on here, especially after he spoke to Doctor Marcos, probably learning about Siddell in the process. He thinks they're connected.'

'Why was he talking to Rosanna?' Monroe asked, and for a moment Declan wondered if the DCI was exhibiting jealousy.

At this, however, Jess shrugged.

'I'm not Billy, Guv.'

'Aye, well, even Billy can't work out the mind of Rosanna Marcos,' Monroe smiled. 'Does he at least say why, after speaking to our divisional surgeon, he now believes his case is related?'

'Because they found traces of mistletoe berries in his beard, and he didn't have them when he started,' Anjli half-shrugged. 'That's probably why he thinks there could be a link.'

'Right then,' Monroe straightened. 'Declan? You're with me. Let's go visit the Southbank, see if we can find any witnesses. Anjli? Go speak to this Mina and find out what the hell she gave him in his soup.'

'Cooper's on her way back,' Jess said, looking back over at them. 'Do you want me to send her anywhere?'

'Aye, she can go with Anjli to this bairn's house,' Monroe almost growled in reply. 'Maybe the sight of a uniform will stun her into speech. Oh, and see if you can find out anything about this Drayson fellow. Like, for example, if he was an investment banker.'

'Oh, he wasn't,' Jess replied with a smile. 'I already found his LinkedIn page. He's a retired barrister. Has been for about ten years.'

'A retired barrister who plays Father Christmas, and a homeless ex-investment broker that likes to wear the hat,' Monroe mused. 'If they are connected, we need to work out how, and fast.'

MINA SUVOSKY SAT IN THE CHURCH, ON THE FOURTH ROW OF pews from the front, and stared down at the bottle in her hand.

Had she done this? She asked herself. *Had she killed him with the power of Christ?*

The man, Santa Mick, had been well liked, but he was angry when he came to the kitchen. He differed from how Lewis had described him, and he'd turned down Lewis's gift, which was good. He was wide-eyed, vacant, and his personality had been different from his usual one, all signs of demonic possession.

Father McNarry had told her of this, back in Romania, before she came over.

Mina had done what anyone would do.

She had killed the demon.

But had she killed the man, too?

She recognised the demon when he looked up at her, asking for the soup. The kind-looking old man with the beard was gone, and in his place, overlaid over it like a double image was his real face, the face she remembered from pictures in her youth, back in Romania – the face of one of Satan's demons.

Rocking back and forth on the pew, just as she had done for the last two days, Mina continued to clasp her hands together, the small plastic bottle in her hand, as she prayed silently for forgiveness and for guidance. And, when none appeared, she sighed, wiped her eyes, took a deep breath, removed the lid of the bottle and drank the remains of the clear liquid held within.

8

ARMCHAIR CONVERSATION

'Okay, don't stress here,' Billy said as he entered the living room, frowning as he looked around. 'Where's Esme?'

'She left,' Davey said, looking up from her phone. She'd parked herself on the sofa, with her feet up, and nodded with her head at the door. 'You were up there a while, and to be honest, we're not the best of pals.'

'Because of De'Geer?'

Davey shrugged.

'She thought I should have been less of a bitch to him, and I thought she should mind her own business, especially if she doesn't have the guts to snag him for herself,' she said, placing her phone down.

'Should you be using that?' Billy pointed at the phone, but Davey just smiled.

'You're the one they're watching, not me,' she replied. 'I'll use the burners to pass messages, but I can still use mine for other things.'

She picked it up, showing an image on the screen of what looked to be a fat cat.

'And the Chonky Cat Instagram page isn't going to read itself,' she finished. 'Who were you talking to? I thought I heard voices?'

Billy nodded.

'As I said, don't stress here,' he repeated softly as he looked back to the door.

After a moment, Andrade, his face and knuckles now cleaned, moved into the room.

'Of course he's hiding here,' Davey sighed, rising to a sitting position. 'So, when the police arrive, we can all be accused of being accessories like one big happy family.'

Billy motioned for Andrade to sit.

'She's helping me,' he explained. 'We're going to clear your name.'

'Or, perhaps, prove you did it,' Davey added, holding up her hands in defence as Billy spun to glare at her. 'What? You know that's the job here. We don't know what happened. Only he does.'

Billy looked back at Andrade.

'Tell us the truth,' he said.

Andrade stared down at the floor.

'You don't want to come with me when I leave the post,' he whispered.

'No offence, mate, but I don't think promotional aspirations are a good idea right now,' Davey suggested. 'The only leaving you're doing right now is in handcuffs and with a bag over your head.'

There was a moment of stunned silence as Billy and Andrade both stared in horror at Davey.

'Just saying,' she said.

'It doesn't matter, he still won't travel with me,' Andrade repeated sadly.

'Now is *really* not the time to do this,' Billy hissed back. 'I went looking for you! I found the body!'

Andrade nodded.

'Who was he?' Davey asked. 'And also, who was he to you?'

'He was my predecessor,' Andrade explained. 'But we'd worked together a year back in Paris. I was on my first posting, and he was on his third, maybe his fourth. He was unhappy though, claimed he was being looked over? *Overlooked*, yes, for promotion. Said he would find his own way to make his fortune, as they did not pay us much.'

'And they placed him in London?'

'Yes, at the start of the year, maybe March?' Andrade counted his fingers. 'Yes. March.'

'Hold on,' Billy frowned. 'If you replaced him, how come you're finishing at the end of the year? You started in June, that's only three, maybe four months after him.'

'He left,' Andrade replied. 'He had enough and quit. They placed him on a flight home and asked me – I had just begun in Madrid at the time – to come over.'

Billy leant back, considering this.

'So, José Almas lived in the Mayfair apartment before you,' he said as a statement of fact rather than a question. 'He decides, after years of being overlooked that he's going to find another way to get rich, takes a transfer to London, leaves after three months, and then around five, six months later he's found, in his old apartment, dead in a bathtub, killed in the traditional execution of the South American cartels and with his toenails missing. Am I close to what's going on?'

Andrade nodded again.

'I've not been at the apartment for a week,' he explained. 'I was being followed. At first, I thought it was someone trying to find out more about you and me, maybe gain some gossip, something salacious they could use against me, against us, but as I carried on doing my duties, I realised they weren't looking at me, just the role.'

'You think they thought you were José Almas?' Davey asked.

At this, Andrade shook his head.

'No, this would have been after his six months ended, and everyone knew he had gone. He left, how you say, under a cloud,' he explained. 'But he came back to London two months ago. He had good clothing, expensive. Not bespoke.'

'Bespoke is off-the-rack, I'm assuming?' Davey looked at Billy, still in his own three-piece suit, although not with the jacket on right now. 'I'm not rich like you.'

'No, off-the-rack is off-the-rack,' he replied. 'Bespoke is a term for several things for several people, but to me, it's where you buy an off-the-rack suit and have it fitted to your shape, while tailored is having it created from scratch.'

'Big difference in price?'

Billy considered this.

'I had this made in *Huntsman* on Saville Row,' he said, patting his waistcoat. 'Whole thing cost about three grand. You buy a five-hundred-pound *Ted Baker* suit, you can have it fixed to fit for a couple of hundred.'

He smiled.

'Obviously, the more expensive the suit, the more it costs to fix.'

'So, when you say, "not bespoke", you mean this was a tailored suit?' Davey looked back at Andrade.

'Yes,' he replied. 'I wouldn't usually know much about this, but ... recent relationships ... have taught me much about tailoring.'

'He wouldn't let me buy him one,' Billy muttered. 'Which I understand, because then he'd have to explain how he got such a thing, even declare it as a gift, but those suits he wears hang hideously on him.'

'I think that's currently the least of his problems,' Davey smiled. 'So, our man José has come into money somehow. Do we know how?'

Andrade shook his head.

'All I know is he'd left something in the apartment,' he explained. 'He hadn't expected to be sent home so fast, he wasn't able to pick it up. He'd hidden it.'

'Hidden what?'

Andrade shrugged.

'He never said, and I could never get him back into the apartment to check,' he replied. 'We met in an art gallery. Or, rather, one I'd gone to, which he followed me into. I never saw him at the apartment, and if I was being honest, I didn't really want him in there. José Almas was a name people spoke of in whispers. He'd very much, how you say, *shit the bed* when he left.'

'Well, he shit the *bathtub* when he died,' Davey muttered. 'Was the apartment trashed when you went in there?'

Davey had looked at Billy as she asked the second part of the statement, and in response he shook his head.

'It was spotless,' he said. 'I assumed this was because the maid had been in before Andrade had returned. He mentioned once they had a weekly one on Fridays. Only thing out of place was the blood on the carpet. I assumed they'd tortured him, pulled out his toenails somewhere like the kitchen and then, when they decided to kill him, they dragged him to the bath, in the process scuffing his bloody feet against the carpet.'

'That fits,' Davey tapped the corner of her phone against her chin as she considered this. 'Gruesome, but it fits. We need to get in there to properly look.'

'I haven't been back since before then,' Andrade shuddered, sitting back in the armchair. 'I don't know how José got into the apartment, either. They changed the security details when he left. They do that every time.'

There was a moment of silence as everyone considered this.

'Shit the bed,' Davey mused. 'What did he do to get such whispers about him?'

Andrade leant forwards, staring at his hands as he thought about this.

'Several things if I am honest,' he said. 'There was talk of an accident, that he hit a teenager while driving. He was on the wrong side of the road—'

'The teenager?'

'No, José. He was drunk, or high on drugs, the teenager died. But as the teenager was on a skateboard, José claimed he'd strayed into his lane, rather than the alternative. There was camera footage, though, and it showed José had lied, or at least hadn't been aware enough of his surroundings. But he claimed diplomatic privilege.'

Billy nodded at this. Under international law, foreign diplomats and often many of their family members could enjoy certain protections, ones created by the *1961 Vienna Convention on Diplomatic Relations*, which allowed them to avoid prosecution for almost any crime – unless the diplomat's home country waived the immunity. Its original intent was to protect diplomats and their families in hostile environments, or from harassment from locals in the countries they were stationed in, but many diplomats had stretched the limits on this. There was even a famous case in New York, back in 1975, when a Barbados ambassador claimed his immunity extended to his pet dog, which had bitten multiple people.

'Could Colombia have waived it?' Davey asked, reading something she'd googled on her phone. 'They did it before. Jairo Soto-Mendoza?'

'He was a Colombian diplomat, true,' Andrade nodded. 'But it was twenty years ago. He was accused of killing the man who had mugged his son in London, and the embassy waived his rights so they could try him. But he was acquitted, and the belief is the embassy knew this back then, and deliberately did this to remove the problem.'

'Because if he'd just walked away, it would have hung over his head,' Billy frowned. 'But going back to José, the murder of a teenager isn't enough to end up murdered in such a way.'

'Depends on the parents,' Davey suggested.

'He did more,' Andrade admitted. 'José was linked to drugs, and the cartels, using his position to get things taken from, or brought into London. This is more likely the reason he left, moments before they stripped him of accreditation and forced him to leave the country.'

'One thing this doesn't explain though ...' Davey waved at Andrade's clothes, still stained with blood. 'If you didn't go home, and you didn't see the body, how come you're covered in, well, *that?*'

'Tell us about the people following you,' Billy nodded.

'They were Colombian, I think,' Andrade replied, choosing his words carefully so as not to give the wrong information. 'Three men, all in their thirties. Fighters.'

'How did you know that?' Davey opened a notepad.

'They were stocky, and they had scars,' Andrade stroked his cheek with a finger. 'The leader? He had a scar down this cheek. Another had one on his eyebrow. They looked more like knife scars than, say, an accident. And they held themselves high, like they didn't expect to meet anything that could affect them.'

'Okay, so tell me what happened with them,' Billy persisted.

'I stayed on a friend's couch for the first couple of days—'

'What friend?' Billy asked, his voice tight. 'Have I met them?'

'Billy,' Davey tutted, looking up. 'He's allowed to have other friends.'

'Yes. Sorry,' Billy reddened.

Andrade smiled, a sympathetic, almost loving one.

'I couldn't come to you,' he said. 'I couldn't bring this to your doorstep.'

'Until now,' Billy may have been a little shamed by his last comment, but he hadn't softened.

'Billy,' Davey looked at him now. 'If you can't be objective, get out of the room.'

Billy looked stricken as he stared back at his fellow detective, but with a reluctant sigh, he nodded.

'Sorry,' he muttered. 'Continue.'

'I stayed on a couch because I'd heard they were waiting near the embassy,' Andrade continued. 'They'd asked for me – not by name, but by my position in the embassy—'

'The same one José had?'

'Yes. I was scared, I didn't know who they were, and I worried it was something to do with my external activities.'

'You mean Billy.'

'Yes. So, I kept away from them as long as I could, but eventually I thought I was safe. I'd left my phone at the apartment when I ran, and I wanted to contact Billy, so I went to get it. However, when I got there, I saw the police.'

Davey nodded at this, writing into her notebook.

'You were there last night?'

Andrade nodded.

'I saw DI Walsh and the others there, and I saw Restrepo,' he continued. 'He's never liked me, and I knew the moment he saw me, I'd be arrested.'

'For what?' Billy now looked up. 'There was no way you could have known what happened in the bathroom.'

'The other people from the building were talking about it,' Andrade replied. 'They too worked for the embassy. One mentioned they'd heard it was José who was dead. They were speaking softly, in Spanish, and I overheard them.'

Nervously, Andrade rose now, pacing the room as he spoke.

'I knew I had to get out of there, but they must have been watching. They caught me as I ran. I fought them, and cut one of them with his own knife, hence the blood on my shirt. They were calling for support on the phone while they held me, and a man, a police officer, pulled up in a squad car. He asked what was going on, and when they turned to speak to him, I pulled free and ran as fast as I could from them. They didn't catch up with me, and I managed to get into Bond Street Station, where I bought a ticket, cash, to Wanstead.'

He looked apologetic.

'I remembered the address of the house from when you invited me here last, and I broke a window at the back to get in. Sorry about that.'

'A window's nothing,' Billy smiled. 'I'm just glad you're safe.'

'What time was this?' Davey closed her notebook.

'About eleven last night?' Andrade shrugged. 'I lost my watch in the fight, the strap broke as I pulled away. I grabbed some food, a sandwich from the refrigerator, and slept upstairs. I hadn't been in a bed for days, so I passed out. But then I heard noises from downstairs, people talking, and I hid. I didn't know who Billy had brought with him.'

'Right,' Davey nodded up the stairs. 'Okay then. You're no good to us looking like that, so go grab a shower, wash that blood off you before any other police turn up. I'm sure Billy has clothes that can fit. Once you're clean, we can discuss the next steps, which is probably Billy checking the dark web or something while I search the apartment—'

She held up a hand to stop Andrade's protest.

'There's no way they're letting you in there,' she said. 'And until you're cleared, the moment they see you, they'll grab you and ship you home to Colombia. Right now? Consider yourself under house arrest.'

Andrade reluctantly nodded at this, and rising from the armchair, he left the room. It was only a minute later, when the faint sounds of the shower could be heard from upstairs, that Davey spoke again.

'There's no way he heard locals talking about José,' she whispered, leaning closer to Billy. 'Rosanna Marcos is known to them, she was around the whole time and she speaks rudimentary Spanish. And you were here when I got the message from her today, with the name of the dead man.'

'Maybe they delayed the information to us?' he replied. 'There's no way Restrepo didn't recognise the body. Maybe Doctor Marcos was left in the dark like we were?'

Davey shrugged.

'Perhaps, but I don't think Andrade's story is a hundred percent watertight. I'm sorry, I know he's your boyfriend and all that, but Rosanna didn't mention a phone being found—'

'They took it with them, or they destroyed it.'

'Again, perhaps, but we need to clear *you*, remember? Not Andrade. That's just a bonus. And currently, he's covered with blood, which I point out again *is not his*, and he's got a convenient space of time away from anyone, with no witnesses to confirm his story,'

'So, what now?' Billy was unhappy with the way the conversation was going, but to his credit, he was still staying the path.

'Get Andrade some new clothes, and toss me down the shirt he was wearing,' Davey rose now. 'I'll check the blood for DNA.'

'Checking if it's José's?'

'Yes,' Davey admitted. 'And no. Worst-case scenario, it is, and he's lied to us. We know where we stand then. Or, it's from one of his attackers, as he said, and we get a hit on Interpol, or one of the Central American databases. Again, it helps. And while I do that, I'll see if I can investigate the room yet, while you check station cameras.'

'Why?' Billy rose now, walking to the door. 'No, wait. You want to see what time Andrade arrived at the underground station.'

'You find him, you find the train,' Davey shrugged. 'You work the timing backwards, you see when he entered Bond Street. That'll prove whether or not he's telling the truth, especially as there'd be a Mayfair copper somewhere who stopped a fight, and had to report it.'

Billy nodded as he started up the stairs. He didn't want to

consider Andrade as a suspect, or even a killer, but he had to look at all options.

He just hoped Andrade didn't turn out to actually be a spy.

He'd never live it down if Monroe found out.

9

SLAY BELLS RINGING

'Well, this is a jolly turn of events,' Monroe said as they walked down the South Bank of the Thames, towards the London Eye and the County Hall. The entire embankment had been dressed up for the season, and taking a deep breath in, Declan could detect traces of mulled wine and gingerbread from the many wooden huts, designed like alpine chalets that now lined the edge of the walkway, the Thames behind them.

'How so?' he asked, frowning.

'Listen,' Monroe grinned. 'It's "*Last Christmas*," by *Wham*. But it's a cover.'

'And that's good because?'

Monroe shook his head.

'You're this many days into December, and you haven't been playing *Whamageddeon*?' he asked. 'I work with philistines.'

'Sorry, no idea what this whamma-whatever is,' Declan admitted, his eyes travelling up, looking at the fairy lights twisted around the trees. It was daylight, and they weren't on, but he could imagine what they'd look like. And he'd already decided to come back later to see the Christmas Market in its full, fairy-lit glory. He'd see if Anjli and Jess wanted to come, although the latter may have other plans, especially if Henry Farrow was still having pre-wedding meltdowns.

He could see cheese stalls nestled next to other ones selling what looked like glowing rock night-lights, and stalls selling knitted "reindeer antler" hats beside German-sausage hotdog stalls. They were only just opening, and his stomach was growling at the sight of them, reminding him he hadn't had lunch yet.

'It's a social thing,' Monroe was explaining as they walked under the Hungerford Bridge, away from the bulk of the chalets and now heading towards the London Eye, the giant Ferris Wheel that looked out across the Thames. 'Rosanna got me into it last year.'

'Oh, so it's not something you'd usually do?'

'Christ, no, laddie. But actually, it's quite interesting. From the first of December, you have to try to not listen to "*Last Christmas*", by *Wham*.'

'Because it's not a great song?'

'You're losing the point of this,' Monroe scolded, glaring at Declan for even daring to scoff at the song. 'To hear it means you are out, and you will now travel to blessed *Whamhalla*, shiny and chrome, and are stopped from continuing the game until next year. However, you can hear covers, or instrumentals, as long as it's not the actual song.'

'Shiny and chrome,' Declan frowned. 'Isn't that from *Mad Max*—'

'I don't make the rules or create the game,' Monroe smiled. 'I just abide by them. If I don't, I get shouted at by the love of my life while she waves a scalpel at me.'

'I get it,' Declan said. 'Okay, so if I'm playing—'

'Oh, no you can't *play*,' Monroe stopped, staring almost in horror at Declan. 'Not from right now. You don't know if you haven't heard the song already this month. You'd be starting with a potential advantage. Cheating, even.'

Declan gave out an audible sigh, already tiring of the game he now seemed to be banned from playing.

'And the point of this is?' he asked, almost expecting the answer.

'To last until Christmas.'

'And if you do that?'

'You win.'

'Win what?'

Monroe looked puzzled.

'The game.'

'I get that,' Declan was getting irritated now as they passed the London Eye to their right. 'But what do you *get* if you win the game?'

'Bragging rights.'

'But what stops you from lying?' Declan continued. 'What if you hear it, but there's nobody around, and you just tell people you're still in? You know, like if a tree falls in a forest and there's nobody around to hear, does it make a sound?'

'Of course it does, laddie. It's a tree.'

'I know that, I'm using the quote,' Declan wanted to punch something. 'If nobody *sees* you hearing the song, how can they know you didn't? You could just say "nope, didn't hear it all month" and claim the win.'

Monroe stared at Declan sadly for a long moment.

'You have no faith in human nature,' he said.

'What, and you do?' Declan almost laughed. 'Guv, you're more cynical than I am!'

'Not at Christmas,' Monroe waggled a finger. 'Not at Christmas.'

By now, they'd reached the London Marriott County Hall, and Declan looked around, confused.

'No police line?'

'It was Sunday night, and it's Christmas,' Monroe explained as they entered the building. 'They'd have cleaned the place up before closing, probably had a brand-new Santa in the Grotto the following day.'

Monroe was correct – the County Hall, now a hotel, was festooned with Christmas trees, and glistening bauble wreaths and sparkling garlands lit their way down the corridor; on the right was a queue of children, each with their parents or guardians beside them, all patiently waiting for something currently happening through a large wooden door on the left, a plaque above the currently closed door explaining the magical location behind it.

SANTA'S GROTTO

As Declan watched, a young woman dressed like an elf, with a deep-green, pointed and conical hat walked out, nodded to the next child and their mother at the front of the queue, and moved to the side as they crossed through the door, the others behind them stepping forwards, and filling the spot.

'Santa lies this way,' Monroe winked, and led Declan down the corridor, towards the door. As they approached it, however, one mother, their small blonde precious daughter in hand, shouted out.

'Oi! There's a queue!'

Slowly, and with great intent, Monroe turned to face the

woman, giving her his fullest "police" glare.

'Madam, do you think we're here to see Father Christmas?' he enquired.

'There's a queue,' the woman muttered, more uncertain of her position now.

As if hearing this, another of the elves, a young man, no older than eighteen or nineteen, peeked a head through the door, and behind him Declan could see mahogany panels with red and gold baubles and garlands strewn across them.

'You have children with you?' he frowned. 'No adults allowed in without children, you know. For reasons.'

'I think you'll make exceptions for us,' Monroe said, pulling out his warrant card and showing the now paling teenage elf. He looked back at the little girl, winking.

'Reindeer Inspectorate, checking if Rudolf is roadworthy,' he said knowingly, before looking back at the elf.

'I'd suggest you get your manager to come have a chat, immediately,' he said, nodding back to the reception area. 'We'll be over there. I think they've been expecting us.'

And, this said, Monroe placed his warrant card away, nodding to the mother, who, realising who these two men actually were, wisely kept quiet, as Monroe followed Declan back to the reception area of the hotel.

It was a couple of minutes before a flushed-looking woman in her forties came scurrying over to them. She was slim, with short red hair, more dyed than natural, and wore a black suit over a pale-blue shirt. The label on her lapel said "Corinne Haynes", and so Monroe smiled as he held a hand out.

'I'm guessing you're our contact, eh, Corinne?' he asked as he shook her hand. 'I'm DCI Monroe, the grinch over there is DI Walsh.'

'Hey, why am I the grinch?' Declan moaned. 'I like Christmas!'

'Aye, but you're not playing *Whamageddeon*, so you're a grinch,' Monroe said before looking back at Corinne. 'Is there a place we can speak? Where there's no bairns around?'

Corinne nodded, her lips thin as she did so, and led them through a side door, into a small back office. There were four desks there, all empty, so Declan and Monroe pulled chairs from two of them, sitting down as Corinne sat behind what was most likely her own desk, straightening a photo on it as she did so.

'You're here about poor Arthur,' she said sadly. It wasn't a question; she'd been expecting them. 'I was the one who called the ambulance on the weekend.'

'We don't know all the facts,' Monroe said softly, giving the woman her space. 'Can you tell us what happened?'

'Arthur's been with us every year for the last five,' Corinne explained. 'Even last year when we had a movie tie-in Grotto with those horrid little yellow people.'

Declan wanted to ask if she meant "Minions" by that, but was scared to ask, in case this turned out to be a racially charged comment.

'He's a family favourite,' she continued. 'People come back every year just to see him.'

'He looks the part?' Declan asked. 'We haven't seen photos.'

'Oh,' Corinne rummaged around her desk, pulling a flyer from a pile of papers, and passing it across. On it was a man, in his sixties, sitting on a leather chair beside a fireplace, a small, red post office box placed inside the opening, smiling at the camera through his half-glasses. He wore a red suit, with white furry cuffs, black boots and a red hat, on top of long, white hair. He smiled through his equally white beard, and while Declan believed the beard was real, he reckoned the hair was definitely a wig, as Father Christmas faced him through the image.

'I can't tell if he's fat or not,' he said, passing it across to Monroe.

'He's stocky, but we don't fat shame here,' Corinne said sternly.

'No, sorry, I just meant Father Christmas is always fat and jolly in the images.'

'Well, ours extols the virtues of vegetables, and is healthy and hale,' Corinne's face was emotionless as she replied. 'Well, he was, until he keeled over three nights ago and died.'

'So, talk us through that,' Monroe placed the flyer in his pocket after receiving a nod he could take it. 'Was he showing signs of sickness earlier on that day?'

'No, none more so than usual,' Corinne clicked at the top of her mouth with her tongue before puffing out her cheeks. 'I mean, he was almost seventy, I think. He was stiff, and sitting in the chair for hours does that. And I think he was coming down with a cold, but he was keeping it at bay with tablets.'

'And he just collapsed?'

Corinne stared up as she visualised the scene.

'He was in the middle of his third shift,' she said. 'He'd do an hour, have a break, then continue. Weekends are always busy, and Sundays are more so. We'd tell them he was checking on the reindeer, he'd go for a pee break, and the kids were usually okay. Parents could be right pricks.'

She reddened.

'Can I say pricks?'

'You can say what you want,' Monroe grinned. 'We're not

arresting you for cussing.'

'Well, they weren't nice people,' Corinne course-corrected. 'But Arthur was a trooper, and although he was a little off, he still worked well.'

'Off because of the cold?'

'No,' Corinne shook her head. 'He had a phone call, and it seemed to shake him. We didn't ask what it was, but we had to speak to him about personal calls, and after that he was in the chair soon after, "ho ho ho-ing" away again.'

Declan pulled out his notebook, writing this down.

'So, he has the call, comes back and then he's sitting in the grotto ...' he said, looking up, waiting for Corinne to continue.

'And then he, well, he died,' she said simply. 'He had a young boy on his lap, and there didn't seem to be anything wrong, but then he started to cough. He covered it until he finished, but you know how you get when you try to keep a cough in, you go red and look bad? Well, that happened. We held back the next child and as he took off his wig, wiped his forehead, still wearing his gloves, which was probably unhygienic as he held children's hands with them, and they must have been sweaty as he was really dripping at this point, we got him some cold milk—'

'Milk?'

'Father Christmas drinks milk,' Corinne insisted. 'He had to stay on brand. Although it was lactose free, because Arthur had a bit of IBS. We'd even considered oat milk, but it didn't look right. Sorry, I'm rambling.'

'It's fine, go on.'

'Well, he always had a glass to the side. Of milk. We thought his beard had tickled or something, and he seemed to be better after a moment, but then, after he finished the glass, he sat back down, pulled the wig and hat back on, called the next child in and the moment the poor boy sat on his knee, he coughed again. But it was bad this time, like really "bringing up a lung" coughing, and the elves quickly hurried the boy out, saying some rubbish about allergies to Rudolph's new shampoo or something, but Arthur was pulling at his tunic, crying out he was too hot.'

Corinne was staring off now, reliving the moment in her mind as she spoke it aloud.

'His face was sweating, he rubbed at his forehead again with his gloves to wipe it off, all while saying he couldn't breathe, that he needed the toilet before he soiled himself ... and then he collapsed onto the floor.'

She shuddered.

'We thought he was having a heart attack. Nathan, he's one of the elves, he's our first aider and he tried to help while we called for an ambulance, but within a minute ...'

She trailed off, and Declan didn't need to know what she *wasn't* saying.

Within a minute, Arthur Drayson, just like Santa Mick, was dead.

'I'm sorry to ask this,' he said, 'but there was something about mistletoe?'

'Oh, yes, there was a strange smell on his lips,' Corinne nodded again. 'It was garlicky. One of the first aiders recognised it as mistletoe. We don't allow it here, as it's poisonous to children. Well, anyone really, but mainly little 'uns. But in his beard, they found bits of it. We thought it must have been placed in the beard, but, as I said—'

'It's not a fake beard,' Monroe finished. 'Could it have been in the milk?'

Corinne nodded.

'That's what I think, as nobody touched his beard, and the only time he touched it was after he wiped his face,' she replied. 'However, by the time we got to the milk to check it, the glass had been cleaned up by one of the elves, so we don't know.'

'The elves,' Declan looked up. 'Were they the ones who would have given him the milk?'

'No,' Corinne shook her head. 'The kitchen would have sent it. Oh, wait, I suppose they would have *technically* given it, because the kitchen would give it to them.'

'So, an elf could have put something in it?' Declan continued.

At the accusation, Corinne was horrified.

'We vet the elves carefully!' she insisted. '*I* vet them!'

She stopped.

'No, wait,' she continued. 'There was one thing. We had too many elves that day. There was a confusion with the schedules I think. But there was no way it could have happened. I didn't see it, but Nathan, he's one of our elves—'

'And the first aider.'

Corinne reddened.

'Sorry, yes, anyway, he said he thought she was a spy.'

'A *spy?*' Monroe almost chuckled, but stopped himself when he realised Corinne was deadly serious.

'Oh yes, Grottos are big business,' she straightened in her chair as she spoke. 'We had the Hilton try to get in here last year. Had their manager turn up with a kid literally from the street, trying to see what we were up to. They only see the Grotto, you see. They don't see the workings behind the curtain, how we get everything ready and all that. But dress as an elf, and you can peek behind, see what we do, and then steal the ideas.'

'So, this spy?' Declan said in an attempt to bring Corinne back on track.

'Oh, right. She was here when Nathan was dressing, but he sent her away. Luckily, she wasn't here long, because when Nathan confronted her about touching Father Christmas's things, she ran.'

'Touching his things?'

'Playing with the hat,' Corinne sniffed. 'Probably trying to work out the material. It's quite plush. Looks expensive. Well, more expensive than some of our rivals, I'll wager.'

'Could she – this elf that is – could she have touched the milk?' Monroe asked.

'You think the Hilton poisoned our Father Christmas just to close our Grotto?' Corinne asked.

Monroe quickly held his hands up.

'We mentioned nothing like that, and I'd ask you not to let your imagination run awry,' he quickly stated. 'I'm just asking, could this imposter, whomever she was and wherever she came from, could she have held the milk?'

'I'll have to check,' Corinne was frowning now, most likely amid a paranoid belief of rival hotels assassinating her Father Christmases. 'Can I come back to you on that?'

'Aye,' Monroe passed across a card. 'You can find me here. One last thing, did you see the hair on this girl? Was she blonde?'

Corinne looked at him apologetically.

'I'm sorry, I don't know,' she said. 'I'll ask Nathan. He's—'

'One of your elves,' Declan smiled.

However, Corinne glared at him.

'I was going to say he's the one who dealt with her, but I'd hate to spoil your little joke,' she replied icily. 'I'll see if we can get an image from the hotel CCTV. Would that help you?'

'Um, yes,' Declan replied, abashed.

Corinne tapped on her keyboard, obviously messaging someone about this. 'If that's everything? I have to get back to work. Those children can be a nightmare.'

Nodding, Declan and Monroe rose, following Corinne back out into the reception, Monroe passing Corinne his business card. There, she shook Monroe's hand warmly, while offering Declan a distinctly colder handshake.

'Someone will email you a printout of the elf,' she said to Monroe, holding up his card to emphasise this.

'Can we not get a copy of the video?' Declan frowned.

'No,' Corinne looked horrified at the suggestion. 'There are children on it!'

'It's not like we're putting it on YouTube or anything,' Declan growled, tiring of this.

'You're right, of course you can have a copy of the footage,' Corinne sniffed. 'As soon as you bring me a warrant.'

As she walked off, Monroe chuckled.

'Aye, she hates you,' he said. 'You'd better hope she doesn't tell Saint Nick to put a lump of coal under your tree, because you're definitely on the naughty list.'

Declan stared for a moment and then smiled.

'What's that?' he asked, frowning as he listened. And, as Monroe strained to hear the music playing, Declan turned and walked out of the hotel.

Monroe narrowed his eyes as he concentrated, and then growled with anger, as through the small reception speakers, the faint sounds of "*Last Christmas*" by *Wham* could be heard.

'Oi, you wee bugger,' he snarled, heading out after Declan. 'Wait right there! I'd like a word with you!'

10

THE POWER COMPELS YOU

The last thing Anjli expected when arriving at the Hampstead Rectory was the ambulance outside the building.

'Can I ask what's happened?' she said to one paramedic, holding up her warrant card as she did so. 'And if it's to do with Mina Suvosky?'

'Young girl?' the paramedic, a woman in her thirties, nodded into the back of the ambulance. 'She's in there.'

'Poisoned?' Anjli felt a sliver of ice slide down her spine. At this, however, the paramedic frowned.

'Why in God's name would you think that?' she asked. 'Panic attack. The priest saw her collapse, called us immediately. We checked her over, gave her a moment to relax, and she's fine. We're just checking her heart before we let her go.'

At the back of the ambulance now, another green-overalled paramedic was helping a young woman, with long, mousey-blonde hair, out of the door, helping her step down onto the tarmac. She looked up at Anjli, and taking this as a moment to identify herself, Anjli held up her warrant card again.

'Mina Suvosky,' she said, 'I'm Detective Sergeant Anjli Kapoor. I wanted to speak to you about—'

In fact, she didn't even get past the word *speak* before Mina's eyes widened in horror, and the teenager pulled her arm from the paramedic's grasp, sprinting off into the grounds of the church.

'Dammit!' Anjli hissed, already throwing her ID back into her jacket pocket as she sprinted after her. 'Cooper! Flank her! Mina Suvosky! Stop right there!'

But Mina wasn't listening. And, worst still, she knew the terrain better than Anjli did.

'Goddammit!' she yelled as she tripped on a bramble. 'Bloody well stop!'

Mina glanced back at Anjli's blasphemy, and that was her undoing, because she stumbled on a tree root at the edge of the garden and sprawled to her knees. And, when she scrambled back to her feet, she was shoulder charged by Cooper against the trunk, pressed into it as Anjli, now caught up, pulled out her handcuffs, quickly cuffing Mina's hands behind her back.

'What the bloody hell was that?' she hissed. 'Why are you making me run like that? I bloody hate running!'

'You're here about the man!' Mina wailed as Cooper spun her to face the detective. 'You think I killed him!'

'Well, what else am I supposed to think when you run like that?' Anjli growled. 'Did you?'

'Yes,' Mina admitted. 'I wasn't supposed to, but I killed the demon within his soul.'

Anjli stepped back at this.

'Demon?'

Mina nodded.

'In Romania we were taught as children, in church, what

demon possession looked like,' she said. 'That man, Santa Mick, he was possessed for many years. I saw this, and that's why I ...'

'Poisoned him.'

At this, Mina's head snapped up angrily.

'Never call the water of Christ poison!' she snapped.

Cooper and Anjli looked at each other briefly at this.

'Wait,' Anjli held a hand up now. 'Are you saying you placed *holy water* into Michael Siddell – I mean, Santa Mick's soup?'

Mina nodded again; her face confused.

'I do it for many of the people on the streets,' she explained as Cooper started leading her back to the Rectory. 'The holy water will protect them from the horrors in the night. And, if they're already taken, the poor souls, then the holy water will burn the evil spirit from them.'

'And you were taught this as a child?' Cooper asked.

'Oh yes.'

A man wearing the vestments of a priest at Mass was now hurrying towards them, holding up his robe so grass or mud didn't stain it.

'Mina!' he exclaimed. 'Is she alright?'

'That depends,' Anjli, deciding to uncuff the teenager, looked up at the priest. 'You are?'

'Father Franks,' the priest replied. Now he was closer, Anjli could see he was around the same age as her, maybe a little older, perhaps late thirties. 'She collapsed. I called the ambulance.'

'She thinks she's exorcising demons,' Cooper stated, 'using holy water. You agree with this?'

Father Franks looked disapprovingly at Mina.

'I told you not to take water from the font, didn't I?' he said, holding out his hand. 'Where is it?'

Reluctantly, Mina rummaged in her jean pocket and pulled out a small bottle, the size someone would put shampoo into when travelling on a plane. Easily hidden in the palm of a hand, squeezy and able to be used on any food or drink.

'She lived in a small village,' Father Franks explained. 'Her family ... there was a loss. Her father killed himself when she was a toddler, and as she grew up, the Church became her home, in particular the local Catholic Priest, Father McNarry.'

'You sound like you don't approve of McNarry,' Anjli said, noting the slightest hint of a sneer that had appeared on Father Franks' face when he said the name.

'I don't approve of his methods,' he replied. 'I'm of a different generation. But he took on training at the Vatican seminary, the *Regina Apostolorum* around twenty years ago, and started working as the exorcist for his local diocese.'

'An exorcist,' Anjli couldn't believe her ears.

'I mean, it wasn't like you see in the movies,' Father Franks quickly corrected. 'Unless you watched them after a few whiskies, but McNarry became infamous for, shall we say, *over-egging the pudding*, and eventually he was encouraged to take a diocese in Eastern Europe.'

'Mina's village.'

Father Franks nodded.

'And he taught you everything you know, didn't he?' he asked Mina, who nodded silently.

'Mina,' Anjli tried her best to make her voice sound calmer and more welcoming. 'You placed holy water in Mister Siddell's soup? Santa Mick?'

Silently, Mina nodded.

'And nothing else?'

A shake of the head.

'But you thought you killed him when you—' Cooper added, struggling to say the words, '—when you killed the demon inside him with holy water?'

'And prayer,' Mina added. 'Holy water and prayer. And yes.'

Anjli wanted to curse, to scream at the sky. The only thing Mina was guilty of was overzealousness and a powerful belief in doctrines taught to her as a child.

'Was this why you had a panic attack?' she asked.

Again, silently, Mina nodded.

'Okay,' Anjli straightened now. 'I don't think you killed Santa Mick, Mina, but I do need you to come with us to my station and give me a statement so we can remove you from our enquiries. Would you do that?'

'Does she need someone with her?' Father Franks looked uncomfortable. 'It's just I'm finishing a rehearsal. It's a big event tonight.'

'Who does she live with?' Cooper asked. 'I'm guessing there's a guardian still?'

'Technically, it's me,' Father Franks replied. 'McNarry sent her here, so she could gain experience in the Church. She wants to be a nun, eventually, you see.'

'So, she lives here?'

'With the verger,' Father Franks quickly explained. 'Lovely woman, and her sons have both moved out now, so she had a spare room. She lives over there, to the east of us. I could see if she could finish early instead—'

'Well, it's not an official chat, so I'll leave it to you to decide who comes,' Anjli interrupted, really not wanting to get into a chapter of *The Secret Lives of Vergers*, passing a card over. 'That's the address.'

'In that case, I'll be there as soon as I can, okay?' Father Franks crouched to face Mina. 'You good?'

'All good,' Mina smiled, nodding. 'I didn't kill him.'

It was said more as a confirmation than a plea; Mina had understood what Anjli had said, and now she was calm, assured.

Anjli wished she could have that kind of self-assurance.

'Right then,' she smiled. 'How about we get you a jacket and your possessions, and then we'll go visit my office,' she said. 'Oh, and bring the bottle.'

'Why?' Mina frowned at the request, but Anjli just smiled in response, glancing at Cooper with a wink.

'I have a few people there who are definitely in need of some blessings,' she said.

DECLAN AND MONROE HAD ARRIVED AT THE TEMPLE INN offices in a foul mood; Monroe because he'd been "whammed", and Declan because he'd spent the journey back being berated for spoiling Monroe's fun by pointing out the song in the reception. Declan had explained this wasn't his fault, and Monroe would have heard the song eventually, especially if he "didn't want to cheat", to paraphrase him earlier, but Monroe didn't think this was funny, and was absolutely sure, despite his protesting otherwise, that Declan had done this on purpose.

Which of course, Declan had.

Jess was waiting for them when they entered the offices with an expression of pride on her face. Declan recognised this, as it was one Billy often wore when he found something out.

'Go on then, out with it,' he said, tossing his coat onto the chair and walking over to her. Monroe was about to join him, but Bullman leant out of her door, nodding at him.

'Jock McScotty,' she curved a finger. 'Need your help.'

Monroe gave one last killer glare at Declan and walked off.

'What's eating at the Guv?' Jess asked, giving the correct term for a change.

'He's annoyed at me because I pointed out some Wham song,' Declan shrugged.

'You sent him to Whamhalla?' Jess was horrified. 'That's dark, Dad. Nobody deliberately Whambushes someone. It's when you ambush someone with—'

'Oh, I get it,' Declan sulked. 'I didn't even know this was a thing. Anyway, stop changing the subject and show me what you found.'

'I have a link between the two of them,' Jess said. 'Drayson and Siddell. They were Liverymen of London.'

Declan pursed his lips as he considered this. To be a Liveryman of London, you had to be a freeman of the City of London, a ceremony only given to people attached to Livery Companies, and specially invited others. But at the same time, there were over a hundred Livery Companies in London, each one with dozens, if not hundreds, of members. To be a Liveryman didn't really amount to much though, it was more a ceremonial title, although they did have the exclusive right of voting in the election of the Lord Mayor of the City of London. And something about taking sheep over a bridge in September, if he remembered correctly.

'Do you have the companies?' Declan asked. 'Maybe they're in the same one. That'd make things interesting.'

Jess read for a moment.

'Michael Siddell was in the *Worshipful Company of World Traders*,' she said. 'Arthur Drayson is ... ah. He's in the *Worshipful Company of Solicitors*, and also a Freeman of the *City of London Solicitors' Company*.'

'So not the same,' Declan frowned. 'Is there anything they could have been at together because of this? Also, Siddell disappeared after the crash in 2008, could he and Drayson have known each other before that?'

'Still checking,' Jess half-apologised. 'I'm slower than Billy.'

'You're doing a stellar job,' Declan smiled.

'They were both members of *The Guild of Freemen of the City of London*,' Jess's face brightened, but then fell. 'But there's over two thousand members there. They're also both members of the *City Livery Club*, which seems to be a gentlemen's club in the City, and also the *Reform Club* and the *National Liberal Club*.'

'That's a lot of clubs,' Declan mused. 'But luckily, I have an "in" into one of them. Can you get lists of members?'

'They're not the Masons, so I expect so,' Jess frowned. 'Who are you looking for?'

'Anthony Farringdon.'

'Granddad's old friend?' Jess was surprised. 'I thought he was only at the National Liberal Club?'

'I'm hoping he might be at a couple of these, and could have met both Drayson and Siddell at some point,' Declan looked back at Bullman's office where Monroe now walked out. 'His eidetic memory could really help us here.'

Monroe walked over now.

'Anjli's just called in,' he said. 'She's bringing in the Mina girl with Cooper. Apparently, she was using holy water to exorcise the demon out of Santa Mick.'

'What, Cooper was?'

Monroe said nothing, allowing the awkward silence to continue, refusing to acknowledge Declan's failed attempt at a joke.

'Everything alright?' Changing the subject, Declan nodded at the door to Bullman's office.

At this, Monroe winced.

'No,' he replied. 'Bullman hasn't booked anywhere for a Christmas party, and now she's stressing. She wasn't in the job this time last year—'

'Her role didn't exist this time last year,' Declan corrected. 'It took you being stabbed to create it.'

'Aye, and that's the problem. She didn't know it was her job to arrange something. So, it looks like we're all in a *Wetherspoons* or something equally dull,' Monroe looked at the screen. 'Gentlemen's clubs. Great.'

'I have a list,' Jess smiled. 'Only the Reform Club's list, though, past and present members. And Anthony Farringdon is definitely there, so he could know them if they were in that and his usual one.'

Declan was looking at the list as she scrolled down, but he placed a hand on her shoulder suddenly.

'Stop,' he said. 'There. Look.'

The three of them looked at the name on the screen.

`DONNAL, SHAUN: 2002 – 2012`

'2012 was when he lost his Labour seat in a by-election,'

Declan breathed, working the dates through in his head. 'Show me Siddell.'

Jess scrolled down.

SIDDLE, MICHAEL: 2002 – 2008

'Looks like he left when he went bonkers after the crash,' Monroe mused. 'But that's six years they were in the same club. Probably even joined in the same intake group.'

Declan thought back to the previous night's conversation.

'Santa Mick. Don't know his name, his full name, we always knew him as Santa Mick, because he always wore a Father Christmas hat on his head, even when it wasn't Christmas. Before that he was Mickey Fish, because he slept near Billingsgate Fish Market and, well, he stunk. The hat was better.'

'Shaun reckoned he didn't know him,' he said. 'But they had to have met.'

'Sure, but this would have been years ago,' Monroe replied. 'People change. And Shaun wasn't exactly in the best state, mental-health wise, when he was on the streets, remember?'

Declan nodded as his phone buzzed. He glanced down at the message.

De'Geer coming back has prints

'Prints?' he asked.

'From the small bottle they found with the body,' Jess said. 'I know they placed it in to be checked.'

Monroe's phone now buzzed. He looked down at it, and Declan had assumed at first it was the same message, but now Monroe looked over to Jess.

'Why don't you take a break,' he said calmly. 'You've been staring at the screen for way too long. Go up to the break room and have a rest.'

'What you're actually saying is "can you go make us a coffee", isn't it?' Jess smiled, rising from the chair and arching her back, stretching as she did so. 'I could do with a stretch of my legs. I'll also see if Detective Superintendent Bullman wants one.'

As Jess walked off, Declan watched Monroe.

'There's a reason you sent her off?' he asked.

Monroe nodded, already sitting at the desk, opening up his emails on the screen.

'Got a hit on Wardour Street,' he said. 'A bar there keeps ninety days on the cloud.'

'Ninety days of what?'

'Camera footage you bampot!' Monroe was searching through an email he'd been sent, clicking on a link and opening up a shared folder. 'Ninety days is three months, and we only need two. So, we can scroll to October, find the right time and date, and we'll see who entered the company. It's the building beside 100 Wardour Street, so we should even get a face.'

He quickly tapped through the footage files, each one dated with a single day's date. And, when he found *October 20* on one of them, he opened it up, scrolling to 9.45am.

'I don't see Shaun,' Declan peered closer.

'He was across the road, you said,' Monroe was watching the screen intently. 'You wouldn't see him on this camera.'

On the screen, a black Mercedes pulled up, and the back and passenger doors opened, with two women emerging from it. The one at the front was just as Shaun had described; the hair was lighter than before and longer, the fringe now a parting, and the woman on the screen, now scanning the pavement in both directions had glasses frames on, black on the screen's low definition, but likely to be blue. She matched the height and build of Francine Pearce, and she looked like the woman who'd made Declan's life hell, but it was the woman beside her, who'd climbed out of the back of the car that sold it for Declan.

She was unexciting, and if anything, blended into the surrounding people, although this was deliberate. She had short brown hair, wore a grey suit with an A-Line skirt and walked straight to the door, opening it for the woman with the glasses, before following her in.

'Trisha Hawkins,' Declan muttered. 'Francine's old number two, and now head of *Phoenix Enterprises.'*

'Isn't Tom Marlowe hunting her?' Monroe frowned. 'For setting him up and almost killing him?'

Declan nodded.

'Last I heard, she was in America,' he said. 'New York.'

'And you know this how?'

'I've had Billy keep an eye on her travel records.'

'That's a reckless use of police funds, but I approve,' Monroe tapped the screen. 'This was two months back, so she could be over there now. But the lassie with her looked very much like Miss Pearce, and the attitude I got from the reception adds to this.'

'So, what now?' Declan asked. In answer, Monroe closed up the screen, signed out of his email and rose from the chair, walking to Declan's desk as the doors opened and Anjli and Cooper walked into the office, a teenaged girl beside them.

'I think Anjli's jealous of your relationship with Jess, and she's kidnapped a daughter all for herself,' Monroe winked at Declan. 'Is that Mina, by chance?'

'It is,' Anjli nodded, and Declan could see she was irritated and tense, possibly from whatever conversations she'd had with the girl. 'I don't think we need to put her in an interview room though, I just need a statement.'

Monroe nodded and as Cooper nodded and left for the break room, Anjli led Mina over to Declan's desk, sitting her down beside it as Sergeant De'Geer also arrived in the office, a note in his hand.

'From Doctor Marcos,' he said, passing it across to Monroe, who quickly opened it, read it, and laughed.

'Rosanna wanted me to know she's won our sweepstakes, as she bet Bullman hadn't booked us a Christmas venue,' he said, continuing to read. 'And, more relevant I suppose, she has found a second set of prints on that bottle.'

'That could be helpful,' Declan said.

Monroe looked up.

'Who was the lassie Shaun told you knew Mick best of all?' he asked.

'Mallory Reed,' Declan replied, reading from his notes. 'Why?'

'Because they're her prints,' Monroe showed Declan the sheet of paper. 'Mallory Reed. Now we need to find out if she's the woman we see going into the alley as well.'

11

TINCTURES

As Shaun Donnal had given Declan Mallory Reed's number, it seemed a better idea for someone to speak to her without uniforms present, rather than turn up with fingerprint matches, and possibly scaring her off. And, as Shaun had probably told Mallory to expect Declan's call, he'd been the one to take this on, while Cooper checked in on Billy, Anjli carried on talking to Mina Suvosky, and Monroe went to have a chat with Anthony Farringdon. Interestingly, Bullman had agreed to come with him on this trip, possibly because she'd met Farringdon before, but also because she probably wanted to check whether the National Liberal Club had space for a small and rather hastily put together Christmas works bash.

Declan had arranged to meet with Mallory in the bar of the Soho Theatre in Dean Street; it was public, quieter this time in the day, just past the lunchtime rush, and close to where she worked off Soho Square.

Mallory was, however, not what Declan expected.

When Shaun had said Mallory knew Santa Mick the best,

he thought she would be in her fifties, not late twenties, her Barbour coat wet from the rain outside, and her clear umbrella placed by the door so it could dry.

Although Declan had to double-take to realise she was Mallory, there was no confusion on her end, and the moment she saw him in a booth by the wall, her lips thinned, her face grew seemingly colder, and she walked over.

'DI Walsh?' she asked.

'What gave it away?' Declan tried to joke, a little insulted he obviously looked a little too "copper" for the bar.

Mallory, in reply, waved around the bar, where young people in jeans and trendy jackets leaned over tables, deep in conversation.

'It's early afternoon,' she said. 'Most of the people in here are wannabe screenwriters and producers, trying to make movies. You, well, don't look like that.'

Declan accepted this.

'I was told you knew Santa Mick,' he said.

'As well as anyone could,' Mallory replied, placing her bag on the chair beside her. 'He was ... troubled.'

'How did you meet?'

'I used to work in the food kitchens years back,' Mallory explained. 'I was in university, up in Bloomsbury, and it was something that helped. You know, on the CV when going for jobs.'

'This was how long back?' Declan asked.

At this, Mallory smiled.

'You trying to work out my age, Detective?' she asked, and Declan flushed. He hadn't meant to instigate any kind of flirting, especially as Anjli would kill him and hide the body, and he wondered if Mallory had the wrong idea about this.

'Actually, yes,' he replied bluntly, hoping it would close

any "banter." 'I'm trying to work out if it was when he was "Mickey Fish", or "Santa Mick" when you first met.'

'Mickey Fish,' Mallory replied, and Declan felt she'd retracted into herself a little with the question. 'I'm thirty-two, Detective Inspector, and I left university just over ten years ago. I was in my second year when I met him, so we're talking 2011.'

'Before Shaun Donnal appeared, as well,' Declan noted the date.

'Yeah, he was still an MP back then, but even when he fell, so to speak, we never knew he was the same man. He was just another of the nameless many,' Mallory smiled as a waiter passed her a glass of water. 'Thanks Neil.'

'When did you stop?' Declan asked.

'I stopped in the kitchens in 2013, but still turned up on special occasions,' Mallory sipped the water. 'Probably helped on and off until 2018.'

'Did you stop because of the degree ending?'

'I had my reasons, and I won't be talking about them,' Mallory folded her arms defiantly as she stared at Declan, who, deciding not to follow that route, changed tack.

'Did you still speak to Santa Mick after that?'

'Here and there,' Mallory said. 'I saw him the night of his death, actually.'

Declan was glad he wasn't holding his own glass at this point, as he may have gripped too hard and shattered it, at the statement.

'You did?' he asked casually. Mallory observed him.

'Wow, you're really shit at lying,' she smiled. 'You already knew, didn't you?'

Declan wondered whether to continue playing dumb and see what else he could get, but decided instead to come clean.

'We have your fingerprints on a bottle,' he said. 'Found in Michael Siddell's possession when he died. Any idea how he got it?'

'Well, of course I know,' Mallory replied irritably, as if this was a stupid question. 'I gave it to him and made him drink it.'

ANTHONY FARRINGDON HAD SPENT MANY YEARS AS THE HEAD of security for both the Houses of Parliament and Downing Street over the last couple of decades, and as some kind of karmic payback for the years of long hours and stress-filled days, he seemed, now he was retired, to simply enjoy sitting in the National Liberal Club, at the junction of Whitehall Place and Whitehall Court; an opulent, white-brick, neo-gothic building that merged in with the surrounding constructions seamlessly, its corner entrance an elaborate arch over a double wood and glass doorway, leading to a doorman who kept the undesirables out, while Farringdon and his fellow members sat upstairs, in opulent leather armchairs, reading newspapers and drinking spirits.

Monroe had known Anthony Farringdon a long time now, from back when he worked the streets with Declan's father, Patrick Walsh, then a DCI in his own right, before they promoted him off the streets and into an office. Bullman, meanwhile, had met Farringdon only once or twice, mainly earlier that year, when she'd assisted Declan while he was accused of terrorism charges.

The bar they were led into was situated in a high-ceilinged room, with red marble pillars running along each side, the space between each one either filled with the green wallpaper the wall was covered in, or a ceiling-high bay window, complete with green drapery framing it.

Glass-fronted mahogany trophy cabinets were beside several of the pillars, and at the rear of the room, beside a bust of William Gladstone, and sitting at his usual low table with three dark-green leather armchairs, Farringdon placed his copy of that day's *The Guardian* down as he rose to shake Monroe's hand.

Still looking as fit as he had when he worked in Whitehall, and sporting the military blazer he always wore, his white hair neatly parted as ever to the right, Farringdon gave a courteous bow to Bullman.

'Congratulations on your promotion to Detective Superintendent, Ms Bullman,' he said, looking back at Monroe. 'And congratulations on still being employed, Alex.'

'Aye, well, that's all because of her,' Monroe jerked a thumb at Bullman as they sat down. 'Thanks for seeing us.'

'Declan in trouble again?' Farringdon asked.

'Not so lucky,' Monroe replied. 'Oh, and thanks for helping young Marlowe. I hear you sorted him some help with a terrorist thing in Westminster Great Hall?'

'You know better than to ask me that,' Farringdon shook his head. 'I don't tell the spooks what the coppers do, and I definitely don't tell the coppers what the spooks do.'

Monroe nodded.

'Fair do's,' he said. 'We're here on a case, actually. One that doesn't involve any of us for a change. Two murders in as many days, and both believed to be club members and Liverymen.'

'Go on,' Farringdon waved for some glasses as he spoke.

Monroe leant closer in case other members in the room could hear.

'Do you remember the names Michael Siddell or Arthur Drayson?' he asked. 'It might be from a while back. Before the crash in 2008, even.'

'Yes, I know the names,' Farringdon nodded, leaning back into his chair as he spoke. 'I knew them well, in fact. Both were members here, also at a couple of other clubs in the city, too.'

'Wait,' Bullman leant closer now, matching Monroe. 'Are you saying that Arthur Drayson and Michael Siddell knew each other?'

'What they did for most of the year, I couldn't say,' Farringdon smiled. 'But I can tell you now, with no word of a lie, that once a year, on Christmas Eve, they knew each other incredibly well.'

He frowned at this, though.

'Why?' he asked, a frown now on his face. 'Are they the murders you mentioned? I see Arthur here now and then, but I haven't seen Michael in ...'

He looked back at Monroe.

'Since, as you said, the crash in 2008,' he finished.

'I'm sorry to say, Anthony, but your suspicions are correct, and they're both dead,' Monroe explained. 'We believe they were both poisoned, within hours of each other, and likely by the same person. Until now, however, we didn't have a way to link them together, as they came from different worlds.'

'No, they definitely worked together,' Farringdon took a deep breath, taking his glass from the low table and downing it one before waving for another. 'Jacob Marley.'

'As in the guy from *A Christmas Carol*?' Bullman frowned. 'What's he got to do with it?'

'Weirdly, everything,' Farringdon smiled as his replacement drink, probably having been waiting for his call already, arrived. 'Let me explain.'

'SEE? PEPPERMINT,' MALLORY EXPLAINED, SHOWING DECLAN the large bottle. 'It's like Gaviscon, or those other anti-acids you can buy, but it's herbal. Got it from a Chinese therapist off Poland Street. But as it's an enormous bottle, I'd put it into smaller ones so I could keep one in my handbag.'

'And where did you get those from?' Declan sniffed it and nodded, placing the bottle back. It definitely smelt of peppermint, but that could be there to mask any other smells.

'There's a whisky shop on Old Compton Street, does mini spirit bottles, like airplane cabin sized ones. I got a couple of Absinthe ones, in the green bottles.'

'Why Absinthe?'

'Because I like Absinthe,' Mallory replied, and Declan wondered if he was being mocked a little. 'So, I drank it, washed it, and then kept it as a tincture bottle, filling it with the liquid and taking it when my IBS started.'

'Why not take a tablet?'

Mallory shrugged.

'I don't like chewing?' she offered. 'Actually, I don't think there was any reason. I just decided it made me look cool. Different. My brother used to do the same thing with his own chemical concoctions. He was a couple of years older, so obviously cooler than me. Could have been worse, he might have been a smoker, and I followed him into that.'

'Chemical concoctions?'

'He was a pharmacist. He tinkered.'

Declan nodded, writing this down.

'And you gave this Chinese tincture to Mick.'

Mallory nodded.

'I was meeting a friend in Piccadilly, so I was cutting through Soho,' she explained. 'I'm walking along, minding my business, and I see him staggering out from the corner. He's pretty recognisable in the hat, so I went to speak to him, but he veered off into the alley, collapsing. I thought he was pissed, and he was suffering from a sick stomach, as he was grabbing it and moaning, so I gave the bottle to him. He drank it, I left, and then later I heard he died.'

'You didn't wait with him?'

Mallory looked away at this.

'It hurt me,' she said. 'He didn't recognise me.'

'Should he have?'

'We spent years talking to each other on the food line,' Mallory straightened up now. 'I thought I'd made an impression. But he'd forgotten me.'

'So, you punished him by leaving when everyone else—'

'Piss off!' Mallory snapped, and several of the people surrounding them stopped their conversations to look over. 'What do you think I am? I told him to rest, let it do its work. He's been like this before, and I've seen it. At best, all he'd do was rant at me again, like he used to. But he didn't know me, and he was suspicious. I gave him some space.'

She rose from the chair.

'And I did call an ambulance, you sanctimonious prick,' she retorted. 'How do you think they got there so fast?'

'Sorry,' Declan waved Mallory back down, noticing one of the barmen, the man named Neil, was watching intently, probably worried there was a fight going down.

He pulled out his warrant card and waved it at him.

'Tough subject, nothing more,' he explained, and Neil

nodded before walking off, as Declan turned back.' I assumed, as you left no statement to the police, that you'd left the scene.'

'I did leave the scene,' Mallory muttered. 'I didn't think he was dead.'

There was a pause in the conversation, as Mallory stared up at the ceiling.

'I should have checked.'

'You said he'd rant at you,' realising the guilt she probably felt to this, Declan decided to change the subject. 'What were the rants about?'

'His old life,' Mallory calmed a little as she spoke. 'What he could remember of it, anyway. It became harder and harder for him to focus on it as he grew older. You know, like how we find it hard to remember before we were five and all that. You'll have an image or two, but no detailed remembrances. It's why all biographies that start when the writer is super young are bollocks.'

'Can you remember anything about his old life?' Declan asked. They knew this anyway, what with his identity now being known, but Declan was curious whether something else could be learnt here.

'He was always on about his club,' she replied. 'Kept saying he'd take me to his club one day, and they'd welcome him back, the long-lost son. But then as the years passed, he became bitter about the club, and I wondered if he'd actually tried to go in it, and was kicked out, you know? He never named it, but he also talked about things he used to own, like his car or his watch collection. But there was one thing he was really proud of, and it was really odd.'

'How come?'

'I never took him as a reader, that's all,' Mallory puffed

her cheeks out as she tapped on the table's surface with her nail, thinking back. 'Although to be honest, I think he bought it as an investment rather than as a passion item.'

'Bought what?'

Mallory shrugged, and there was a slight, sympathetic smile to her lips, as if remembering something nice but melancholy at the same time.

'Charles Dickens's *A Christmas Carol*,' she said. 'He was lucid once, said he'd bought the first edition, incredible condition, with the red and green title page. Was really proud of this. Spent like twenty, maybe even thirty grand on it. I thought he was joking, so I found a picture of one, sold a few years ago and he cried, saying "that's the one" and that he deserved to lose it. It was probably then I realised he wasn't one of the common or garden homeless people. He'd come from – and lost – money. Big money.'

'Did he ever say why he deserved to lose it?'

Mallory nodded.

'He said the story was about Scrooge becoming better, while he went the other way,' she said. 'Never explained what he did, but started crying, saying he hurt people, that the ghosts had been angry at him.'

'Sounds like hallucinations.'

'I said that too,' Mallory replied. 'But he was convinced they were real people.'

'THE CLUB STARTED AROUND FIFTY, MAYBE SIXTY YEARS AGO now,' Farringdon explained. 'A club *within* a club. A secret society that met once a year on Christmas Eve, rain or shine, snow or hail.'

'Okay,' Bullman frowned. 'So far it just sounds like a Christmas piss up.'

'Oh, it was definitely one of those, but the club was small, exclusive. Never over nine at a time, always people who'd been vetted by the others, who had history in at least two clubs. And, strangely, people who were Freemen of London.'

'Why?' Monroe asked.

'Never found out,' Farringdon shrugged. 'I was invited to a bash one year, went along, felt it was all a bit silly and then left.'

'Why silly?' Bullman smiled as the waiter passed her a glass of water, taking a sip.

'They made us wear these red fluffy Father Christmas hats, except for four of them,' Farringdon explained. 'The three ghosts got green ones, and the Scrooge had a black one.'

'Sorry,' Monroe held up his hand. 'Ghosts? Scrooge?'

'Oh, yes, sorry, should have explained that part,' Farringdon smiled weakly. 'The whole point of the Jacob Marley Society was to be philanthropic. Giving money to those in need. The members would all put around five thousand pounds into a kitty, so we had about forty or fifty thousand to be spent. Then, three members would be chosen to be ghosts for the next year – one of Christmas Past, one of Present and one of Future. Their jobs were to find willing candidates for the money, someone who had terrible luck in the past, one who was having a terrible time right now, and one who was heading towards a terrible time in the next year.'

'Past, present and future.'

'Exactly,' Farringdon sipped at his drink. 'The ghosts would then put their cases to the Society, who would then vote on which gained the money. If there was a tie, the Scrooge came in and decided.'

Farringdon thought about this for a moment.

'Actually, the Scrooge could also veto choices,' he said. 'If the Scrooge decided nobody was worthy, then the money was held over to the next year, like a lottery rollover.'

'So let me get this right,' Bullman puffed out her cheeks. 'Three ghosts are chosen, they turn up at Christmas Eve with candidates, they talk about them, the Society votes, the Scrooge decides or confirms, the money is sent to the winner and you decide the next years ghosts and Scrooge?'

'That's pretty much it. But the candidates don't turn up. Sometimes they don't even know they're being talked about. I think there's an interview process, perhaps.'

'How do you decide the ghosts?'

'They pulled out billiard balls,' Farringdon explained. 'Ghosts can't be ghosts two years on the trot, but you can be a Scrooge and then a ghost, and vice versa. Some people never get to be either, as it's all the luck of the draw.'

'And because of this, Siddell and Drayson were in the same room, maybe even arguing cases against each other, every Christmas Eve.'

Farringdon nodded.

'I went in 2005, before the Society had the problem, though,' he said. 'But that doesn't mean I didn't hear about it.'

'Hear about what?' Bullman frowned.

'Well,' Farringdon leant closer. 'In 2007, there was an issue, as the pre-decided Scrooge wasn't impressed with the candidates, barred the others from voting and claimed there was no winner, delaying the fund to the following year.'

He raised a conspiratorial eyebrow.

'Can you guess who that was?'

'Siddell or Drayson?'

'Siddell,' Farringdon nodded. 'But Drayson, the Ghost of Christmas Past, was furious his candidate had been cast aside so simply. They got into quite a fight, so I heard.'

'Can you remember the other two ghosts?' Bullman straightened in her seat.

Farringdon nodded.

'Eidetic memory,' he said, tapping the side of his head. 'The other two were Neil Robertson and Colin Walters. Neil passed away a few years back. Shame, he was a good-natured fellow.'

'And Colin?' Monroe was writing the name in his notebook.

'No idea,' Farringdon shrugged. 'But if someone's taking out the 2007 Jacob Marley Society, then he'd be my next candidate.'

'Because he was a ghost?'

'God no,' Farringdon laughed. 'Because Siddell stole the money that year, and split it between the four of them, rather than give to the poor buggers that needed it.'

12

FACE OFF

Billy had needed space once Andrade finally got to sleep in the bedroom.

He didn't want to move through the CCTV footage of train stations with Andrade in the house, in case he walked in on Billy doing this, asked why Billy was checking in on him, and the whole thing collapsed around them as Billy admitted he didn't trust him.

So, while Andrade slept, Billy grabbed his laptop and snuck out of his house, heading down to a local café on Wanstead High Street, where he could leech the Wi-Fi while checking the footage.

There was also the slightest thought in the back of his mind that said *to do this away from his house might be a better idea, in the grand scheme of things.*

Jess had emailed him three times now; he felt bad for her. Thrown into his position, she was rapidly finding his shoes were hard to fill. Which, even if a little arrogant, was also by design; Billy's filing system was all over the place, created in a way only he knew, specifically to ensure nobody could ever say they could do without him.

Of course, this didn't help when they were forced to do so.

Sitting by a yellow-painted wall and sipping at a Flat White, Billy had his screen open, faced away from anyone else in the café, as he scanned through footage.

On the screen now, Billy was watching the camera on the eastbound platform of Wanstead Underground Station. Andrade had said he'd arrived around eleven the previous night, so Billy had started there, working backwards to no avail.

So far, he'd reached ten pm, and nothing had flagged up anything on the algorithm he was using. He wondered if Andrade had been mistaken, and had gone to Snaresbrook, the Central Line underground station on the other end of the High Street, no more than half a mile away and on another spur of the line, but if he had, there would be another long hour of staring at trains ahead of Billy.

There was also the timing issue.

Andrade had said he'd seen Declan and the others, but they arrived around half an hour after Billy called, which was shortly before nine in the evening.

To see them meant Andrade had to arrive between nine and ten. To leave, run to Bond Street, be attacked on the way and then escape to the station, this would have taken up to half an hour.

Billy should have seen him by now.

Frustrated, Billy was about to turn off the feed and start again when the screen paused – the algorithm had picked up a hit, based on the images of Andrade Billy had fed into the system.

And, on the screen, Billy clearly saw Andrade leaving a

Central Line train on the Wanstead East platform. The number on the bottom left gave the time.

21:48

Billy stared at the number for a long moment before understanding what it meant. *Andrade didn't arrive around eleven, he arrived a good hour earlier.* And, working out the trip from Bond Street to Wanstead, a half-hour trip according to a train app Billy had, meant he caught the train at nine-twenty pm *at best.*

The station was a ten, fifteen-minute walk from the apartment, and this was without the chase Andrade had mentioned, and Billy had followed the train back to Bond Street now, and was watching in reverse as the passengers walked backwards off it, pausing the feed as he saw Andrade.

Noting the time, he pulled up the CCTV of the main booking hall, reversing back a few minutes until Andrade appeared once more. Then Billy moved to Oxford Street, flicking through cameras at the entrances to Bond Street Station until he saw Andrade emerge. This took longer, as he wasn't sure of the entrance, but eventually he saw him walking backwards towards Mayfair.

And on the screen, he was *talking on his phone.*

Billy leant back from the laptop at this.

'I'd left my phone at the apartment when I ran, and I wanted to contact Billy, so I went to get it. However, when I got there, I saw the police.'

The words of Andrade echoed in his head as he stared at the screen.

If Andrade didn't have his phone, then what was this in his hand?

Watching the footage as it now moved in the correct direction, Billy saw Andrade finish his call, waving his hands. He wasn't close enough to read facial expressions, or hear any sound, but he knew Andrade well enough to see he was angry.

And, on the screen, Andrade took the phone, splitting it apart and tossing it into a bin. If Monroe had been here, he would have claimed this to be "typical spy stuff", and for once, Billy kind of agreed with him.

Billy opened a map up in a different browser. If Andrade had come here straight from his apartment, then he would have headed north from Hays Mews and Davies Street to the east of Grosvenor Square; luckily for Billy, that entire area was a literal "diplomats row", and security was tight. And, checking through traffic cameras, Billy could just about make out Andrade as he travelled north.

There was no confrontation and no police. In fact, after around ten minutes, Andrade was outside his apartment. There was no camera here, but Billy could estimate from the speed Andrade had been walking, the time of his arrival. If he was correct, then Andrade had started his journey at five past nine that evening, almost the same time Billy had been in there, and definitely before any of the Last Chance Saloon turned up.

'When I got there, I saw the police.'

The police hadn't been there. Andrade had left before they arrived, and had made a call on a phone he claimed he didn't have during this time. Billy couldn't check the number called or calling, as diplomatic privilege would have covered the phone so, unless Andrade told him truthfully, there was no way to know who that was to.

Andrade had lied about everything.

Billy felt sick. If Andrade had lied about that, what other lies had he told? Were *they* a lie?

Tapping out a message and sending it to Davey, Billy slumped back into his chair.

He didn't want to go back to his house, but he knew to get answers, he had to do so.

Sighing, he gathered his items.

This was going to be *really shit.*

DAVEY HAD BEEN SURPRISED TO BE LET INTO THE APARTMENT, but mentioning her past as the assistant to "The Barracuda" opened more doors than she expected, and after a wait of less than five minutes, she was allowed by a miserable-looking guard into Andrade Estrada's one-time home.

It was cleaned now; the body was gone, the blood removed from the bath, and the carpet still damp from whatever steam cleaning company had done their best to turn it from a blood-covered horror show into a slightly darker shade of smudge. Davey had hoped to gain a sample of the blood, something to use against the DNA on the shirt she'd taken from Andrade, but she also knew Rosanna Marcos had probably gained a few samples from when she'd been here, and the shirt had been sent to her for examination. The speed of the clean-up, though, felt suspicious; why do this when there was a criminal case ongoing?

That's if there is one ongoing, she thought to herself as she entered the living area. *The Colombians probably want it to all go away right now. They even tried to pretend they didn't know who José was—*

'It looks nice, does it not?' a male voice spoke behind her, and Davey spun around to face an apologetic older man, shorter and stockier than her, but holding himself up straight, as if trying to gain an inch in height, so as to match her better.

'They said I could come in,' she blurted.

'I know, Detective Constable Davey,' the man smiled. 'I told them to. I am Pablo Restrepo—'

'Ah,' Davey smiled. 'Doctor Marcos spoke about you.'

'Nothing good, I hope?' Restrepo raised an eyebrow.

'Well, she said you still owe her for keeping your arse out of the fire,' Davey replied. 'Does that count?'

Restrepo laughed; a genuine, belly one.

'I do,' he replied. 'But I am afraid I cannot help you.'

'That's okay,' Davey smiled. 'I'm not sure I understand how you missed recognising a guy you worked with every day, but it does make anything you tell me a little bit suspect.'

Restrepo stared at Davey for a long, uncomfortable moment, and she knew this relationship wasn't going to improve anytime soon. Which was fine, to be honest. In fact, if he didn't like her, he'd stop with the fake "friendship" act, and she might actually learn something.

'What do you think happened?' Davey looked around as she spoke, deciding to test this theory. 'Personal opinion, not official statement. That way I get the truth, not bollocks political soundbites.'

'You really don't care what we think of you, do you?' Restrepo raised his eyebrows in surprise. Davey noted the *we* in the sentence, and simply smiled back at him until eventually, tired of the silence, he spoke.

'I think Andrade and José had a fight, and it got out of hand,' Restrepo eventually shrugged. 'Why they fought, I do not know. Where Andrade is now, I also do not know.'

He leant in now, his face cold and emotionless.

'Do *you* know?'

'I'm here as a favour,' Davey replied icily, hoping her poker face hid any answer to the last question.

'You are not the first using favours,' Restrepo straightened, nodding to the back bedroom. 'Another is in there.'

Frowning, and realising Pablo Restrepo had kept her out here deliberately while someone else worked the scene instead of her, Davey marched over to the door to the bedroom, opening it to see an elderly man checking through the drawers.

'Hello,' she said, as he turned to face her.

He was in his sixties, or a well-looked-after early seventies, with brown curly hair peppered with white that showed more in the bushy beard that sprouted from his chin, a Harris tweed jacket, waistcoat and deep-burgundy corduroy trousers. The jacket was a deep-blue, while the waistcoat seemed to be a traditional grey tweed in colour, the white shirt underneath collarless.

'Detective Constable Davey,' Chivalry Fitzwarren boomed. 'I thought it'd be Billy that appeared.'

Davey smiled; she'd only met Billy's great-uncle once, a few months earlier, but it was one of those meetings you remembered, as Chivalry was definitely a larger-than-life character.

In fact, he was just that, as his real name was Steven, and his day-to-day business seemed more humdrum than someone of his current look and name would affect.

'Mister Fitzwarren,' she said. 'Can I ask how you're here?'

'Fitzwarrens have a lot of history with Colombia,' Chivalry said, rubbing his thumb and fingers together in the international sign for *money*. 'When I heard Billy was being investigated by them, I came to check into it. I assumed he'd be gaining help from one or two of you.'

He looked around.

'No miserable Scot, or the other fella?' he enquired casually, but Davey knew he was playing for time, working out how many of the *Last Chance Saloon* were about to appear in the apartment, possibly giving his own investigation some issues.

'No such luck,' she replied. 'I'm no longer part of the Unit. I'm ... well, I'm *between* units right now.'

Chivalry looked like he wanted to ask what had happened, but instead nodded, looked around the room and sighed.

'I'm guessing you'd like a sitrep?' he asked.

'Sure,' Davey relaxed a little. With Chivalry's offer of a situation report, it looked like he wanted to play friends rather than competitors. 'Go wild.'

Chivalry turned from the drawers fully now, facing Davey as he spoke.

'Nothing found yet,' he admitted, 'but you're likely to be a far better forensics examiner than I am. Have at ye.'

So that's why you want to play friends, you slippery old bastard. You have nothing.

Davey went to look around, but then stopped as something came to mind.

'Why are you *really* here?' she asked suspiciously. 'And don't tell me it's because of Billy being held earlier, because he's been gone for hours now, and is currently in the house you own.'

Chivalry smiled wider now, and was about to reply, but then the smile faded, as if he'd been ready to give a glib reply, but then thought better of it.

'Billy contacted me to ask for advice, knowing I had connections in the country,' he said, nervously checking the door to the room, in case Restrepo had emerged within eavesdropping distance. 'I don't care about the Colombian. He's a distraction to my great-nephew, nothing more. In a couple of weeks, he'll be gone, and good riddance to him.'

'Not a fan, then?'

Chivalry shrugged.

'It's not a colour thing, or a sexual judgemental thing, if you're worrying,' he added. 'I mean, the things I've seen and done over my lifetime make Billy look like a monk. But there was always something *wrong* there with that lad, something I couldn't explain.'

He waved around the room.

'Until now, that is.'

'You think he did it?'

'You tell me,' Chivalry smiled. 'Why are you here, DC Davey, formerly of the Last Chance Saloon?'

Davey didn't quite know what to say, because she didn't really know herself.

'I was asked,' she replied. 'Billy's off the team until this is cleared up. So, I'm someone who can help, but isn't part of ... well, his current life.'

'So, you're not here either to find Andrade innocent,' Chivalry nodded in understanding. 'You're here to clear Billy, no matter what.'

Davey looked around the room, deciding that not answering this was probably the better and more diplomatic answer.

'Am I wrong?' Chivalry insisted.

Sighing, Davey leant against the back of a chair as she gathered her response.

'I met Andrade exactly once,' she said. 'I wasn't impressed. But then I've never been the romantic type. He was pretty, but there was always something a little needy about him. I thought Billy could do better. I never told him though, and then it was too late, and I left the Unit.'

'Because?'

Davey glared at Chivalry for a long moment of icy silence, and eventually, realising he wasn't going to get an answer to this, the older man held his hands up in mock surrender.

'Go on,' he replied. 'I won't pry any further.'

'I'm here because Billy Fitzwarren was – no, *is* – a mate, and I don't want to see him used as a scapegoat.'

Chivalry said nothing, but his slight smile showed relief, and possibly gratitude, within.

Davey paused, looking down beside the bed. Carefully, she held up a watch, the leather strap broken.

'This isn't wear and tear,' she said, staring at it closely. 'This has been ripped off. Like someone grabbed your wrist and pulled you one way while you went the other, forcing tension on it.'

She paused, remembering a line Andrade spoke.

'I lost my watch in the fight, the strap broke as I pulled away.'

'I think this could actually be Andrade's,' she breathed. 'But if it is, it's about three hundred yards in the wrong direction. He lost this on the streets towards Bond Street.'

'And you would know this how?' Chivalry smiled, knowing Davey knew more than she was saying. Silently, she cursed her idiocy.

'Billy checked the CCTV,' she lied.

'Maybe Billy would recognise it?' Chivalry enquired after a long moment of suspicious silence, as if he now disbelieved everything Davey now spoke.

'Did you find Andrade's phone?' Davey said loudly, changing the subject as she pocketed the watch quickly, calling out to Pablo Restrepo, through the door. 'I wondered if he'd left it here, especially if he did some kind of moonlit flit.'

Restrepo poked his head around the door.

'There was no phone found,' he replied.

'Would you tell me if there was?'

'I have no need to lie,' Restrepo shrugged.

Davey walked over to the man now.

'You told Billy's colleagues you were waiting to identify José Almas, when he'd worked under you every day for months, and there were no injuries to the face to stop you recognising him,' she said. 'And today, you said you thought they had a fight that went out of control, but José was found tied and naked in a bathtub, killed by a manner of torture known as a Colombian necktie, and with half his toenails missing. I think you've needed to lie a lot, Mister Restrepo, and I've yet to work out why.'

She leant closer.

'So, give me this one question. Answer it honestly for once. Do you honestly believe Andrade Estrada could do this?'

Restrepo didn't even take a moment to compose an answer before replying.

'I do.'

Davey stepped back, surprised by the answer, but noting there was nothing in Restrepo's manner or tone that suggested he was lying right now.

Chivalry stopped examining the drawers, turning to face the man.

'And what makes you so sure he could do this?' he asked.

At this, Restrepo made a sad half-smile.

'Because this is not his first time doing such a thing,' he replied.

'WHERE THE HELL ARE YOU, *YOU SON OF A BITCH?*'

Billy slammed the door behind him, looking around for something to use as a weapon, in case Andrade was violent. He was angry, maybe even enough to cause some actual damage. After all, he'd been lied to, his nature had been taken advantage of, and he wanted answers.

At the side of the door was an umbrella stand, and in it was a sturdy length of walking stick, one of those country-walk types that was longer than a cane, and had a bone 'Y' in the top, for some unknown reason. Pulling it out, he gripped it in his hands as he stalked up the stairs.

'Andrade?' he called out, waiting for an answer and receiving none. 'You up there?'

The anger was dissipating now, replaced by concern, and, as Billy walked to the top of the stairs, he got nervous.

What if someone had got in and killed Andrade? What if by leaving, he'd doomed Andrade to a death worse than José Almas?

But there was no Andrade upstairs. In fact, the bedroom looked like a bomb had hit it, with clothes strewn everywhere. Billy wondered for a moment if he'd been burgled, until he saw his *Bellroy* overnight bag was missing from his wardrobe, as well as a small collection of shirts, jeans and jumpers.

Andrade was the same size, give or take.

Billy slammed his fist against the side of the door in frustration. There were two options here, and neither was good.

There was a third one, an option that suggested Andrade had been taken, but nobody would do that and then take the time to fill out an overnight bag.

No, the options were that Andrade had filled a "go bag" of sorts and run before he could be found, or he'd filled a bag and run because he knew Billy was about to learn he'd lied, and would either come looking for a fight, or would return with the authorities.

He wasn't wrong there, Billy thought as he looked at the stick in his hand.

Either way, Andrade was gone. He hadn't waited for Billy and Davey to clear him, which also meant he didn't have faith in their ability to.

Possibly because there wasn't a way to, as he was the killer he was pretending to be running from.

Billy closed his eyes, clenching his hands tight around the walking stick. He wanted to swing it, smash things, walk away from this. But the fact of the matter was, no matter what Andrade had done right now, where he'd gone or even who he'd gone to, Billy was now tied up in this, for better or worse, until he could clear himself. Not just of the murder in the apartment, but of any connection to Andrade's crimes while in London. Because currently, it was looking like Andrade could have been breaking quite a few laws while they'd been together, maybe even using Billy's police contacts.

Which would make Monroe right about him from the start.

It was around now when the hammering started on his front door.

Walking down, and expecting an armed police unit to be on his doorstep, he opened it to find Davey and his Great-Uncle Chivalry standing there, both staring at his weaponed hand. Billy stared back at Chivalry's own weaponed hand, currently gripping a First World War *Webley Mk IV* revolver.

'Is he still here?' Chivalry asked, pushing past Billy, looking around the house. As he did so, Billy looked imploringly at Davey, who nodded at the walking stick.

'That for us, or for him?' she asked.

'Him,' Billy admitted to them both. 'He lied to me. He didn't run from anyone last night. I saw the footage. He was calm as anything.'

'You'd better get yourself a stiff drink and sit down,' Davey smiled. 'Because that's not the only lie he's been telling recently. You have a lot to catch up on.'

13

BACKGROUND CHECKS

JESS LOOKED NERVOUSLY AT MINA FROM ACROSS THE OFFICE, currently sitting at the side of Declan's desk, staring blankly at a patch of carpet exactly two feet from the chair.

'Should I get her a drink or something?' she muttered softly.

Anjli, standing beside her, smiled.

'You've smacked down killers who were attacking you with power tools,' she said, patting Jess on the shoulder. 'Why are you stressing about a teenage girl who might not even be connected to this more than a slightly zealous belief in God?'

'I'm not sure,' Jess frowned as she watched Mina. 'I think it's because she's the same age as me.'

'And that's why I'm asking you to speak to her,' Anjli winked. 'Look, I've been trying for an hour now, and I've not got anywhere with her. The priest she lives with will be here soon, the verger seems to be non-existent. Once either of them turns up, we won't get anything else from her, and I'm bloody sure there's something we're missing here.'

She sighed.

'She won't talk to me because I'm a copper and I'm double her age. You're not a copper, and you're the same age as her. Take her to the break room, make her a drink. See what you can get from her. It's not like it's the first time you've built an asset.'

Jess looked horrified at the comment.

'Are you saying Prisha was moulded, or groomed by me?' she said, aghast.

'Oh, God, no, I forgot that's how the two of you met,' Anjli reddened. Jess had helped them in the *Red Reaper* case by talking to and effectively infiltrating a group of students who'd all known the victim, Nathanial Wing, before he died. In the process, she had become close to one student, Prisha, and after a few months had even started dating her.

Which, if looked at the wrong way, could look like that, even if it wasn't what Anjli meant.

'Let's just say that was a happy accident, eh?'

Still not looking convinced about this, Jess walked across the office towards Mina.

'Hey,' she smiled. 'I'm Jess. I'm helping out around here. You want a drink?'

'Are you police?' Mina looked up at her.

At this, Jess grinned.

'More official mascot,' she said, motioning for Mina to follow her. 'I'm doing my first year of A Levels in North London right now.'

Mina rose, and Jess noted she'd picked up the little bottle of holy water she'd brought with her. Anjli had wanted this to be very informal, until the moment it wasn't, and as such, she'd been allowed to keep it.

Jess just hoped Mina wouldn't start trying to exorcise *her* with it.

'Do you want tea, coffee, or something cold?' Jess asked as they walked up the stairs. Mina considered this carefully, weighing up all the options.

'What sorts of tea do you have?'

'*Tea* tea,' Jess replied. 'I think, anyway. What my dad calls "builder's tea". I don't think we have anything else. But we do have milk and lactose free milk, so you get a choice there.'

'Builder's tea is fine,' Mina gave a small, nervous smile. 'Father Franks drinks that.'

'He's the priest of the church you live in, right?' Jess entered the kitchen area of the break room and put the kettle on. 'He's coming to pick you up?'

'He shouldn't,' Mina sat at a table after being instructed to by Jess. 'I'm an embarrassment to his Church.'

'How?'

'The first time I do God's will, I end up in a police station,' Mina smiled.

Jess couldn't help herself and chuckled at this as well.

'I think this is a far different situation than if you were arrested,' she said, placing a tea bag in a mug. 'I wouldn't be doing this for you, for a start.'

As she waited for the kettle to boil, she looked back at the scared teenage girl in front of her. 'Anjli – that is, DS Kapoor – said you'd lost your parents,' she said. 'I'm sorry for your loss. I can't imagine how I'd feel if that happened.'

Mina looked up. 'You still have both parents?'

'In a way,' Jess nodded. 'My mum and dad have split, and Mum's getting married again, and I don't see much of Dad apart from when I'm on holidays, but at least I can still see them.'

She leant back, letting a long breath out.

'My mum is mental at the moment though,' she carried

on, wondering if something personal given might help here. 'She's marrying this guy – Henry – nice man, they've known each other for years, but he also used to be my dad's old boss, and he has a real chip on his shoulder about another wedding happening next year, so now their marriage has to be the "best ever", and neither of them are backing down on this, even though I don't think Mum or Henry really care.'

'Sounds complicated.'

'Yeah, it's the other reason I'm spending a lot of time here right now,' Jess waved around. 'Believe it or not, helping solve crimes is actually easier than wedding planning.'

'I still see my parents,' Mina replied after a moment's silence. 'When I shut my eyes. And I know they both watch over me.'

'Can I ask what happened?' Jess asked, and then wrinkled her nose. 'No, sorry, that's super rude of me.'

'Not at all,' Mina nodded at the kettle. 'Your water has boiled.'

Jess turned and filled the mugs, going to the fridge and pulling out the two cartons. Mina nodded at the full-fat milk and, after sorting out the tea bag, Jess placed a splash of milk into the mug.

'Sugar?'

'One, please.'

This done, Jess took the two mugs and brought them over to the table, passing one over to Mina. However, as she went to sit down, she saw Mina open the small bottle and drip two small drops of water into the drink.

'Armour,' Mina said as she saw Jess watching her. 'It's my vaccine, as you say, against evil.'

Jess nodded as she sat, sipping at her own tea.

'My nan was like that,' she said. 'She'd say prayers as she

ironed my grandad's shirts. She wasn't religious or anything, but he was a police officer, and she always said that she was ironing in the protection, like creating a spiritual Kevlar vest.'

'And did it work?'

Jess's face fell.

'The daughter of a serial killer murdered him, so not really,' she said. 'Although it was a car accident and a heart attack that did him in, so maybe if she'd tried to stab him or shoot him, it would have worked. Or maybe the prayers wore off. She died a few years before him, you see. He ironed his own shirts after that.'

There was a long moment of silence, and Jess worried she'd given too much information now.

'My father killed himself,' Mina eventually broke the silence with this bombshell. 'I was two, I don't remember him.'

'Wow,' Jess leant back in her chair. 'I didn't know. You don't have to say anything else—'

'He had money problems, bad ones,' Mina explained. 'He worked in the City, in London, as a broker I think, and he sent his money home to us. It was good money, and my family had a good life, so I've been told. But then his finance deals collapsed because there was a big financial crisis or something, and his company fired him. Without a job, he couldn't stay in the country, but he couldn't keep us fed and homed if he came back to us, and so he took anything he could get in London. But without legal citizenship, the jobs were off the books, cash in hand, and rare. And my father had spent his life working with numbers. He didn't know how to wire a fuse or build a wall. The jobs dried up.'

'Harsh,' Jess didn't really know what else to say to this. 'What happened to your mum? If you don't mind me asking?'

'Cancer,' Mina replied, her voice devoid of emotion. 'I was ten when it happened. I should have gone into the system, but Father McNarry, he was a friend of hers, said I should stay with him. And, earlier this year, Father Franks invited me and another boy from the village to come to London as part of an exchange visit, on Father McNarry's suggestion. They know each other.'

'You want to be a nun, I believe?'

Mina nodded, and her face broke out into a beatific smile.

'Oh yes, very much so,' she said. 'It is the best way to honour him, to be his bride.'

'Christ?'

Mina looked at Jess as if she was an idiot.

'Of course, Jesus Christ,' she intoned. 'I cannot take holy orders until I am eighteen, though, so I'm helping the Church until then. That's why I help with the soup kitchen.'

'I thought it was a charity service, not a Church one?' Jess frowned.

'The Church provides volunteers for St Benedict's,' Mina explained. 'Father Franks knows Lewis Hoyle, he's the man who runs the soup kitchen most nights, and he needed some helpers. It's nice. I get to help the people I meet, prepare them.'

'Prepare them?'

'For their fights with Satan,' Mina lowered her voice now. 'It is a daily battle for them all.'

Jess wanted to continue down this path, to ask more questions, but she also knew from Anjli's notes that Mina had believed Santa Mick had been possessed by a demon.

Although she'd seen stranger things in her time helping her father in the Unit.

'Did you know Santa Mick?' she asked instead. 'Before the food lines?'

'Yes, but not for long,' Mina nodded. 'He turned up at church one day. He was very sad, and was mumbling at the back of the Nave, all alone. He looked like he hadn't slept in days.'

'But he came to what, Mass?'

'No, he came for confession,' Mina shook her head at the question. 'Father Franks wouldn't speak to him though, said he had to take a bath before he'd let him into the confessional.'

She looked across the room at this point, lost in the memory.

'Mina?' Jess pressed on.

'That's when I knew he was a demon,' Mina returned to the current as she spoke. 'Father Franks wouldn't take his confession. He was scared of him.'

'Did he do that often?'

'I never saw him refuse a confession, ever,' Mina said, finishing the tea. 'This was very nice. Can I have another?'

Before Jess could reply, however, there was the sound of people walking up the stairs, and Anjli and a Catholic Priest, in his clergy shirt, collar and jacket, appeared in the doorway. Jess assumed this was Father Franks and smiled.

'I was making Mina another tea, Father,' she said. 'Would you like one?'

Father Franks frowned.

'You're an officer?'

'No,' Anjli said from the side. 'She's the daughter of our Detective Inspector, but as she's the same age, I thought it might be nicer for Mina to have someone to talk to.'

'Has she given her statement?' Father Franks asked Anjli,

his head moving from side to side as he tried to split his attention between Anjli and Mina.

'She has, and she's ready to go whenever you want to,' Anjli smiled. 'Thank you for allowing her to clear up one of the issues.'

'What issue was that?' Franks looked concerned, but then a wave of relief crossed his eyes as he remembered. 'Oh, you mean the holy water in the soup? I'll make sure she never does it again.'

'Unless it's actively banned by the Church, I see no reasons to stop it,' Anjli shrugged as she nodded for Mina to rise and join the Father. 'We'll call if anything else is needed.'

'Do you expect to need Mina again?' Father Franks halted.

Anjli pursed her lips, considering this.

'Well, she was a witness with Lewis the night Michael Siddell died, so she may have seen something, maybe classed as unimportant at the time, which could help us immensely down the line,' she said.

Father Franks nodded understanding at this but, as he turned to leave with Mina, Jess spoke up.

'Father Franks?'

He paused, looking back.

'Yes, my child?'

'I have a quick question if you don't mind?' Jess asked. 'I'm not a police officer, so you don't have to answer, but I'm just curious. A couple of things, actually.'

'Go on.'

'Mina said you knew Lewis Hoyle, who runs the soup kitchen,' Jess started. 'I wondered how you knew him?'

'He was in seminary school with me,' Father Franks replied calmly. 'He didn't finish, though. We stayed friends afterwards and as we both did God's work, I looked for ways to help him. The charity he started, St Benedict's, helps a lot of people.'

'He started it?' Anjli looked up at this.

'Well, he was involved in the original planning and funding for it, but then he joined seminary school,' Father Franks scratched at the back of his collar as he thought back. 'Eventually he realised his future was with the homeless, and he left.'

He looked back at Jess.

'And the other thing?'

'Mina said Santa Mick came to ask for confession, but you refused him,' Jess asked, and Anjli noticed Father Franks turn away slightly, his expression darkening. 'I wondered if there was a reason for it?'

'He stank,' Father Franks replied. 'Urine, vomit, it was ... it was overpowering. That was it.'

'And you haven't allowed people who smell to take confession before?'

'I've answered your questions, and as you said, you're not a police officer,' Father Franks straightened suddenly, his tone becoming officious. 'Therefore, I—'

'She might not be a police officer, but I am,' Anjli said icily. 'So how about you answer the girl before you leave?'

Father Franks looked conflicted, but then sighed.

'He'd caused issues in the church,' he said. 'In the past. Disturbances and suchlike. He was a drunk, he ranted and he would shout and scream loudly now and then, when a flash of his past would appear. But then it'd go as quick as it came, and we'd be left with a confused old man who'd scared the parishioners. I'd told him he wasn't wanted there, that he should go to one of the other churches, there's a few in Soho even, but he wouldn't listen. He wanted forgiveness from me, not someone else.'

'And why do you think that is?' Anjli continued.

'I don't know!' Father Franks was getting agitated now. 'I'd say to ask him, but that's not an option now. Maybe it's because I was younger than my local peers, and he thought I'd go lighter on penance? Some of the others could be quite Fire and Brimstone.'

Anjli nodded at this, stepping to the side, allowing Father Franks and Mina to leave.

'Thank you for your candour, Father,' she said. 'And thanks for your time, Mina.'

Mina smiled shyly as she followed Father Franks out of the break room, but then paused.

'Jess, are you free tonight?' she asked.

'I can be,' Jess half-glanced at Anjli as she replied. 'Why?'

'We have a service tonight,' Mina looked at Father Franks as she spoke. 'A carol service to help the homeless. It's life-affirming.'

'You're welcome to come, but it's very, well, *Catholic*,' Father Franks smiled weakly.

'I'm a practising Catholic, Father,' Jess grinned. 'I'm well used to the bells and smells. I'll see if I can come by.'

Mina smiled and ran down the stairs after Father Franks as he left, leaving Anjli and Jess alone.

'So,' Anjli puffed out her cheeks. 'What did you learn?'

'That Father Franks seems to have more secrets here than Mina,' Jess leant back against the counter as she thought. 'He knew the guy who ran the soup kitchen, he wouldn't let Santa Mick take confession, and he pretty much had a meltdown when I questioned him on it.'

Anjli nodded.

'Yeah, there's more going on than we thought there,' she said. 'You sure about tonight?'

'I'll raise it with Dad later.'

'You can do it right now,' Anjli replied, turning back to the doorway. 'Everyone's downstairs as Monroe wants to have a briefing.'

Jess went to leave, but paused as Anjli smiled.

'I'm doing the teas first though, aren't I?' she asked.

'Now you're getting it,' Anjli's grin grew wider. 'You'll be a cracking police officer one day. Don't forget to add two sugars for the Guv.'

And, with that wise piece of information imparted, Anjli left Jess alone with the kettle and coffee machine.

She was about to start when her phone beeped a message. It was from Billy.

Have they got you making drinks yet?

Yes

There was a pause, and then Billy replied.

Make terrible ones. If you're shit at making teas, they'll move onto some other poor bugger.

Reading the text, Jess grinned.

Now *that* was something she could do.

14

BLACKBALLED

'Michael Siddell, the one-time Scrooge of the Jacob Marley Society,' Monroe said, pointing at the image on the plasma screen. It was of Siddell before the 2008 crash, a face of arrogance and greed that stared down on the people watching him. The current members of the Last Chance Saloon were all sitting in the briefing room now; Declan and Anjli in their usual spots, De'Geer, Doctor Marcos and Cooper at the back, and Bullman perched at the doorway. Jess had taken Billy's usual spot on the laptop after passing the drinks around, and was sitting eagerly at her station, waiting for a nod, a motion of some kind to ask for the image on the screen to change.

'Also known as Mickey Fish and Santa Mick,' Declan added, watching Jess with a modicum of amusement.

'Aye, laddie, a man of many names, found dead, seemingly from stomach issues, but then believed to have been poisoned,' Monroe nodded. 'But there we hit a strange twist in the tale. Doctor Marcos?'

'Santa Mick wasn't poisoned,' Doctor Marcos said from

the back. 'Or, rather, he didn't ingest poison. There wasn't any sign of it in his stomach, even if he showed all the signs of it.'

Monroe nodded to Jess, and she eagerly clicked on her mouse. The image now showed Arthur Drayson, an image taken from his Barrister days, decked out in his "silks" – his wig and gown.

'Arthur Drayson also didn't ingest poison,' Doctor Marcos continued, and smiled as the noise rose in the briefing room. 'Yes, I know, there was mistletoe on his beard, and there were traces found of the same mistletoe in a glass left in the kitchen area, but it wasn't enough to kill, especially with a reaction as quick as the one he had. And, more importantly, we now believe he did it himself.'

'Suicide?'

'Self-medicating,' Doctor Marcos shrugged. 'It's been a herbal healer for centuries. *Getafix* in *Asterix* uses it to help with the magic potion—'

She stopped, realising she was going off on a tangent.

'Anyway, over the years, trials carried out using oral mistletoe in moderation have found it can reduce the symptoms of high blood pressure, headaches, and dizziness. This was apparently what Drayson was doing, using the mistletoe in the garlands as some kind of health tonic, crushing a couple up and tossing them in the milk as he was probably feeling a little stressed with all the little darlings around. Although, this is still hearsay based on people who'd been working with him.'

'So, if he drank the mistletoe deliberately, and neither ingested anything else, how did they die?' Declan frowned.

'Oh, they were poisoned,' Doctor Marcos smiled. 'But not orally.'

She nodded to Jess, who frowned.

'Sorry,' Jess said. 'I wasn't told you had any other images to show.'

Doctor Marcos took a deep breath but relaxed it.

'Sorry,' she said. 'I'm just used to Billy having this almost psychic way of knowing what I want up on the screen. Look in my folder, under "*Bleugh*" please.'

Jess typed on the laptop's keyboard, and after a second or two, an image of a third man appeared on the screen. It was the photo of a young man, in his twenties or thirties, in the green uniform of an emergency paramedic.

'This is Charlie White,' she said. 'He was one of the first paramedics on the scene when Arthur Drayson collapsed, trying to keep him alive. And, about an hour after he did so, he was violently sick in St Thomas's Hospital, and was admitted into a ward himself.'

'What was wrong with him?' Anjli asked.

'Same symptoms as the other two, but far more minor,' Doctor Marcos replied, checking her own notes. 'But, as he was in a hospital when it hit, he could be treated quickly.'

'Let me guess, he also didn't have anything in his stomach?' Monroe leant against the table, scowling as he sipped at his tea. He glanced at Jess, who stared back innocently as he placed it back onto the table beside him, but then looked back at Doctor Marcos. 'It's a contact venom?'

'I think "venom" is a little dramatic, but you're on the right path,' Doctor Marcos nodded. 'Charlie White didn't touch Arthur Drayson until he'd pulled on a pair of latex gloves, but before he did this, he pulled off Arthur's "Father Christmas" gloves as they got him into a more comfortable position. The black leather ones with the white fluffy edgings.'

'The *gloves* gave him the poison?' Declan was surprised at this.

'Actually, we believe so,' Doctor Marcos nodded. 'But only trace elements.'

'There was a first-aider elf,' Declan read his notebook. 'Nathan. He also checked on Arthur Drayson, so why didn't he contract it as well?'

'Because he didn't touch the gloves, focusing instead on the chest and the heart,' Doctor Marcos nodded. 'We looked into him. The moment we heard about Charlie, however, we checked the gloves. And, on the tips of the fingers were trace elements of sweat, and also some unknown toxin we're still checking, but something that definitely contained Viscumin.'

'Mistletoe,' Anjli said. 'Could it have spilt onto his fingers from when he drank it?'

'Then we would have had traces of milk, too,' Doctor Marcos shook her head. 'But it started us thinking. And we —' she pointed at De'Geer here '—or, rather, the Viking had an idea.'

There was a long silence as De'Geer, not realising it was his turn to continue, stared blankly at Doctor Marcos, eventually standing with a jerk as he finally realised it was his opportunity to speak.

'Witnesses said they saw Arthur Drayson sweating, and rubbing at his forehead,' he said, now looking at Declan who, realising quicker than De'Geer did that it was his turn to speak as part of this hot potato, opened his notebook, reading aloud.

'*We held back the next child and as he took off his wig, he wiped his forehead, still wearing his gloves, which was probably unhygienic as he then held children's hands with them, and they must have been sweaty as he was really dripping at this point,*' he said. 'This was word for word from Corinne Haynes, the manager of the grotto.'

'Exactly,' De'Geer pointed at Declan. 'He wiped his forehead while wearing his gloves. But the problem with this is there aren't many toxins that work fast through the skin.'

'There's that one the Russian spies use,' Cooper suggested.

'True, but we're not in a spy movie,' Doctor Marcos commented. 'Also, things like Thallium take months, even years to work, and if this was something like Novichok, we'd have kiddies collapsing too. The point is usually for the target not to be aware they've been poisoned, so they go home, do other things, and the killer gets to walk away. This was pretty instantaneous compared to that. And because of this, we knew we had something different.'

'But there are ways to bypass this,' De'Geer beamed as he spoke, and Declan knew he'd come up with this idea. 'DMSO, for example.'

'Okay, and what's that?' Monroe frowned.

'Dimethyl sulfoxide,' De'Geer replied. 'It's an industrial solvent that comes from wood. It's non-toxic and is used in a ton of stuff.'

'Not liking the "non-toxic" part of that, laddie,' Monroe muttered. 'Not sounding like "fatal poison" to me.'

'The DMSO isn't the poison, it's the way to make it work, Guv,' De'Geer continued. 'It's been used a lot recently in holistic medications, as if you have it on your skin, it allows a far quicker absorption of anything that touches it, moving into your body through your skin.'

'It effectively removes the barrier of the skin,' Doctor Marcos added. 'So much so that you're actively told, when using any kind of DMSO, to wash your hands before using anything else, in case that bleeds through into your body. And because of its many uses, it's available without a prescription, and can be purchased in health food stores, by mail order, and on the Internet.'

'So, you're saying the contact poison didn't actually *need* to be a contact poison?' Declan asked.

'I'm saying this definitely helped,' Doctor Marcos nodded. 'There's usually a faint garlic odour, but the mistletoe and viscumin's smell would have covered it, as they're similar.'

'Corinne said they could smell a strange garlicky odour on Arthur Drayson's lips,' Declan replied.

'Mixing DMSO into the poison meant they could put something like a batrachotoxin into the mix with some viscumin, smear it on his forehead, and in a couple of hours, thud,' Doctor Marcos continued. 'Boom. Dead person alert.'

'How did they get it on his forehead?' Jess spoke without realising, and then reddened. 'It was the wig, wasn't it?'

'No, that's what I thought,' Doctor Marcos took over again. 'But when we checked, we found it was actually on the inside of the hat. So, we went and had another look at Michael Siddell. He had welts on his forehead, and the cap was long gone, but I think he also had poison smeared on the inside of the hat he was wearing.'

'How long would it take to work?' Monroe asked.

'Hours,' Doctor Marcos tapped the back of her teeth with her tongue, a tapping noise that echoed around the room. 'It would have had an advantage with the DMSO, but it would still have been a slow-acting toxin. Drayson was on his third shift; he'd been wearing the same hat for hours. And Santa Mick told Lewis, the soup kitchen guy, he'd been given a new hat by a lady earlier that day, and he'd been wearing it ever since.'

'A health worker,' Monroe tapped at his beard. 'Or maybe an "elf" worker? Maybe Santa Mick wasn't slurring?'

'A health worker makes more sense, as a nurse would have a better knowledge of poisons than Tinker Bell,' Anjli commented.

'Tinker Bell's a fairy, not an elf,' Declan replied, and then flinched as Anjli looked at him. 'Either way, someone made sure they laced both hats with poison at the same time. Anything on this mysterious elf?'

'Oh, aye,' Monroe nodded at Jess. 'It's in my folder. Labelled "*I got this because the manager hated DI Walsh.*" Have a look.'

Jess grinned as she looked into the folder system, and Declan pouted as he looked at his boss.

'Enjoy Whamhalla,' he said, and Monroe mimed an arrow to the chest.

'Ah! You got me!' he cried as, on the screen, an image turned up of a slim woman in an elf costume in the hotel grotto. The image was from a camera high in a corner of the room, and only gained a section of the face, enough to just about make out the jawline, but showed the incredibly blonde hair, which was long and pulled back.

'It's like the lassie in *Game of Thrones*,' Monroe said. 'Probably peroxide or a wig.'

'Is that the best we have?' Anjli asked.

Monroe nodded.

'Apparently, she was very good at avoiding the cameras,' he said. 'This was literally the only time we don't see the back of the head.'

'Any idea where she got the costume?'

'Any costume shop could do it,' Declan said, leaning

closer to look at the image. 'She might even have gained it from someone there.'

'Well, that's all we have, so we need to look into this,' Monroe checked his notes. 'Any news on who spoke to Drayson by phone? Corinne said he was spooked by it.'

'A Colin Walters,' Jess said, reading the screen. 'It's being looked into by Cyber Crime.'

'Walters? Aye, good, keep on at them,' Monroe said. 'And if they give you any shite, tell them I'll be the next one calling. We need any news we can get on Colin Walters right now.'

'Guv?' Anjli frowned. 'Is there something you want to share with the class? We haven't heard that name before.'

'Oh, aye, I was chatting to Farringdon with Bullman earlier today,' Monroe nodded, realising his mistake. 'Interesting development with the two victims, they were both in some stupid bloody kiddie club.'

'What DCI Monroe is trying to say is that Drayson and Siddell were in a small club-within-a-club called the Jacob Marley Society,' Bullman smiled from the doorway. 'Which basically meant they met once a year and decided which of three poor randomly chosen buggers received a fifty-grand windfall to help them on their way.'

'But in 2007 it all went to shite,' Monroe, annoyed at the interruption, now continued. 'Because Siddell made sure there was no winner and kept the money, pocketing it and splitting the cash between himself, Arthur Drayson, Neil someone-who-doesn't-matter as he died years back, and Colin Walters, who were the other people involved in this windfall plan.'

'You think this is someone gaining revenge on this Society?' Declan frowned. 'That's fifteen years gone. A hell of a long time to wait for this.'

'Siddell went AWOL the following year,' Anjli suggested. 'Maybe it's taken this long to find him?'

'I suppose, as Michael Siddell and "Santa Mick" are technically two different people,' Declan mused. 'Bloody hell, between him and Shaun Donnal, how many others are on the street hiding?'

'Sadly, too many,' Bullman intoned. 'Too many indeed.'

'Apparently they did this thing every year where they chose three needy cases, and picked one over the others,' Monroe returned the briefing onto its correct track. 'That year's winner got nothing, though. And, as they were the most in need, it probably pissed them off greatly.'

'Do we know who won?' Declan asked.

'Farringdon's checking into that,' Monroe replied. 'But there was one thing that makes this whole thing a definitely more believable revenge story. Farringdon said when he was invited to attend one year, he was made to wear a Father Christmas hat. Apparently they all did this in the Jacob Marley Society, except for four of them – the three ghosts wore green ones, and the Scrooge, the person who decided who got the money, had a black one. Siddell was the Scrooge that year, and Drayson was one of the ghosts, as was Colin Walters, who called him the day he died.'

'Bloody hell, this was a definite message,' Declan whistled. 'So, what happened with the girl?'

This was aimed at Jess, who blushed.

'DS Kapoor was the one who interviewed her,' she stammered.

'Yeah, and I got nowhere,' Anjli added. 'Go on.'

'Mina Suvosky, sixteen years old, pretty much killing time until she can become a nun at eighteen,' Jess started, speaking from memory. 'Dad died when she was two, broker of some kind who worked in London, mum died of cancer a few years later. Fell in with the Catholic Church, a Father McNarry brought her in, but he was a bit of a zealot.'

'How so?' Monroe asked.

'He was a Catholic exorcist,' Anjli interjected. 'Still is, I suppose. Haven't got hold of him yet as he's in the middle of nowhere and they don't seem to like Wi-Fi or phone signals in the depths of Romania. Sorry, carry on.'

'Father McNarry then sent her to London as part of an exchange a few weeks back, where she now stays in the church of Father Franks, who knows Lewis Hoyle, the soup kitchen manager. That's how she got involved helping, but she started taking holy water from the font and dripping some into the soups, as she wanted to help the homeless fight the evils of Satan.'

'That's why she spiked Siddell's soup?'

'Yes and no,' Anjli spoke again now. 'She believed he had a demon inside him, and she was exorcising it, using things she'd been taught by Father McNarry.'

'Sounds like a solid reason to move her to the back of the list,' Monroe said, but paused as he watched Jess purse her lips at this. 'Good intentions and zealotry – zealotism – whatever the damn thing's called, they don't make you a killer, well, most of thc time, anyway. You think differently?'

'I'm not sure, Guv,' Jess spoke slowly, nervously. 'She believed Santa Mick was more troubled than the others because she'd seen him in the food queues a couple of times, and Lewis had mentioned him. However, Santa Mick also came to her church asking for confession from Father Franks, and he didn't give it to him.'

'His reasons?'

'Personal hygiene,' Anjli looked at her notes. 'But when

he was pressed on it, he became quite irritated, saying Siddell had "caused issues" in the church, but not stating what they were, just that he was loud and shouting.'

'Hampstead is a fair distance from Soho,' Cooper mused. 'If Siddell was Catholic and wanted confession, he could have gone to a dozen different places.'

'She's right,' Declan nodded. 'The Church of Our Lady of the Assumption and St Gregory is on Warwick Street, literally a five-minute walk. And there's even St Patrick's in Soho Square itself. He wouldn't need to go that far.'

'Mina and Father Franks both mentioned they have a link with St Benedict's kitchen, so maybe he felt more comfortable there?'

Declan frowned.

'Seems a reach,' he muttered. 'But I think Cooper's right. There's something there.'

'Maybe we should look into Father Franks then,' Monroe mused. 'Billy – sorry, lassie, Jess – could you check into his past, see if there's anything we can use? Especially as he has a personal link with both the soup kitchen and the victim.'

Jess nodded, typing away as Monroe looked around.

'Anything else I missed?'

Declan half raised a hand and then put it back down.

'Sorry, force of habit,' he smiled. 'I saw Mallory Reed. The bottle was a peppermint tincture, bought from a Chinese therapist off Poland Street.'

'We checked the bottle,' Doctor Marcos piped up from the back, where she'd returned to. 'It's just some herbs and spices, all aimed at soothing a stomach.'

'Mallory said she saw Siddell, but he didn't recognise her. She left this with him, but when he collapsed, she called the ambulance for him,' Declan said, flicking through the notes.

'One thing though, she talked about the conversations they used to have, before he became so far gone he didn't recognise her. She said he'd once owned a first edition copy of Charles Dickens's *A Christmas Carol,*' but when she showed him a picture online, he started crying, saying "that's the one" and that he deserved to lose it. Started saying Scrooge became better in the book while he went the other way, saying he hurt people, that the ghosts were angry at him.'

'If you steal the money from them one year, maybe the ghosts do become unhappy,' Monroe suggested.

Declan, however, shook his head.

'I suggested they could be hallucinations,' he replied, 'but Mallory was convinced he believed they were real people.'

'Maybe someone's been playing a trick on him?' Anjli spoke up. 'Someone turns up and wears a green Santa's hat, he sees it, it triggers a memory, and he thinks they're a current Marley Society ghost? Maybe he means this?'

'Possibly,' Declan replied. 'She didn't see him that much, and was only in town by coincidence.'

He stopped.

'One more thing,' he added. 'She was with the soup kitchen after Lewis started, but left nine years ago, only coming back now and then. I got the impression there was a problem.'

'With Lewis?'

'I'm not sure,' Declan shook his head. 'But there's something going on there.'

'What do we need to be looking for here?' Monroe glanced back at Doctor Marcos. 'Poison wise?'

'Whoever put this together has to have serious training as a chemist,' Doctor Marcos replied. 'I can't believe a sixteen-year-old could get the items and put them together, although stranger things have happened, I suppose. We should look into chemical backgrounds.'

'Mallory mentioned her brother was a pharmacist,' Declan suggested.

'Check into it,' Monroe looked at his watch. 'We're unlikely to be getting anywhere else today, so check up on your leads and then call it a night.'

Jess went to put her hand up, but stopped.

'Go on, lassie.'

'Mina invited me to her church service tonight,' Jess replied. 'They're feeding the homeless, with St Benedict's Kitchen's help. I'm Catholic, so I know all the secret handshakes and such, and I thought it might help the case if I turned up, had a look around?'

'Aye, if you're up for it, go help some homeless, and see if you get anything,' Monroe nodded. 'Declan, Anjli, you're with me. We've been invited to the pub for a Christmas drink.'

'Who by?' Declan frowned.

'Tiny Tim and the spirit of Charles Dickens,' Monroe smiled. 'Everyone keep on with this. And find me this bloody elf girl.'

As everyone walked out of the briefing room, Declan walked over to Monroe.

'Any news on Billy?' he asked softly.

'We'll know more soon,' Monroe nodded sagely. 'After all, that's the drink we're about to have, laddie.'

On that comment, Monroe looked forlornly down at the mug on his desk.

'Your daughter,' he whispered. 'Has she been in touch with Billy lately?'

'I don't think so,' Declan frowned. 'Why?'

'Because her tea-making is suddenly as abysmal as his is,' Monroe moaned as, picking it up, the two of them left the briefing room. 'It's like she's deliberately making it bad, so we go back to Cooper doing it.'

'She's a chip off the old block,' Declan grinned. 'Because that's exactly what I did, too.'

15

BLOOD WORK

After the briefing had ended, Doctor Marcos had returned to her office on the ground floor, but De'Geer had been asked to take a minor diversion, taking his motorcycle and heading down to South London. Although he was a Sergeant now, he was still historically a motorcycle police officer, and because of this it was his police-issue motorcycle that pulled up on the junction of Pratt Walk and Lambeth Road, De'Geer clicking down the stand and pulling off his helmet as he stared across the street at the four-storey brown brick and glass building on the corner. Although housing the *Metropolitan Police Central Communications Command Centre,* it was also the home of the *Metropolitan Police Forensic Science Laboratory*, a Brutalist-style police complex with external concrete staircases, brick infill and a large concrete ventilation shaft that protruded out on the street corner.

Doctor Marcos wasn't the biggest fan of it; she'd only really used it as a place of last resort, gaining intelligence on a potential murder weapon that would clear Declan when he was accused of terrorism, or hunting down rogue forensic examiners during a gang war. And, now she had De'Geer to do it for her, she made a point of avoiding arriving here whenever she could, sending him instead.

And so, De'Geer placed his bike helmet under his arm and entered the building's reception, where they scanned his ID, and pointed the way to the blood works floor.

It wasn't actually called that; it was more a forensic screen unit, but as Doctor Osborne, De'Geer's contact here focused primarily on blood and DNA profiling, the name kind of stuck.

'De'Geer,' Osborne said as he stared into a microscope, not looking up at De'Geer's arrival. He was a young black man in his late twenties, but looked older because of a premature greying of his hair. He was stocky and unshaven and wore a Wrexham Football Club hoodie, even though he wasn't Welsh. 'Take a seat.'

'How did you know it was me?' De'Geer did as he was told.

'Because you're ten-foot tall and sound like an army of soldiers when you stomp into a room,' Osborne finally looked up. 'Oh, I see it's fluorescent day today.'

'Came by bike,' De'Geer replied. 'Following the safety guidelines.'

'I thought guidelines were only for human-sized people,' Osborne reached to the side and picked up a half-eaten sandwich, munching on it as he stared across the room. 'Marcos send you for the results?'

De'Geer nodded.

'And we couldn't email them because they're all hush-hush?'

Again, De'Geer nodded.

Osborne laughed at this.

'Bloody Marcos never changes,' he said. 'She still marrying the Scot?'

'I believe so,' De'Geer replied, fidgeting.

'Bloody hell. "I believe so." You know, they did well when they built you in the Temple Inn basement, because you're the perfect robot,' Osborne mocked. 'I bet you haven't done any of the things we talked about last time you were here.'

De'Geer reddened.

'The case,' he explained. 'It's taken up time.'

'You said you'd ask the girl copper out for a drink,' Osborne spun in the chair now to fully face De'Geer. 'You haven't, have you?'

'I have,' De'Geer straightened indignantly. 'We've been on a couple.'

'Alone or with others?' Osborne asked, and at no reply, he laughed. 'Did she even know it was a *drink* drink?'

'Probably not,' De'Geer muttered, staring at the ground now. 'And there were always others there. Anyway, it's got complicated. Joanne's back.'

'For good?' Osborne, having known Doctor Marcos for years, was obviously well acquainted with De'Geer's predecessor.

'For a case,' De'Geer pointed at some papers on Osborne's desk. 'That one.'

'Ah, and this is why you're here,' Osborne placed the remains of his sandwich down. 'Not to see me, but to get the results for *her*.'

De'Geer didn't reply.

'You need to decide what you want in life,' Osborne stretched out his arms, making small groans of relief as his spine audibly cracked. 'Right then, let's see what we have.'

He pulled up a sheet of paper, staring at it.

'Okay, so these are evidential samples, taken to facilitate comparison against case-related DNA material, right? Rather than CJ samples for the DNA database?'

'Yes,' De'Geer nodded.

At this thought, Osborne smiled, winking theatrically.

'Although I'm not to *officially* compare it against case-related DNA material, right?'

'For the moment,' De'Geer wanted to wink back, but fought the urge to. 'Currently we can't explain how we received the item.'

'Yeah, that's not the first time I've had that excuse from Rosanna Marcos,' Osborne was already reading the sheet again.

'So earlier this week I received a sample of blood, which Marcos named "candidate X,"', he said. 'Having checked the blood on the shirt, or, rather, a cut piece from the shirt, I can tell you the blood on it is a ninety-eight point-nine match for candidate X. Is that what you wanted to hear?'

'Not really,' De'Geer slumped against the chair. "Candidate X" was José Almas, a sample of blood taken from the bath scene and passed to Lambeth before the Colombians could stop them. If the blood on Andrade's shirt matched the blood in the sample, then it was looking even more likely Andrade Estrada had killed him.

Which, considering the manner of the death, was almost unthinkable.

'Well, maybe this will help you,' Osborne grinned. 'We identified the other DNA.'

'Other DNA?' De'Geer sat up. 'There was more than one sample on the shirt?'

'Three in total,' Osborne replied. 'No hit on the sweat and skin samples from inside the shirt, but I'm guessing you already know who wore it, but the second blood traces—'

'Two sets of blood?'

Osborne paused, watching De'Geer.

'Bloody hell,' he said. 'You really didn't expect this, did you?'

Reddening, De'Geer shook his head.

'To be honest, I wasn't sure what to expect,' he said. 'But you said you identified it?'

'Carlos Pascal,' Osborne tapped on his keyboard, and on the screen the image of a Spanish man appeared. He was middle-aged and stocky, a scar running down his cheek. 'We have the records through Interpol. Colombian native, born and raised in Bogotá. Last seen in Chile about eight months back, was brought in after a bar fight in Puente Alto, but was freed without charges, even though witnesses saw him ram a broken bottle into someone's eye. Not a nice man, from all accounts.'

'How much blood was his?' De'Geer was on the edge of the seat now.

'Not much, but we only checked a sample of the shirt. I'd say a slight cut's worth, while the other blood, your "candidate X" left a ton on the front.'

De'Geer took the offered sheet, looking down at it. Andrade Estrada had been there at the death of José Almas, or at least had been there shortly after when the blood was still flowing, and had gained the blood onto his shirt.

But at the same time, he'd also got the blood from Carlos Pascal on the shirt.

'Is it old blood?' he asked automatically.

'As in "did the wearer of this shirt cut Carlos a good while before they opened an artery on candidate X", right?'

Osborne shook his head. 'Saw nothing that'd corroborate that. I'd say the two samples were provided onto the shirt within an hour of each other. Maybe even at the same time.'

So, Andrade had been here, but so had Carlos Pascal.

Rising, De'Geer nodded thanks.

'Can I keep this?' he waved the paper.

'I never did the tests as it was off the books,' Osborne shrugged. 'Therefore, there's no bit of paper, comprende?'

De'Geer smiled.

'Appreciated,' he said, turning to leave.

'Hey,' Osborne rose from his chair before De'Geer could continue out. 'Any chance of a little quid pro quo? After I've helped you?'

De'Geer paused, intrigued.

'What's the problem?' he asked. 'And don't tell me you need something pulled down from a top shelf.'

'No, it's something your boss might be interested in, and I'd like off my tables,' Osborne was already typing on his keyboard. 'We had something come in a few days back. Not really paid attention to, the only reason I looked at it twice was because of Marcos's current fetish with Christmas hats.'

'It's not really a fetish—' De'Geer started, but then shut up. 'Sorry, go on, what do you mean?'

'A friend of mine works the Shoreditch patch,' Osborne leant back in his chair as he waited for an app to load. 'A few days back, there's a dead homeless girl called in from one of the morning crews. Shelly Garraway.'

'Murdered?'

'Nope. Dead in her tent,' Osborne looked back at him. 'She'd found a corner of the underside of a railway bridge she could put it up underneath, and she'd been there a few days. There are some community support coppers who check in with the homeless around there, you know, make sure they're all okay, make sure the women have tampons, all the usual.'

'But this girl died?'

'Yeah, poor cow,' Osborne showed a photo on the screen, a candid shot of a short, skinny woman in her early twenties, smiling at the camera at some kind of birthday celebration, her hair cut into a mousey blonde bob. 'She didn't look like this in the end though, she'd been caught by Captain Jack.'

De'Geer didn't need to ask what Osborne meant; "Captain Jack" was street slang for heroin.

'Overdose?'

'Maybe,' Osborne nodded. 'She was seen three nights back in Central London having a fight with Stitch, who's apparently a real person and not a Disney character. Anyway, she was seen telling Stitch, who's a woman in her thirties, by the way, that she was a "stinking coward" for not getting some ice for her—'

'Crystal meth?'

'Either that or she really wanted a slush puppy,' Osborne joked. 'The impression the community officer that wrote this down had though was it was more a drug-addict lover's spat than anything else. This was around nine-thirty at night.'

'Three nights ago?'

'Yeah,' Osborne checked the screen. 'Same day as the tramp you're checking into died.'

De'Geer wasn't overjoyed at the usage of "tramp", but he kept silent.

'What's the connection with Christmas hats?' De'Geer frowned. 'Because currently it just sounds like an overdose case, or some kind of death by natural causes.'

'Oh, yeah, sorry,' Osborne smiled. 'She was wearing a

Father Christmas hat when they found her. Lying in her sleeping bag, peaceful as anything.'

De'Geer considered this.

'This might not be connected, though,' he said. 'I mean, it's the time of year to wear these things.'

'I know, that's why I only mentioned it now in passing,' Osborne turned from the screen. 'I raised it because she was seen in Soho on Sunday night, and then later wore a hat and died.'

'Is she in a morgue?' De'Geer continued to write the notes down. Osborne was right to pass this to him, as there was a chance this could be connected. However, a homeless girl wasn't in the same wheelhouse as ex-Liverymen, so there was a very strong possibility this was nothing more than a sad endnote to someone's life.

'Three floors down,' Osborne pointed, as if De'Geer could see the body through the floors. 'It becomes a bit of a dance when a rough sleeper dies. If they're not known by anyone, then usually it's someone from *Spires, Crisis, St Mungo's,* all those charities that have to identify the body. If nobody claims it, even after it's identified, it falls to the local authority to pay for and arrange a burial or cremation, in what is called a "public health funeral", which is basically a pauper's funeral. Burials usually see the deceased placed in a communal grave of up to three bodies.'

'Bloody hell,' De'Geer muttered.

'Yeah,' Osborne nodded. 'They're miserable bloody affairs. Minister, Funeral Director and pall bearers. And they're usually brought in for the job.'

He straightened, shaking off the melancholy.

'Anyway, she's downstairs if you want to have a look. She still has her belongings in a bag, but they'll probably be burnt soon, because they bloody reek. Was in there with another body yesterday, and I had to move morgues.'

De'Geer finished writing this down, nodding.

'Thanks, Peter,' he said, rising back to his feet. I'll give it a once over before I return to the boss.'

'Hey, one other thing,' Osborne leant back on his chair now, relaxing. 'You said DC Davey's back?'

'Kinda,' De'Geer replied cautiously. 'She's off the books, working with DC Fitzwarren on something.'

'It stirring old memories?' Osborne smiled. 'Gonna go for another crack at it?'

'Definitely not,' De'Geer started to the door, feeling uncomfortable as to the direction the conversation was going.

'Oh,' Osborne said, crestfallen. 'I thought you might be looking back at her, so I could have a shot at the pretty PC you work with.'

'What, Esme?' De'Geer stopped in the doorway. 'You fancy Esme?'

'She's beautiful,' Osborne smiled, most likely imagining her. 'Gutsy, too. If you're okay with me having a try?'

'I'm nothing to do with it,' De'Geer replied noncommittally. 'She's her own woman.'

Walking out of the lab, De'Geer frowned at the way he was now feeling. He hadn't really considered Esme Cooper in that way for a few weeks now, not since Milton Keynes, but this was also because he'd been so busy in his new role, and with the promotion now official ...

You're jealous.

De'Geer shook his head. No, this was silly. Why would he be ...

Osborne and Cooper, in the mortuary, K-I-S-S-I-N-G—

'Enough,' De'Geer spoke harshly to his inner thoughts.

'We can think about this after we examine a dead body, yeah?'

And with the voice in his head silent once more, De'Geer continued down the stairs, his thoughts conflicted, and distracted by images of a black-haired woman by the name of Esme Cooper.

16

TINY TIM

THE *OLD BANK OF ENGLAND* WAS A PUB BASED ON THE OTHER side of Fleet Street from the entrance to Temple Inn and the Last Chance Saloon, and therefore had become one of the go-to locations for the team, when any of them were working late in the office.

An imposing Grade II-listed building, the pub was once the Law Courts branch of the *Bank of England* from 1888 to 1975, but after falling into disrepair, it was restored by *Fuller's* brewery two decades later in neoclassical style, complete with marble, specially commissioned murals, chandeliers and sculptured high ceilings.

Now a *McMullen's* brewery, the pub was homely and welcoming.

Of course, two weeks before Christmas, the place was heaving with drunken office parties as Declan, Monroe and Anjli arrived.

'Bloody hell,' Monroe muttered. 'How are we supposed to see—'

He stopped, sighing as he pointed at a sign.

'The upstairs is booked for a private party,' he muttered. 'I'll wager the Fitzwarrens have bought the blasted pub to make sure they get that.'

Walking past the sign and making their way up the stairs, they weren't surprised to find the upstairs area far quieter than the lower level.

In fact, only two people sat up here.

'Declan!' Chivalry Fitzwarren bellowed across the upstairs bar, rising to his feet and extending his arms for what looked to be an upcoming manly hug. 'How the devil are you?'

Declan avoided the embrace, turning it into a shoulder-check handshake. He was amused at Chivalry's use of the word "devil" in his greeting; after all, the first time they met, they brought Chivalry in as an occult expert.

'Where's DC Davey?' Monroe asked, nodding to Billy as he sat opposite.

'Checking in with Doctor Marcos,' Billy said and, as Declan sat at the table next to Monroe, he thought he caught the slightest hint of regret and sadness. 'We have a shirt being checked for blood residue.'

Declan had heard Andrade's shirt had been passed to Doctor Marcos, but decided it was probably better not to comment on this.

'You okay?' he asked instead.

At this, Billy looked up, his eyes haunted, as he shook his head.

'Not really, no,' he replied. 'Everything I knew about Andrade seems to be a lie.'

'Andrade killed José?' Monroe looked at Chivalry as he spoke, almost as if expecting the older man to give a more honest answer. However, any answer that was to be given paused as Anjli walked up with three drinks in her hand.

'Oh, good, it's you,' she deadpanned as she saw Chivalry rise to help her. 'What did I miss?'

'Possibly the worst day in Billy's life,' Declan said as he took his Guinness. 'So, what happened?'

'Andrade was at the Wanstead house,' Billy leant back in the chair and stared up at the ceiling as he replied. 'When Cooper, Davey and I arrived.'

'Aye, we know that,' Monroe nodded. 'Cooper told us when she returned. Explained how he'd been attacked or something outside his apartment, and ran for a train.'

'Yeah, well, she returned to the Unit before the fun stuff started,' Billy continued. 'Davey suggested we confirm his story, so I went to a local cafe to do it without him seeing me, well, try to disprove his alibi. I found him on the train CCTV and worked his journey out. He was outside the apartment when I was in there and then went straight to Wanstead. There wasn't an attack, there was nothing. And he arrived a good hour before he claimed he did.'

There was a half-finished whisky in front of him; he knocked it back in one go before carrying on.

'He had someone's blood on his shirt. As I said, Davey's checking right now if it's José's or not. I would have laughed at this until everything else came out.'

'Everything else?' Anjli had bought herself a white wine and was sipping at it, her attention now drawn to Chivalry as he cleared his throat.

'I met with your DC Davey in Andrade's apartment,' he explained. 'I'd been called in by Billy—'

'I hadn't called you in at all,' Billy interjected. 'I didn't even know if you were in the country. When I messaged you, I asked about any contacts you might have in Colombia.'

'I decoded the hidden message, that you needed my help.'

'There wasn't a bloody decoded message,' Billy was getting irritated. 'I just asked—'

'Well, I'm here now, and let's face it, you need my help,' Chivalry interrupted.

In return, Billy made an audible and pissed-off sounding sigh and slumped back into his chair.

'We have business interests there,' Chivalry explained to Monroe, changing the subject from his invitation to the party. 'Anyway, I never trusted the Colombian, and so rather than ask around, I thought I'd go straight to the source.'

'The Colombian being Andrade?' Anjli asked.

Chivalry didn't reply, just nodding curtly at this.

'And how did that work out for you?' Monroe replied, raising an eyebrow.

'Not that great,' Chivalry admitted. 'Pablo whatshisname, the security fellow explained Andrade was their prime suspect, because, well—'

'Because he'd killed before,' Billy finished, straightening in the chair. 'He was a member of a Cartel in his teens, and was alleged to have killed two men in that time.'

'I think it was more than alleged.'

'Until we have proof or some kind of confession, I will not harbour that thought,' Billy snapped.

At this, Chivalry rose in his seat to face his great-nephew.

'They said he'd given others the Colombian necktie,' he spoke calmly, as if trying to defuse an argument.

'No, Davey said he'd been there when others had done that!' Billy's voice was rising now. 'That doesn't mean he held the knife, or even did anything! Just because you never liked him, stop trying to make everyone hate him!'

There was a moment of uncomfortable silence, punctuated only by drunken cheers from downstairs.

'Okay, what happened next?' Declan stepped in now, bringing attention back to him.

'I'd already returned home to confront him,' Billy admitted. 'While following him on the CCTV, I'd seen him make a call and throw the phone away – the phone he claimed he didn't have as it was still in the apartment.'

'I'm guessing he wasn't there when you got back?' Declan asked.

Billy glared at Declan.

'You don't have to make it sound like you were right all along,' he muttered.

'Billy,' Declan leant closer. 'I'll give you that as you're hurting. But do you *seriously* think *I'd* do that?'

There was a second, awkward silence before Billy shook his head.

'No,' he replied with a slight smile. 'It's more the Guv's remit.'

'Damn right,' Monroe grinned.

'We also found a watch in the apartment, the strap broken in a scuffle,' Chivalry added. 'One Andrade had claimed was lost in the fight on the street, in a fight that never happened.'

Monroe nodded at this.

'Any idea where Andrade went to?' he asked.

Billy shook his head.

'I'd only just realised he was gone when Chivalry and Joanne turned up,' he said. 'Opened the door to find a bloody gun in my face.'

'You have a permit for a gun?' Declan asked as Chivalry smiled winningly back at him.

'Poor boy's delusional,' he replied casually, with a wave of his arm, dismissively moving aside the weapon-related question. 'Opened the door wielding a walking cane. Man wasn't seeing straight.'

'Well, I appreciate the gesture,' Monroe said as he pursed his lips. 'So, the laddie is back on the run, and the Colombians peg him as the culprit.'

'I still don't think he did it,' Billy said into his glass. 'But is that because I can't bear to have been made a fool of?'

'No, it's because you only see the best in people,' Anjli placed a hand on his, halting him. 'And I'd rather have that any day.'

Billy smiled weakly at this.

'So, how can we help?' Declan asked.

'You can't,' Billy replied. 'You know that. The rules—'

'Bugger the rules,' Monroe snapped. '*What can we do to help?*'

Billy looked at Chivalry for a long, drawn-out moment.

'We can't allow you to help,' he said. 'Not until we have something better to show the Colombians. And if Andrade's shirt has José's blood on it, then we're in a completely different state here. But we might be able to help you.'

'And how do you see that?' Monroe frowned.

'Jess gave me a heads up on where you were, on this Santa Killer case,' Billy held up a hand. 'Don't be angry at her, she wanted information on how I structured my file system, and this was my payment.'

'Not enthused with the "Santa Killer" name,' Monroe growled. 'But I suppose it's better than the alternatives.'

Chivalry smiled as he leant forward across the table.

'I just so happen to know the Jacob Marley Society,' he said. 'We travel in the same circles.'

It had taken Jess almost an hour to reach Hampstead, and when she arrived at the Rectory, she had to take a step back and stare at the church beside it.

It was well known why her father had been effectively banished to the Last Chance Saloon; he'd taken down two corrupt police officers at Mile End, and the police had found him to be a bit of a pariah to most officers in the area, but before that he'd been suspended for punching a priest on live television.

A *Catholic* priest.

At a Hampstead church.

This Hampstead church.

In fairness, the way her dad had explained it, he'd been provoked. The priest in question, Father Corden, had been running a dog-trafficking scam from the church. With dozens of affluent members of his Hampstead congregation, Corden had realised many of their dogs were high-end pedigree and, while the owners took confession with him, leaving their dogs tethered outside, Corden had accomplices take the dogs and examine them. If they were spayed and neutered, they were no good for breeding, and Corden let them run free, nothing more than a dog which had slipped their lead for a fun-time escapade around Hampstead Heath.

But the ones that weren't spayed or neutered? That could breed more pedigree doggies, and they went for a cool couple of grand a dog. Minimum.

It'd been beneath her dad's pay grade, but he liked dogs, and he'd taken the case on. And, when he was utterly convinced he had the answer, he'd asked a local parishioner for her help – well, more accurately, her dog. What he hadn't realised, as he set up the sting, was that the woman whose dog he'd borrowed was an Instagram influencer, and, the moment the sting was in operation, she called up the local papers, using this to gain her "brand" some much needed exposure. And, as it was a slow news day, those local news outlets turned into an ITV broadcast unit, showing the arrest live on the six pm news.

This, however, would have been fine; the villain was arrested, and the dogs were saved. A great news story. It could even have helped her dad become a DCI in Tottenham North. However, Father Corden not only believed dogs didn't have souls but also, when learning Declan was Catholic, tried to bargain with him, claiming not only would Declan's soul go to hell for arresting him, but that *Jess's* soul would go to hell as well.

It was at this point, on the steps to the church and on the ITV News, after hearing a priest damn his daughter's soul to hell, that Declan punched Father Corden squarely in the face.

The same steps that Mina now walked down, smiling.

'You made it,' she said. 'Are you okay?'

'I'm having a terrible case of déjà vu,' Jess replied. 'So, what's the plan for this evening?'

'It's a Christmas meal, Mass and carol service,' Mina linked an arm through Jess's, leading her up the steps and into the church. 'A lot of the locals get a little twitchy when the homeless turn up in their post codes, but it's a really enjoyable night.'

'How do you know?' Jess frowned. 'You weren't here last Christmas.'

Mina faltered at this, but the smile was still plastered on her face.

'Lewis told me,' she said. 'He comes to the church.'

Jess was actually surprised at this, but that Lewis and Father Franks were at the same seminary school meant there was every reason he'd continue supporting his friend when he took on his own church in the area.

'When did Father Franks take over here?' she asked, and instantly regretted it.

'When your father arrested my predecessor,' Father Franks smiled from the doorway to the church. 'Which was good on two fronts. First off, it removed a rotten apple from our flock, and second, it brought me here.'

He took in a deep breath.

'Right then,' he said. 'Let's feed some people.'

'I WASN'T AT THE 2007 DEBACLE, BUT I HEARD ABOUT IT THE following year,' Chivalry explained. 'They didn't have a Society meeting in 2008, because of the stock crash wiping out all their piggy banks. Bloody idiots. But they still had their gentlemen's clubs, and they still had their gossip.'

'What did they say?' Anjli asked, a millisecond before Declan could utter the same words.

'You understand how the bloody thing worked, right?' Chivalry asked as he saw the affirmative nods in return. 'They each had their *Cratchits*. That's what they called the three candidates for the money. One from the past, one in the present, and one who needed money for the future.'

'We heard there was a winner who didn't get paid,' Monroe replied. 'That Siddell took the money and split it.'

'Not quite,' Chivalry tapped the side of his nose. 'Yes, he took the money, but not everyone took the money from him. In fact, Colin Walters offered to pay the full amount back the following year, even though he never took a single penny. Apparently, he felt terrible, especially when Siddell disappeared after losing everything a few months after this all happened. They thought he'd jumped into the Thames or something.'

'Fifty grand's a lot to pay back if you didn't steal it.'

'Not to these people, it isn't,' Chivalry sniffed. 'To some back then it was the monthly coke bill.'

'We think his murderer could be the winning *Cratchit*, gaining revenge for losing out on the money,' Declan suggested. 'But we can't find out who won.'

'I remember bits,' Chivalry tapped at his chin with his index finger. 'There was a start-up that hoped for a fee, something charitable, that was Colin's *Cratchit*, I believe there was a medical chap who had lost funding for a cancer research project – that was Arthur's one, and finally there was a City banker who'd fallen down on his luck, and needed something to help him back on his feet. This was Neil Robertson's one, a friend of his, someone known by a few of the group, I think. Shame that; the death.'

'Death?'

'Neil Robertson,' Chivalry sniffed. 'Nice man. Cancer literally ate him away. Anyway, the other guy, the City banker, died too, though. Took his own life during the stock market crash.'

Declan felt a chill run down his spine at this, and looked at Anjli, obviously coming to the same conclusion.

'Was his name Suvosky?' she whispered.

'You know him?' this surprised Chivalry. 'Or, rather, *knew* him?'

'We've met his family,' Anjli replied. 'And this makes things very interesting.'

'It also gives us a suspect with a motive,' Monroe leant back on his chair, puffing out his cheeks as he rubbed at his goatee. 'Bloody annoying though, that we had her in the Unit and let her go.'

'Jess is with her now,' Declan pulled out his phone. 'I should warn her—'

'About what?' Chivalry smiled, and Declan had an irritated feeling he was deliberately keeping something back.

'That the daughter of a man, who killed himself after money owed to him was withheld – the same daughter who had befriended the person who withheld it, shortly before his murder, might have a reason for not wanting to come in again for questioning,' he replied calmly. 'Unless you know something else?'

Chivalry bellowed with laughter.

'You *know* I do, and you still play along!' he boomed. 'Oh, Declan, I've missed sparring with you.'

He cleared his throat, and Declan had a sudden fear he was about to tell another tall tale.

'Valentin Suvosky's story is more melancholy because not only did he *not* gain the money after Siddell absconded, but when Siddell decided he didn't want to choose a winner, he wasn't even in the lead,' he laughed. 'I mean, a financier losing money? That sort of thing was commonplace, and the society wanted entertainment, not stark mirrors into their own potential futures. They reckoned Neil only offered Suvosky up because he hadn't bothered to find anyone else.

The bloody start-up Colin Walters had been pushing was looking like it was going to win—'

Anjli half rose from the chair.

'How common is this knowledge?' she hissed, interrupting.

Chivalry shrugged.

'I was told from the horse's mouth, but few people ask the horses for tips these days,' he said. 'Why?'

'Because if Mina Suvosky thinks the money was stolen from her dad, and she's looking for revenge, then she has every reason not only to kill Michael Siddell but also every other member of the Jacob Marley Society,' Declan replied. 'And also, anyone else who gets in her way, including my daughter.'

17

PRODIGAL SON

DECLAN HADN'T EXPECTED TO BE BACK HERE ANY TIME SOON.

'Are you sure there are no cameras?' he muttered as he climbed out of his Audi, Monroe and Anjli emerging from the back seats like bodyguards.

'For Christ's sake, laddie, nobody cares about your indiscretions with Father Corden,' Monroe hissed. 'Except God, maybe. Oh, and any parishioners who still attend.'

He stopped, considering his words.

'Actually, this might not be that great for you.'

Declan had ignored a lot of this conversation, as Monroe had been mocking him with a rather devilish sense of glee since they left Temple Inn, throughout the drive, and all the way up to walking the steps towards the church.

The lack of cameras and television news crews right now was a good thing, but the music coming from inside showed there was likely to be a full house in there, and he really didn't want to relive old problems.

'Maybe we wait until it's over?' Anjli suggested. 'Mina isn't going anywhere, and Jess can look after herself.'

Declan nodded, leaning against the outside wall of the porch.

'I'm happy with that idea. They wanted to excommunicate me, you know,' he said. 'DCI Farrow was pressured incredibly heavily to remove me. They kicked Liz out of a Catholic book club.'

'It was over a year ago now,' Monroe smiled. 'They'll probably have forgotten who you even are—'

'You've got some nerve coming here,' a woman's voice suddenly spat, the venom in it audible. 'After what you did.'

Declan looked around to see an old woman, short, white-haired and bitter, leaning against her walker as she glared at him.

'Evening,' he smiled, even though he didn't feel like it.

The woman grunted some kind of response and then carried on into the church. The service was almost over, and Declan assumed she was part of the Church, rather than a late-arriving parishioner.

'Yeah, they've totally forgotten,' he said. 'No problems there.'

'That might not be about the Priest,' Monroe suggested innocently, enjoying every moment of this. 'Maybe she's just not a fan of your friendship with Charles Baker?'

'I don't *have* a friendship with Charles Baker.'

'Says the man invited to Charles Baker's Number Ten Christmas bash,' Anjli grinned. 'Were *you* invited, boss?'

Monroe mimed hunting for an invitation in his pockets.

'You know, lassie, I don't think I was,' he said in mock surprise. 'What a bloody oversight.'

Declan mimed a "dying laughing" motion at the pair of them, but stopped as the music from inside the church ceased.

'Looks like the service is ending,' Monroe checked his watch. 'Earlier than I thought, to be honest. They would have fed them first—'

'Surely they'd feed them after the service?' Anjli frowned. 'Make sure they'd stay for it and all that? You know, stop them running off into the night with full bellies on free food?'

'Your problem, Anjli Kapoor, is that you're way too cynical,' Monroe bemoaned.

'I find it keeps me warm at night,' Anjli grinned. 'Well, that and public enemy number one here.'

Declan decided enough was enough, and was about to walk to the door when it opened, and parishioners exited out into the night.

Quickly, Declan pivoted his head, making sure he wasn't recognised, but the old woman returned, pointing at him while leaning against her walker. The amount of time she'd been in the building was minimal, and Declan realised from the moment she left his view, she must have walked straight to the person she was now talking to, bringing them out with her.

'See? He's still here,' she hissed. 'Be careful, or he'll come for you, too.'

Father Franks now walked out onto the porch, smiling at Declan as he did so.

'You might want to come in before others recognise you, DI Walsh,' he said. 'Thanks for waiting outside until we'd finished. And for not punching me, too.'

Declan groaned. When he'd seen Franks at the Unit, the Priest hadn't mentioned he was Corden's replacement, or that he knew Declan was the "Priest-Puncher" of Hampstead infamy, and he probably didn't realise until he and Mina had returned to the church, but now that he knew, Declan realised he was going to get this all night.

And so, taking a deep breath and blowing it out as he counted slowly to five, he followed the other two into the church.

'I'M GUESSING THIS ISN'T A SOCIAL CALL?' FATHER FRANKS asked. 'You're here to speak to Mina?'

He gestured across the room, where Jess and Mina were in conversation.

'She doesn't have many friends her age,' he smiled. 'I think your daughter's arrival has helped a lot.'

'How well do you know her?' Monroe asked.

At this, Father Franks frowned, looking from Monroe to Declan to Anjli to Monroe once more.

'What's happened?' he asked, his voice lower now. 'You literally had her in your station a couple of hours ago, and were all smiles, sending her home quite happily.'

'That's because she was a witness then,' Monroe replied calmly, moving the four of them to the side of the church, moving past parishioners as they left. 'Now we have reason to believe she could be a suspect.'

By now, Mina and Jess had noticed the three new arrivals and were walking over.

'I don't understand,' Father Franks shook his head. 'How is she a suspect?'

'We believe the victim, Michael Siddell had knowledge of her father,' Declan continued. 'As, in 2007, Michael Siddell actively stopped him from gaining a charitable donation of around fifty grand, which could have helped him get onto his feet.'

Father Franks stared open-mouthed at Declan.

'He *won?*' he whispered.

At this, Declan looked confused at Monroe.

'No, he didn't,' the Scot replied. 'There wasn't a winner as Michael Siddell never declared one, but it's believed one of the others was the front runner, but you already seem to know about this. Could you please explain how?'

Father Franks sighed, looking over at Mina as she approached.

'Because I knew Valentin Suvosky,' he admitted. 'Back in the day, before I was a priest, I worked in the City. I was a trainee broker back then. But the crash in 2008 changed everything. It sent me on a new journey, into this.'

He tapped his chest to emphasise the point before continuing.

'I worked for Valentin before the crash happened though,' he carried on. 'Just an intern, you know, learning the ropes, nothing more. I think I made more cups of tea than trades, and I always felt I could help him, but I failed.'

'You were with him when he died?' Anjli asked.

At this, Father Franks shook his head.

'I had my own troubles then,' he looked to the church's flagstones as he continued. 'I was watching my entire world collapse around me. Institutions around for centuries were gone in mere hours. Because of this, I was distracted. I wasn't there for him. And then he was gone.'

He sighed again.

'I could have followed him down that dark path too, but luckily for me I found God shortly after, and it led me here.'

'You're young for quite a large parish though,' Declan

commented. 'I'd have thought they'd have placed a more established priest here.'

'Nobody wanted it,' Father Franks smiled. 'And the bishop thought some "new blood" would work here, now Hampstead is becoming trendy again.'

'The Father heard about my mother from Father McNarry, who he'd trained under,' Mina added, stepping forward. 'When he learned the church had embraced me, he asked if he could sponsor me until I was of age to join the nunnery.'

'Well, I seem to recall it was more McNarry telling me I had to take you in because you were driving him mad,' Father Franks smiled in response. 'I had half a dozen emails from him, and at least two phone calls from his assistant, all saying Mina needed to face her demons before she took vows. And London? It's where her demons remain.'

'And you're telling me the fact you were working at the same soup kitchen Michael Siddell ate at is a coincidence?' Monroe looked sceptical. 'Lassie, you're gonna have to do better than that.'

'Now hold on, she was in the kitchen because of me,' Father Franks spoke quickly now, moving in front of Mina, as if worried the police officers were about to take her. 'My friend, Lewis—'

'Lewis Hoyle, who runs the soup kitchen,' Anjli interrupted. 'Mina said he knew you.'

Remembering his own conversation with Lewis earlier that day, Declan nodded.

'He was at seminary school with you, wasn't he?' he asked. 'He told me he'd trained to be a priest, but it didn't work out.'

Father Franks nodded.

'He was,' he looked across the church where, by a table and passing out what looked to be mugs of soup from a large pot, was Lewis Hoyle. 'He's a good man. Been with the charity since it started. When I had the news Mina was coming over, I mentioned this to him. He knew of my past, of my failure to save her father—'

'How?'

'Because I told him. I had to unburden myself of past sins in the seminary, and that one ... well, it proved harder to do so,' Father Franks explained. 'Anyway, he listened, forgave me, and years later, when he heard she was connected to my past, he offered to bring her onto his team. But she's only been there a few times so far.'

'How come?' Declan looked at Mina, who blushed.

'Father Franks doesn't like me talking to the homeless,' she explained. 'He thinks I see demons everywhere, and he worries I might do something.'

'Like what? Like putting a wee nip of holy water into their tea?' Monroe smiled. 'Is that really terrible?'

'It can be, if you look at it with PR goggles on,' Father Franks admitted. 'If it came out that the Catholic Church was sticking holy water into non-denominational homeless people's food, there might be a bit of a backlash.'

He looked back at Declan.

'And we've already had our fair share of drama and scandal around here, wouldn't you say, Detective Inspector?'

Declan made a weak attempt at a smile and wished more than anything for the flagstones to swallow him up. He didn't know if the church had a crypt, but right now he really wanted to be in it, rather than up here.

Not noticing her father's discomfort, Jess looked at Mina.

'Did you know who Santa Mick was?'

Mina didn't speak, instead shaking her head.

'Did you ever hear the name Michael Siddell before this week?'

Again, a shake of the head.

'Lewis told me about Santa Mick, and when I saw him, I saw his demon,' she replied. 'But I've told you this before. Lewis offered him a new hat to replace his old one, like he'd done before, but Santa Mick turned it down. He was very shouty too, throwing it into a puddle. Said he already had a new hat.'

'You mentioned he was a demon,' Declan looked over at Mina now. 'Was this something Father McNarry taught you?'

'Father McNarry taught her a lot of things, it seems,' Father Franks's face darkened as he spoke. 'Most of which was irresponsible. I've been trying to contact him and tell him what happened, but he's very hard to get hold of.'

'Maybe we could have a go?' Monroe suggested.

Declan puffed out his cheeks, looking at Monroe.

'We could—' he started, but stopped as Monroe's phone rang.

The old Scot held up a hand to halt Declan.

'Aye?' Monroe answered, frowning as he listened.

'It's Doctor Marcos,' he mouthed, walking away from the group.

'I didn't know Santa Mick was Siddell,' Father Franks said as Monroe carried on talking, away from the group. 'But if you're looking for someone with motive, then you need to arrest me as well, as I have a closer link to her father's death than Mina has.'

Declan frowned at the comment.

'Hold on. If you didn't know he was Siddell,' he asked, 'then why did you refuse him confession?'

Father Franks paused at this.

'Honestly? I know it's not very Christian of me, but it was mainly because he wouldn't take a bath.'

'I also heard he "caused issues" in the church,' Anjli added. 'What issues could they be?'

'I'm sorry, am I under suspicion for refusing a confession?' Father Franks laughed. 'I don't know what you're talking about. Maybe other people had problems with him?'

However, at this Declan stepped closer.

'A minute ago, you said you had a closer link to Valentin Suvosky's death than Mina, and you had motive,' he said. 'Surely you can see why refusing the confession of the man who caused Valentin's death could be seen as suspicious?'

'I didn't know he was Siddell,' Father Franks repeated. 'I've already told you this.'

Declan was going to reply to the comment when Monroe, a sour look on his face, walked back to the group.

'Mina, did you ever speak to a homeless woman named Shelly Garraway?' he asked.

Mina thought for a moment and then shook her head.

'I don't think so,' she said, frowning. 'Should I have?'

Monroe looked at his phone as it beeped, and then turned it so the screen faced the others. On it was a short, skinny woman in her early twenties, smiling at the camera.

'She would be skinnier now,' Monroe said sadly. 'Not in a good way, either. She was addicted to heroin.'

Again, Mina shook her head.

'Who is she?' Father Franks asked.

'Another dead person,' Monroe sighed, placing his phone away. 'My sergeant had a tip from a friend in forensics. Seems Miss Garraway was found a couple of mornings ago, in her tent, dead. Wearing a Father Christmas hat.'

'She was poisoned?' Declan raised an eyebrow. 'Did she know Michael Siddell?'

Monroe shrugged.

'De'Geer is checking into it, and Rosanna is looking at the body right now, after they found traces of the same substances the other two bodies had on her forehead,' he said softly, just enough for Declan and Anjli to hear, but enough to muffle the bulk of it from Father Franks and Mina. 'From what the Viking could see, she may have known Siddell in passing, from the streets, but she'd disappeared from her home in Cardiff two years back, and with her age difference, there's no way she was connected to his prior life or the Jacob Marley Society.'

Anjli's face darkened.

'Maybe this isn't that after all,' she growled. 'Maybe we're looking at the wrong suspects?'

'Two of which are standing right here?' Father Franks, catching the end of this comment, raised an optimistic expression. 'Are we safe to go?'

'Aye, don't take any long trips, though.' As Father Franks and Mina walked back towards the tables, Monroe was already staring back at the phone, looking down at the photo of the bobbed-haired woman whose whole life was ahead of her in it. 'And if you think of anything that can help us, let us know.'

Declan glanced across the church again, but stopped as he saw another familiar face.

'Guv,' he said, nodding towards Shaun Donnal, helping clear up some paper plates.

'Aye, we should probably have a wee natter with him while we're here,' Monroe growled. 'Anjli, could you have a quick chat with Mister Hoyle, see if he knew Miss Garraway at all?'

As Anjli nodded, pulling out her notebook and walking off, Jess pulled at Declan's arm.

'What do you need me to do?' she asked.

'Finish up with Mina, see if you can get anything else out of her,' he said. 'And then go home. I need you at your best tomorrow, as I have a feeling it's going to be a very long day.'

Surprisingly, Jess didn't argue this, simply nodding and walking over to where Mina stood. Watching her for a moment, Declan was brought back to the task in hand by Monroe, lightly clipping him around the back of the ear.

'Wake up, you eejit,' Monroe smiled. 'We have conspiracies to talk about, so grab your tin-foil hat.'

'It's not really a tin-foil hat situation when we believe him,' Declan muttered, rubbing at his neck as they approached Shaun Donnal.

Who, as he saw them approach, placed the tea towel he was currently cleaning mugs with down, and walked a little to the side to allow privacy.

'Is this where you tell me I'm insane and dreaming things?' he asked, almost confrontational.

'Actually, no,' Monroe replied. 'I had a look at the place in question, and you definitely saw Francine Pearce. Well, maybe saw Francine Pearce. That is, we're pretty confident that you did see the currently declared dead person known as Francine Pearce.'

Shaun shivered, and Declan knew he'd probably been hoping for the first answer, that he'd simply mistaken someone else for Pearce, and that everything would continue on as normal.

'Are you sure?' he whispered.

'We found CCTV,' Declan nodded. 'It definitely looks like her. She's alive. Well, she was a couple of months back.'

'She was with another woman,' Monroe added. 'Trisha Hawkins. Does that name mean anything to you?'

Shaun shook his head.

'Sorry, I don't think I ever met her,' he said. 'Just Frankie, and the attack dogs she always had.'

He looked to the doors of the church, almost like he was expecting Francine and her bodyguards to burst through right now. Declan understood the fear. He'd had it himself for weeks after he'd been accused of terrorism.

'We believe she's in New York now,' he whispered, placing a hand on Shaun's shoulder. 'I don't think she's coming back, so you're safe for the moment.'

'Although, if there's anything else you can find out about the Wardour Street address, we'd appreciate it,' Monroe winked. 'Maybe speak to Baker? I think he might listen to you more than us right now.'

Dumbly, Shaun nodded.

'Also, while we have you here, can we ask you some questions?' Declan asked. 'When we met, at the party when you first aimed me at Santa Mick, did you know he was Michael Siddell?'

'No,' Shaun replied. 'I'd never met him in our previous lives. Or, if I did, I never really classed it as important, I suppose.'

'You never saw him at the Reform Club, where you were both members? And where you were both new joiners at the same time?'

'Were we?' Shaun was either truly surprised, or good at feigning surprise at this. Declan couldn't tell which one. 'I must have met him, then. But that was before ... well, before the years of this.'

To emphasise his point, he waved a hand at the still-present rough sleepers in the church.

'Can you confirm you only knew him as Santa Mick?' Monroe pressed.

'No, I'd seen him a few times when he was Mickey Fish,' Shaun corrected. 'Smelled him, rather.'

'Did you ever see him here?'

'Couple of times,' Shaun nodded. 'Although the Father didn't like him here.'

'Because he smelled?'

'When he was Mickey Fish, sure,' Shaun frowned. 'But that was before Father Franks arrived. No, he may have used that as an excuse, but he seemed a little scared of Santa Mick. Threatened, even.'

Declan looked up, but Father Franks had already left the Nave of the church.

'And you don't know why he was threatened?'

Shaun shook his head.

'Sorry.'

'One more thing,' Monroe showed the photo of Shelly Garraway. 'Do you recognise this woman? She might not look the same anymore—'

'Yeah, I knew Shelly,' Shaun nodded. 'She was an addict from Shoreditch, Hoxton, maybe Haggerston. Came into Soho for the evenings, mainly as there were more tourists to beg from around. Is she okay?'

'Not really,' Monroe placed the phone back into his pocket. 'She's dead as well. Same Santa hat and everything.'

Shaun looked horrified at this, and Declan couldn't help but wonder if this was "faked for the cameras", so to speak.

'I'll let her family know,' Shaun eventually spoke. 'I'd been working with her through the outreach programme, so I have her details.'

Declan looked at Monroe, and the older man got the unspoken message, walking off, allowing Declan a moment alone with Shaun.

'Did you know my history here?' he hissed. 'With Corden?'

Slowly, Shaun nodded.

'Is that why you brought me in?'

Again, Shaun nodded.

'I thought the fact Santa Mick came here was the universe lining things up, you know?' he replied. 'I never came here when the other guy was around. Father Franks and Lewis were old friends, so it was a natural fit for the church to help. Thought it might give you some closure, too.'

'I have closure,' Declan smiled darkly. 'I had it over a year back when I smacked a dog-trafficking priest in the nose.'

'You were going for DCI, weren't you?' Shaun asked. 'I was told by Charles.'

'And how did he know?'

Shaun smiled. 'Mate, after Devington, he had a folder on you, bigger than most lobbyists,' he said. 'He made it a personal mission to learn everything, and he mentioned this when we started working together again.'

He leant in.

'But after you were suspended, after you moved, you haven't even applied for the test,' he said. 'Why's that?'

'I like things as they are,' Declan muttered, unsure as to his actual reason.

And, at this, Shaun nodded.

'I know that one,' he said. 'I lived my life by that one. But while you don't go for DCI, what about the others? The DS over there or the young blond DC who was outside Devonshire House that day? Are you stopping them from progressing by not doing it yourself?'

'Of course not—' Declan started, but then stopped. *Why hadn't they gone for promotions in the last year?*

Unaware of what he'd started in Declan, Shaun Donnal nodded at him.

'Just think about it,' he said as he walked off. 'God has plans for you, maybe.'

Declan stared after him as Monroe walked back to him.

'You look like you just received a bollocking,' Monroe smiled.

'More a sermon, I think,' Declan shook his head slightly to clear the cobwebs. 'Could he be a suspect? He knew Siddell and Garraway, and he was in the Reform Club at the same time, so he could have been a Marleyite.'

'A Marleyite? I like it,' Monroe muttered. 'But if he is, he's a bloody idiot. We're only on the case because of him.'

He looked across the Nave, where, by the door, Shaun spoke quickly to Lewis Hoyle before leaving.

'Although *that* laddie might be worth talking to.'

Declan started for the door, but an old man in a tweed jacket appeared in front of him.

'You have some nerve coming here,' he hissed. 'After what you did. Brute.'

'Father Corden was a criminal,' already knowing what the argument was about, Declan replied as another woman, a middle-aged one this time, walked up beside the argumentative old man.

'You'll burn in hell for your sins,' she said. 'Hell.'

'So, I've been told.'

Declan looked back to the door, but Lewis had now left as well.

Moving past the two people, Monroe and Anjli following, he made it to the door to the church, looking out across the churchyard and the path that led to the street.

Lewis Hoyle was gone.

'You think this was deliberate?' Monroe asked from beside him. 'He saw us and left?'

'He was dismissive,' Anjli muttered, obviously annoyed she'd been unable to get anywhere. 'I gave him a moment to finish up and then he was gone. If that's not suspicious behaviour, I don't know what is.'

'I don't know,' Declan replied. 'What I do know, though, is this is bigger than one man killing himself, and a daughter gaining vengeance.'

Declan looked back into the church, past the accusatory glares, and up at the statue of Jesus on the cross above the altar.

'I just don't know what it is yet,' he finished.

18

REUNION

'I LOVE WHAT YOU'VE DONE WITH THE OLD PLACE,' DAVEY SAID as she entered the downstairs forensics lab of the Temple Inn Command Unit.

Doctor Marcos, currently sitting at a table, with a microscope to her eye, looked up with a half-smile.

'We haven't changed anything,' she replied.

'I know,' Davey sat on her old chair. 'That's why I like it.'

She frowned at the chair's settings.

'Why is it so low?'

'Because De'Geer's twice your size,' Doctor Marcos grinned, turning to face her one-time protégé. 'What did you need?'

'I wondered if you'd checked what Osborne gave Morten about the shirt?' Davey looked at her.

'Ah, so this is an off-the-books question then,' Doctor Marcos tapped on the keyboard beside her and her screen, currently on screensaver mode, burst into life. 'I know De'Geer sent it across, so let me check ...'

She looked back, her face darkening.

'Yeah, you were right,' she said. 'It's José Almas.'

'Damn,' Davey leant back on the chair. 'I wasn't really expecting a different answer, but I was holding out for one, you know?'

'Life gives you lemons sometime,' Doctor Marcos shrugged. 'Although, is this a lemons scenario? Blood on Andrade Estrada's shirt shows he was there when Almas died, surely this helps clear Billy, especially as we have a witness who claims Billy was alone when he arrived, looking for Andrade?'

Davey shook her head.

'He's cleared by this, but then we have to explain *how* he had this shirt in his possession. Which means currently we can't use it as evidence, without pointing out Andrade was in his house. Which—'

'Makes him a suspect again,' Doctor Marcos nodded. 'And, of course, you still don't know if the shirt was covered during the death, or after. It could have transferred while Andrade was checking a dead body.'

'Does it look that way?'

'Well, as De'Geer probably told you, as Osborne told him, there's another sample found,' Doctor Marcos turned her laptop screen so Davey could see it. 'Carlos Pascal.'

Davey leant in as Doctor Marcos read from the page.

'Colombian from Bogotá. Last seen in Chile about eight months back, was brought in after a bar fight in Puente Alto, but was freed without charges.'

Davey, however, wasn't listening, instead pointing at the screen.

'The scar,' she said, pointing at the vicious puckered mark that ran down his cheek. 'Andrade mentioned that. He said the men that attacked him had knife scars, were stocky, and the leader had one down his cheek. Does that look like a knife scar?'

Doctor Marcos peered closer, nodding.

'So, the imaginary people Andrade claimed he was running from outside might not be so imaginary, but they didn't face him where he said,' she said. 'Looks like there was more than just Andrade in the room the night José Almas died.'

'He also said they broke his watch strap in the scuffle,' Davey tapped her pen against her lips as she stared at the screen, deep in thought. 'But I saw it in the apartment. It's like he had the fight, but he moved it to make it fit his narrative. I'll get Billy looking into Pascal, though, as if he's Colombian drug Cartels, then he might have a history with Andrade – from when he worked for them.'

She smiled, waving a hand to stop Doctor Marcos from asking more questions about this revelation.

'Long story, and we're still checking,' she said. 'But I think I'm starting to see what happened here. And there's a chance that although Andrade didn't kill José Almas, he was definitely there when it happened, or at least shortly after. And in that moment, he gained two sets of blood on his shirt before leaving.'

'Running?' Doctor Marcos closed the laptop now.

'I don't think he ran from anything,' DC Davey shook her head sadly. 'And neither does Billy's great-uncle.'

'Yes, I heard the old occultist was back on the scene, although I'm not sure I'm too happy about that,' Doctor Marcos rose from her chair, stretching as she did so. 'Still, if anyone can cause trouble with the best of them, it's that man. Coffee?'

'Please, but as I don't want to see anyone, I'll stay here,'

Davey replied, almost apologetically. 'It's still a little raw sitting in this building, and I'm still not too happy about *being* here, you know?'

'That's understandable,' Doctor Marcos replied, walking to the door. 'After all, you definitely shit over the friendships you had with everyone here.'

'Wow, way to sugar-coat the message,' Davey forced a smile. 'But truthful.'

'Well, you're okay for the moment, because they're all out doing proper police work. You remember that, don't you?' Doctor Marcos grinned. 'So, you're safe for a while. Only Bullman's around.'

She stopped as the door to the lab opened, and De'Geer stood there like a deer in headlights, staring at the two women in the room.

'Oh, and De'Geer,' Doctor Marcos continued. 'He's here too, it seems.'

'God, how did you react?' Billy half-laughed as he looked up from his laptop.

In response, Davey simply shrugged.

'What do you think I did?' she exhaled, looking up at the ceiling. 'I made my excuses and left.'

They were sitting in the living room of Billy's Wanstead house; it was almost eight-thirty in the evening and Chivalry, complaining at Billy's lack of anything worthwhile within his collection of takeaway menus, had stormed off into Wanstead to arrange some kind of restaurant delivery service from the brasserie on the other end of the High Street.

'You know, he wouldn't have bitten,' Billy grinned. 'You should have stayed, caught up with him.'

'It's bad enough having Cooper around as the ghost of Christmas Past,' Davey muttered, quickly glancing to the door in case Esme Cooper was loitering around again. Seeing they were alone still, she visibly relaxed. 'Anyway, what do you have?'

At the question, Billy became all business.

'Carlos Pascal was a member of the Colombian Cartels, in particular Los Lideres,' he said. 'We know a little about this, as when Johnny Lucas was accused of murdering Jeffrey Tsang, I learnt all about them while checking into Jackie's past in La Modelo jail in Bogotá.'

He shifted in his chair.

'Although they don't call themselves Cartels anymore,' he explained. 'For the last fifteen years or more, they've preferred the term *neo-paramilitary organisation* to explain themselves, even though they do the same thing. Los Lideres, for example, funds itself primarily by trafficking cocaine, marijuana and heroin, but also by doing illegal gold mining.'

'They're *gold* miners?'

'Apparently so.'

'Okay,' Davey gave a half-shrug at this. 'Remind me not to go against you on a pub trivia team. Did you find anything else?'

Billy nodded, but this time he didn't look happy to share.

'Osborne was right when he found the Interpol record for Carlos Pascal,' he said, scrolling down the sheet. 'He's Colombian born and bred, did his time on the other side of the law in Bogotá, was pretty visible there about ten years ago.'

'When did Pablo say Andrade was connected to the

Cartels? Or whatever they're called now?' Davey reached for her notebook. 'It was around the same time, right?'

'Yeah, and in Santa Librana, which is a small village just south of Bogotá,' Billy nodded. 'According to the notes, Carlos Pascal was in Puente Alto, in Chile about eight months back, was brought in after a bar fight but was freed without charges, even though witnesses saw him glass someone in the face.'

'He had connections?'

'He had diplomatic ones,' Billy replied ominously. 'Checking the Chile records, he was whisked out by the Colombian Embassy in the middle of the night and stuck on a plane.'

'He worked for the embassy?'

'No, he worked for Los Lideres, it seems,' Billy leant back, obviously frustrated. 'But someone in the Colombian Embassy in Santiago learnt about the arrest and squashed it.'

'Okay, so we're talking April this year,' Davey counted off on her fingers. 'Where was Andrade at that point? Or José?'

'According to Andrade, and the records at the embassy Doctor Marcos got from Restrepo, José arrived in London in mid-March. It's around two, three weeks before the attack in Chile.'

'And Andrade?' Davey frowned. 'He said he was in Paris a year back, pulled into London in June, so that's six months of time we have a hole in.'

Billy nodded.

'His details are locked,' he muttered. 'But I remember talking to him once, we were discussing restaurants, and he said he had a love for Chilean food. I never thought of it before, but what if he gained that while in Chile before he moved embassies?'

'What you're actually saying is "what if Andrade was the one that freed Carlos Pascal," basically,' Davey shuddered. 'And, whether he had a long-time connection to the man in the Colombian drug gang. But how do we work that out?'

'Chivalry has already asked a few of his contacts,' Billy rose from his chair. 'Bloody hell. What did I get myself into, Joanne?'

'I think we need to find Andrade to get that solved,' Davey replied, still seated. 'His shirt is evidence, but we need to explain how we got it. Far easier to have him officially come in.'

'I don't think that's likely,' Billy sighed. 'He comes in, he's involved in the murder and probable torture of José Almas. We'll need to destroy his life to clear mine.'

'No offence, Billy my boy, but he's destroying yours right now,' Davey rose now, walking over and placing a hand on Billy's shoulder. 'It's a race to see who comes out with more intact right now. And if we can't find Andrade, maybe we can find Carlos Pascal. After all, he has to be known by someone, and he's injured, if there's blood on the shirt. How badly, we don't know.'

'I should try hospitals,' Billy nodded. 'Private ones that diplomats use. Off-the-books—'

He paused as his phone beeped.

'That's not the burner,' he said, picking it up and reading the text. 'It's Declan. He's asking me to check into something for him.'

'I thought you were suspended?' Davey raised a slightly mocking eyebrow at this.

'Yeah, but this is something a little more off the books,' Billy looked back up at Davey now. 'It's connected to Trisha Hawkins.'

'Christ, just once I'd like a case that wasn't connected to that bitch,' Davey laughed. 'Still, good to see you're embracing the life.'

'The life?'

Davey waved at the phone.

'You're doing something off the books while working off the books? You really have embraced the fugitive lifestyle,' she explained.

At this point, however, her own phone beeped.

'Looks like he needs you too,' Billy chuckled. At this thought, Davey shook her head.

'It's Bullman,' she said, reading the message. 'She wants us both in tomorrow morning.'

'That doesn't sound ominous at all,' Billy mock-shuddered, but this stopped as there was a crash behind them, and both officers spun, hastily grabbed makeshift weapons in their hands. In the front doorway, Chivalry Fitzwarren stood triumphantly, three paper bags of takeout food in his hands, held out to the side like a hunter showing off his trophies.

'Now we can eat!' he exclaimed. 'I hope you don't mind, I took the liberty of ordering for you, mainly because I know Billy has an extraordinarily terrible taste in French cuisine.'

He stopped, looking at the two expressions that faced him.

'What did I miss?' he asked.

DECLAN HAD RETURNED TO THE TEMPLE INN UNIT ALONE after the conversation with Father Franks and Mina; Monroe and Anjli had gone for a drink in Hampstead, but after returning to such a notorious location, Declan hadn't wanted to hang around, especially as he didn't want to risk walking into one of the couple of dozen elderly Catholics that had been glaring at him as they left the service.

And so, he'd returned by car, Monroe and Anjli promising to be back, by tube, shortly after. Declan hoped it wouldn't be a late one, as Anjli had come into work with him that morning, which meant if he returned to Hurley without her, first she'd have to go home by train, which was a nightmare after nine pm, but second, he'd never hear the end of it.

And life was too short for that kind of hassle.

As it was, PC Cooper was in the office when he arrived, claiming she was finishing up some paperwork, but Declan wondered if she was hanging around on the off chance De'Geer might pass through. She offered him a cup of tea, and Declan was about to accept when a text from an unknown ID appeared on his phone.

Have a lead on your case. Meet me in the Phoenix Garden.

Declan stared at the message for a moment before replying.

Who is this?

After a minute, a reply came through.

Not on here. Phoenix Garden. If you're not there by 10pm, I leave.

Declan looked at his watch; it was only just past nine, and the Phoenix Garden was a mile's walk from here, in a small cutting off Shaftesbury Ave, situated behind the Phoenix Theatre. He could be there in fifteen minutes.

It could be a trap.

There was a part of Declan's mind that didn't trust this. *Who was this, sending him a message?* And was the case the current one, or the one Billy was working on? Phoenix Garden was close to Soho, so there was every chance this was connected to Michael Siddell, and to be honest, he had nothing to lose by checking it out.

Gathering his jacket, he nodded to Cooper.

'Got a meeting, it seems.'

'You sure, Guv?' Cooper frowned, checking her watch. 'It's late.'

Declan shrugged.

'Crime doesn't work nine-to-five,' he said, instantly regretting it.

'You think this is crime?' Cooper raised an eyebrow. 'Sounds like you shouldn't go alone.'

'I'll be fine,' Declan forced his most reassuring smile onto his face. 'What's the worst that can go wrong?'

Calmly, and as if talking to a child, Cooper told him.

IT WAS ALMOST NINE-THIRTY WHEN DECLAN ARRIVED AT THE west end of Phoenix Gardens, at the junction of Phoenix Street and Stacey Street. It was dark there, the noise of Shaftesbury Avenue's traffic muted by the buildings on either side of him.

He was alone now, standing at the corner and looking around. There was nobody else looking suspicious, and Declan wondered if he'd made a mistake, whether this was some kind of wild goose chase, but before he could consider this any further, there was a movement from the side, and a man walked out of the shadows.

He was tall, slim, and held himself like military. Declan recognised the look, the walk, the "squaddie swagger" he'd seen so many times. It was the walk of a man readying himself for a fight.

A trap, then.

'Okay, so you can tell me who you are *now*, eh?' Declan said, turning to face the man. 'No phones here.'

The man stopped, watching Declan, and for a moment Declan flashed back to a moment outside his old apartment in Tottenham, when the man with the rimless glasses, known only as DI Frost, had attacked him in the street, leaving him for dead over a year earlier.

'You're peeking through windows you shouldn't be near,' the man said casually. 'You and that old bastard with the goatee.'

'You mean Wardour Street?' Declan replied, trying to match the casualness of the stranger. 'You mean the office where Francine Pearce and Trisha Hawkins went into, a couple of months back? That window?'

'See? Now you're just making it harder for yourself,' the man said, looking to the side, presumably checking for witnesses. Declan let his arm loosen in the sleeve of his coat, and felt the reassuring weight of his extendable baton slide into his right hand.

'You didn't think I'd walk into this blindly?' he smiled, watching the stranger as he paused mid-stride, his eyes now staring down at the baton.

But then the stranger smiled.

'You didn't think *I'd* come here alone?' he replied, and from the shadows to Declan's left, another man appeared.

This man was built like a brick shithouse, shorter but stockier, a mass of curly black hair and a beard hiding his olive complexion.

The stranger, now emboldened, took a step closer.

'Paul Stringer says to back the hell off,' the stranger continued. 'It's above your pay grade, DI Walsh.'

'Is he the security guard who talked to Monroe?' Declan frowned. 'Why's he hassling me? Tell him to go beat up Monroe instead.'

His eyes widened in mock realisation.

'Oh, wait,' he said. 'You tried that before and failed, when Rattlestone was still about. You're ex Rattles, aren't you? You've got that arrogant swagger and stench of failure all over you.'

'This time we won't fail, and this time we're gonna hurt you.'

The stranger seemed to have had enough now, as he moved in close, and Declan saw he had some kind of a black device in his hand. It looked like a taser, and Declan stepped back from it as the bearded man moved from the other side.

Declan realised quickly this was a dangerous position to be.

But luckily it didn't last long, as the stranger suddenly arched back with a scream, dropping the black device as prongs from an X26 police issue taser jabbed into his spine, fired by PC Cooper, standing in the shadows and waiting for her moment. And, as she bodily slammed into the stranger, sending him to the floor, the bearded man now turned, charging into her, knocking her to the side as he pulled the stranger, still twitching, up from the ground, half carrying him out of the street.

'We should go after them!' Cooper, flushed with adrenaline, said, already fitting a new cartridge into the taser. But Declan held up a hand; the adrenaline had already left his system, and there was no way of knowing if there were more friends of the stranger waiting for them if they followed.

'We know where they came from, and we have DNA,' he said, pulling out his phone and turning off the *record* function. 'We'll sort it out tomorrow.'

He patted Cooper on the arm.

'Good shot, by the way.'

'I told you it was a trap,' Cooper grinned as they walked back to Shaftesbury Avenue. 'But you suits never trust us uniforms.'

'Fair point,' Declan smiled. 'Fair point indeed.'

19

CLOSURE

'You're a bloody idiot,' Monroe hissed as he stared at Declan across his desk. 'A bloody, bloody idiot.'

'I had backup,' Declan replied sullenly. 'I had Cooper with me. And she's damned good in a fight.'

'She is, Guv,' Anjli, sitting at her own desk admitted. 'I've seen her take down guys double her size.'

'It makes sense you'd take his side and support him on this,' Monroe spun on Anjli now, 'But this idiocy—'

'Oh, hold on one damned moment,' Anjli rose now, angry. 'I don't support him at all on this, and if we'd been here last night, I'd have handcuffed him to his bloody chair.'

'She's right,' Declan admitted. 'I had this all the way home. And at home. And all the way here this morning. And we even took separate cars.'

'The joys of Bluetooth connections and car speakerphones,' Anjli glared at Declan. 'You could have been hurt.'

'It was a calculated risk!' Now getting annoyed at being the punchbag here, Declan shouted the response across the room now, pausing as he realised that everyone was watching him; Jess had stopped working at her monitor station and was deliberately *not* staring across the office at him, while Bullman was now leaning out of her own office.

'All good?' she asked.

'All good, boss,' Declan replied.

'Apart from you being a bloody idiot, right?' Bullman smiled, and before Declan replied, she ducked her head back in.

Declan sighed, allowing his anger to dissipate.

They were all right, of course.

'Look,' he started, his voice calm now. 'Cooper was there, I was ready for a trap. And when they kicked off, we took them down.'

'I see no bodies in the cells, though,' Monroe replied icily. 'Let them run away, did you?'

'Actually, yes,' Declan leant against his desk as he nodded. 'They would have been out within an hour, and it would never have gone to court. Or they'd have been removed quietly, and nobody would have been wiser. It was the Pearce Associates way, the Rattlestone way, and now the Phoenix Industries way.'

'Or the Robinson Finance way,' Monroe mused.

'Exactly,' Declan straightened. 'They wanted to send a message, nothing more. I sent one back. And now they're on the back foot, so we can keep on at it.'

'You're still a bloody idiot,' Monroe muttered, but stopped as the doors to the office opened, and Billy and Davey walked through. Both were dressed for work, but there seemed to be something off in their mannerisms. Like they didn't want to be there.

'I didn't realise your suspension had been lifted?' Monroe said, walking over and giving Billy a reassuring pat on the shoulder. 'Or has the lassie on your computer dragged you into work?'

'Different lassie,' Davey replied, nodding at Bullman's office. 'Actually, can you still be called "lassie" when you're Bullman's age?'

'I heard that,' the faint sound of Bullman's voice could be heard through the door to her office. 'Send *Tintin's* Thompson Twins in here, please.'

'You heard her,' Monroe said, winking at Davey. 'Better get on with it.'

As Billy walked past Declan, however, he passed across a folder.

'Found this out last night,' he said. 'Should help.'

'You did all this last night?' Declan flicked through the folder, but at this, Billy flushed.

'Well, um, no. I outsourced a little,' he admitted. 'I couldn't ... I couldn't get through the firewall.'

'I understand,' Declan replied with mock reassurance. 'You're stressed. It's hard to perform under pressure. I'm guessing this was Trix Preston's work?'

Billy nodded, hurrying to catch up with Davey, walking through the door to Bullman's office, the door closing behind him.

Declan looked at Monroe.

'Bollocking?' he asked, nodding his head at the door.

'As long as it's not me in there, I don't care,' Monroe smiled. 'What did he find out, then?'

Declan started rifling through the papers.

'There's no way even Trix did this in one night,' he said. 'There's land deeds, financial information, connections between Robinson Finance and Phoenix, even travel reports for Trisha Hawkins flying to New York.'

'Tom,' Monroe nodded as he leant over Declan's shoulder, looking down at the papers. 'He has an axe to grind after they almost killed him, and he's out of MI5's good books, so he's probably working with Trix on this.'

Monroe looked back to the door, a slight smile on his face.

'Let's not tell the boy, though, eh?' he suggested. 'If he thinks she could do all this in a matter of hours, it might up his game when he comes back.'

'If he comes back,' Declan closed the folder, placing it on the desk. 'I think—'

He stopped as his phone rang. Picking it up and identifying himself, he listened for a long moment before looking back at Monroe.

'That was the front desk downstairs,' he said. 'We've got a walk in. Colin Walters.'

'The third ghost?' Monroe stroked at his goatee. 'This could be the break we need.'

He looked across at Jess.

'Do we have anything from Rosanna?' he asked. 'I mean Doctor Marcos?'

'The hat Shelly Garraway was found dead with definitely had the same mixture of poisons and solvent as the other two had,' Jess read from the screen now. 'But I can't find anything that connects her to this.'

'Which means she either died by accident, or because we're looking at the wrong case,' Monroe sighed. 'Let's hope it's the former, eh?'

'Dad,' Jess rose now. 'There's not much to do here until around lunchtime, as I'm waiting on emails—'

'And you're wondering if you could bunk off, have a morning break?' Declan grinned at his daughter. 'Jess, you don't work here. You're going above and beyond just sitting at the desk, so anything you do is fine.'

'I'm not bunking off—' Jess went to argue, but then paused as her brain, realising Declan was giving her permission, caught up with her mouth. 'It's just Mina invited me to help with the soup kitchen this morning, as they're a little low on staff. And I thought it might help me check into things. You know, Lewis and Father Franks, her dad, all that.'

She looked away, shuffling her feet.

'And ... and I really enjoyed doing it last night,' she said. 'I felt I really helped people.'

'And you don't think you help people here?' Declan asked.

'Oh, no, I know I do,' Jess quickly back-pedalled. 'But there it's a lot more instant, you know? You give the food, and you're instantly helping.'

Declan smiled and pulled Jess in for a quick hug.

'You're doing great,' he smiled. 'And I'm proud of you for thinking of doing this. Go help the kitchen. When the emails come in, you can head back. I'll be in Soho myself later, so I'll pop by and see how you're doing. Deal?'

'Deal,' Jess grinned, already grabbing her jacket. As she left for the door, however, Monroe looked across the desk at him.

'Back in Soho later, aye?' he asked.

'Yeah, I think it's time I had a chat with Paul Stringer,' Declan growled before heading to the door himself. 'But first, let's have a chat with Mister Walters.'

'Sit down, the pair of you,' Bullman said, looking up from her chair. 'Christ, you look like you've been brought in for detention.'

'Well, I was under the impression I was suspended and banned from coming in here,' Billy replied, taking the seat on the right. 'You know, when I was told to get my things and all that, boss?'

'That was for the cheap seats,' Bullman replied knowledgeably, and Billy had to wonder for a moment who she was talking about. But, before he could speak more on this, she continued. 'I brought you in because I've had some updates. Ones I didn't want to share on the phones, even if they're burners.'

She pulled out her notebook, opening it up, and Billy realised as she flipped through the pages, looking for her notes that this information was so dangerous, she hadn't even written it down on her computer.

'I had Cooper's update,' she said, still scanning the pages. 'And I also had the forensics report. First off, were you aware a murder suspect was in your house?'

'No, ma'am,' Billy responded.

'Good,' Bullman nodded at this, obviously not believing the lie. 'I was talking to Dav—Chief Superintendent Bradbury, and he had some updates for me on this.'

'Why would one of the top bods of Scotland Yard be looking into this?' Davey, surprised, asked. 'Ma'am?'

'Because I asked him to, and he likes me,' Bullman didn't look up as she carried on looking through the notebook. 'Sorry, still trying to find it. I was worried someone might find it, so I wrote parts on differing pages, like a secret code. *Da Vinci* style.'

Billy wanted to point out that Bullman may have been

taking the "cloak and dagger" part of this a little too seriously, but decided to keep wisely silent.

'Aha,' Bullman eventually found what she'd been looking for. 'So, we have some news on your second suspect. Carlos Pascal.'

'Has he been found?' Billy sat forwards now, perching on the edge of the chair.

'Not yet, but we have found out some other secrets,' Bullman replied. 'Such as he definitely had a connection in the Colombian diplomatic service.'

'We know,' Billy sat back now, dejected. 'We think Andrade worked for him as a teenager.'

'Really?' Bullman was surprised by this. 'Okay, stick a pin in that, because mine came from somewhere else. It seems our section head, Pablo Restrepo, is a cousin of his.'

There was a long, stunned moment of silence here.

'Pablo knows Carlos,' Davey nodded as she considered the news. 'Yeah, that makes sense. It also explains why he was slow to give details. Probably knew his family was in town and was giving them a chance to get out. Especially if he knew they were bleeding.'

'So where does this put us, though?' Billy frowned, tapping on the arm of the chair unconsciously as he did so. 'Do we hunt Andrade? Carlos? Watch Pablo and see if he takes us anywhere? It's just the two of us, boss. And Cooper, who's only with us part-time, and Chivalry. Which technically makes three, I suppose.'

'I can't suggest anything,' Bullman replied. 'But I can say, whatever you do, we'll be there to back you up, and bugger the protocols.'

'At least Pablo Restrepo is more likely to be found,' Billy mused, a little emboldened after the comment from his superior. 'Okay then, we have a plan. Thanks, Guv. And thank Chief Superintendent Bradbury for me, too.'

Bullman nodded.

'Sorry I had to drag you in for this, but I don't trust spies. And even if we're not claiming Andrade as one anymore, his blasted boss looks to be one for sure.'

This finished, and rising, Billy and Davey walked out of Bullman's office and into the main area. It was quieter now, with Declan and Monroe both gone now, Jess having left as well.

Davey went to continue to the exit, but Billy paused her, nodding at De'Geer, currently in the briefing room.

'Go and speak to him,' he said. 'Make friends. You might not have another chance to.'

Sighing, Davey nodded at this.

'Fine,' she hissed. 'But only because you're not technically police right now and I feel sorry for you.'

Pulling out her phone, she threw a quick text into the ether, and then left Billy to his own devices, knowing he'd likely run to his precious computer station, to see what damage Jess had done in the two days she'd been there.

Walking into the briefing room, Davey knew she'd be seen through the glass walls talking to De'Geer, but at the same time, nobody would hear what they were saying. That said, the only people in the office were Billy and Anjli, and they were now deep in conversation, each catching the other up with the events of the previous day while Billy, Davey could see to her amusement, desperately wanted to check the computer, only keeping from doing this because of his politeness to Anjli.

De'Geer looked up as Davey walked in. She didn't know what to say, really, and automatically made her way to her old chair at the back of the room, sitting down and facing him before speaking.

'Hey,' she said.

'Hey,' he replied, a little cautiously. 'You all better? You bolted from Marcos's office like you saw a ghost last night.'

'Food poisoning,' Davey lied. 'All good now, though. Wanted to say sorry, though.'

'What for?' De'Geer now sat on a desk, facing the back of the briefing room, and Davey. 'You didn't do anything.'

'I led you on, and that was bad of me,' Davey replied. 'Fact of the matter is, Morten, I am attracted to you. But that's not enough for me. I'm not choosy, I'm not playing hard to get, I'm just ... meh. I look at you and go "he's attractive," but I don't thirst for you.'

'Um, thanks?' De'Geer frowned.

'Look, I'm what people call asexual,' Davey continued. 'That means—'

'Asexuality's the lack of sexual attraction to others, or a low interest in or desire for them,' De'Geer smiled. 'We did a course on sexuality. It came up.'

'Oh, good,' Davey added. 'So, being "ace" means I know you'd be an amazing boyfriend, partner, whatever, but just not with me.'

'That's fine,' De'Geer nodded. 'Wasn't looking to be with you, anyway.'

Davey went to reply, but all she did was open and shut her mouth.

'You seem to think that I'm some kind of puppy dog, pining for you like Greyfriars Bobby,' De'Geer straightened now. 'But honestly, I think I fixated on you because deep down I knew I couldn't have you, that you were unobtainable, and that was safe. I realised on our first date—'

'It was only a drink—'

'Our first *drink,* that there was nothing there. Sure, I was attracted to you, but I soon realised there were more options out there.'

'Like Esme,' Davey raised an eyebrow as she suggested. At this, however, De'Geer's expression darkened.

'Yeah, well, I screwed that one up,' he said.

'How come?'

'I had an opportunity there after the Robin Hood convention,' De'Geer squirmed a little as he replied. 'You weren't on that case, but we were overnight in a hotel and we shared a room.'

'I heard,' Davey grinned. 'So, what did you do to screw it up?'

'Missed my chance, and threw myself deep into the friend zone,' De'Geer mocked throwing a rugby or American football. 'Score! Yay me!'

'You missed your shot? Take another one,' Davey glanced at the door, as if checking they were still alone.

De'Geer, however, stared at the ground.

'You know Pete Osborne at Lambeth?' he asked.

'Course I do,' Davey replied. 'Why?'

'I saw him last night; he asked if I was still going after you.'

'Probably wanted the gossip,' Davey shrugged, settling back in the chair. 'It's lonely in the morgues.'

'Yeah, but he only asked because he wanted to know if Esme Cooper was free,' De'Geer replied icily. 'He thought I was after her, and if I was after you, then he had a shot himself.'

'Ah,' Davey leant forwards on the chair. 'And what did you tell him?'

'I told him the truth, that we weren't an item,' De'Geer said. 'But when I left, I felt angry. Like he was pushing in on my turf.'

'That's very alpha male and misogynist of you.'

'No, I'm not explaining it right,' De'Geer continued, waving his hands. 'I was—'

'You were jealous,' Davey interrupted. 'You were jealous that Osborne might succeed where you failed. Or, more rather, succeed where you didn't even bother trying.'

'... yeah,' De'Geer muttered. 'Pretty much.'

'So do something about it,' Davey rose to her feet now. 'Tell her how you feel. You fancy her, right?'

'Yeah, I do.'

'And you'd like to ask her out, right?'

'I ... I don't know.'

'Would it be easier if she asked you out, you big girl's blouse?' Davey grinned. In response, De'Geer flushed red as he rubbed at his neck sheepishly.

'I suppose.'

'Good,' Davey looked past De'Geer and towards the door. 'Then ask him out, go on a date and let's get past this whole bloody mess, the pair of you.'

De'Geer spun around to see a red-faced Cooper at the door, her phone in her hand.

'I had a text from DC Davey,' she said by explanation. 'It said to get here ASAP. I wasn't eavesdropping, I swear.'

'Esme, do you fancy Morten?' Davey asked. 'Actually, don't answer that, as I already know you do. And Morten, you fancy her. So, I suggest you stay in here together and sort it out, yeah?'

Walking past Cooper, though, Davey paused.

'But if you hurt him, I'll hunt you down and hide the body so well, not even Rosanna Marcos will find it, yeah?'

She paused, paling.

'That sounded better in my head,' she said.

'It was fine, exactly the right level of menace,' Cooper replied. 'Now, can you leave us for a moment? I need to talk to this stupid Viking.'

BILLY HAD RETURNED TO HIS COMPUTER STATION JUST TO "check the CPU", and while he did this, Anjli popped out to her car; she'd forgotten to bring in her purse, and even though it was probably fine in a car park effectively outside a police station, there was an element of concern in her head.

And therefore it was Anjli, exiting out of the building and onto King's Bench Walk, that saw Mallory Reed, waiting nervously to the side.

'Can I help you?' she asked.

'I'm not sure,' Mallory replied, obviously uncomfortable. 'I was looking for DI Walsh, but ... no, this is silly.'

'Not at all, I work with him, I'm DS Kapoor,' Anjli smiled. 'Would you rather talk outside? It's a little cold, but there's a coffee shop around the corner.'

'It's nothing, I swear,' Mallory shook her head. 'I'm Mallory Reed. I work—'

'I know who you are, Ms Reed,' Anjli stepped forward, holding a hand out to be shaken. 'Your statement helped us a lot.'

'It wasn't everything, though,' Mallory replied. 'I only learned this morning about something else.'

'Okay,' Anjli let the hand, unshaken, drop. 'Like what?'

'You have another dead body, don't you?' Mallory added. 'Shelly Garraway?'

'Yes, we do,' Anjli said, questioning quietly if she had time to pull her phone out and record it. 'What about her?'

'She had a Father Christmas hat, didn't she?'

'Okay, you're either super psychic, or you have an inside scoop,' Anjli spoke slower now, wondering where this was going. 'Because as far as I know, only a handful of people know that, and nearly all of them are in that building.'

'Someone overheard your boss asking Father Franks about it. Last night, at the church,' Mallory carried on. 'But they hadn't put it together. I did, after I spoke to DI Walsh. Shelly was wearing a Father Christmas hat when she died, because she took it earlier that night, from the Soho St Benedict's Kitchen. It had been thrown to the floor by Michael Siddell, after Lewis Hoyle tried to give it to him.'

'How do you know this?' Anjli asked, frowning.

'I'm right, aren't I?' Mallory insisted. 'Lewis tried to give "Santa Mick" a new hat, but he said no. And that hat, one picked up by Shelly killed her. It was accidental, but the intent wasn't.'

'And why would Lewis Hoyle want Michael Siddell dead?' Anjli shook her head. 'We've not found any connection between them.'

'Then you're not looking deep enough,' Mallory replied. 'You're not looking at why he walked away from the priesthood.'

'Pretend I'm an idiot,' Anjli snarled. 'Tell me what I'm missing.'

Taking a deep breath and trembling, Mallory Reed nodded.

'I only worked it out last night, after I learnt about Shelly,' she said. 'Lewis knew Michael Siddell, but he only knew Santa Mick by *that* name. A week before Michael died, I told Lewis what I'd learnt about him from our talks, how he had a guilt to the past, a fascination with Dickens, *A Christmas Carol,* Scrooge, all that. And Lewis went pale.'

She looked around, as if expecting Lewis Hoyle to appear.

'He told me he knew Michael,' she whispered. 'He said it couldn't be, he was shocked. Because back in 2007, when the St Benedict's Kitchen was starting, Michael Siddell refused them a monetary prize.'

'Wait,' Anjli held up a hand, shaking her head. 'Are you saying St Benedict's was one of the three *Cratchits*, the candidates for the Marley Society's funding?'

'I don't know about that,' Mallory said. 'All I know is although he claimed it was old news, and Santa Mick had suffered enough, I saw hatred in his eyes. And Shelly Garraway died because of wearing a hat, one Lewis Hoyle tried to make Santa Mick wear.'

20

START-UPS

'You know the basics of the Society, yes?' Colin Walters asked as he sat in the interview room, Monroe and Declan facing him. It wasn't an interview and would usually have been conducted in a far more informal situation, but Colin was convinced he was about to be murdered, and the room had been chosen to give him a little relief and security, to keep people out, rather than keep him in. He was a man in his late sixties, with a square shaped head, which with his hair and beard, both cut to sharp angles, made Declan feel this was a deliberate attempt to emphasise it. He was overweight but not too much so, more flabby than fat, but hid this with oversized clothing that made Declan wonder if he'd lost a lot of weight recently, and had once been far bigger.

'Yes,' he replied. 'Anthony Farringdon and Chivalry Fitzwarren have both explained aspects of it.'

'Good,' Colin nodded. 'Farringdon's a good egg. Chivalry, I can't remember someone called ... good God, is that what *Steven* Fitzwarren's calling himself these days? Bloody dramatist. Although if anyone can be an authority on Christmas ghosts, it's that spooky bugger.'

Declan kept quiet, allowing Colin to continue with his story.

'Anyway, yes, so 2007,' Colin continued, taking the hint. 'We had three candidates. *Cratchits*, they were called.'

'Explain to me how you'd get these,' Monroe asked, sipping from a mug of tea in front of him. Mugs weren't usually allowed in interview rooms; the drinks were another attempt at making the whole place seem cosier.

'Well, personally, I had three interns at my company,' Colin said. 'Although I suppose back then they were just apprentices. Maybe they were paid, too. I don't remember. We didn't have a lot for them in the last quarter of the year, so I had them look around for some interesting characters.'

'And these characters were just lying around, were they?' Declan asked.

At this thought, Colin fixed him with a withering stare.

'It was 2007, not 1907,' he said simply. 'The Internet might not have been the social media beast it is now, but there were still forums and LiveJournals and all that stuff. Places where you could learn of hard luck stories or people with their eye on the future. I was the ghost of Christmas Future, so I was looking for start-ups, or people with plans for helping others.'

'And the others?'

'Neil was the ghost of Christmas Present, and had someone who'd had a fall, wasn't doing that well right now. And Arthur had Christmas Past and picked a researcher who had lost his grant earlier that year.'

'It sounds to me like the Cratchits of Past and Present

were pretty much the same,' Declan commented, determined not to wither under the glare.

'Yes, well, they were, pretty much,' Colin admitted. 'It was one night a year, and we were mainly there to get pissed and donate some money. It wasn't like the *X Factor* or anything, with all these rounds and stuff. The three Cratchits weren't even there on Christmas Eve. They turned up to a meeting of the Ghosts only, when we were getting our ducks in a row. And even then it was a night in November, they all came in one by one, explained their problems and left. *Dragon's Den* for beggars.'

Declan considered this.

'So, there's every chance they all could have met?' he asked.

'Oh, they definitely all met,' Colin sniffed. 'They were all in the side room waiting their turn. But they were rivals for what they believed was a grant. They were all paranoid the others would take the money from them, so they weren't making chums, if you get my meaning.'

'So can you go through it all for us?' Monroe leant back on his chair.

'We brought in our candidates; we made cases for them. In the past, we've had ones that were too close, and because of this, we now had this buffer. A Cratchit doesn't work out? We have a month to replace them, and a list of options. But in 2007 we didn't need to. All three worked, entertainment wise. Pulling on the heartstrings and all that. I think Neil's was someone we knew, too, so there was a little pathos to it, too.'

'It seems a little heartless to look at three people, all in dire need of funding, as entertainment,' Declan snapped. 'Feels a little more like rich people making poor people fight for their amusements. No better than medieval lords playing with the peasants.'

Colin nodded.

'You're right,' he replied. 'It was like that. We had the money, and we fed our own egos with this philanthropy. But we weren't wicked men. And karma came for us when the stocks crashed.'

'Who were the three Crat—candidates?' Monroe asked now. 'Do you remember?'

Colin nodded.

'I had a start-up charitable company,' he explained. 'Aimed at helping homeless people. I think they wanted to sort a shelter, do soup kitchens in London, all that.'

Declan felt ice slide down his spine.

'St Benedict's?' he asked softly.

At this, Colin's face brightened.

'You know it? Wonderful!' he exclaimed. 'Yes, they were just starting, needed funding to buy equipment. Lewis, the chap I spoke to, he said—'

'Lewis Hoyle was a Cratchit?' Monroe almost stood up as he spoke. 'You're bloody kidding me!'

'I don't see the issue here,' Colin looked at Declan, confused.

'Michael Siddell, after the crash, became homeless, sleeping rough on the streets,' Declan explained. 'Years later, his mind ravaged by drugs and whatnot, he called himself "Santa Mick" and ate at the same soup kitchen Lewis runs. In fact, Lewis was one of the last people to see him alive.'

'Aye, and now we have a man who lost out on a money tree, finding the same man now in front of him,' Monroe added. 'That's motive right there.'

'We also know Valentin Suvosky was one of the others, but we don't know the third,' Declan finished.

At this, the now shocked Colin nodded.

'Yes, absolutely, it was Brian something. Not my Cratchit, so I don't know everything, just that he had some kind of bone marrow cancer thing going on, I think terminal as well, and he wanted to use himself as a research subject for some unorthodox, but effective cures. He was going on the basis that if he failed, he died anyway, but he might be able to find things that could help others. And, of course, survival was a definite bonus here for him.'

'Can you find the name?'

Colin shrugged.

'He shouldn't be too hard to find,' he said. 'He died in 2012, but had made great strides in bone marrow research. Amazing chemist, incredible outlook on life. Was actively looking at nature to cure cancer, rather than science.'

He stared off, frowning.

'I think he called his lab "BMR" something, as it stood for Bone Marrow Research,' he added. 'I wish I could help more.'

'No, that's fine, we can use that,' Declan was writing this down. 'And whose Cratchit was he?'

'Oh, that was Arthur's puppy,' Colin nodded. 'Suvosky was Neil's.'

'And who was going to win?'

'No idea,' Colin shrugged slightly, but there was an awkwardness to it, like he didn't want to answer. 'That was all up to the Scrooge.'

'And Siddell hadn't seen any of them before Christmas Eve?'

'Not to my knowledge,' Colin replied. 'But then we were never close.'

Declan noticed Monroe texting on his phone, probably telling the others Lewis Hoyle could be a prime suspect.

'What happened on the night?' he asked. 'Why wasn't anyone picked?'

'Siddell was a prick,' Colin snapped. 'He took the money and ran. I mean, we didn't know this at the time, but he had gambling debts. Horses, mainly. He held the decision over, which had been done before, but not at the last minute. And then he told the treasurer he'd changed his mind. Had a fifty-grand cheque made out to cash as he hadn't one hundred percent decided yet, and then ran off and cashed it. Claimed it was an administrative oversight, that his secretary had put it in with other payments by accident, but we all knew that was bollocks. He needed quick cash, and he used us to get it. Obviously, there was a massive barney over this, everyone was mortified and he was accused of throwing the Society into disrepute.'

'You only met once a year, though,' Declan frowned. 'Surely an accusation like that didn't really hold water?'

'No, and that was the point,' Colin moaned. 'Whereas people like us tried to uphold the tenets, people like Siddell, were utter scumbags of the lowest degree.'

He barked out a bitter laugh.

'You know what he used the money for in the end?' he snapped. 'We thought it was for the debts, but no. He bought a book with it. Bloody thing was up for auction in the New Year and he used our money to buy it.'

Colin laughed again, and once more it wasn't a humorous one. But then Declan realised he knew what the book was, remembering the words Mallory Reed had spoken.

'Charles Dickens's A Christmas Carol. He was lucid once, said he'd bought the first edition, with the red and green title

page. Was really proud of this. Spent like twenty, thirty grand on it.'

'It was *A Christmas Carol,* first edition, wasn't it?' he asked. 'I heard he owned one, and it cost him around half as he would have stolen.'

'Yes. Wanker. He split the rest of the money between Arthur and Neil, like ten grand each, I think' Colin folded his arms and glared at the table. 'I was glad when he was bankrupted by the crash. I offered to repay the debt, you know. The other buggers just looked innocently away, claimed they didn't know anything. But by then, the crash had changed everything. We didn't hold another meeting for three years.'

'So there never was a winner?' Monroe closed his notebook. 'Not even a bookie's favourite?'

'St Benedict's was the favourite,' Colin said with a hint of pride. 'I knew it'd do well. Rich people always feel a little guilty when they're publicly seen not helping the poor.'

'And Suvosky?'

'He made his own bed, made poor business decisions. Why should we bail him out? And the other one, the cancer guy, he wasn't going to find a cure anytime soon, he'd die before he'd win. He might last a few years, but the sand was already spilling through the hourglass. We'd be throwing the money away.'

Declan watched Colin as he spoke, deciding he really wasn't a fan of the man.

'You called Arthur the day he died.'

'Absolutely,' Colin nodded. 'I talked to him a lot. It was only Siddell who was blackballed.'

'So, the call was purely coincidental?' Declan asked now, leaning closer. 'It was nothing to do with the murders?'

'God no!' Colin exclaimed. 'I was calling him from Devon.

I'd had someone trying to get hold of me, a female journalist or something doing a piece on the Marley Society. I said they should speak to him as I didn't talk to the press, and was calling to give him a heads up, as he loves all that hearts and flowers rubbish. I didn't get back until last night, and found bloody police officers banging on my door.'

Declan sighed inwardly as he leant back.

'Well, thank you for your time, Mister Walters,' he said, rising from his chair. 'If you can just wait here, I'll speak to DCI Monroe here about protection.'

'Protection from what?' Colin genuinely looked confused.

'I don't know if you've worked it out, but someone's murdering your little Dickens class of 2007, and you're the last on the list,' Monroe gave a dark smile. 'I'd like to keep you alive until we at least catch the bugger.'

With Colin Walters staring now in horrified realisation of his current predicament, Monroe led Declan out of the room, closing the door behind him.

'Bloody Lewis Hoyle,' he hissed. 'How did we miss this?'

'We didn't,' Declan replied, checking his notes as they walked down the corridor. 'Father Franks told us everything from the start. When he picked up Mina, he told Jess and Anjli that Lewis Hoyle was involved in the original planning and funding for St Benedict's, but then he joined seminary school. He then said Hoyle left, returning to the charity, realising his vocation was with the homeless. What if he tried to become a priest after he lost the money?'

'Then he'd have every reason to hate Siddell, and we've been letting him into every step of our investigation,' Monroe said as they entered the office. 'What do you reckon to this journalist?'

'I think he gave a killer the address where they could find

Arthur Drayson, without realising he'd damned his friend,' Declan replied.

Monroe nodded, looking across the office as they entered.

'Cooper, good, I need you to get some uniforms to stay with Colin Walters for a while—'

He stopped.

'Why the hell are you smiling?'

'No reason,' Cooper said, walking off with a definite skip in her stride. 'I'll get some uniforms.'

'I'll never understand women,' Monroe growled as he spied Anjli across the office. 'Lassie! We have news!'

'I have some too,' Anjli said, not allowing Monroe to continue. 'Lewis Hoyle killed Shelly Garraway.'

Monroe went to speak, but just stood there, dumbfounded.

'That is, Mallory Reed thinks so,' Anjli hastily corrected. 'Says the Christmas hat Lewis tried to give Santa Mick was thrown into a puddle and Shelly took it and wore it. And then, a few hours later, in the middle of the night, she died in her tent, still with it on. When forensics checked it—'

'They found the same toxins,' Declan finished the sentence, guessing correctly. 'We have another link to Hoyle too. Am I right in thinking Father Franks said Lewis Hoyle set up St Benedict's?'

'He was one of the team but left briefly, yeah,' Anjli frowned. 'Why?'

'Because St Benedict's was a Cratchit in 2007 and Michael Siddell ripped them off,' Monroe said, rapping the edge of a chair with his knuckles as he thought aloud. 'They were the apparent winner, too. But this doesn't fit right. Where am I going wrong here? Lewis starts up a charity, tries for a grant as such, doesn't get it, goes to be a priest, changes his mind, returns to the street. I get that as a story, it works fine. And sure, ten, twelve years later, maybe he realises one of the homeless is the guy who screwed him over. But to kill him over this? Seems extreme.'

'Also, if he failed to give Santa Mick the poisoned hat, how did Santa Mick get the replacement?' Declan asked. 'I mean, I know the woman he met that morning gave him it, but if Lewis was working with someone, surely he knew this? He wouldn't try to give Siddell another one?'

'Maybe he thought Santa Mick would already be dead?' Anjli suggested. 'And, when he saw him in the line-up, he made a back-up hat just in case, thinking the hat given earlier hadn't worked?'

'Possible,' Declan nodded. 'Which would mean he had an accomplice. But who?'

'Have you told Jess yet?' Anjli paled slightly as she looked around the office. 'She went to help out, remember?'

'I'll let her know now,' Declan said, pulling out his phone and typing a quick message.

Keep an eye on Lewis. Might be more there than we thought. Heading in to speak to him. Let us know if he leaves.

This sent, he looked back at Anjli.

'How did you hear this from Mallory?' he frowned. 'Was she here?'

'She caught me outside while I was popping out to grab my purse from the car,' Anjli shrugged. 'Right time, right location. I also had a text from Jake, the bouncer I spoke to on Broadwick Street. He has a witness that claims he saw the blonde woman who gave Santa Mick his new hat.'

'I thought she gave it to him around Liverpool Street?' Monroe looked up.

'No, we know he walked into town from Liverpool Street that day, but apparently it was given in Soho around noon.'

'You should go see them right away,' Declan said. 'Show them the elf photo too, for what good it could do. We'll share a cab.'

'So, we're going into Soho then?' Monroe watched Declan. 'You want to go arrest the wee scroat?'

'I think he has some questions to answer, yes,' Declan nodded. 'And we could also swing past Wardour Street, too.'

He picked up his extendable baton, currently on his desk, and fitted it up his coat's sleeve.

'And this time I'm coming prepared,' he growled.

21

CALL THE ENGINEER

DAVEY HAD TAKEN THE FIRST SHIFT, AND NOW STOOD ON THE corner of the street that faced the Colombian Embassy, watching the door for any sign of Pablo Restrepo.

She knew anyone watching her would laugh, for this was not how spies worked. She was too visible, too obvious, even for her attempts at blending into the surroundings, which, considering her short ginger hair contrasted with everything around her, was a little difficult.

'How's it going?' the voice of Billy Fitzwarren whispered in her Bluetooth earpiece and, not for the first time that day, since leaving Bullman's office; in fact, she wondered if she'd made the right choices in her life.

'Nothing so far,' she said. 'But I'll—'

'I meant with De'Geer and Cooper?' Billy's voice continued. 'Like, has anyone said if they're an item yet?'

'Honestly? You'd know if they were,' Davey hissed. 'They'd tell you first. People like you more than me.'

'We can fix that,' Billy continued. 'I could—'

'Shut up, I've got company,' Davey hissed as, walking out

of the embassy and looking pretty irritated, Pablo Restrepo made his way across the street, stopping as he reached Davey.

'A tree,' he said, looking at the slim foliage she'd tried to hide behind. 'This is what you came up with?'

'I'm waiting for an Uber,' Davey lied. 'It's running late.'

'You're spying on a diplomat of the Colombian government,' Restrepo snapped back, bored now of playing the game. 'I could have your government arrest you.'

'You could, because I'm being a pretty shit spy right now,' Davey shrugged. 'And they could arrest me, it wouldn't be the first time this year, either, but then I'd have to talk about Carlos Pascal.'

Restrepo paused.

'What about Carlos Pascal?'

'You know, how his blood was found in the apartment,' Davey continued, deciding that if the shirt was where the blood was, and the shirt had been in the apartment at some point, this was a calculated guess at the situation. And, by the stony expression Pablo Restrepo now gave her, she knew she was on point here, and that he likely knew the blood was there too. 'And how he likely killed José Almas for Los Lideres, throwing it onto Andrade. Who used to work with him. And them. Crazy.'

She smiled, patting Restrepo on the side of his torso, as if checking the fitting of his jacket.

'Hmm. You don't really work out anymore, do you?' she asked. Restrepo was so shaken, he didn't even try to stop her, as she continued to speak. 'I wondered how you knew about Andrade's past – I mean, you're a spy and all that, but you seemed really knowledgeable. And then we realised, you just asked your cousin Carlos! The one you, or Andrade, or both even, have been covering for. Was it you that cleared him in Chile? Actually, don't worry. We don't care.'

'You do not know what you're getting into,' Restrepo hissed, his voice cold and dangerous.

Davey, however, laughed at this.

'Man, for a spy, you're really shit at doing research,' she said. 'If you did, you'd know my whole life has been a public relations horror show, and scarier pricks than you have tried to threaten me.'

She tinkered with his lapel, brushing off some dust as she did so.

'We don't know where Andrade is, and it's annoying,' she said. 'Billy has this whole martyr complex thing going, but we don't care about the man's safety. We just want Billy cleared.'

'By "we" you mean you and his great-uncle?'

'Yeah, and pretty much every copper who's ever met Billy,' Davey grinned. 'He's superb at getting people to like him. Like a Cocker Spaniel. And the people who owe him? Wow! A list. Prime Ministers, entire army regiments, underworld gangs, don't even get me started on the people with weapons, just anyone who could be out there, looking to help him.'

She leant in.

'You think you have power? We're the City of London police, mate. We *are* the power. And we'll make your entire life a living hell while you're here.'

'I have diplomatic immunity,' Pablo Restrepo puffed out his chest. 'You are nothing but a minor cog, and if you or your friends try to arrest me, I'll—'

'Who said we were going to arrest you?' Davey frowned, shaking her head. 'I was taught everything I know by the Barracuda, Pablo. Do you think I'd go legitimate on you, when there's so many other, more fun options? Tell Carlos Pascal it's open season on him, too. Unless he gives us something we can use to free Billy.'

'And Andrade?'

Davey stepped back.

'Couldn't give a shit about him,' she said. 'Get him somewhere we can arrest him, drop his immunity and we'll forget all about this. As long as someone who was there when José died, pays for the crime, we're good.'

Restrepo stared at Davey for a long moment.

And then, with a smile, he reached to his lapel, fiddled with it for a long moment and pulled off the small, sticky tracker she'd placed there.

'You are right,' he smiled. 'You are a shit spy.'

Tossing the tracker to the floor and stamping on it, he turned around, walking back to the embassy.

'Go home, little fish,' he said. 'You are no barracuda.'

Davey waited a long moment before breathing out.

'Did you get all that?' she asked.

'Laid it all on a bit thick about me, didn't you?' Billy's voice was hurt.

'Selling the story,' she smiled. 'Is it working?'

'Yeah, until he works out you stuck another tracker on his jacket pocket, we're good,' Billy replied. 'With luck, that'll happen as he goes through the security scanners.'

'Got to admit, I don't understand that,' Davey said, watching the embassy. 'Why did we waste a second tracker?'

'We put one on him, he goes "nice try" and carries on,' Billy explained. 'We put two on, he still thinks "nice try", but now he's wondering if there's a third, a fourth, on and on. Did we clone his phone? Are we tracking his car? The paranoia will kick in and he'll start second guessing.'

'And this helps how?'

'He won't phone Carlos, he'll need to speak to him face to face.'

'You think he'll do it in person?' Davey turned and walked away now.

'Let's hope so,' Billy's voice was more uncertain now.

'And then what?'

'Then we see if Andrade's the spy Monroe's always claimed he was,' Billy replied. 'And then we get him, Pablo and Carlos in a room together, and hope they don't kill each other before we learn what the hell's going on.'

IT WAS LATE MORNING BY THE TIME DECLAN ARRIVED AT Wardour Street with the others. Climbing out of the cab and paying the driver, he looked up at the building ahead of him.

'We have about an hour before the kitchen closes,' he said. 'Jess texted, saying it's moved today, it's north of Oxford Street and off Rathbone Place, but it's only a ten-minute walk.'

'I'll go speak to the witness on Broadwick Street,' Anjli was already heading off. 'Let me know when you're off there and I'll catch you up.'

'Or we'll catch you,' Monroe smiled. 'I don't think this will take too long. We can then go speak to Hoyle together.'

Nodding and giving a little wave as she walked away, Anjli left the two detectives alone in the street. Monroe, shifting his grip on the umbrella he held in his hand, looked at Declan.

'You still want to play it the way we discussed?' he asked.

'Absolutely,' Declan was already heading to the entrance, opening the door and walking through as he spoke.

The lobby hadn't changed since the last time Monroe had been in there, and the girl behind the reception counter was the same one as well, looking up at the entrance, and wrinkling her nose when she saw Monroe again.

'I think you're—' she started, but Declan held up a hand.

'Shut it,' he said commandingly. 'Press your little button and bring Paul Stringer here right now.'

'Or what?' the woman glared back defiantly.

'Or I will call in every favour I'm owed and have you destroyed,' Declan said with utter conviction. He didn't know if he could do such a thing, but the fact of the matter was he sounded like he believed he could, and the woman swallowed, pressing a button.

'You're making a mistake,' she said.

'No, the mistake was when your boss sent men out to attack me last night,' Declan smiled, but there was no humour behind it. 'That made it personal. I'm making it *more* personal now.'

The elevator doors opened, and Paul Stringer walked out through them, his eyes darting around the reception, both wary and confused.

'Paul, right?' Declan looked at Monroe, who nodded slightly, before turning back. 'No need for introductions, right? We should probably find a place to talk.'

'And why would I want to talk to you?' Paul asked, frowning.

At this, Declan pulled his phone out, pressing a button on the screen. The voice of the attacker from the previous night echoed through the tinny speaker.

'Paul Stringer says to back the hell off. It's above your pay grade, DI Walsh.'

'Is he the security guard who talked to Monroe? Why's he

hassling me? Tell him to go beat up Monroe instead. Oh, wait, you tried that before and failed, when Rattlestone was still about. You're ex Rattles, aren't you? You've got that arrogant swagger and stench of failure all over you.'

'This time we won't fail, and this time we're gonna hurt you—'

Declan paused the recording.

'I don't know what he's talking about,' Paul shrugged. 'I never spoke to him.'

'How do you know?' Monroe asked. 'We haven't shown you a photo.'

Paul didn't reply, and in response Declan walked up to him, now uncomfortably close.

'You tried to taser me,' he hissed. 'You tried to set me up and hurt me. I'm sure if I looked into it, I mean *really* looked into it, I'd find the burner phone you texted them their orders from. Would it have your fingerprints on? Should we check?'

'You don't have a warrant,' Paul held his chin up as he replied.

'We're well past warrants now,' Declan smiled again. 'So, let's find a place with no windows where we can have a proper chat. You can even have others in there, but we are having that chat right now.'

Paul nodded, a rapid up-down as he considered his immediate options, and stepped away, pressing the elevator call button.

'I'm taking them to meeting room three,' he said to the receptionist. 'Let the others know they can meet us there.'

He looked at Monroe.

'You can leave that here, you know,' he said, nodding at the umbrella.

'It's a family heirloom,' Monroe was appalled at the

suggestion. 'It's not leaving my side. Although it does have a nasty habit of opening up randomly, so I'll hold it close.'

The door to the elevator opened, and Declan and Monroe entered the car, Paul coming in last, pressing the button for the third floor. The space inside the car was tight, and there was a CCTV camera in the top left corner. Monroe stood there and, as the doors closed, his umbrella snapped open—

'Oh, bollocks,' he said, trying to close it, flailing around as the car started upwards.

Paul turned, trying to help close it—

Monroe quickly raised the umbrella, blocking the camera as Declan leant forwards, slamming Paul against the wall of the car, his extendable baton across Paul's throat, pressing the "LIFT STOP" button, feeling the car stop moving between the second and third floors with a sickening lurch.

'What are—' Paul croaked out before Declan exerted a little more pressure on his throat, halting him.

'Interesting thing about those cameras,' he said, nodding at the umbrella, currently blocking the car's CCTV view. 'They're cheap. Most of them have no audio. And, if you check building records, you can get an idea on which ones were built in. So, if you cover one, say with an umbrella, making it look like an accident on the video, the person watching genuinely has no idea what's actually going on. Are we trying to close it? Are we arguing about it? Or am I about to break your windpipe with a length of high-quality, hardened, extendable police baton, with a rather unforgiving steel shaft?'

'What do you want?' a weaker, more whispered response.

'You're going to send a message,' Declan said. 'To Francine, to Trisha, to both, either, I don't care. Tell them I'm not coming after them, and they don't need to worry about us trying to arrest them. That's a friendly message, isn't it?'

Paul looked confused, and Declan leant closer.

'I know she's alive, we saw the video footage. And I don't care. Because of one important thing. I'm – no, *we're* not the threat she should be worried about.'

'We know they're both in America, and they probably think they're safe, but they're forgetting a couple of things,' Monroe added from the corner of the car. 'First off, the MI5 agent they almost killed when freeing Karl Schnitter was my effectively adopted nephew, Tom Marlowe. And now, he's been blacklisted from the agency and has nothing to lose on anything he does.'

'And he wants revenge,' Declan said. 'It'd be terrible if he was told where Francine and Trisha currently were, wouldn't it? And then there's Karl himself, who, before handing himself into the CIA, actively tried to blow Francine up. Imagine how creative he could get if he was told where she was right now?'

'And remember, he's not with the CIA anymore,' Monroe grinned. 'They would have given him a nice new identity. One even Trisha Hawkins couldn't get. He could do it and nobody would ever know.'

'But how could this information get to them?' Declan asked. 'Oh, yes, another person she was blackmailing who not only runs a secret, black-bag *Star Chamber*, but is also now the Prime Minister. The two of them are really racking up the shit lists they're on.'

He pulled away, lowering the baton.

'We're not the enemy here, because we don't need to be,' he said. 'We don't need to end Francine and Trisha because someone else inevitably will. So, *tell* them this. In fact, tell them we're their only friends.'

'Because, laddie, if they come back to the UK and give themselves up, we might – and I emphasise *might* – be the only people who actually care if they survive,' Monroe finished. 'I'd also suggest, though, that you find a new line of work. Because between you and me right now? We're pretty pissed at you for trying to hurt one of us.'

To emphasise this, Declan kneed Paul viciously between the legs, letting him crumple to the ground as he pressed the "LIFT STOP" button a second time, allowing the car to continue up.

'We're watching you,' he said, stepping back as Monroe took down the umbrella. Now, anyone looking at the screen would just see the two of them standing back, allowing Paul to roll around on the floor, his knees almost up to his chin.

As the doors opened, two men stood waiting. The one thing they weren't expecting, however, was for Paul Stringer to be thrown at them, sending them all tumbling to the floor as Declan pressed the ground floor button.

'Good talk,' he said as the doors closed. 'Stay safe now.'

Now alone in the car, Declan looked at Monroe.

'Too far?'

'I think that may have been just far enough,' Monroe was securing his umbrella again. 'But I think we'll keep checking on this place, just to be sure.'

Declan's phone dinged. Pulling it out, he checked the message.

Going with Mina to the boxing ring for more stock.

'Jess is leaving the kitchen,' he said. 'That means nobody's monitoring Lewis right now.'

'Boxing ring?'

'Probably auto correct,' Declan shrugged.

'Then we'd better hurry then,' Monroe said as the doors to the reception opened, and the pair of them walked out, nodding to the open-mouthed receptionist as they did so. 'Because if someone lets him know we're on our way, he's gone.'

22

PENCIL DRAWINGS

ANJLI HAD BEEN SPOTTED BY JAKE, THE BOUNCER OF THE "Lucky" nightclub before she even saw him. It was almost lunchtime, and from the looks of things, the club was getting busy. It was more a gentlemen's club than dancing club, though, and Anjli assumed the doors never closed there. She'd heard rumours that the Tsangs owned the clubs around here, but after the gangland coups, and the subsequent land grabs that occurred a few months back, she no longer knew for sure the state of play in London.

Still, she wasn't here for the club, or the bouncer. And for the moment, if they were doing anything dodgy, it wasn't her problem.

'Morning,' she said, walking over. 'You have something for me?'

'Yeah,' Jake wasn't tall for a bouncer, but what he lost in height, he gained in girth, with shoulders that looked wider than the door he was currently guarding. 'See that guy over there? He reckons he saw the woman who gave Santa Mick the hat he was wearing.'

Anjli looked across the road; in the tabard of a BIG ISSUE seller, a middle-aged, scrawny man with wild hair stared nervously at her.

'Thanks,' Anjli nodded, walking across the street, watching the man pull back slightly, as if worried she was about to attack.

'I'm Anjli,' she said, deciding to keep this casual. 'What's your name?'

'Tick,' the man replied.

'You were christened "Tick?"' Anjli frowned.

The man, however just smiled.

'I like Tick, people call me Tick,' he continued, relaxing a little as he spoke. 'You're the copper looking for the woman, right?'

'I am,' Anjli nodded. 'But I'm confused how you saw her. We thought it was around Liverpool Street where Santa Mick got his hat?'

'Nah, that's because Mick sleeps near there,' Tick shook his head. 'He didn't get the new hat until around lunchtime on Sunday.'

'And you know this because?'

'Because I was there when she did it,' Tick smiled. 'About two streets away, near Soho Square.'

'We have a witness who said that Santa Mick claimed she was "an elf lady, spoke to me when she walked to work," before he then lost his temper,' Anjli read from her notes. 'We thought this meant he met her in the morning. You're saying it was later?'

'Yeah, the lady was definitely not a nine-to-fiver,' Tick replied. 'Not with what she was wearing.'

'You mean a nurse's uniform?'

Tick frowned, as if trying to explain it.

'Nah. It was kinda like a stage costume,' he said. 'Greens and reds and a pointy hat.'

'A Santa's elf costume?' Anjli felt a sliver of ice slide down her spine as she asked the question. If this was correct, then it was definitely "elf" and not "health" that had been said by Santa Mick on the Sunday before he died.

At it, though, Tick's eyes brightened.

'That's it exactly!' he smiled.

'And where was this?' Anjli asked. 'We know Mick would walk down Fleet Street—'

'Covent Garden,' Tick interrupted, his eagerness to tell the story overcoming his politeness in allowing Anjli to finish. 'Just south of the Jubilee Market. A lot of rough sleepers go there, some of the street performers help them out. He usually grabs a bacon roll there.'

'And you know this because?'

'It's one of my patches,' Tick puffed his chest out. 'Official and everything. I have a permit. I'm only here right now because Jake said to stay around for you.'

He leant in, whispering conspiratorially.

'I shouldn't be selling here, but I reckon you'd get me off if I get into trouble, right?'

Anjli smiled.

'Oh, I think something can be arranged.'

LEWIS WASN'T ALONE IN THE KITCHEN WHEN DECLAN AND Monroe arrived. They'd intended to stop by Anjli's location first, but the knowledge he was now unsupervised had sped up their pace, and now they were walking up from Oxford

Road, seeing the last of the morning queue being served by two other young helpers.

'Officers,' Lewis smiled, obviously unaware of their intent. 'Can I help?'

'Aye, you can,' Monroe nodded at the two helpers. 'Can they hold the fort while we have a wee chat with you?'

Lewis's smile faded as he realised this wasn't the cordial conversation he was expecting.

'Um, sure,' he said as he pulled his apron off, nodding to the girl closest to take his spot. This done, he walked out of the gazebo area and, with Monroe and Declan flanking him, walked across the street, out of earshot of the others.

'Shelly Garraway,' Monroe said, showing the photo they had of her, the pretty woman at the party. 'You know her?'

Lewis peered at the picture.

'I know Shelly, but she never looked like that. She was more ... wasted away,' he explained. 'What about her?'

'She's dead,' Monroe continued, his voice emotionless. 'Killed by the same poison that took the lives of Michael Siddell, or "Santa Mick", as he was known, and Arthur Drayson.'

'Why?' Lewis frowned. 'How was she connected?'

'Oh, she wasn't,' Declan spoke now. 'This was an accident. You see, she picked up the hat you tried to give Santa Mick, and she ran off with it. Wore it all night, and the toxins you smeared onto the inside of it killed her in the early hours of the morning.'

Lewis stared dumbly at Declan.

'Where did you get the hat from, Lewis?' Declan asked.

'I-I, that is, there was a shop, did five for three pounds—'

'And where did you get the contact poison from, Lewis?'

Monroe interrupted. 'Viscumin and batrachotoxin, mixed into some MSCO and wiped on the inside?'

'No, wait, you think I did this?' Lewis was bobbing his head from one face to the other.

'Well, you admitted you tried to give him a hat, but he said no,' Declan leant closer. 'A hat you lost when Shelly Garraway stole it and put it on. An act that later killed her.'

'No, wait, I couldn't ... why would I do such a thing?' Lewis was realising why both detectives were close now, hemmed in against a shop front.

'Oh, we think poor Shelly died because of an accident,' Monroe admitted. 'But Michael and Arthur? That was because of the Jacob Marley Society, and the fact they stole your money.'

'I was so stupid,' Declan hissed. 'You told me the first time we met. You said to me "Christ, they didn't even know if Mick was his real name." You said *they*, Lewis. *They* didn't know. Because *you* knew, didn't you? You knew when you told me this that Michael Siddell was Santa Mick.'

Lewis stared, wide-eyed at Declan, without moving a muscle for a good ten seconds.

And then he started to cry.

'I wanted him to die,' he said. 'Jesus, forgive me, but I wanted him to die.'

'It's alright,' Declan said soothingly, realising the man in front of him was close to a breakdown. 'Just tell us—'

'But I *didn't do it!*' Lewis looked up, tears streaming down his face. 'I didn't even know it was him until I was told!'

Declan frowned at this.

'Who told you his identity?' he asked.

'Mallory did!' Lewis wailed. 'She'd been talking to him, and he gave away something that revealed his true history!'

'But why would Mallory Reed care?' Monroe looked around now, checking they weren't being observed. 'I would have expected Mina Suvosky to say something, but Miss Reed—'

'You don't know, do you?' Lewis spoke suddenly, his voice calmer as his surprise took over. 'You don't know who she is, do you?'

'I'm thinking we don't, laddie,' Monroe growled. 'So why don't you start by explaining yourself?'

'YEAH, THAT'S HER,' TICK NODDED AS HE LOOKED AT THE IMAGE on the phone. They were now walking through Soho Square as they talked, and Tick passed the phone back. 'I mean, I can't see the face properly, but the costume's exact.'

Anjli looked at the image of the elf girl, taken from the South Bank Hotel CCTV. This was taken not long after Michael had met the same girl north of the Thames, but it was less than a mile's walk from the market to the hotel.

She could have done it in less than fifteen minutes.

'We can't see the face here,' she said as they reached Oxford Street. 'You might be the only person who could describe the woman to us.'

'Oh, I can do better than that,' Tick grinned, reaching into his BIG ISSUE bag. 'I drew her for you.'

'You drew her?'

'Yeah,' Tick looked at her, pausing his search. 'I was trained at the Royal Academy. Just because I rough sleep, don't mean I'm some kind of second-rate person.'

'I didn't mean that,' Anjli shook her head. 'I was just surprised, that's all.'

'Well, that's okay then,' Tick smiled as he returned to his rummaging. 'Here you go.'

The image was drawn on a sheet of printer paper, and looked like it'd been done in biro, but it was spectacular. It was a portrait, from the bust upwards, with the pointed green hat shaded but uncoloured, fading as it reached the top of the page.

The peroxide hair was pulled back, the neck tightly collared with a "Santa's Elf" tunic, but the face was perfectly clear. She wasn't smiling, like you would when having your painting done, nor was she aware she was even being drawn, the face caught from memory.

'It's not a great one,' Tick admitted, apologised, even. 'I only drew it after Jake mentioned you were looking for someone who could help, and it's from memory, so probably a little off. He lets me sell my copies outside the club sometimes. But it was a couple of days, and I think I got her, but I'm not a hundred percent correct.'

'Oh, you're a hundred percent here, alright,' Anjli said as she looked at the image.

'You sure? How can you tell?'

Anjli looked back up at Tick.

'Because I know her,' she said, folding the paper up and placing it in her jacket pocket. 'Come by the Unit tomorrow and we'll buy all the copies you have, while we take your statement.'

Tick nodded, more amazed he'd caught the likeness than at the potential money he'd make the following day, and carried on towards Tottenham Court Road as Anjli pulled out her phone. She needed to text Declan and Monroe. But then, at the same time, they were only a couple of minutes north of her right now, if they'd gone straight to Lewis Hoyle.

Throwing caution to the wind, she set off at a run up Rathbone Place, heading towards the last known location of the St Benedict's soup kitchen.

ESME COOPER WAS FLYING ON A CLOUD RIGHT NOW. MORTEN De'Geer was actually going to have a proper drink with her, and had expressed interest in her. This was further than she'd got in months, and there was every chance this was a Christmas miracle.

Right now, she was alone in the main office. She'd been working on research into the Cratchits, in particular the Bone Marrow Research company that had yet been unidentified. She'd put out a few requests, hoping someone on the HOLMES2 network could help, but it was actually another asset that brought the answer.

'Thought I'd find you here,' Chivalry Fitzwarren said as he entered the office. 'I seem to have lost my great-nephew and DC Davey.'

'How did you get in?' Cooper rose, confused. 'Did you just walk through reception?'

'Oh, was I supposed to go through reception?' Chivalry seemed surprised at this, and Cooper, unaware of any other entrances, frowned at him.

'I haven't heard from them either,' she said, deciding to ignore this, pointing at the spare computer she was working at. 'I'm trying to find a bone marrow expert.'

'Really?' Chivalry walked around, looking at it. 'BMR ...'

His face brightened.

'This is the Cratchit, isn't it!' he exclaimed joyously. 'Oh, you found him! Well done you!'

'Well, all we have is Brian, and Bone Marrow Research,' Cooper explained. But, as she went to continue, Chivalry laughed.

'It doesn't stand for that!' he exclaimed. 'Was that Colin telling you this? Bloody fool. BMR was his name. I remembered it because it's the same name as my son. Although my Bryan used a "Y" in it.'

'What did it stand for?' Cooper asked, not caring too much about the family history. 'We've been trying to work it out for an hour.'

'Oh, yes, sorry,' Chivalry nodded. 'It stands for Brian Matthew Reed.'

Cooper stared at him.

She then turned to the computer and started typing, staring at the screen.

'Boss!' she cried out.

A moment later, Bullman poked her head out of her office.

'What is it—' she started, seeing Chivalry standing there with a smile. 'Oh God. Shouldn't you be avoiding police stations? Doesn't lightning hit you in them?'

'You're mistaking that with churches,' Chivalry gave a nod.

'Boss, Mister Fitzwarren just gave us the third Cratchit's name,' Esme said excitedly. 'It's—'

'BRIAN REED? THE THIRD CRATCHIT WAS MALLORY REED'S older brother?' Declan stared in shock at Lewis. 'Seriously?'

Lewis nodded.

'I didn't know until later, but she'd sought me out,' he

explained. 'Her brother had failed in his research without any funding and had died a few years later. She wanted to launch some kind of civil suit or something, but it never came to pass. And then she stopped working at the soup kitchen and I kind of forgot about it.'

'You didn't tell us *you* had a connection to Michael Siddell, and you didn't tell us *she* had one either?' Monroe was almost apoplectic with rage right now.

'I knew if you learnt of my connection, I'd be a suspect, especially as I saw him right before his death,' Lewis whined. 'And if I couldn't tell you that, how the hell was I supposed to tell you about Mallory?'

Monroe was about to respond to this, possibly even with the use of the umbrella, when a faint shout of his name could be heard, and Monroe looked down the road to see Anjli running towards them, a sheet of A4 paper in her hand.

'You okay, lassie?' he asked.

'I have a sketch of the woman who gave Santa Mick his new hat, and who doctored Arthur Drayson's hat shortly afterwards,' she said, slowing down and gathering her breath. 'It was elf, not health.'

'Was it Mallory Reed?' Declan asked, looking back at Lewis. 'Because our friend here just told us she's the younger sister of Brian Reed, the Cratchit who was trying to cure his cancer.'

'And she wanted to sue Michael Siddell a few years back, so it makes sense she would want to kill him,' Monroe added.

Anjli, however, shook her head, showing the sketch.

'It's not Mallory Reed,' she said as the three men facing her stared down at it. 'I might not have an eye for art, but even I can make that out,'

'Ah, shite,' Monroe looked at Declan. 'That's Mina Suvosky.'

Declan glanced back to the kitchen, his stomach flip-flopping.

'What time did they leave?' he whispered.

'What?' Lewis frowned. 'Leave where?'

'*What time did Jess and Mina leave the kitchen?*' Declan shouted, looking back at him.

'About twenty minutes back,' Lewis replied, his face whitening as he realised the importance of what Declan was saying. 'Mina had been here since breakfast, but she had a phone call from Father Franks. He was very unhappy. I couldn't hear the words, but he was shouting down the phone. Mina spoke to your daughter after she disconnected, and then they both left. Didn't say a bloody thing.'

Declan pulled out his phone, dialling Jess's number. After a single click, the phone went to voicemail, a sure sign it was away from a signal or underground.

'Declan, she'll be alright,' Monroe reassured. 'She's faced down the worst we've gone up against. And she's a good fighter.'

Declan stepped away from the group, looking around the street.

'Boxing ring,' he said. 'She didn't say it by accident. It was a joke. Father Corden. She's going to the church in Hampstead.'

He looked back at Lewis.

'Is Father Franks involved in this?'

'God no!'

'Could he be *unintentionally* involved?'

Lewis frowned, and then silently nodded.

'You're coming with us, and you can tell me all about it in

the car,' Declan said. 'Until I know for a fact you're innocent, you're glued to my side.'

'What do you want me to do?' Anjli asked, but it was Monroe that answered.

'Get the word out,' he said. 'To everyone. Get to Hampstead, and fast. And find Mallory Reed because I'm buggered if she's not involved somehow. And find out about this McNarry fellow who brought young Mina up, because I'm starting to think this is a very long-term plan here.'

23

ARMED CLOSURE

BILLY'S PLAN HAD SURPRISINGLY WORKED; AFTER TEN MINUTES inside, Pablo Restrepo had left the embassy by the back entrance and walked south, observing for anyone following.

Billy had been in the entrance to a building down the road, half hidden behind a Georgian column as he watched the man leave. While Davey had been the visible one out front, he'd spent the last hour merging into his surroundings in an attempt to not be seen. He wasn't an expert in tactical reconnaissance or anything, but he was an expert in what Andrade Estrada looked like, and so he hung back, allowing Restrepo to disappear from sight.

A second later, another shadowed figure peeled away from the entrance to a closer building, following. He had a hooded jumper on, and this covered his face, but the clothing was Billy's, which meant it had to be Andrade, having changed clothes before running from the house.

The game of cat and mouse had carried on after that. Andrade wasn't bothered about anyone following him, instead focusing wholly on Restrepo, who seemed confident he was alone, and headed towards Green Park, taking the smaller cut-off roads and passages, in case a car had somehow followed.

Andrade, however, seemed to have an almost psychic connection where Restrepo was going, and frequently had walked in other directions, almost finding ways to get ahead of his one-time boss, so Restrepo didn't realise his tailer was actually guessing his moves before he did.

But eventually, after around twenty minutes of feints, double-backs and strange directional choices, Pablo Restrepo must have entered the opulent entrance of the Sheraton Grand Hotel on Park Lane, as this was where Andrade stopped, as if trying to work out what to do next.

Billy knew what to do next.

'Worried about the cost of the place?' he asked, walking up behind Andrade. 'Don't worry. I can cover it.'

Andrade spun around, his hand in the pocket of his hoodie now pointing something at Billy in an automatic reaction, but his expression of surprise and the relaxing of whatever was in the pocket showed Billy that currently, he was safe.

'What are you doing here?' he asked incredulously.

'Looking for Carlos Pascal, same as you,' Billy replied.

However, at this, Andrade shook his head.

'You might look for Carlos too, but it's not the same,' he said carefully. 'Because I mean to kill him.'

'How about you don't do that, and allow us to clear your name and get you out from under his thumb?' Davey said, walking up from the Green Park end of the street. She'd been following Billy on a tracker he'd placed on his own phone, and now both of them stood on either side of Andrade. 'Or we could just arrest you right now and clear the whole thing up for Billy.'

'You don't understand,' Andrade moaned, but Billy stood his ground.

'Then explain it,' he said. 'Because currently all we have is you working for Los Lideres and Carlos Pascal since you were a kid, and Pablo Restrepo being his cousin.'

'There's more to it than that,' Andrade nodded.

'So, let's fix it,' Billy smiled. 'Without the gunplay.'

He looked at Davey.

'Did you call in the favour?' he asked.

Davey nodded, checking her watch.

'Andrews will be here in five,' she said. 'We should get things moving.'

'Who is Andrews?' Andrade frowned.

'Specialist Firearms Officer, SCO19,' Davey smiled. 'He's our backup for when this goes wrong.'

She nodded to the doorman, who had been staring at the three mis-matched people standing in front of him for a few seconds now.

'You might want to tiptoe people out of the lobby,' she said, waving her warrant card at him. 'You're about to have a lot of weapons and diplomatic incidents happening at once.'

THE DUTY MANAGER OF THE SHERATON GRAND HADN'T BEEN expecting such a circus for a weekday morning, and stared in almost horror as the SCO19 armed police unit, comprising five men and women, walked through the main entrance, led by SFO Andrews, nodding at Billy as he approached.

'You intending to get shot again?' he asked, and Billy

knew this was a comment relating to a simunition exercise they'd been on a year earlier, where Billy, playing a terrorist was taken down by Andrews and his men before letting off a single shot. But before Billy could reply, SFO Andrews was already looking at Davey.

'Your boss here?' he asked, and Billy could sense a little trepidation in his voice. 'She still has one of my guns. And my guys won't work with her while she still has those little 3D kill trophies she made up.'

'Doctor Marcos isn't my boss anymore,' Davey smiled. 'And I think the trophies were just to put you off your game.'

'No,' Billy corrected. 'She has them around her computer screen. She's still proud of them.'

He looked back at the duty manager.

'You're sure it's the sixth floor?' he asked.

The duty manager nodded, and Billy looked at the armed officers.

'We're hoping this will be easy, but if not—'

'Come in and save your arses again, like we did at Devington House,' SFO Andrews grinned.

'I seem to recall I had to stop you entering and shooting everyone,' Billy frowned.

'We beg to differ,' SFO Andrews winked. 'Who's the hoodie?'

'Andrade Estrada,' Billy explained. 'He's our bait.'

'Well, he can give me his gun,' SFO Andrews held out his hand. Andrade was surprised they had seen it, but agreed, pulling out a snub-nosed revolver and handing it across.

'You have a licence for this?' SFO Andrews asked as he opened it up, emptying the chambers.

'Diplomatic immunity,' Andrade smiled.

'That's fine then,' SFO Andrews passed the bullets to

someone behind him. 'You can have the ammunition back when we're done.'

Another officer had checked Andrade while SFO Andrews had done this.

'He's clean,' she said. 'No more bullets.'

'Good, then the worst you can do is throw this at someone,' SFO Andrews finished as he passed the now empty gun back to Andrade. 'Here. In case you need it for show.'

He looked at Davey again.

'And we contacted the Ambassador, as per your request,' he said. 'If this goes wrong, a lot of people might lose their jobs.'

'Well, let's do it right, then,' Davey looked at Billy. 'Detective Constable Fitzwarren, if you will?'

'Thank you, Detective Constable Davey,' Billy smiled. 'Let's do this.'

ROOM 645 WAS A MID-CORRIDOR ROOM, AND LOOKED NO different to the ones along the corridor beside it, but that was the whole point. If you were hiding someone, you didn't make it easy for everyone to find them.

Billy motioned to Andrade to stand to the side, out of immediate view, and then banged on the door.

'*Carlos! Pablo! Room service!*' he shouted out. 'Open the door before I have security smash it in!'

There was a muffled argument from within the room, a sound of a bolt, probably the hinge at the top of the door that stopped opening being pulled back, and the door opened a slit to show Pablo Restrepo glaring balefully at them.

'You are interrupting Colombian diplomatic work,' he snarled. 'You need to leave now—'

He stopped as Andrade rolled around the door, gun aimed at his face.

'Back away now,' he said, cocking the empty gun, and likely hoping Restrepo's shock would overcome his inbuilt spy ability to realise the weapon was empty.

Billy didn't want to risk it, and pushed the door open, moving Restrepo back as he led his companions into the room, where, standing behind the bed and with his own weapon held up, was Carlos Pascal, shirtless, and with a bandage wrapped around his torso.

'Put the guns down, we're here to talk,' Billy said, his hands in the air. 'You need this over, and we need this over.'

'You bring a killer into my room—' Restrepo started, but Andrade stepped past Billy, ramming the gun under the older man's chin.

'Go on,' he hissed. 'Call me a killer again.'

'Guys!' Billy shouted again. 'Back up! All I want are some answers!'

The three men stopped, staring at him.

'Look, I know Andrade worked for you,' Billy continued, looking at Carlos. 'I know you're Pablo's cousin. What I can't work out is why you killed José. What did he know?'

Carlos looked at Andrade.

'You didn't tell?'

'Nobody would believe me,' Andrade replied, before turning to face Billy. 'José was ambitious, I already said this. And he started working for Los Lideres when he realised he wouldn't get higher. What I didn't mention was he left after he learnt of my connection to them.'

'Did you leave Los Lideres?' Billy asked, already knowing the answer.

'I'm sorry, Billy, but no,' Andrade admitted. 'They are my family. But I didn't want to do what they asked me to do anymore. I wanted to leave the family, leave the embassy, and be with you.'

'This doesn't feel that much like that,' Billy admitted.

'That's because he said no,' Andrade pointed at Restrepo. 'He wanted me to continue, as my next posting was back in Madrid, as he had plans to build shipping routes for Los Lideres there. I'd had an argument, said I would not follow his orders anymore.'

'This was a week ago, right?' Davey said. 'You told our colleagues there was a fight.'

Restrepo nodded at this.

'Ungrateful bastard wanted out,' he growled at Andrade. 'After what we did for him. I called my cousin. Told him to come talk sense into his boy.'

'I'm not his boy,' Andrade hissed.

'Let me guess,' Billy said. 'You turned up, but Andrade wasn't here, because he knew this was what you'd do, and he went off grid.'

'I bought a camera,' Andrade admitted. 'One of those Ring ones, which tells you on your phone when someone arrives. Motion detected, battery operated, connects to the Wi-Fi. I set it up and ran. About three, four days later, it pings, showing me Carlos in my apartment, looking around, checking mail. I realised then I wasn't getting out. He put something on the mantlepiece, but I couldn't see what it was, as the camera I had didn't move. And then he left.'

'But then José arrived,' Davey stepped forward now. 'He had his own key from when he was there, and he broke back in, looking for something he'd hidden before he was removed, something he hadn't had time to pick up.'

Andrade nodded.

'My camera picked him up too, and I realised I had to tell him, warn him he was likely to be grabbed by Carlos. But when I got there, it was too late.'

'Because Carlos had left his own motion detector,' Billy looked across at the injured man. 'One that would let you know if someone turned up. You had a hit, thought it was Andrade, but when you found José, who worked for your rivals, it was Christmas.'

'I thought he was there to kill Andrade, but after questioning him—'

'Torturing, you mean,' Davey snapped. 'We saw the injuries. The blood.'

'Whatever,' Carlos shrugged. 'After I gained my answers, I realised he was looking for money he'd hidden there. And after learning there was treasure secreted in the apartment, I decided I should be paid for what I was doing. But then the Boy Scout arrived.'

'I tried to stop the killing, but I was too late,' Andrade explained. 'José was dead in the bath. I got his blood on me when I checked. But then Carlos grabbed me, saying I needed to be punished for going against Los Lideres, and in the struggle I cut him along his ribs with his own knife, and got away.'

'Breaking your watch strap in the process,' Davey nodded with comprehension now.

'I grabbed the camera and ran,' Andrade looked to the floor now.

'Why the camera?'

'Because anyone watching the footage would see me there,' Andrade shrugged. 'No camera, no footage.'

'Who did you call on the phone?' Billy now asked. 'When you headed towards Bond Street?'

Andrade, finally realising Billy knew more than he'd expected, slumped.

'Pablo,' he said. 'I wanted him to know what his cousin had done. By then, though, he'd already learnt from Carlos.'

'And they pinned the murder on you,' Davey said, looking back at Andrade. 'Do you still have the Ring camera, and the footage?'

'I do,' Andrade replied. 'But it's inadmissible, because—'

'Because it's on embassy property,' Restrepo smiled now. 'So, as I said before, this is something the Colombians will fix. Let us take Andrade into our custody, and we will ensure he gets excellent treatment for—'

He didn't finish, as Andrade screamed, launching himself at the embassy's head of security. As they went down, Billy dove in also, pulling them apart.

Restrepo, however, had picked up the snub-nosed revolver. He went to fire it at Andrade, but paused, testing the weight before laughing.

'Empty?' he chuckled. 'You threaten me with an empty gun?'

He looked back at Carlos.

'Shoot them,' he smiled.

'I wouldn't do that,' an unfamiliar voice spoke, and Chivalry Fitzwarren walked around the still-open hotel room door. 'It'll just hurt your case more.'

Restrepo stared in a mixture of surprise and horror at the older man, an expression that grew even more when another suited man walked around with him. He was in his sixties, his white hair and beard cropped short against his olive skin.

'You know the Colombian Ambassador, I'm guessing?' Chivalry smiled. 'He's an old friend. We were just having a chat out there, in the corridor, when we heard noises. We were going to interrupt, but then we didn't, and we just, well, stood and listened to everything you said.'

Carlos raised his gun, but Chivalry raised his own Webley, aiming at Carlos as he waggled his finger.

'Uh-uh,' he said. 'You see, we weren't the only ones who heard. Come in, chaps.'

At this, SFO Andrews and his team burst into the room, screaming, rifles raised.

'Drop the gun!'

'Get on the ground now!'

As Restrepo and Carlos reluctantly complied, Restrepo glared up at Andrade.

'You're a dead man,' he hissed as he was pulled to his feet by SCO19 officers and dragged out of the room, Carlos behind him.

Billy looked at Andrade, watching his two one-time mentors with a mixture of sadness and shame.

'You okay?' he asked.

'Not really,' Andrade replied. 'But I will be.'

'Good,' Billy replied, pulling out his handcuffs. 'Because, Andrade Estrada, I'm placing you under arrest.'

24

CHURCH CONFESSION

FATHER FRANKS WAS PACING IN THE NAVE OF HIS CHURCH WHEN Jess and Mina arrived through the main doors.

'Is everything okay?' Mina asked as she walked over to him, making a cross and curtsying as she approached the altar.

'Is everything okay?' Father Franks was shaking his head now. 'No, Mina. It's very much not okay. I spoke to Father McNarry.'

Mina paused as she approached now.

'You did?'

'I did,' Father Franks nodded slowly. 'You see, the police had contacted him. Probably her dad.'

He aimed this part at Jess.

'He wanted to know why he was being asked about you and me, in connection to a murder of a man he didn't know.'

'Sorry,' Jess didn't know what else to say.

'Oh, no, I should thank you,' Father Franks smiled across the church at her. 'He hasn't been replying to my messages.

He's been working in communities off the grid. Has been for months.'

He now looked back at Mina, who stood beside the altar.

'That's what you were hoping for, weren't you?'

'I don't understand,' Mina frowned. 'Have I done something wrong? Are you unhappy with me?'

Jess felt a buzz in her jacket. Pulling out her phone, she realised she'd had three missed calls from her dad, likely from when she was out of range on the London Underground, and one very worrying text message had just arrived from him.

Mina's the killer.

'Yes, I'm bloody well unhappy!' Father Franks shouted. 'What have you got me into? I get Father McNarry calling, and when I mention you, he's clueless! Seems he didn't email me, telling me to bring you in after all! Seems he actively barred you from his services, because he found you were mentally unstable when it came to talk of exorcisms! You were more of a zealot than he was!'

'Demons exist! They exist and we need to stop them!'

'With holy water?'

'Yes!'

'And what about this?' Father Franks pulled out another bottle now; it was a pink, steel water carrier, probably half a litre in size. 'I smelt it, Mina. It's not water, it's not spirits, it's something with garlic. Is this what you fed them?'

'You went through my things?'

'*You lied to me!*' Father Franks cried out, arms extended. 'You don't want to be a nun! Father McNarry told me the nuns said you'd be unsuitable! But your written English isn't that good, so who sent the email for you? Tell me, who's working with you as you kill these people—'

There was a sickening *crunch* as Mina, grabbing a golden cross from the altar, swung it like a mace, catching Father Franks in the side of the head, sending him to the ground in a pool of his own blood.

'*Shut up!*' Mina cried at the unconscious body. '*Shut up!* You don't understand!'

'Understand what, Mina?' Jess asked carefully, backing away from the altar.

'That some people have to die so that others can live,' another voice, a woman's voice replied, and Jess turned to face a new entrant, a young woman, a familiar one in hooded Barbour coat, dark-brown hair and pale-grey glasses.

'Mallory Reed,' Jess said.

'You must be his daughter,' Mallory smiled. 'I can see the resemblance. Please, take a seat. I need to calm Mina down, and I could do with your help.'

'You killed them?' Jess stepped back, confused.

'Don't be silly!' Mallory exclaimed, almost horrified at the suggestion. 'I didn't kill anyone! *She* killed them. *She* exorcised the demons.'

Mallory shrugged, a little bashfully at the next admittance.

'I just gave her the means to do it.'

'SHE TOLD ME,' ANJLI GROWLED AS SHE SAT IN THE BACK OF THE police squad car as it hurtled towards Hampstead, lights flashing, siren blaring. She sat next to Declan in the back, Lewis wedged between them, while Monroe sat in the front, next to Cooper, driving at breakneck speeds through the London streets. 'Well, she as good as did.'

'How?' Declan asked.

'When she told me about Lewis here giving Shelly the hat,' Anjli looked out of the window, clenching and unclenching her fist. 'There's no way she could have known about the poison, unless she knew what the plan was with the first hat.'

'I didn't know the plan with the hat!' Lewis moaned.

'But Mina did, right?' Declan asked, shuffling a little more towards the door to gain some space, before falling back onto Lewis as the car screeched around a right-hand turn. 'She had to if you're innocent.'

'Yes,' Lewis nodded, like a drowning man reaching for anything to keep him afloat. 'She saw the hats when I arrived. I'd been bringing them each day in case I'd see him. When I saw him in the queue, I grabbed one.'

He shook his head, pursing his lips as he considered this.

'Before I did that though, she was buggering around behind me, for maybe twenty seconds?'

'More than enough time to wipe something onto the hat,' Monroe said from the front. 'Did she have gloves on?'

'Yeah, marigolds,' Lewis nodded. 'The new people do. It's a way to make sure they don't—'

He stopped.

'Get infected by the nasty homeless people?' Anjli raised an eyebrow. 'Was that what you were about to say?'

'She took them off,' Lewis said instead. 'She was wearing them, but she wasn't later on.'

'She may have got some liquid on them, and didn't want to either get any on herself or contaminate anyone else,'

Monroe suggested. 'It was probably backup in case Michael Siddell had lost the hat she gave him a few hours earlier.'

'When did Mallory Reed tell you who she was?' Declan asked.

'I think it was a few years back,' Lewis scrunched his face up as he tried to remember. 'I never met her at the start, I met her brother for literally a heartbeat in 2007, and then the funding didn't happen, and we couldn't start. That's when I went to the seminary.'

'What changed your mind?'

'God,' Lewis looked at Declan, and for the first time, Declan saw peace in the man's eyes. 'I was in the same class as Gary – Father Franks, that is. He told me how he'd turned to God after failing his previous mentor, Valentin Suvosky, and when I learnt I'd met that same man in 2007, and that he too had been lost by the theft of the money, I realised this was a message, telling me that St Benedict's was my future. I mean, what were the chances of meeting someone from the exact same problem that caused my decision?'

'Stranger things have happened, I suppose,' Declan replied. 'So, you returned to St Benedict's what, a year? Two years later?'

'A year, 2009,' Lewis nodded. 'The other partners had tried to continue, but they were struggling. I'd been the—bloody hell!'

The last part had been as Cooper slid between two lorries, her hand hammering on the horn as she screamed obscenities at them.

'Sorry, I, um, I was a catalyst for change,' Lewis trembled. 'Mallory turned up a couple of years later, part of her University degree, but as time went on she kept asking me about the beginnings of the food kitchen, saying she'd heard rumours of the Marley Society screwing us over. I thought nothing of it, assumed she was looking for gossip. I didn't know it was her brother who was scammed as well.'

'Was he dead by then?'

'No, but he was sick. She looked after him ... look I'm sorry, I assumed she'd told you all this. In 2013, she tried to convince me to sort out a class action suit against the surviving members, saying she reckoned she could get the other two families involved, still not saying she was one of them. She was way more into this than I was. I asked Gary what he thought, as he had connections to the Suvoskys, but he said they'd had issues of their own, with the mum being ill. I said I wasn't interested, and a week or so later Mallory stopped attending kitchens.'

He sighed.

'She would come by now and then, and she was talking a lot with some of the rough sleepers. In hindsight, she must have known Siddell was Santa Mick, because she spent a lot of time with him, but his mind was burnt out by then. She probably couldn't tell for sure.'

'And then Mina appeared.'

'A few weeks back,' Lewis nodded. 'Look, she's a good kid. Misguided, but good. I don't think—'

He stopped as Declan held a hand up.

'Hold that thought,' he said, watching Cooper as she spoke into her radio. 'What's going on?'

Monroe looked back at the three on the seat.

'Bullman,' he said. 'Just had Father McNarry call her. Seems he had no idea Mina was in the country, and hadn't sent Father Franks any emails.'

'No, that can't be right,' Lewis shook his head. 'Gary wouldn't do anything like this.'

'My daughter's in his church right now,' Declan growled. 'For your sake, I hope you're right.'

He looked out of the window; they were getting close now.

'Turn the sirens off,' he said to Cooper, who did so automatically. 'I don't want them knowing we're coming.'

'Laddie, the chances are we're not the only ones heading there right now,' Monroe replied.

'I know,' Declan nodded. 'But I reckon we'll be there first, and any advantage we can get helps Jess.'

JESS SAT ON THE FRONT ROW PEW, STARING DOWN AT FATHER Franks.

'He should be in a hospital,' she said. 'That's a vicious wound.'

'It's just a cut, he'll get over it,' Mallory snapped. 'It's not like Mina's father or my brother.'

Jess said nothing; she'd had Mallory ranting about her brother for the last couple of minutes, and had worked out exactly who she was in the grand scheme of things.

'How did you make the poison?' she asked. 'My ... I mean, the Unit's divisional surgeon took ages to work it out.'

'My brother,' Mallory seemed to relax a little as she spoke. 'He was researching into viscumin as an option against bone marrow cancer, and he used MSCO to help get his mixtures into his body.'

'He tested on himself?'

'Who was he supposed to test on?' Mallory snapped, now angry again. 'He didn't get the grant!'

'Look, Miss Reed, I'm sorry, but you can't keep using that

as an excuse,' Jess folded her arms now, glowering at the woman. 'The amount he would have gained was somewhere around fifty grand. For the sort of research he needed, you had to be looking at hundreds of thousands in funding, if not millions.'

Mina, sitting on the raised step of the altar, head in her hands, was staring down at Father Franks, as well.

'He's a good man,' she muttered. 'I shouldn't have done that.'

'You needed to,' Mallory replied, looking back at her. 'He would have stopped everything.'

'Stopped what?' Jess asked. 'You've killed Michael. You've killed Arthur—'

'Colin Walters,' Mallory hissed. 'He didn't fight for us.'

'He offered to pay back the stolen money.'

'For next year!' Mallory snapped, straightening as she half-shouted the response. 'Not for us! He was soothing his ego, and next year's candidate would get double the money for doing nothing! Is that fair?'

She looked at Mina now.

'Is that fair, Mina?' she cooed. 'Is that fair to your father? Your poor, dead father, killed by these bastards?'

'Father Franks is a good man,' Mina looked up defiantly. 'I shouldn't have done that.'

Mallory sighed loudly, finally looking at Father Franks.

'Mina, find a first aid kit. You're right. It's not his fault McNarry came back early.'

As Mina ran off to find something, Mallory turned her attention back to Jess.

'It was the first pebble, anyway,' she said. 'The money my brother would have got when he won.'

Jess ignored the *when* rather than *if* spoken by Mallory.

She'd already decided she was the wronged party; there was no way she'd admit someone else could have won.

'Pebble?'

'Yes, a pebble. He needed money, so he had to start small. *"An avalanche starts with one pebble. A forest with one seed. And it takes one word to make the whole world stop and listen. All you need is the right one."* Forty, fifty grand was a sizeable chunk to raise awareness. That would have led to bigger things.'

'Let me guess, that's from Confucius or something?' Jess wasn't impressed by the quote.

'Jay Kristoff, actually, from his novel, *Endsinger*,' Mallory replied. 'You should try it sometime.'

'Well, you didn't find one word. You found a *murder*,' Jess shook her head. 'Three murders, in fact. Possibly four if Father Franks isn't helped.'

She nodded to the door Mina had recently left through.

'And one of them seems to be a mistake, because your weapon out there was a little too gung-ho about giving your toxins to people.'

'That's not my fault!' Mallory cried out. 'Things were already in motion. I wanted to stop it, I really did!'

'Ah,' Jess smiled now, leaning back on the pew. 'In that case, *"the avalanche has already started. It is too late for the pebbles to vote."* Like that? Ambassador Kosh, *Babylon 5*. I'm watching the first series with my girlfriend at the moment. I think it's pretty apt, don't you?'

Her expression darkened.

'And you don't get to play the victim, seconds after you admit there's still someone you want to kill.'

'What do you know?' Mallory mocked. 'You're a child.'

'I'm the same age as Mina,' Jess folded her arms. 'And yet you're quite happy to use her.'

Before Mallory could reply, Mina walked back into the room, pale faced.

'Did I do this?' she asked, now crouching beside Father Franks, waving some smelling salts under his nose. 'I did what you told me to do. I exorcised the demons and allowed the tortured souls to go to Heaven. Did I do wrong?'

'Is Father Franks a demon?' Jess rose now.

'Of course not!' Mina shook her head. 'He's been nothing but kind to me!'

'And yet you tried to kill him with that cross,' Jess said, pointing at the discarded and bloody cross on the floor. 'Are *you* the demon?'

This thought had obviously never occurred to Mina, and she staggered back, staring at her bloodied hands as, groaning, the now conscious Father Franks weakly tried to sit up.

'Shut up,' Mallory hissed. 'You're confusing her.'

'No, it was you,' Father Franks muttered weakly. 'I should never have given you her details. I didn't know what evil you planned.'

He winced, clutching at his head.

'You got to him, too,' Jess said, looking from Father Franks to Mallory, who shrugged.

'I met the Father when he took over this place,' she said, waving a magnanimous hand around the Nave. 'Lewis told me he was a friend of the third Cratchit, so I told him my story. Said I was looking for closure, asked if I could speak to Mina. He gave me Father McNarry's details and suggested I called, but instead I hopped on a plane and visited the church over there.'

'You poisoned her mind,' Father Franks croaked.

'I didn't need to do anything of the kind,' Mallory actually laughed at this. 'McNarry was bonkers. Believed he was a bloody exorcist, like in the movies. It was so easy to convince him of my good intentions and the evils out there. And, as he did whatever mad old priests do in the middle of nowhere, I worked on Mina. I groomed her, I suppose.'

'But if you had her kill them, why go see Michael Siddell?' Jess shook her head. 'If you hadn't done that, we might never have found you.'

'Oh, you would have,' Mallory shook her own head in response. 'I wanted to get ahead of the curve. By giving a tincture, one of my brothers own recipes, I got to be an early suspect, and then get myself removed from the list. And it meant I could chat to them again tonight and aim them square at Lewis.'

She walked over to the altar now, relaxing as she looked over at Mina.

'Yeah, he's probably in a squad car now, being taken to a station,' she said. 'But if I'm honest, really honest? I saw Michael Siddell in his last hours because I wanted to watch the bastard die. Horribly. Shitting his pants and knowing it was me that did it.'

She stopped, staring up at the statue of Jesus above the altar.

'But the senile bastard had the last laugh,' she whispered. 'His burnt-out brain didn't even recognise me. I gave up on him, walked off. It wasn't justice. He didn't deserve to die in the company of someone else.'

'You seem to have forgotten one thing, though,' Jess said, her voice quavering a little. 'Lewis might be suspect number one, but what about me and Father Franks here? The moment we tell the police what you've said, they'll be after you.'

'True,' Mallory smiled as she bent over and picked up the

stainless-steel bottle, the one Father Franks had held in his hand when he first confronted them, now turning back to Jess as she opened the bottle's lid. 'Unless the death count rises. A smear on the forehead kills in hours. I wonder how fast you die when you drink the whole damned thing?'

25

MEDICINE GO DOWN

MALLORY STOPPED AS, IN THE DISTANCE, THEY COULD HEAR THE first of several police car sirens approaching.

'You called the police on us?' she hissed at Jess, who shrugged.

'No,' she replied calmly, 'but that was mainly because I didn't need to. My dad's an awesome detective, and I knew he'd work out the truth, especially when he saw I'd returned to Hampstead.'

She looked at Mina, now cleaning Father Franks' wounds. Father Franks, however, wasn't happy with this state of affairs, and kept weakly batting her hands away as he tried to keep her from him.

'I always knew there was something wrong with you,' she explained. 'Not *wrong* wrong, but there was something off. You weren't telling us the whole story. And because of that, I decided to keep an eye on you. I hoped you'd give up a clue or something, not give me all of this.'

'This wasn't supposed to happen,' Mina muttered. 'She said the demons would go, that we would free them.'

'Yeah, probably best not to listen to the crazy person over there,' Jess couldn't help the smile that appeared on her face. However, all it seemed to do was anger Mallory, who held up the bottle.

'Well, you've just volunteered to drink this first,' she growled, approaching Jess, who brought her hands up, moving into a fighting stance.

'Just try it, bitch,' she hissed back, but her voice wavered, nervous as to what would happen. But before Mallory could continue, there was a flurry of movement at the back of the church.

'That's probably not the best of ideas,' Declan said as he walked out from the shadows of the Nave. 'I hear there's a strong taste of garlic in it, and I only like that in butter.'

If Jess was relieved to see her father, she kept it quiet as she stepped back, watching Mallory like a hawk.

'How long have you been there?' Mallory asked.

'Not long,' Monroe now spoke, appearing from the other side of the church. 'Give up, lassie. You're surrounded.'

He listened as the sirens grew even louder.

'And it's just getting worse for you,' he finished.

'I locked the door behind me as I entered, so there's no way—'

Mallory stopped, glowering at Mina.

'You! You did this!'

Mina didn't reply, instead staring at the ground quietly.

'She let us in when she was looking for the first aid kit, yes,' Declan said. 'She saw us approaching the back door and, unlike you, she's not too far gone to realise she's done a terrible thing.'

'Righteous vengeance isn't a bad thing,' Mallory snapped.

'Either way, it's time to put the bottle down and come in,' Declan continued, stepping forward.

At this, though, Mallory raised the bottle to her lips threateningly, halting him.

'Don't come any closer!' she shouted, her voice echoing around the Nave. 'You don't know anything about what happened!'

'I think I do,' Declan replied softly, looking over at Jess. 'Based on what I've just heard, and what we worked out on the way here.'

Mallory stared silently at Declan, and he took this as a tacit offer to continue.

'We know you were the younger sister of Brian Reed, who needed money for his cancer research,' he started. 'Unfortunately, Michael Siddell took that money and ran back in 2007.'

'It was Brian's money,' Mallory growled. 'He needed it.'

'But he was never going to get it,' Monroe said, nodding at the side door, where Lewis Hoyle now stood silently. 'Unfortunately, your brother would never win the money. The fifty thousand in prize money was destined to go to Saint Benedict's.'

'Is this true?' Mallory glanced at Lewis, who shrugged.

'We'll never know,' he replied.

'You didn't know,' Anjli spoke now, walking in from the other side of the church, effectively surrounding Mallory. 'But still, you were annoyed on his behalf, even if he'd just given in and carried on, so you started looking into lawsuits to find out if there was any way you could get back at the Marley Society for what they did.'

'You needed allies if you were going to do this, though,' Declan said now. 'You found out about St Benedict's and

Valentin Suvosky. A couple of years had passed now, and your brother's work hadn't progressed as far as you hoped. A class action suit of some kind, for the money you believed owed to him, would help a lot. And so, you took on volunteer work at Saint Benedict's, hoping to get to know the people who were involved, and see if their stories matched with your brother's.'

Mallory nodded.

'I learnt Lewis was the man who'd originally gone for the grant, so I tried to get in close, but slowly, so as not to spook him.'

'And how did that work out for you?' Monroe asked sadly.

'Not well,' Mallory admitted. 'I worked with him for years, building up the courage to ask them to join me. By then I'd already found out Valentin had committed suicide, and Lewis was my only choice.'

'But then Lewis mentioned another person,' Declan looked at Father Franks, sitting on the floor still, reluctantly being attended to by Mina. 'Gary Franks, who Lewis met in his brief change of careers, during his attempt to become a priest.'

He looked over at Lewis now, shifting uncomfortably by the door.

'You ask Father Franks for his thoughts on this, and he passes the buck to Mina, the surviving daughter. But now the problem was that nobody knew where Michael Siddell was. He disappeared right after the crash, and as far as anybody knew, he was dead.'

'But you didn't care, lassie,' Monroe said as he watched Mallory carefully. 'You wanted revenge and, after your brother passed on, you planned something worse.'

'It's no secret that your brother was working on ways of

curing cancer and it probably worked the same way as chemotherapy,' Declan explained. 'What he was looking at to kill the cancer would cause him physical problems as well. Perhaps he was looking at mistletoe, or the viscumin inside it, maybe batrachotoxins. Either way, when he died, you realised that you could use it in your revenge.'

'But around now you met Michael Siddell again,' Anjli had reached Jess now, moving her behind. 'But you didn't know it was Michael, as he was calling himself Santa Mick at the time, and looked completely different. You'd got to know him as you'd been looking to help rough sleepers, but there must have been a moment where the penny dropped, the lock opened, and you saw the man in front of you as he truly was. You realised this was the man who stole the money, but had no clue who he was.'

'Now you have a target, and you also know Arthur Drayson and Colin Walters are still alive, so there's a chance to kill all three birds with one stone. But, if you did this, you'd need to cover your steps. Be clever.'

'You learnt Mina's mother had died, and the lassie had spent the last few years of her life being trained up by a mad exorcist in Romania,' Monroe said, but paused as Mina rose.

'Father McNarry wasn't mad!' She exclaimed. 'He saw the truth!'

'A *passionate* exorcist in Romania,' Monroe countered, and Mina shrugged, sitting back down.

'It wasn't hard, was it, to gain information on Mina from Father Franks, to go to Romania, talk to her and convince her that her father had been a victim of demonic possession, a death caused by people *also* under demonic possession, and that it was up to her to save his soul by removing the demons from them.'

'It was true,' Mina snapped.

'We'll never know, lassie,' Monroe replied sadly, his face darkening as he looked back at Mallory. 'You kept on priming and pushing this poor wee child, and then one day, when Father McNarry went off grid for a few weeks, you pretended to be him in emails, and then his assistant by phone, all to suggest to Father Franks that McNarry, the man he trained under, had suggested to bring Mina across while she was waiting to become a nun.'

'And of course, you'd do this,' Anjli added. 'This is the daughter of a man you used to work for, a man you felt you betrayed. The guilt of this was enough to sway you. And once she came over, it was suggested she help Lewis in the kitchen.'

'Why?' Father Franks frowned. 'Why Lewis?'

'Because she needed a patsy,' Declan replied calmly. 'Lewis also had a motive. He could be blamed for everything. Hell, we almost did that.'

He looked back at Mallory now, his tone deepening.

'And then came the day itself of the murder. The chances are Mina didn't even realise what she was doing with the hats. She probably thought she was doing something similar to the holy water, simply cleansing the soul. And she was a good worker. She found Santa Mick, gave him a hat and went to the hotel and did the same to Arthur Drayson.'

'You can't prove this,' Mallory insisted.

'We have a real good witness,' Anjli held up the sheet of A4 paper with the sketch on it, and Mina paled.

'Once she did this, she went to work as if nothing had happened,' Declan watched Mina again. 'But then Santa Mick turned up; he hadn't died yet, now standing in the queue waiting for food. You realised Lewis was about to swap the hat for a new one, got scared and rubbed some more "holy mixture" into another of the hats, so he'd still take the "exorcism" when the hats were swapped. But he wouldn't take it and he walked away, and in the process, your backup was taken by Shelly Garraway, who died six hours later.'

Mina sobbed gently at this, but Mallory remained emotionless as she listened.

'An old Santa with high blood pressure dies of a heart attack. A homeless man dies in the street. No ingested poisons, and alone, they're not a case for murder. But even if they were, you could blame Lewis for this. Unfortunately for you, we're superb detectives.'

The sirens had stopped now; Declan knew the whole church was likely surrounded.

'You did this through grief, but you killed innocents,' he said.

'I didn't kill Shelly! She did!' Mallory pointed at Mina. 'I never told her to add to another hat!'

She stopped, looked around, hearing the hammering on the double doors at the end of the Nave, and sighed, realising there was no way out of this.

'I did it all,' she said. 'I killed Michael, I killed Arthur, and I killed Shelly.'

'We have a witness that says he—'

'I don't care what you have,' Mallory snapped. 'He has what, a sketch? I'm giving a confession. I poisoned them all.'

She trembled as she finished.

'All four victims.'

'Four?' Declan looked at Monroe before a horrifying realisation took hold. 'Mallory, don't—'

But it was too late.

Before anyone could get to her, Mallory brought the

bottle to her mouth and drank deeply from it, spluttering as the poison tried to come back up.

'Stay back!' Monroe shouted. 'That bloody stuff can kill you if it touches. Gloves! Now!'

Mallory had already dropped the bottle, now falling to her knees, retching up traces of the liquid and blood onto the stone floor as Declan ran to her.

'You didn't have to do this,' he said. 'We could have fixed things.'

'There's no fixing this,' Mallory started before groaning, gripping her stomach and falling to her side. 'Taken way more than they had. I should pay for what—grruuugghhhh ...'

As she moaned in pain, Declan saw paramedics running to her.

'Get that shit out of her,' he said. 'Don't let it touch you.'

As the paramedics closed in around Mallory, Declan was pulled away by Monroe.

'There's nothing you can do, laddie,' he said. 'Let them do their job.'

Declan wanted to hit something, to smash something. *He'd been so close.* Looking over at Jess, he saw her staring in horror at the crowd around Mallory, and he walked over, pulling her to him.

'You did well, kid,' he said. 'Come on, you should get some fresh air.'

As he turned, he saw Father Franks being helped to the door. Seeing Declan, he waved off the officer helping him and, with his head now bandaged, he walked over to Declan and Jess.

'I'm sorry for bringing all this to your door,' Declan waved at the head wound. 'I seem to be bad for priests every time I come here.'

Father Franks weakly laughed.

'Have you considered this was God showing you a path back?' he asked. 'I've spoken to people, and I know your history. Lapsed Catholic, right? Probably didn't help much when the entire Catholic Church decided you were public enemy number one.'

'You should speak to my ex-wife about that,' Declan almost winced at the memory.

'This case might have ended badly for people, but it brought you back to the Church,' Father Franks smiled. 'Maybe next time you could even come by without sirens.'

It was Declan who laughed now.

'I'll consider it,' he said as, nodding gently so as to not kick off more pain, Father Franks shook him by the hand, allowing the officers to help him out of the door.

Declan looked back to the altar, but instantly regretted it, as he saw the paramedics placing a silver "space blanket" over the face of Mallory Reed, as Anjli pulled the weeping Mina Suvosky away, once more in handcuffs.

'Come on,' he said to Jess. 'Let's get the hell out of here.'

'Can I *not* walk out with you?' Jess asked, looking up at him. 'Like, could you go first, and I'll come out a couple of seconds after?'

'Why?' Declan frowned.

'Because you brought a whole ton of police to the church again,' Jess smiled. 'And all the old ladies who hated you before are going to have a field day when they see Father Franks with a head wound. I thought I'd do better not being seen with you.'

Declan laughed.

'Fair point,' he said. 'Fair point indeed. Wait here, while I face the music.'

Jess shook her head, linking arms with him.

'I was only joking,' she said. 'We're Walshes. We face the world together.'

'Yeah, but you're soon to become a Farrow,' Declan pointed out. 'When your mum remarries—'

'Never happening, Dad,' Jess said. 'I'm keeping your name. Now come on, let's go have some blue-rinse grannies shout at us.'

She walked off with a smile, and Declan watched after her.

This was another time she'd gotten into danger while working with him, he thought to himself. He couldn't do it anymore.

He knew she wanted to join the Unit when she qualified, but for the moment, Declan needed to speak to Bullman. Jess had to be kept from these sorts of cases. She needed to stay safe.

Because you do so well at that.

She's a child.

She knows what she want. Besides, you tried to keep her in the office. You made her the computer person.

'Because it was safe! I didn't mean to let her out!' Declan snapped aloud, realising he was talking to himself. Then, shaking off the darkness and forcing a smile, he followed his daughter out of the church.

EPILOGUE

THE ROOM THEY'D PLACED ANDRADE IN WAS DARK AND windowless. It wasn't a punishment, or some kind of underground cell, but mainly a place he could be held, where nobody could see, or get to him.

Apart from Billy, of course.

'You okay?' he asked as he stood awkwardly by the door.

Andrade, in jogging bottoms, trainers and a grey hoodie, shrugged.

'My life is over,' he said. 'Well, I mean, this life is over.'

Billy nodded. He'd been told what was due to happen next. Andrade was out of the service, and the Ambassador had waived all diplomatic privileges for Andrade and Pablo Restrepo, which meant they could be punished for any crimes they had committed while previously protected.

'I'm sure they'll take into consideration what you—'

'No,' Andrade rose, facing Billy now. 'This life. You. Me. Us.'

Billy refused to react.

'There was never an "us",' he said calmly. 'There was me,

and the "you" I was shown. The Andrade I knew, I dated, I *loved,* isn't the man I see before me. And if you truly loved me, you wouldn't have put me through this.'

'And how could I have done that?' Andrade, realising this wasn't the romantic reunion he'd hoped for, looked away.

'You could have been honest from the start,' Billy snapped. 'Hell, you could have been honest when I found you in my sodding wardrobe! We could have worked together on this! Instead, you carried on lying.'

Andrade nodded, looking at the ground.

'Have they said what's likely to happen?' Billy asked.

'I've agreed to testify against Carlos, and the Los Lideres,' Andrade nodded. 'They won't put me into prison because I wouldn't last the night. I can't go home as I wouldn't last the week. So, they'll put me in witness relocation. I don't know where or *who* I'll be. But it'll be the rest of my life. I won't ever see you again. You'll never be able to find me – not that you probably want to.'

He looked up, and Billy saw desperation in his eyes.

'You could come with me,' he said. 'Leave all this, come start a new life with me. You always complain about your family, well here's a chance to start afresh without them! No more dangerous situations! Just the two of us, out on our own.'

'Living yet another lie,' Billy replied, probably a little harsher than he meant to. 'It might just be one to add on the list with you, but to lie like that ... it's unthinkable to me.'

'So that's a no, then?' Andrade had known the answer, but Billy realised he'd been hoping for a last-minute reprieve.

'No.'

'Heh,' Andrade barked a small laugh. 'At least your boss can feel vindicated.'

'My boss thought you were a spy, not a Los Lideres murderer,' Billy snapped. 'And even though he never truly trusted you, he still welcomed you into our family.'

'That's not a family, that's a prison,' Andrade shook his head sadly. 'You're better than them.'

'Unfortunately, as much as I'd love to believe that, you've recently proven to me you're a shit judge of character,' Billy stepped backwards, already leaving the room mentally, if not physically. 'All I wanted to do was to see you one last time, tell you to stay safe, and that no matter what you did, I'll always remember you fondly.'

Andrade looked up, and there were tears in his eyes.

'I didn't want this,' he whispered. 'I wanted us. To grow old together.'

Billy couldn't meet Andrade's eyes.

'Me too,' he said. 'But dreams are just that.'

'Thank Davey for me,' Andrade said suddenly. 'And Chivalry. They did their best to help me.'

Billy nodded, deciding not to tell Andrade that neither of them had his best intentions at heart, and had only got involved to make sure Billy was freed.

And, as he turned away, about to open the door, Andrade spoke one last time.

'Imagine,' he said. 'A few years from now. You're in Madrid or Barcelona, somewhere pretty and hot. You have a coffee, and you look up and see a handsome stranger watching you. He's not the man you once knew, but he's similar. Almost as if only his name is changed.'

Andrade was openly crying now.

'I hope you'd speak to him,' he continued. 'Maybe have a drink, create new times together.'

'Goodbye, Andrade,' Billy said, his face emotionless. 'I hope you find the life you wanted.'

Before Andrade could reply, Billy opened the door, slipped through and closed it, and his one-time lover, behind it.

And now, alone in a corridor, Billy Fitzwarren collapsed to his knees and sobbed.

'SO, WILL YOU COME BACK?' BILLY ASKED AS HE STOOD OUTSIDE New Scotland Yard, where Andrade was currently in custody. He'd gained his composure back and, with a wipe of the eyes in a bathroom, looked more like a man with allergies than someone who'd just walked away from the potential love of his life.

DC Joanne Davey, eating a pretzel, took a moment to finish her mouthful before replying.

'No,' she said. 'Look, I'm sure everyone would be awesome and all that, but I'm not the same person. I haven't done what I need to do yet. And, to be honest? It felt super awkward when I went back yesterday. I mean, yay for sorting De'Geer out, and it was nice to see Rosanna, but I'm not needed there anymore. I have to find somewhere else I'm needed.'

'Any ideas where?' Billy asked.

Davey shrugged.

'Maybe not the police, no matter what Walsh did to keep me in,' she said. 'I might take a sabbatical, spend a year looking into other things. Monroe's already put some feelers out for me, and that Reckless woman said she could always use a consultant forensics person who wasn't tied to the law, so I might have a chat with her, and Chivalry offered me a job—'

'As what?'

'I honestly have no idea. But, if the money's right and it sounds interesting, I might look into it.'

Davey smiled, looking at Billy.

'You've checked your watch three times since you came out,' she said, nodding back at the building. 'You got somewhere to be?'

'Work,' Billy smiled. 'I had to stay off until the end of the weekend, but I can start again today.'

'Good for you,' Davey placed a hand on Billy's shoulder. 'But listen, seriously. What you just had to do in there? Speak to Andrade, knowing you'll never see him again? You might think you're okay now, but later on, it's going to punch you in the face hard. And when it does—'

'Call you?'

'God no!' Davey laughed. 'I was going to say have a chat with Bullman or Rosanna! Don't bring *me* your sad flowers shite!'

And with this said, Davey held a hand out, flagging down a cab.

'Keep in touch, though, yeah?' she said, giving Billy a quick embrace.

'I will,' Billy nodded as Davey climbed into the cab, gave an address and, as if forgetting Billy was even there, and already moving onto the next thing, DC Davey started reading Instagram posts on her phone as the car drove off.

Billy stood alone outside the building.

It was a short drive back to Temple Inn, or around a mile's walk.

Taking a deep breath, and doing his best not to look behind him, Billy started eastwards.

It was a long day ahead of him, and he needed to be ready.

DECLAN FOUND JESS SITTING ON THE BENCH OUTSIDE TEMPLE Church.

'You okay?' he asked, already knowing what the answer would be. It had been several days since the face-off at the church. Mallory Reed had been declared dead on arrival at the hospital, although Declan knew she'd died well before then, Father Franks was already back doing services, having vindicated Declan, claiming he saved his life, and Mina ... well, she was in the midst of a ton of red tape.

Even though she'd killed people by wiping a squeeze bottle of toxin onto the inside of festive hats, she hadn't done it to kill, and at best would be given a manslaughter charge. Throw in the issues she had thanks to the overzealous Father McNarry, added to her own traumatic past, and there was every chance she'd get a reduced sentence, if not a simple caution.

After all, it was Christmas.

Surprisingly, Father Franks had been her biggest supporter, claiming the Catholic Church would stand behind her every step of the way, but this could have been partly because of his own past with her family, and partly because he knew exactly how crazy the exorcist they sent to Romania was, and therefore the Church felt a little responsible here.

Lewis had returned to the soup kitchen, and Declan

thought he could see a little coldness in the man's eyes, as if he'd trusted the wrong people and got burnt in the process.

Which, in a way, he had.

Jess looked up from the door of the church, where it looked like she'd been trying to burn a hole through the wood with her gaze.

'Me?' she asked. 'Why wouldn't I be?'

'Billy's taking your job away from you,' Declan smiled, deciding if his daughter didn't want to mention anything, then neither would he.

'Oh. Ah.'

Jess smiled. They sat together for a long moment before she spoke again.

'She was the same age as me. Give or take a few months, anyway.'

'Her life took a different path,' Declan replied. 'She was so desperate for answers, she listened to anyone who claimed they had them. Hopefully she'll gain some help.'

Jess nodded.

'I don't know how you do this,' she said finally. 'All my life I wanted to be a police officer, but it's hard.'

'If it was easy, then everyone would want to be one,' Declan grinned. 'You're doing good. You stopped Mina from doing worse. Probably even saved Father Franks' life.'

'I didn't know if you were going to get to me in time,' Jess admitted.

'Sure you did,' Declan grinned, pulling her in close to him. 'Sure you did. And look what you got out of it. Father Franks is so happy you saved his life, he'll probably reinstate your mum to the Catholic book club.'

'Oh, didn't she tell you?' Jess looked a little uncomfortable now. 'She rejoined a couple of months back. Henry spoke to his bishop and sorted it out.'

'Of course, he did,' Declan leant back against the pillar. 'Well, at least that's one thing off my shoulders.'

'She still blames you for it.'

'Of course she does,' Declan smiled, rising. 'Go on, get into work. We still have you for the next week and a half, and we intend to use you.'

Jess furrowed her brow.

'Bullman said she wants to talk to me,' she said softly. 'I think she might be reducing my time with the Unit.'

'Well, you are doing your A Levels, and next term is a busy one,' Declan kept his face impassive - Bullman was reducing Jess's risk because he'd asked her to.

'Are you going to the party tonight?' Jess asked as she rose. 'Apparently Bullman found a venue.'

'We'll see,' Declan started walking in the other direction. 'Tell Anjli, when you get in, I'm just checking in on Monroe, he reckons he has something to show me.'

Jess tapped her fingers on her forehead in a mock salute and headed off eastwards. Declan watched her, his smile fading.

If Anjli hadn't been shown me the sketch, we might have fumbled around for hours before working out the link. And by then she would have been dead.

'Or, she'd have kicked the shit out of Mallory Reed and arrested her,' he spoke aloud, surprising a middle-aged tourist walking past. He turned to leave Temple Inn through the north entrance, aiming to grab a taxi to Monroe. 'After all, she's done it before, and she is a bloody Walsh.'

Monroe nodded to Declan as he entered through the glass doors of 100 Wardour Street.

'Not quite as it looked before, is it?' the Scot said.

Declan took a moment to look around, slowly nodding. The reception had been sparse before, but now it was even emptier; the table and chairs to the side were gone, and only the reception desk was still there, with the phones, computer and even the high chair to sit upon taken away.

'Apparently, the old owners left three days ago,' Monroe said with a smile. 'Left in the middle of a Saturday evening, skulking away like thieves in the night.'

'You think we did this?' Declan examined around the back of the reception.

'I think they realised we knew where they were, and that we weren't going to sit back and watch,' Monroe nodded. 'I think they realised they were exposed.'

'And now they're back in the shadows,' Declan muttered.

'For the moment, laddie, for the moment,' Monroe took a deep breath in, as if he was breathing in the surrounding room. 'We'll find them again. And now they know we can, they'll be watching over their shoulders.'

Declan stepped away from the reception, but then stopped. Reaching into his jacket, he pulled out a business card, one with his name, email address and Temple Inn phone number. Turning it over, he pulled his tactical pen out and wrote a message.

SEE YOU SOON

This done, he put away the pen, placed the card, face up, on the reception and walked away.

'Never liked the Feng Shui of the place, anyway,' he

muttered. 'Come on, I hear we have a party to go to.'

'You know, I expected a pub,' Anjli said as she picked up a small savoury canape, thrusting it into her mouth like she expected it to escape from her grasp before she could chew. 'But this is good.'

The location she was complaining about was the opulent setting their Christmas drinks were now in; a beautiful and ornate dining room facing out across the Thames, and in the middle of the Houses of Parliament.

'Anthony Farringdon sorted it out,' Bullman beamed. 'And of course, the moment Charles Baker realised we were here without his help, he made sure people knew that he, too, had arranged something.'

'I thought we were on his shit list?' Anjli frowned. 'Or are we all friends again?'

'We're friends as long as we have a mutual enemy,' Declan said, snaffling two small prawn things in pastries from a passing silver tray and slamming them into his mouth. 'I'm happy with that.'

He looked across the room; by the window he could see De'Geer and Cooper deep in conversation, some Temple Inn uniforms he couldn't name were beside them staring in awe out of the windows, and on the other side of the doors that led out onto the patio were Monroe and Doctor Marcos, laughing at some unknown joke with Bradbury, who'd decided he should turn up the moment he learnt the Temple Inn party was a higher class of Christmas piss-up than usual. And, by the far wall, standing next to the half-high wooden panels were Billy and Jess, probably catching each other up on the various computer expertise they'd had to use during their respective cases.

Declan made a note to check in on Billy and make sure he was okay; he knew more than others how a sudden loss could destroy someone, take them to a dark place, and the last thing he wanted was for that to happen to Billy.

But, that said, the laughter he could hear from the two of them meant that, for the moment, he didn't have to worry about either of them right now.

He felt an arm link through his, and looked down at Anjli, wine in hand, a blissful smile on her face.

'I love the little green things,' she sighed, pointing with the wineglass at a waitress, walking past with a tray of what looked to be avocado slices. 'You learn how to make me those, I'll love you forever.'

'Wait, our love is currently finite?' Declan frowned. 'Not sure if I like that.'

'Me neither, actually,' Anjli was watching Billy now. Jess had been called aside by Bullman and, now alone, Billy's facade had dropped, and he now stared mournfully out of the window.

Nodding, Declan led Anjli over to Billy who, the moment he saw them approach, was all smiles again.

'You don't need to,' Declan said. 'There's no need to put a face on with us. We're here for you, whatever you need, yeah?'

'Currently, I could do with friends,' Billy took Anjli's embrace as she pulled away from Declan.

'Well, you're lucky,' she said as she looked around the room; at De'Geer and Cooper, trying to innocuously slide out of the party together, at Monroe and Doctor Marcos, now speaking animatedly at Bradley and Bullman, at Jess, on the phone in the corner, likely calling Prisha, and then back to Billy. 'Because that's what we're all here for.'

And, with her drink placed on a table, and with Billy locked in one arm, and Declan in the other, Anjli started towards the patio doors.

'Come on, let's get some fresh air,' she said, walking up to the doors and throwing them open. '*God bless us, Every one!*'

The wave of torrential rain that blew in before someone slammed the doors closed soaked all three of them instantly.

'Well done, you eejits,' Monroe, caught slightly by the downpour, glared at them. 'Now you can see why it hasn't been opened all afternoon.'

But Declan, Anjli and Billy didn't care, and as Jess joined them, they found themselves caught in the moment, laughing uncontrollably, soaking wet in the doorway.

In some ways, it was a perfect way to begin Christmas, especially if this was the best that Christmas offered.

LEWIS HOYLE GRIMACED AS HE WATCHED THE RAIN COME DOWN; he felt sorry for anyone caught in this tonight on the streets, and the queue of downtrodden, soaked rough sleepers already queuing for the meal later that day depressed him.

'Come on,' he said to the volunteer beside him. 'Let's start heating everything up. Sooner done, sooner fed.'

And, with a nod to the people at the front of the queue, Lewis Hoyle set out the paper bowls for the meal.

Because for many of the people here, *this* was the best that Christmas offered.

ACKNOWLEDGEMENTS

When you write a series of books, you find that there are a ton of people out there who help you, sometimes without even realising, and so I wanted to do a little acknowledgement to some of them.

There are people I need to thank, and they know who they are.

People who patiently gave advice when I started this back in 2020, the people on various Facebook groups who encouraged me when I didn't know if I could even do this, the designers who gave advice on cover design and on book formatting, all the way to my friends and family, who saw what I was doing not as mad folly, but as something good.

Editing wise, I owe a ton of thanks to my brother Chris Lee, who I truly believe could make a fortune as a post-retirement copy editor, if not a solid writing career of his own, Jacqueline Beard MBE, who has copyedited all my books since the very beginning, and our new editorial addition Sian Phillips, all of whom have made my books way better than they have every right to be.

Also, I couldn't have done this without my growing army of ARC and beta readers, who not only show me where I falter, but also raise awareness of me in the social media world, ensuring that other people learn of my books.

But mainly, I tip my hat and thank you. *The reader.* Who once took a chance on an unknown author in a pile of books, and thought you'd give them a go, and who has carried on this far with them.

I write Declan Walsh for you. He (and his team) solves crimes for you. And with luck, he'll keep on solving them for a very long time.

Usually, I end there, but this time I have a little more to ask of you. Homelessness is something very important to me, especially at this time of year. If anything in this book has affected you to the point you want to donate to a homeless charity this Christmas, or even whenever in the year you read this, I'd like to offer some suggestions.

Crisis UK - www.crisis.org.uk
Shelter - www.shelter.org.uk
St. Mungos - www.mungos.org

Thank you for reading.

Jack Gatland / Tony Lee,
London, November 2022

ABOUT THE AUTHOR

Jack Gatland is the pen name of *#1 New York Times Bestselling Author* Tony Lee, who has been writing in all media for thirty-five years, including comics, graphic novels, middle grade books, audio drama, TV and film for *DC Comics, Marvel, BBC, ITV, Random House, Penguin USA, Hachette* and a ton of other publishers and broadcasters.

These have included licenses such as ***Doctor Who, Spider Man, X-Men, Star Trek, Battlestar Galactica, MacGyver,*** BBC's ***Doctors, Wallace and Gromit*** and ***Shrek***, as well as work created with musicians such as ***Ozzy Osbourne, Joe Satriani, Beartooth*** and ***Megadeth.***

As Tony, he's toured the world talking to reluctant readers with his 'Change The Channel' school tours, and lectures on screenwriting and comic scripting for *Raindance* in London.

An introvert West Londoner by heart, he lives with his wife Tracy and dog Fosco, just outside London.

Locations In The Book

The locations and items I use in my books are real, if altered slightly for dramatic intent. Here's some more information about a few of them...

St Benedict's isn't real, but is synonymous with so many homeless kitchens, around the world. The people who give their time, especially in the cold and wet winter conditions of winter in the UK are absolute saints.

I'm not sure what **100 Wardour Street** is now, but it does exist, and many years ago it used to be a cigar shop and lounge, where people would smoke cigars while drinking expensive coffee. I had several meetings in there over the years with visiting US screenwriters and producers, and it was always warm and welcoming.

I believe it's now just an extension of the bar next door.

The Marriott Hotel at County Hall is an opulent, five-star hotel that was once the home of the *London Film Museum,* a collection of film and TV props, with a comic artist in residence. There was originally a section on how films are made, including information on all the major studios, and original pieces included costumes and props from British films, the autogyro 'Little Nellie' from *You Only Live Twice*, an original *Superman* meteor, the Rank Organisation gong used in their opening titles, and armour made by Terry English for *Excalibur*.

This moved to Covent Garden in 2014, and now the County Hall is a must-visit location, and the Father Christmas experience is apparently, according to reviews, one of the best in London.

No Santas, or Father Christmases, even, have died so far.

The Jacob Marley Society is fictional, but the clubs mentioned in the book are real, as is the club that Liverymen are allowed to use in the City of London.

The Old Bank of England pub is real, and the description and the history written in the book explain more than I could here, although one thing I don't mention, which is currently (as of writing) true is that in their 'sun garden' is a double decker bus that you can drink in!

Finally, I never name the **Hampstead Church,** as it's an amalgamation of several in the area. So don't go looking for dog-trafficking priests!

If you're interested in seeing what the *real* locations look like, I post 'behind the scenes' location images on my Instagram feed. This will continue through all the books, and I suggest you follow it.

In fact, feel free to follow me on all my social media by clicking on the links below. Over time these can be places where we can engage, discuss Declan and put the world to rights.

www.jackgatland.com

www.hoodemanmedia.com

Visit Jack's Reader's Group Page
(Mainly for fans to discuss his books):
https://www.facebook.com/groups/jackgatland

Subscribe to Jack's Readers List:
www.subscribepage.com/jackgatland

www.facebook.com/jackgatlandbooks
www.twitter.com/jackgatlandbook
ww.instagram.com/jackgatland

Want more books by Jack Gatland? Turn the page...

DI Walsh and the team of the *Last Chance Saloon* will return in their next thriller

BENEATH THE BODIES

Order Now at Amazon:

mybook.to/beneaththebodies

But if you want to read something different by Jack Gatland...
read on...

T-MINUS TEN

DEVIN MACINTOSH WAS IN THE MOOD FOR A CELEBRATION.

The champagne was on ice; the lights turned down low, the room-service oysters now room temperature and, if he was a little honest, not up to the par he'd expected from the hotel.

The Madison Hotel was as "five star" as you could get, and to rent a suite, even for a Sunday night, was more than most of the staff at the hotel earned in a month.

Devin called it "pin money".

To be brutally frank, Devin wouldn't spend so much on such a frivolity; he wasn't one for bells and whistles. Sure, he enjoyed a steak dinner like the next guy, but he was just as happy chomping down on a Burger King Bacon Double Cheese with onion rings – as long as he didn't have to sit in the bloody restaurant, that was. The places stank of poverty.

And Devin Macintosh hated poverty.

This wasn't some kind of irrational hatred; this was because one time, many years earlier, Devin had been one of those poor, penniless bastards, scraping a living in any way he could, regardless of the legality of the situation. In fact, it was why, many years later, Wrentham Industries poached him from their closest rival with a rather impressive benefits package, including his own box at Madison Square Garden, and the use of a couple of executive suites at the Madison Hotel.

As he'd said, Devin wouldn't spend on such a frivolity. He expected someone to cover the cost for him.

Lying on the bed, the satin sheets crumpled, Devin ran a hand through his hair. For a man in his late forties, he looked great for his age; at least a good five or ten years younger. This was partly because of his exercise regime, and also because of the hair plugs he'd gotten around five years earlier, when he'd seen his family's genetic disposition for balding had knocked upon his own door.

His wife had called it a vanity exercise and a waste of money, saying he didn't need to do such a thing, that he was "still attractive without hair." But he'd called her a hypocrite, pointing out she'd happily let him pay for her new breasts, and the conversation drew to a close.

Still, they both got what they wanted.

But, for all his complaints about costs, Devin had his fancies. His underwear, currently the only thing he was wearing right now, was worth more than the average suit of his corporate team, and his watch, currently on the sideboard next to his expensive, top-of-the-range phone cost six figures.

But neither of them were as beautiful as the woman laying breathless on the bed next to him. In her late thirties, her own expensive and incredibly flimsy lace underwear had been half removed already, during their first play fight, her incredible breasts free from restraint and quite frankly, in Devin's opinion, spectacular, no matter how much they cost.

Rising, Devin leaned across the woman, grabbing one of the two champagne flutes on the side table. Downing it, he toasted her.

'Happy anniversary,' he said, and was about to speak again, to say something more, maybe even about love, or something equally sappy when the woman grinned, leant closer, and bit him hard on the arm.

'Ow! You bitch!' he hissed, snapping back as the woman laughed at his response. 'Dammit Rebecca! Don't leave marks! I exercise with the board tomorrow morning! How will I explain teeth marks to Myles when we're on the treadmill?'

'Tell him you have a very healthy sex life, while his cock's covered in cobwebs?' Rebecca lounged now against the bed, her hands gripping the silk sheets, inviting him to retaliate against her.

To retaliate on her.

'You should punish me,' she said, in an apologetic "little girl" voice. 'Punish me, Daddy.'

Devin smiled in response, tossing the now-empty champagne flute across the room as he rose on his knees, towering over her as they—

The phone on the sideboard *pinged*.

'Leave it,' Rebecca ordered.

'It could be important,' Devin's attention was now split between the gorgeous, half-naked woman in front of him, and the glowing screen of his phone, just that little too far away to see what the message was.

'I'm important,' Rebecca snarled, and gone was the apologetic little girl. 'If it's life-threatening, they'll send you an email. Or they'll call your PA and she can call you.'

The phone *pinged* a second time. Not a reminder for the message, but a new, second message.

'I swear to god, Devin,' Rebecca hissed. 'You touch that goddamned phone and I'll punish you.'

'Be serious,' Devin replied, the fun now drained from the situation, rolling across the bed and grabbing the phone. Rebecca tried to stop him halfway, but he slipped past her, grabbing the phone and holding it high, out of her reach as he looked up at the message displayed on the screen.

9-1-1 BOARDROOM

'Crap,' Devin slumped down, showing Rebecca the message. 'I've been called in.'

Rebecca snatched the phone from him, staring down at the message, as if hoping that by doing this, she'd somehow change the text on the screen.

'It's all in capitals,' she said. 'It's never in capitals when they send this.'

'I know.'

'This probably doesn't mean anything good,' Rebecca looked up at Devin now. 'Are you in trouble?'

'Why the fuck would you think I'm the one in trouble?' Devin now hissed, straightening, as he faced Rebecca. 'There's ten of us on the board. Well, something like that. I've never counted. But why can't one of them be the one in trouble?'

'Because you're a sneaky, backstabbing shit, and you've always been half a step ahead of everyone else and a firing squad?' Rebecca suggested. 'Tell them you're sick. Tell them it's a fucking Sunday night and God said you could have the day off.'

'Not with that code,' Devin shook his head, already walking over to his trousers and pulling them on. 'You don't get the 9-1-1 unless someone's shit the bed on a massive scale.'

'So, let someone else clean it up,' Rebecca replied.

'I'm the one who usually cleans it up!' Devin exploded. 'This isn't a debate or a negotiation, Rebecca! I've got to go in! Bloody Victoria will go, and she's at her kid's recital.'

'Yeah, but she hates her kids,' Rebecca pouted. 'You can't go! It's our anniversary!'

Devin, currently pulling on his dress shirt, paused, nodding.

'It's not fair, and I get it,' he said, now sitting on the bed placing a hand on Rebecca's arm. 'And it's really not how I wanted to spend the night. But I have to do this. It's why I get the money I get. It's why I get ...'

He waved a hand around the suite.

'... this.'

Rebecca said nothing, but her confrontational body language was softening as she glared at Devin.

'This is shit,' she said.

'I totally agree,' Devin leant in, kissing Rebecca lightly on the lips. 'It'll only take an hour or so. Wait here, crack open another bottle. Go wild on room service.'

Rebecca frowned at this as Devin rose, tucking his shirt into his trouser band.

'Do you pay for room service?' she asked suspiciously.

'Fuck no!' Devin laughed. 'Do you think I'd suggest it if you were spending my money?'

Rebecca folded her arms now, still angry at what was happening.

'I'm not happy about this, Devin,' she said as he pulled on his socks. 'There might be ... consequences ... when you come back.'

Devin slipped his shoes on and, grabbing his jacket and tie, he blew Rebecca a dramatic kiss.

'Promises, promises,' he mocked.

'I'm serious!' Rebecca shouted at Devin as he walked to the door of the hotel suite. But by then he'd already gone, the memories of the beautiful, topless woman in the lacy underwear now replaced with concern about what was so fucking bad that the DEFCON text had been sent.

He knew it wouldn't be good.

THE DRIVER WAS WAITING FOR HIM OUTSIDE THE HOTEL AS HE stormed out, still doing up his tie as he nodded at him.

'Got your message,' the driver opened the door, allowing Devin to enter before closing the door behind him, walking around to the driver's side, and taking off his own cap as he entered.

Now looking over his shoulder, the driver smiled.

'Home or work, sir?' he asked.

'Why the fuck would I be going home?' Devin snapped, looking at his watch as he did so. The time read 7:08. 'Take me to the office. And knock that stupid fucking smile off your face.'

He'd had the driver, a young, irritatingly handsome Albanian for at least three months now, and as he berated him, Devin realised he'd never once asked what his sodding name was. He had a very brief moment of concern, a wonder whether he should ask the driver now, but this was wiped away quickly by the simple fact Devin didn't really care.

Now admonished, the driver turned back to the road, and

Devin pressed a button to his side, relaxing as the privacy window rose between them.

Devin hated having to make polite conversation with the drivers. He hated to make any conversation, to be honest. Again, the issues of his past, of having to converse with lower classes rose its head. Devin reached across the limo seat for the small drinks cabinet held within a side compartment, pulling out a bottle and then pouring himself a whisky, downing it in one hit, and wiping his mouth with his hand before pouring another glass.

Looking out the window, watching Manhattan pass by, he sighed.

'Fuck.'

Pulling out his phone, he stared at the message one more time.

9-1-1 BOARDROOM

What the hell had happened? Was it a takeover? Maybe Mika Tanasha, that backstabbing bitch, was finally making her play. Either way, he'd lied to Rebecca; this would not take an hour. Just getting the contrary fuckers to sit at the table was going to take half that.

Sighing audibly, Devin dialled a number on his phone, holding it to his ear and waiting for it to connect, watching the privacy screen intently, as if expecting it to drop at any moment.

After a couple of seconds, the call was answered.

'Hey, it's me,' Devin smiled as he spoke into the phone. He didn't feel like smiling, but he'd been told once by a director of sales that if you smiled when you spoke into a phone, you sounded friendlier. Personally, Devin thought it was bullshit, but he was happy to try it. 'I've been called into a board meeting.'

There was a pause as Devin listened to the voice on the other end of the line.

'It's the message,' he said. 'The message is the bad one, and you know what that means. I could be there all night.'

Another pause, another conversation from the other end of the phone.

'I know, but there's nothing I can do,' Devin rubbed at the bridge of his nose as he replied, trying to keep his voice calm, to not shout. 'It's gonna be a late one, so kiss the boys for me and I'll see you when I get home.'

He looked back at the privacy wall; it was up, but the glass was opaque, and he could see the driver's eyes through the rear-view mirror, watching him, judging him for the conversation he was having right now with his wife, at home, with his children, unaware of any anniversary tonight.

'I love you too,' he said, looking out of the window, unable to allow the driver to see his eyes as he lied, disconnecting the moment he said this, holding the phone in his lap.

He'd fire the driver tomorrow, he decided, as he poured himself another whisky, settling back into his seat. The nosey bastard was too interested in what his betters were doing. And, rather, who they were doing.

And that simply wasn't the way they did things around here.

You had to gain *power* first, before you started blackmailing.

The office was dark, and he liked it that way. He could have put the lights on and seen better what he was doing in the light, but he didn't need to. The light from the chrome and glass building opposite was enough for him, bleeding through the windows of the office, casting shadows across the room, hitting the rifle on the floor.

He crouched now; the window was floor-to-ceiling glass, tempered and strong, but not strong enough to resist the glass cutter he placed against it, making a rough circle before using a suction cup to bring the now detached piece of glass back into the office.

The last thing he wanted was for it to fall the other way, crashing to the pavement a dozen floors below him. Someone might call the police, and that would not do.

They weren't in his plan until later.

Now with a hole in the window around a foot off the ground, he climbed down onto the carpet tiles of the office and, now prone, he took the rifle, placed the muzzle through the opening, only an inch or so out into the night air, but enough to provide a clear shot. The rough circle was large enough to aim his sight through, too, focusing on the lit up boardroom on the other side of the street, as he unclicked the arms of his stand and readied the rifle, aiming it at the window.

This done, he started on the second part of his plan, pulling a roll of Gaffa tape out of his duffle.

The night hadn't even started yet, and he was already excited about what was about to happen.

For tonight, *justice* came to Wrentham Industries.

T-MINUS FIVE

THE LIMO PULLED TO A STOP OUTSIDE THE MAIN ENTRANCE TO Wrentham Industries at seven-fifteen pm; for the journey, through midtown and in the middle of theatre traffic to only take that long was actually good, but Devin wasn't going to let the driver know this, instead stepping out of the car the moment the door was open and slamming the now empty whisky tumbler into the driver's hand.

'You should have been faster,' he hissed.

'I couldn't have been any faster,' the driver replied with a surly 'sir,' added after a second delay. 'The only way we could have been quicker was if I jumped every red light—'

'Next time, jump the red lights,' Devin snapped back, emphasising each syllable with a tap of his index finger on the driver's chest. 'Your delay of even a minute could have cost the firm billions.'

'I'll try to remember that, sir,' the driver replied, stone-faced. Devin almost laughed. He was starting to like the driver. He could even see a future for the man – if he wasn't firing him first thing in the morning, anyway.

'Do you want me to wait for you?' the driver asked, still staring dead ahead, not even trying to catch Devin's eye.

'No, you're done for the night,' Devin yawned. 'I'll get an Uber back to the hotel when we're done. It'll be faster than you can do it.'

'Very good, sir,' the driver replied and, irritated by this, Devin waved his hand dismissively.

'Just piss off, yeah?' he said, turning away from the car and already starting towards the door. 'You're making the building look lower class.'

As the driver, silently fuming, walked stiffly back to the driver's seat, Devin smiled. He didn't have to be such a dick to the guy, but if you didn't use the power, what good was having it? That great power and great responsibility bullshit was the stuff of superhero comics, and those arrogant, spandex-wearing fags weren't real.

Another car pulled up before he reached the door, and Devin turned to face it as the driver, almost identical in looks, size and uniform as his one, walked around hurriedly and opened the door. Devin wondered whether there was a particular company that only hired chauffeurs that looked like that, but then stopped with a grimace as he realised who was getting out of the car, and therefore would be sharing an elevator with him.

Victoria Harvey was a grade-A, diamond-carat bitch. In her late thirties, but constantly claiming she was five years younger, she was fit as hell – Devin had to give that to her – and currently wore an expensive mink jacket, with an extortionate handbag under the arm.

She seemed to have a better relationship with her driver than Devin did, too, as shown by the slight but visible finger trace along the driver's arm as she told him to wait for her.

They're probably fucking, Devin thought to himself as he faked a smile for the cheap seats. *And if not already, they will be later.*

Walking up to Devin, Victoria didn't even acknowledge the fact he'd held the door open for her, waltzing through and into the lobby as if she expected him to do such a selfless act.

Devin *hated* Victoria.

As they fell into step, walking across the lobby and nodding at the security guard behind the counter in that way people do when they really don't expect to be stopped, Victoria looked over at Devin.

'You smell of fucking,' she said. 'Can't be your wife, it's not her birthday.'

'Always a pleasure,' Devin ignored the jibe as he motioned for the guard at the elevator to call for the carriage.

'Do you know what the hell this is about?' Victoria continued. 'Bloody cloak and dagger bullshit always gives me ulcers.'

Devin raised an eyebrow at this.

'Wait, you didn't call it?' he asked. 'I assumed this was as dramatically drama queen as you can get, so it had to be you or the Asian.'

Victoria sniffed as they entered the executive elevator, the guard leaning in to press the button for them, because God forbid they should have to lower themselves to such an act.

'I was at my daughter's recital,' she muttered irritably. 'Had to leave three songs in. Are they called songs? I don't know. All I know is someone had better have died for this, because I'm missing important moments in her life.'

'They usually do die when we get calls like this,' Devin puffed out his cheeks as he watched the number slowly climb upwards. 'I've only had the 9-1-1 once since I arrived. And that was when Ryan whatshisname jumped out the fucking window.'

'God, I forgot about that, the stupid bastard,' Victoria tutted. 'Still, you should be careful, Macintosh. You almost sound like you give a shit.'

'Just stating a fact,' Devin flashed an incredibly insecure smile. 'How was the recital?'

'Fucking abysmal,' Victoria moaned. 'You'd think with the amount of money I was paying, she could play a vaguely recognisable tune.'

The doors opened onto the twenty-third floor, and with a wave of his hand, Devin offered Victoria the option of leaving the car first.

'Fuck no,' she said, motioning for him to take the lead. 'If the shit's hitting the fan, I'm not the first one walking in. You're junior to me. You can be the meat shield.'

Laughing, Devin walked out into an empty, open-plan corridor, the workers on this floor long gone. Only a single cleaner still worked at this hour, a man in his thirties, brown hair under a red baseball cap, headphones on over the top, his face half-hidden as he cleaned the marble floor beside the doors.

'Piss off and do that later,' Devin snapped, backing away a little as he walked past the man, resisting the urge to pull out some antibacterial hand gel. Watching him, Victoria was amused by this.

'Worried you might catch "poor" if you stand too close?' she mocked as they continued down the narrow corridor that led to the boardroom. 'Prick.'

She stopped as a sudden thought came to mind.

'What if they're already making alliances?' she hissed, trying to look through the glass walls of the boardroom. The angle wasn't good for spying, but she could see Myles Fenton in the doorway. The CEO of the company was fat, balding, red-faced from years of neglect, and was currently checking his watch. 'We should team up. Strength in numbers.'

'Yeah, right up til you stab me in the balls, Brutus,' Devin shook his head. 'I'll take my chances alone, thanks. Besides, I think it's Miko.'

'You do?' Victoria almost clawed at his arm, to pull him back to ask more, but Devin had already walked into the boardroom, and it forced her to follow suit.

The boardroom itself was swish and futuristic. One side, facing into the office, was opaque glass, blocking the view into the office space, giving secrecy – and the main reason Victoria hadn't been able to count the deals happening inside. The other side of the boardroom was a wall of full-length glass windows, looking out into Manhattan. It would have been an incredible view, if it wasn't for the fact that fifty yards away another building, a half-lit floor matching the level of this room, stood, a black monolith in the night, blocking any postcard panorama.

Devin hated the location here; it meant his office, up on the top floor, could only see half of Manhattan. And, annoyingly, nobody else wanted to help him get the other buildings destroyed, even when he'd drunkenly mentioned he knew men with demolition experience, and was happy to "Fight Club" the whole damn city to get an unobstructed view.

The room itself was nothing more than a boardroom table, with twelve seats at it. In the middle of the table was a conference call phone, a remote next to it, and this remote controlled the massive flat-screen television on the wall at the end, mainly used for presentations and suchlike, or when one of the board couldn't be bothered to attend and "Zoomed" in from their homes, or even, on one occasion when he was so hung over, from his office two floors up, as Devin simply couldn't muster the strength to walk to the elevator.

Apart from that, the room was quite sparse. Against the opposite wall was a mahogany side cabinet, where the bottles of water were placed, and the bottles of scotch hid in the deep-filled drawers. Devin paused as he realised each drawer now had a small gold number on it – probably some other bullshit HR idea for productivity, decided by Myles while fucked on Ketamine.

Devin was sure Myles took that. Or something similar.

Because nobody could be as mind-numbingly boring as Myles Fenton and not be on horse tranquillisers.

On top of the cabinet were a coffee machine and a microwave, and Devin made his way straight towards it. He had a feeling this was going to be a long one, and he needed caffeine.

'You're late,' Myles chided both of the new arrivals.

'Piss off, Myles,' Victoria snapped, also ignoring him as she walked past. 'You're only here on time because you've got nothing else to do.'

Myles looked abashed at the insult, but said nothing as Victoria turned her attention to the rest of the room.

'And that goes for you brownnosers too,' she said, pulling off her mink and slumping it onto the back of a chair, effectively claiming the space before anyone else could.

There were six other people in the boardroom, either

sitting already at the desk or standing, talking in hushed whispers to each other, probably considering the same short-term alliances that Victoria had, or texting angrily on their phones, annoyed to be called out.

First, there was Jason Barnett. In his late thirties, and in fact only a year older than Victoria, he was Wrentham Industries' fast talking sales director – immaculately dressed in a sharp suit and a trendy tie, his hair on point, desperately trying to be in his twenties, and looking almost as if he'd been waiting for the call, or hadn't actually gone home yet. Which, even though it was a Sunday, was probably the case. He seemed to live in the office.

Next to him was Tamira May. She had just turned forty, as she'd had a really shitty party recently, where she spent the whole night getting more and more shitfaced while telling everyone she was fine, and life began at forty, all that self-help bullshit, before collapsing after doing some MDMA and telling everyone her life was over. As far as Victoria was concerned though, it wasn't her age that was stopping her from getting laid; it was the fact she was a mixture of angry Mom and stern accounting governess in her outward appearance; harsh and cold, wearing simple clothing that belayed her status and position in the company. If Victoria was honest, Tamira was probably the one person here she was intimidated by, and not because she looked like an extra from the *Addams Family*.

Now with a coffee in hand, Devin also looked over the group, his eye instantly drawn towards a stunningly attractive Asian woman by the wall. Miko Tanasha was one of the older members of the board, only a year or two younger than Devin, but she still looked in her twenties, the bitch. A

Japanese woman with steel in her eyes, she wore a simple yet expensive suit, and was watching everyone while pretending to examine her phone.

Devin wanted more than anything to take her there and then on the table, but even if she wanted to – and he knew she definitely didn't – he already had Rebecca.

Oh, yeah. And his wife.

Beside Miko, however, was the complete opposite. Hayley Moran, plump, bubbly and with a fondness for pastels puffed nervously on a Vape, pulling her cardigan close around her as she stared out of the window, looking out across the city – or at least as much as she could see, with a thousand-yard stare, her mind far away.

Devin tapped the top of his mouth with his tongue as he watched her, considering what he was seeing, and deciding it was a nervous, guilty woman. *Was HR Hayley the reason they were all here?*

There was a loud, bellowing laugh from the other side of the boardroom table, and Devin looked across to see Eddie Purcell, an early fifties gangster of a man, in particular a man built like a brick shit house and who looked like trouble no matter how expensive his suit was. His gold jewellery and cygnet rings rattled as he shook with laughter at something Myles said, but the moment the decrepit CEO turned around, his face became one of bitter anger, a stare that was literally burning through the back of Myles Fenton's skull.

The Wrentham Industries board was here. All that was missing was Corey Gregson, but he was always late.

There was, however, someone new in the room. Someone Devin didn't know. A young, scared-looking woman with long, mousey-blonde hair, and no older than her mid-twenties, sitting at the table with the look of a woman who really didn't know why the hell she was there.

'Hello,' he said, walking over and sitting down. 'Who the fuck are you?'

'She's Donna,' Hayley replied for her, sitting down a space away from Devin. 'She's from the secretarial bay. To note the minutes.'

Devin nodded at this, and the others, seeing people now sitting, made their own way over.

'Well, sit there and shut up,' he hissed, while keeping his smile plastered on. 'Two ears, one mouth, yeah?'

'And if anything we say off the record turns up online?' Myles added, sitting at the head of the table, 'I'll personally end you.'

'She's just doing her job. No need for you both to be dicks about it,' Hayley snapped irritably as Donna reddened, as if horrified to find herself the subject of attention.

'Yeah, she's stuck here with you,' Jason joined in now. 'Give her a break.'

He finished this by giving a friendly wink at Donna, sitting back and looking at Myles, a smug expression on his face. Devin forced the smile off his own face. The two of them were as bad as each other. The young bull and the wounded old bastard.

Shame neither of them would end up on top. Not while he was around.

'If I wanted your opinion, Jason, I'd look for it in the gutter,' Myles muttered, and was about to continue when Jason rose angrily to his feet, the chair clattering behind him.

'Now listen here, you dusty old prick—'

'Guys!'

The word wasn't shouted, but it was spoken with such

force that everyone stopped, even Jason, turning to look at Eddie, sitting beside the television.

'Can we just sort out why we're here and get on with it?' he asked, almost patronisingly. 'I dunno about you, but I got better things to do tonight.'

There was a consensus of nods, before Victoria, frowning, spoke.

'Where's Gregson?'

'No show, so far,' Eddie shrugged.

'Probably pissed up in a bar. Again.' It was Tamira who added that, and as the two of them discussed the uselessness of Corey Gregson, Jason took this opportunity to look over at Victoria across the table.

'How was Jenny's recital?'

'Fuck off, Jason. Like you give a shit.'

Reddening, Jason backed off.

'Right then,' Myles eventually spoke. 'Let's get this board-room meeting started while we wait for Gregson.'

HE WATCHED THEM THROUGH HIS NIGHT-VISION SNIPER SCOPE, stroking the barrel of his rifle as he saw them sit at the table, still arguing. They were probably wondering where Corey Gregson was, unaware that he was tied up and sadly unable to join them tonight.

Or ever, even.

They had no idea he was watching them.

They had no idea what he was about to do to them.

He smiled, pulling the bolt back, clicking the bullet into the rifle's chamber and smiling wider as the *ka-chuk* echoed around the empty office room.

It sounded good. *Righteous.*

Soon, there would be blood. Soon, there would be death.

Soon, there would be *justice.*

It was time to start both the clock – and the game.

'Right then,' he whispered. 'Ninety minutes on the clock ... and go.'

Hooded Man
MEDIA

PAINT
THE
DEAD

Hooded Man
MEDIA

SLEEPING
SOLDIERS

Printed in Great Britain
by Amazon

35651998R00209